When Wicked Runs South

Written by Marissa Miller

Based loosely on:
Alice's Adventures in Wonderland
Through the Looking Glass
Peter Pan
The Wonderful Wizard of Oz

This book is a work of fiction. The names, characters, and events in this book are all fictitious. Any similarities to persons real or living is not intentional for this derivative book, and would be the work of the original creators. This retelling has a unique plot, and while it uses derivative sources*, the plot as a whole is the creation of the author.

When Wicked Runs South
ISBN:

Published by Marissa Miller via IngramSpark
14 Ingram Blvd, La Vergne, TN, 37086
www.ingramspark.com

*Derivative sources in this book fall under public domain, or under the "fair use" policy for character and location usage. All credit to original authors has been given in accordance and is recorded under the copyright registration in the United States Library of Congress.

Acknowledgments

Thank you to the original creators of these characters and worlds:

J. M Barrie for *Peter Pan*

Lewis Carroll for *Alice's Adventures in Wonderland* and *Through the Looking Glass*

L. Frank Baum for *The Wonderful Wizard of Oz*

This book is a work of fiction, using the characters and locations from the above books.
The plot is completely original.

Thank you to the Sullivan family for helping sponsor the publication of this book, and thank you to usual rag tag support team. Your presence is invuable to me.

A special thanks to my CP, DE, and dear friend, Deonna, as well. This book would not exist without you.

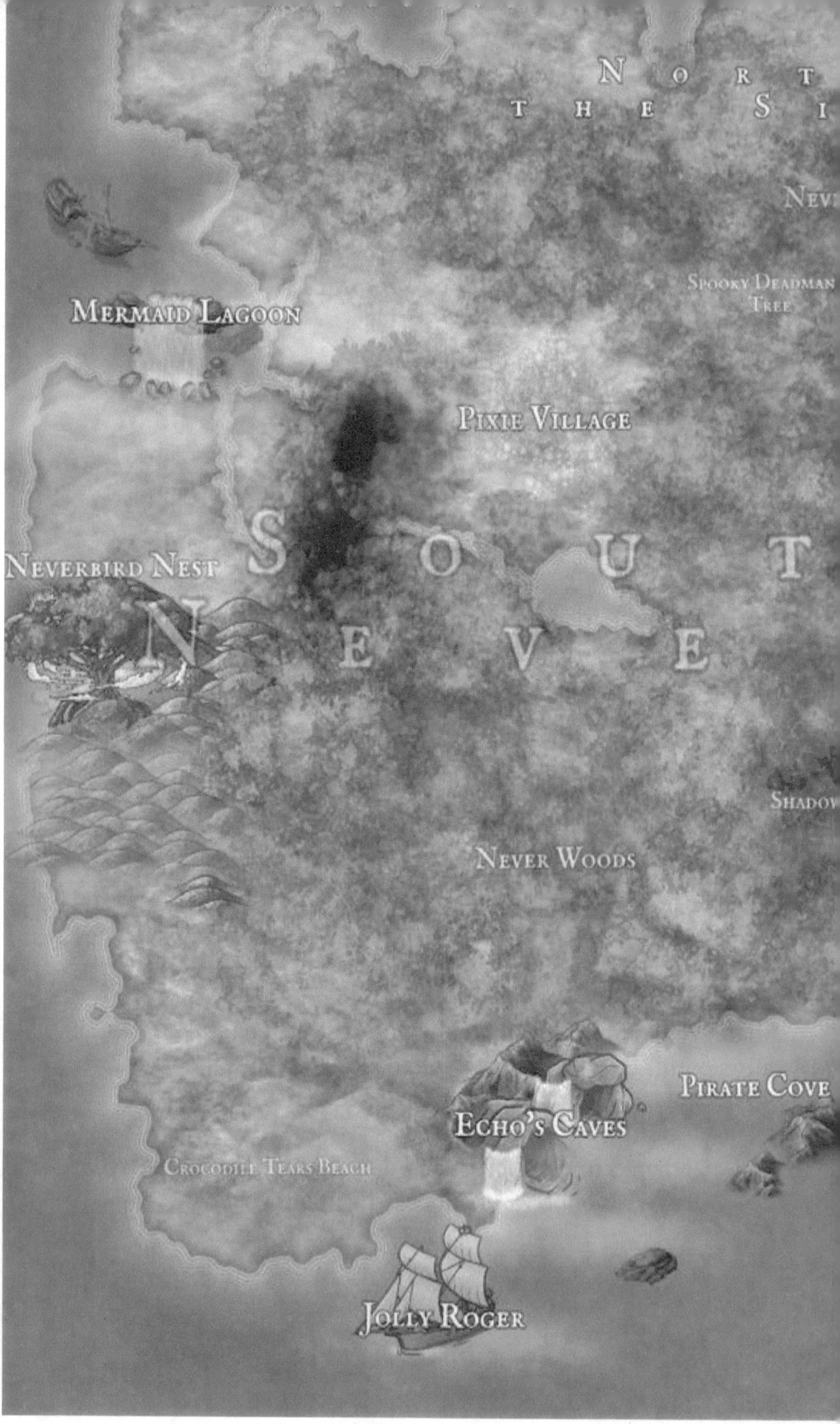

NORT
THE SI
NEV
Spooky Deadman Tree
Mermaid Lagoon
Pixie Village
Neverbird Nest
SOUT
NEVE
Shadow
Never Woods
Pirate Cove
Echo's Caves
Crocodile Tears Beach
Jolly Roger

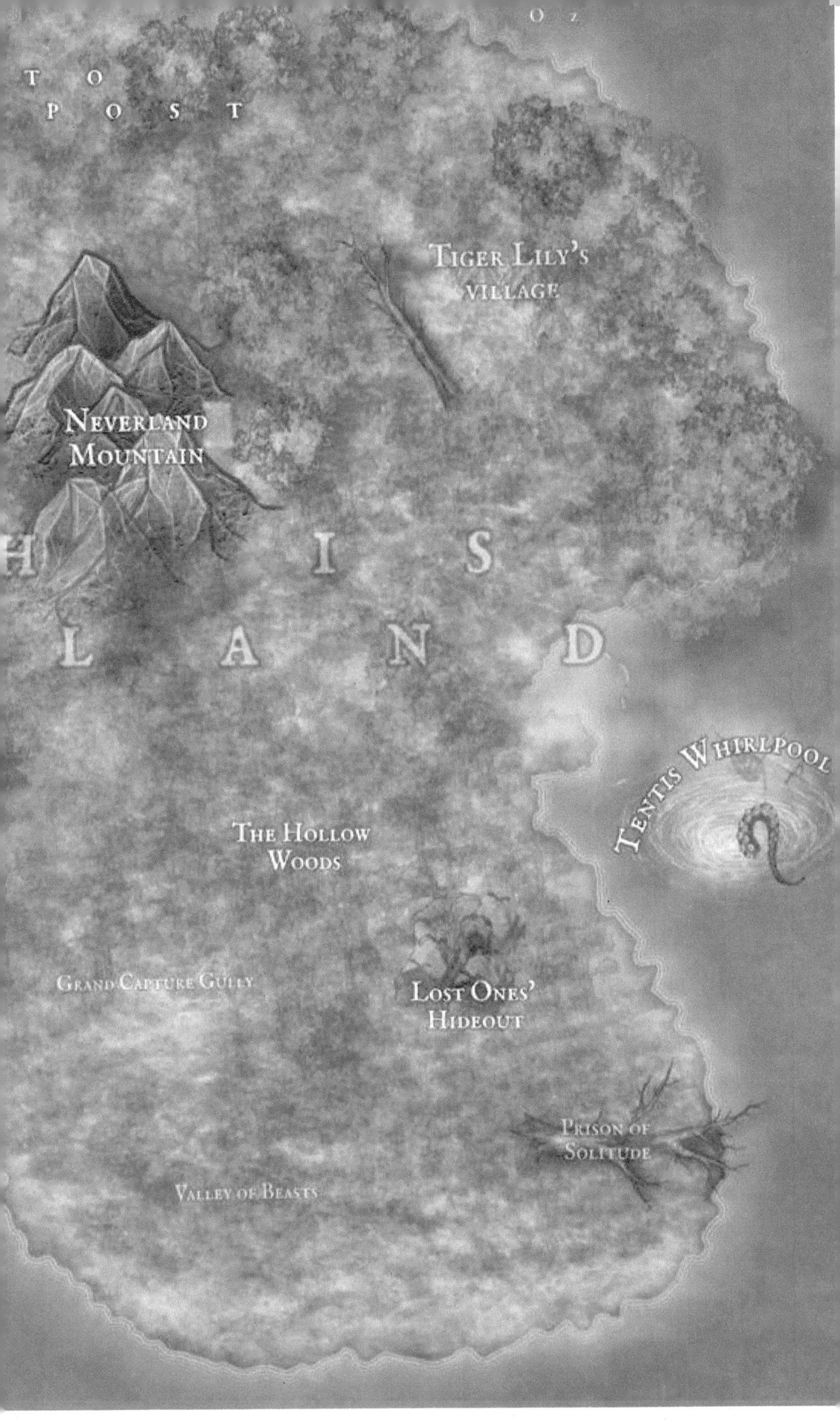

O Z

T O
P O S T

Tiger Lily's
village

Neverland
Mountain

H I S
L A N D

Tentis Whirlpool

The Hollow
Woods

Grand Capture Gully

Lost Ones'
Hideout

Prison of
Solitude

Valley of Beasts

When Wicked Series
Book Three
When Wicked Runs South

I kept my eyes tightly closed as the increasingly familiar sensation of teleportation engulfed me. My ears were ringing, but my mind was simultaneously echoing the conversation I'd had with The Wizard before he'd teleported me away.

Right, best let's get on with it. And Alice, dear, don't worry about Wonderland while you are away. I assure you it will be in good hands. In fact, don't bother coming back at all.

Before me, it had been Peter, waved away, to who knew where, with a simple flick of the hand. I'd challenged the Wizard's power and he was showing me just how easy it was to deal with us. We were nothing more than pests to him. Shamefully, I realized on some level, being the Wicked Witch of the West had made me feel powerful. Relying on the broken moral compass around my neck to get me through the hard bits of wielding power had given me a false sense of invincibility.

Frustration welled within me until the heat of it, mixed with the burning electricity of despair, boiled over into a surge propelled by my already spinning compass. I felt my emotions rend themselves from my body in acrid energy that burst forth like spears of lightning.

"Gah! Stupid, ignorant girl!" I shouted as I allowed the torrent of feelings to purge from my body. Then I sagged to the ground that I could now feel firmly beneath my feet. The heat of my outburst steamed off of the remaining water that the Wicked Mombi had doused me with, and my hand raised instinctively to my throat where she had choked me with my compass.

I was somewhere gloomy and moist. The vast darkness smelled of the kind of misted air that came from countless years of waves lapping at stone. It stung my eyes, and I couldn't tell if the salty tang on my lips was from the air, or from the stray tears that slithered down my cheeks.

"Spontaneously exploding isn't going to be something you do often, is it?" I whirled around at the sound of a semi-familiar voice behind me.

In fact, I am so confident in our team, I think I'll even allow your teams. But, let's mix it up! I recalled The Wizard's final crow before he sent me away, as I looked at the tall dark-haired young man leaning against a stone wall. Despite the dim lighting, I recognized him as Peter's childhood friend, and one of Dorothy's traveling companions.

"No," I sniffed, then sighed in resignation. "Well, actually, yes, it can happen often. It depends on this blasted moral compass and its whims."

"Right. Well, I will just be keeping my distance from you then. I'm Tip, if you didn't remember, by the way. I know we already technically met but it wasn't exactly the main focus of the hour." Tip jerked his chin in my direction, remaining slouched against the wall.

"Yes, Peter sort of stole the spotlight there." I nodded halfheartedly, images of Peter's surprising display of magical power in the dungeons of Oz flashing before my eyes.

Tip squinted at me, guarded and judging. He looked a far cry from the supportive friend to Peter back in Oz— or even Wonderland, for that matter. Something had changed his demeanor now that it was just me and him.

"What? Why are you staring at me like that?" I asked, clutching onto my necklace self-consciously, instantly feeling a wall of defense spring up between me and the Lost Boy.

"Dorothy mentioned a Wicked witch trying to kill her in Wonderland, and escaping a psychotic girlfriend of Peter's. Seeing as the latter is most definitely you, and Dorothy connected some dots back in your *castle,* Queen of Wonderland, that had escaped me in all the hubbub. Then, there was your little display of honesty and general disregard for others…"

"And, your point?" I pressed, waving him on impatiently.

"You're a Wicked."

"Yes, I am. I thought that had been made pretty clear. Big bad Alice, the Wickedest Witch West of the Signpost, and all that nonsense."

"It's hardly nonsense if it's true."

"Alright then, it isn't nonsense. But, to be fair, I am also currently the only witch west of the signpost," I added with a shrug. Despite his loyalty to Peter, and the small glimpse of enthusiasm he'd displayed towards his friend, something told me Tip wasn't too sure about me.

"Look," Tip sighed, picking up on my assessment of him. "I don't want to be offensive, but I just don't really have a soft spot in my heart for you Wicked witches. Peter is my friend, so I owe it to him to show some pleasantness, but he's not here, so there it is."

"Well!" I huffed, taking offense anyway.

"Mombi is a Wicked witch—"

"Clearly, I am not exactly in league with her!" I snapped, interrupting his explanation indignantly, as I pictured the white-haired ice witch mocking me, and felt my compass tick with anger.

Tip squinted at me for a moment before pointedly continuing, "She kidnapped me and held me hostage for some time as a child. Only in the past several years did I even begin to really grow older. She played all sorts of mind games, and used all manners of magic and manipulation on me to suit her whims." His words were clipped and jagged, like even referencing that period of time was a struggle to force through his lips.

"You trusted Dorothy, and *she's* a Wicked witch too," I pointed out, folding my arms crossly.

"Well, she's different." Tip mumbled and shoved his hands in his pockets in a defiant and surly gesture.

"Is she now?" I quirked an eyebrow and smiled. "Oh, I see. Little Miss Freckles is special, is she?"

"Don't go jumping to conclusions, Witch." Tip warned me with a sharp look. "You may be young by choice, but you and I are clearly not as blissfully ignorant of some more adult factors of life. Dorothy either. Peter is a lot of things, and blissfully ignorant just happens to be one of his creeds. He has had a tough time, and if everyone else vanished, leaving him alone for who knows how long, how do I know you didn't take advantage of that for your own needs?"

"Taken advantage of him?" I demanded incredulously. "Up until a day ago, I was worried that he was the one manipulating me for *his* gain."

"Peter doesn't have much experience with women, let alone a Wicked one, but his getting extremely attached to one at all may alter his judgment. He didn't even know about puberty until a few hours ago. He is a Good person, and he has suffered horrors as a child that no one should, but in other ways, he is entirely innocent. The Wicked witch *I* knew liked to use her wiles to baffle men. She'd say or do anything to get something she wanted out of them."

"Goodness," I couldn't help but scoff. "You're afraid I am some sort of succubus who is preying on your friend, aren't you?"

Tip stared boldly back at me but didn't respond. I felt heat rise in my cheeks from equal parts indignation and embarrassment.

"Well, you're wrong. Tell me, why are you so quick to judge me, but *Dorothy* got a free pass? Is it just because I happen to be involved with your friend, or rather, do you *actually* think she's an exception to your preconceived notions on morality?" I squinted at the boy and took a step closer, my arms still folded, body rigid with increasing annoyance and mutual mounting hostility.

"I didn't know she was Wicked when we first met. I just knew she wasn't friends with The Wizard, so it wasn't preconceived at all," Tip replied, raising a hand for silence when I opened my mouth to interrupt. "However, hearing her story, she has only been in this world for a matter of days and the girl clearly has no idea what she is doing. Most of this terrible stuff has been thrust upon her. It isn't something she chose. She's just been reacting to what *Wickeds* have been putting her through."

"I didn't make her drink the tea!" I hissed, practically baring my teeth at him.

"No, just swung a knife at her throat, right?" Tip's gray green eyes bored into mine, judging and unrelenting. "One of those little details she mentioned in passing back at the castle."

"Yet I was the one who got cut with it." I had half a mind to zap the glare off his puckered little face. I gestured pointedly to my injured arm that was still bandaged from the gash of the knife.

"You know what they say about karma, Witch." Tip replied evenly, and I ground my teeth together, seeing that this back and forth was going to go nowhere. He'd clearly made up his mind about distrusting me already. *He* was the one feeling very two-faced right now. Pleasant to some and sour to others.

"So, Little Miss Freckles gets a free pass because she's only been here a few days? How about those of us who have been here for years? I certainly didn't burn a village down in *my* first few days here." I snapped. "Whether you like it or not, she is as Wicked as I am."

"She risked her entire mission to actually save a mouse caught in a giant spider web. It was stupid, but not exactly something one would categorize as Wicked. She's not interested in Peter in the slightest either." Tip's eyes flitted away and his voice was soft.

I thought for a moment about how I had left Peter behind in Wonderland after our quarrel. Had that been Wicked? No. I simply was trying to make pragmatic decisions for my future. And I was hurt that it seemed he didn't want any part of that future with me at the time. It was emotionally based, of course, but it wasn't set in malice. My fingers fidgeted against my arms.

"You've been here for a while by the sound of it, and your reputation is the *Wickedest* Wicked Witch. Now, if Mombi is just a regular Wicked witch, I wonder why I would have my doubts with her apparent superior." Tip's tone returned to its dry, sarcastic self, and his eyes rested on me, unblinking and accusatory.

"Didn't Dorothy saving that mouse lead you into a trap? And

what about the little bird? She's clearly interested in Peter— for whatever relevance that holds." I rolled my eyes.

"*Wendy* isn't Wicked, and Dorothy didn't set that trap, Mombi did. It's a staple of hers." Tip's tone could cut through glass with the layers of animosity buried under his captor's name.

"Fine, don't trust me," I seethed. "Your opinion is about as important to me as a thorn in my foot."

"Doesn't a thorn in your foot draw a lot of attention?" He bickered needlessly, eyes beginning to rove around us.

"You're so painfully irritating. If it weren't for Peter, I—" I stopped myself before finishing the incriminating sentiment.

"Kill me? Cut off my head? My, how very Wicked of you," Tip snorted, and I kicked myself for falling right into proving him right.

"Whatever issues you have with your Wicked witch, sort it out with her and leave me out of it." Tapping my fingers rhythmically against my temple, I winced at the throbbing inside my skull. "My head is pounding from whatever dreadful potion The Wizard used on me, and I just want to get out of this place and back to the others. So, if you can just stomach it long enough to do that, let's figure this out together, then we can go back to not knowing each other. I'm really not planning to smite you or anything."

Tip merely grunted in a noncommittal manner to my statement, but shrugged and began exploring our immediate environment best he could in the dim lighting. I groaned at the notion that I had been paired with such an unhelpful brute, and made to plunk myself on the ground to try to think up a plan, only to immediately plop into a layer of water. It was cold and had movement, trickling through my fingers as I splayed them on the ground.

"Where'd this water come from?" I grumbled aloud, and switched to crawling around on my hands and knees to take a more tactile approach to discerning our ominous environment.

After stumbling over my dress, I cursed inwardly, forgetting how tedious exploring in a long dress was, and waved a hand over my attire to return it to that of a red blouse, fitted black trousers, and sturdy boots.

I continued to follow the trail of running water until I traced it back to a small crevice in the pitted wall. "Curious," I mumbled as I felt around the opening. A piece of the surrounding wall broke off into my hand and the stream of water increased its flow. "Oops."

Summoning a small flame to my hand, I inspected the hole more closely, unease coiling down my spine as I followed a crack that began at the crevice and ran the length of the stone to the ceiling. It would have been an easy enough thing to repair magically, had water not already started spurting from the seam, extinguishing the flame in my hand in a pitiful hiss.

"Oh dear," I breathed, no longer able to see the crack to repair it. My eyes plummeted back into darkness in stark contrast to the orange glow that had been there a moment before.

"What did you do, Witch?" Tip called through the gloom to me, his tone patronizingly longsuffering.

"Yeah, Witch, what did you do?" Tip's voice rang through a second time in a hollow echo that didn't quite mirror his original statement.

"What?" I barked back, trying to hold back the water telekinetically as best as I could. Pain pulsed through my arms as the raw flesh of both my burns and my wound from fighting Dorothy stretched to their limits from the effort.

"Did you hear that voice?" Tip shouted back at me, this time sounding closer. The scuff of his soggy boots sloshing through the shallow water now coating the gritty stone floor also told me he was coming to join me.

"That voice, did you hear it?" The echo came once more, bouncing between my ears from somewhere overhead.

"It's quite the uncanny impression," I grunted behind gritted teeth. The weight of the water I was holding back was getting heavier by the second, and I couldn't risk dropping my hold by freeing up one hand to light the area again.

"I think we are in Echo's Cave…" Tip muttered mostly to himself, distant and forlorn. His indistinct form was beside me, and my eyes were finally beginning to adjust to gloom.

"I could use a little help here!" I snapped, my muscles screaming. "Can you find a way to plug this, light the area so I can fix it, or know a way out? You can play a game with your echo another time."

"I could help! Play with your echo." My own voice reverberated back at me. A cold chill ran down my spine.

"That's not what I said..." I swallowed hard, I squinted at the spluttering shadow of water spitting from the crack as it began writhing with additional mass. Two red, glowing eyes cut through the dark, the embodiment of malice.

"That's not what I said!" My own voice growled at me from where the crimson gaze was pinning me down, it's down slipping into something low and raspy and more akin to a monster.

A shriek of surprise erupted from me as two cold shadowy tendrils curled around my wrists— equally eerily both tangible and intangible against my prickling skin. In a single fluid motion, the shadow pulled my arms apart to spread like wings at either side of my body. My hold on the water followed suit, splitting the wall in two, unleashing the hidden geyser of pent up frigid salt water. I was pelted with the burst, sending me slipping from the shadow's grasp as I was repelled backwards into the flooding cave. The water level had already grown from a trickling depth of a few centimeters to flowing freely at my waist in a seat position.

"Witch?" Tip called for me, wading clumsily through the lapping current. "We need to go. Now."

I spat the water from my mouth and rubbed the salt spray from my eyes. "What was that?"

"Come on!" Tip yanked me to my feet and ushered me forward.

"What are you doing? We can probably fight it," I panted as we broke in a labored run in the water.

"I hope you're a fast swimmer," Tip commented absently, then released his guiding hold on my hand. "Something isn't right. That should have been Echo, a harmless voice that calls back incorrect statements in your voice at you. It was never tangible before and definitely never hostile."

"It looked like a shadow-thing. Maybe I can blast it with fire or something." I mused.

"If that *is* Echo, then that means we are in Echo's Cave."

"Should that mean something to me?" I snapped.

"It's a cluster of caves on the southernmost coast of Neverland near Pirate's Cove."

"So, we are in Neverland?"

"Pay attention, Witch." Tip sighed, irritation sparking in his voice. "We are in a cave on the coast of the Neverland Sea. Something has made Echo violent, and the cave is now filling with that sea. If you start a fire now—unless you can keep it going continuously despite the water— will only hinder our vision against the dark when it goes out. So, if you want to stay behind and drown, throwing your Wicked magic fireballs at a violent shadow, go ahead. I'm getting out."

My lips puckered in annoyance and my jaw set. He had a point, but his condescending attitude made me want to join forces with the creature and drown him. Maybe it'd let me go if I helped…

The compass ticked, reminding me that this was yet another of my many Wicked thoughts filtering through in a tense situation.

"Do you at least know where you're going then?" I grumbled, my feet beginning to lift from the ground with each lapping pull of the rising tide.

"Not exactly." Tip admitted and my heart fluttered anxiously. "I'm familiar with these caves, but it's been a long time since I've been here and I'm not exactly sure *where* we were put. But we can at least try following the current and hope it leads up to an opening to the sea."

"How did The Wizard even know to teleport us here in the first place? Is he familiar with Neverland geography?" I asked, my curious mind beginning to sift through theories and ideas.

"Must be." Came the monosyllabic reply.

"I can't run anymore," I puffed, pushing off the ground to a horizontal position to begin swimming instead. My shorter height was a disadvantage, but even Tip's tall frame was struggling to run sluggishly through the water.

"Guess we'd better swim for it from here," He conceded, dropping fully into the current.

"You'd better swim for it!" That garbled echo called back to us, setting my teeth on edge.

My eyes darted around wildly at the unnerving sound of claws grinding against stone in rapid succession, couched in a low hissing and snarling that snaked through the ambient air of the cave. I dared look up when a few pebbles tumbled from the ceiling against the top of my head. Above me, I saw the dark outline of humanoid wraith skittering after us on all fours. Its malevolent scarlet gaze bored into mine, a hunter fixed on its prey, and now that my eyes had adjusted, I could make out a row of sharp teeth spreading from ear to ear on the creature.

"It's coming after us," I tried to keep the fear out of my voice, paddling as fast as I could beside the Lost Boy. The water was now filling half of the cavern. "I really hope we find a way out of here soon."

"Me too. We are running out of rope here. You don't have any water magic?"

"Stooping to my Wicked abilities?" I scoffed.

"Is now the time for that?" Tip bit impatiently.

"No, I don't have any control of water. The best I have is telekinetic movement to a limited degree." The end of my reply was drowned out by a terrible rumbling noise.

"Where'd it go?" Tip hissed, scanning the ceiling for signs of the wraith, but there were no signs of the ominous Echo beast.

We both slowed to a pause, treading water in place to try to discern our surroundings. All I could hear now was the sound of water lapping around us.

"Something just occurred to me," I began as unease curled through my chest. "The water keeps rising in here and we are getting alarmingly close to the ceiling."

"That *just* occurred to you?"

"No," I snipped. "If the water is still rising like this, I don't think there is an outlet."

"It could be high tide." Tip countered with a shrug. "We just need to not have a roof over our heads and we will be fine."

"But the current wouldn't still be going directionally if it were meeting with a large body of water pushing in, would it?" I queried, looking down at where my long hair was being pulled by the water.

Tip's scowl of annoyance turned into one of contemplation. "That might mean we are in the cave by the waterfall. If we—"

Another loud rumbling thundered around out, the sound causing ripples of disturbance on the surface of the water.

"Look out!" I shouted, slipping in front of the vexing Lost Boy, just barely catching a falling rocking from crashing into him with my telekinetic hold.

The weight of the boulder started pushing me down, and I kicked out hard to stay afloat long enough to drop it away from us.

The effort caused me to wheeze for a moment. My lungs were still burning from all of my smoke inhalation in Oz, and my body was sore and tired.

"Look out!" The growling echo sounded to repeat my warning, and the bright gleaming eyes appeared above us again.

I expected another rock to be dislodged at us, but to my horror, the beast itself pushed off the ceiling, pouncing right for us.

"Ah!" I squawked, just before the monster made contact with me, and we both submerged below the murky water.

Dark bubbles billowed around me, and scarlet colored the water as the wraith's talon-like claws raked across my shoulder. One nicked the compass, scratching the silver metal, and for a brief moment of reprieve, the shadow recoiled with a growl.

Bringing my hands together, I materialized a knife and tried to stab it, but like a true shadow, my blow sailed right through it.

As panic began thundering in my chest, I felt Tip's rough hands grab hold of my wrist and yank me up.

When my head broke the surface, the shadow mirrored me, its

demon-like head slowly rising above the water. Its eyes narrowed into chips and it's too-wide mouth of fangs glistened as beads of water tinged with my blood rolled down its body.

My heart hammered in my chest wildly with fear, and my compass began spinning to match my heart rate. I reached up a hand and grabbed at the ceiling with my mind, cracking the rock to send large fragments tumbling down toward the wraith.

It hissed at me and flitted backwards in the direction we had come from, the shower of rubble separating us.

"That was reckless!" Tip snapped at the water rolling us up and down from the impact of the broken stones. "Not only does adding that much mass to the water push the level higher, you could have let in *more* water and drowned us all the faster!"

"Did you want to get eaten by that thing?" I shouted back at him. Frustration mounting to greater heights from my spinning compass. "It tore into my shoulder and my knife went right through it like it wasn't even there."

"You have a knife?"

"I dropped it." I replied flatly. I could easily make another one for him to have but his attitude was making me feel stingy. And, since we couldn't stab the shadow, it didn't seem like it would better our odds for him to have one anyway.

"Of course you did."

"You know what—" I stopped as my head bumped against something solid—The ceiling. We were out of time. The cave had filled. "Oh no."

Tip glanced upward, alarm glistening in his eyes. I needed to break us out of here or we were going to drown. But Tip had also been annoyingly right, and if I aimed the wrong direction, I'd kill us that much faster.

"Where can I hit? It's our only shot at this point."

"Can't you teleport us?"

"I don't know where I am, so I could just as easily teleport us into somewhere worse or into a rock." I tilted my chin, my cheek now brushing the top of the cave. "Just tell me where I can blast!" My voice pitched with panic, before I was forced to suck in a deep breath, the water brimming the top of the cave.

Blinking rapidly to try to peer through the dark water, I felt Tip tug my arms to our right, and I had no other option to comply with following him. I knew my vision in the dark wasn't fantastic but I was beginning to think this man had some sort of hidden ability to see in the dark. Beyond that, the salt water was stinging my eyes terribly, causing me to have to squeeze them shut repeatedly.

I could just barely make out his arm gesturing to an area against the wall. In the dull pulsing sound beneath the water, I noticed I could hear a sort of *whooshing* sound, and realized my hair was still being pulled toward the tiniest glimmer of bleak light.

Tip had found the source of the current— and not a moment too soon. My vision was already starting to flicker, and my head was pounding while my lungs screamed for air. It was dulling my magical strength the more my physical body weakened, so I didn't think I could hold the collateral weight of the stone. I focused my power in my hand and pounded it against the rock desperately. I repeated the motion again and again, until finally, the stone cracked, a tall gleaming fissure against the stark black.

I struck again, deepening the cracks. Then, in a final desperate attempt to break through, I resorted to using my remaining strength to rend the rock in two at the seam. In an instant, Tip and I were sucked through the new opening, freefalling blindly. Rocks tumbled around us, one the size of my fist struck the compass with a thud, and I felt a jolt of pain course through me from head to toe.

Gulping in as much air as I could around the spraying water, I looked around me wildly. Pain seared behind my eyes at the sudden light, but from what I could tell, we were seconds away from smashing into the rocks at the base of the waterfall so I was glad I looked.

Thankfully, Tip was tumbling within arms reach so I latched onto his hand and teleported us a few feet away, safely from both the falling rubble and the rocks waiting to crack our bodies beyond repair.

"This… this way," Tip coughed weakly beside me, and began swimming to where I could now see a beach.

I followed sluggishly behind him, reducing my strong strokes to meager paddlings. Eventually, I could finally feel solid ground beneath me again and crawled forward on my hands and knees. Twice I had been to Neverland now, and twice I had nearly drowned thanks to some creature trying to drown me. Pausing in the shallow lapping waves, I looked down at my dented compass, scowling at the damage done by the shadow and rocks.

"When did she give that to you anyway?" Tip asked, grimacing as he continued to draw in deep breaths while we dragged ourselves forward through the sand.

"When did who give what to me?" I sniffed.

"Mombi."

"What are you going on about? She didn't give me anything other than a splitting headache."

Tip squinted at me with a pause of confusion before tapping the base of the throat with a leading raise of his brows. "The moral compass. It's Mombi's."

"Where are we? What happened?" I demanded. *Take deep breaths. Stay calm.* I willed myself as my brain caught up to my current precarious situation. The tips of my silver shoes peeked over the edge of the cliff Wendy and I had been stranded on. Wind pulled at my hair, and I could feel the buildup of salty ocean mist mix with the sweat on my face.

"I think we are in Neverland," Wendy answered from beside me. Her gentle eyes were narrowed against the wind, bittersweet nostalgia swirling wildly.

"Great, another wacky world to figure out? I've barely managed to walk through the other two and keep my life. Or my feet at the very least." I grumbled.

"Well, I am familiar with Neverland, at least, so we have that going for us." She offered kindly, clearly trying to scrounge up some sort of silver lining for me.

I bit my tongue. Wendy was very nice as far as people went, but heaping piles of optimism in dire straits was grating to my nerves and turned my stomach. After swallowing down a biting retort that would ultimately be unhelpful, I took a more productive and contained approach.

"Alright, so do you know how to get us off this cliff?"

Wendy scanned the horizon, even daring to lean forward enough to crane her neck to look above us.

"I think we are near the Neverbird Nest." She answered finally, leaning back against the crumbling dirt and stone.

"Is that bird something we need to worry about eating us?" I asked with a lame laugh, half attempting a joke, but Wendy merely shrugged.

"Probably not."

"That's very reassuring." I replied tartly.

"We could try jumping into the water. There aren't any rocks and the water is deep." Wendy suggested, squatting precariously to get a better vantage point of the tumbling sea below us.

A cold chill ran down my spine at the thought of submerging in the infinite water. I shook my head slowly. "I'd rather not."

Wendy looked at me curiously before switching to a seated position on the bluff, her legs dangled from the crook of her knee down. Her casual fearlessness was increasingly unsettling.

"We could climb up the roots. They are all over the side here and will likely lead us to the Neverbird Tree."

"That sounds dangerous," I sniffed.

Wendy huffed a sigh and raised her arms in defeat. "Well, Dorothy, I'm afraid short of staying here indefinitely, we have to either go up or down."

I glared at the Lost Girl, though I knew she was merely stating the truth. I furrowed my brows and tried once more to steady my breathing.

"I just don't want to die here, falling off the cliff like some brainless idiot."

"I'm sure Alice won't let you die. She wants your shoes, right? If you die here, I think The Wizard gets them for putting you here."

"Alice isn't here!" I snapped. I had only known her a handful of hours longer than Wendy, but her moods were dangerously unstable. She had been ready to kill me one moment, and then be allies the next. Was I supposed to just blindly trust that the alliance would hold when things got rocky? For all I knew, she'd push me just to take the shoes.

"It's all going to be fine, Dorothy. You just need to calm down and believe you will be alright. Neverland picks up on strong convictions."

I tried really hard to not keep looking down at the drop in front of me. I could hear pebbles being dislodged from the shaking of my legs. I felt the strange dizziness slither through my brain, and tasted the phantom remnants of insani-tea on my lips. *Not now.*

"What about you?" I breathed, closing my eyes, trying to quell the rising storm ballooning in my head. I couldn't lose it. Not here.

"What about me?" Wendy tilted her head, her blue eyes reflecting the shimmering ocean below us. Something about the image yanked at my subconscious with a vague sense of familiarity.

"How do you know that *you'll* be alright?"

She smiled. There was a mature sense of peace, I couldn't even hope to grasp at, radiating from her. "I don't. One thing I learned in Neverland— that I had almost forgotten until I saw Peter again— is that all you need is a little faith and trust to carry you from any situation."

Gee, how cliché. I forced my eyes not to roll. Happy thoughts were not going to get us off this cliff. Silence lingered to an awkward length.

"So what do you suppose we do? Just wait and hope we don't tumble to our doom?" My voice cut through the quiet like a knife. I was trying to resolve myself to the possibility that one of the others would find us, eventually.

But, Wendy's back straightened and she lifted her chin with a strength I hadn't seen in her yet. "No." Her voice was full of adamance.

"No?" I quirked an eyebrow, sweat beading down my back, and another wave of anxious chaos tumbled through me.

"No, I do not intend to do anything of the sort."

"Well then, now what?"

"I lived here in Neverland for a while too, you know."

"And?" I couldn't help but scoff.

What could this dainty little doll possibly accomplish? No doubt, she'd had Peter with her at all times, if not her brothers, or other Lost Ones like Tip, and was only shown the finer elements of this place. Sure, she'd been held captive in a dungeon, but she'd been more or less safe. And, I highly doubted that she had drank any contaminated tea or had her heart twisted in moral obscurity to toughen her up like Alice or myself.

"*And*, it wasn't all just fun and games. Neverland is just as dangerous as Wonderland or Oz. One doesn't simply just survive without magic and not learn a thing or two. There is always a way out."

"But, The Wizard took you and faked your murder…" I pressed, unsure if she was trying to convince herself as much as me that we would make it off this cliff alive.

"The Wizard is a different story. I can admit that I am defenseless against magic and I will not stoop to a Wicked witch's level by murdering someone. No offense, of course."

"Of course," I sniffed.

"Plus he only got me when I wandered into his territory. But, being able to navigate a place like this is a completely different story. Now, can you inch yourself to the left a bit?"

"Why?"

"Because I've decided we are climbing up."

"What?" I gasped, the tensing of my entire body in apprehension sending more rubble tumbling away.

"We are going up. Worst case, we end up going down. But, something tells me you'd fancy avoiding the swim." She expertly swung her legs under her and rose back to a standing position beside me.

I knew she was right, and we needed to do something but anxiety was wreaking havoc in my chest, like a bowling ball, sending the pins flying in every direction.

With no small amount of reluctance, I shifted a little to my left as Wendy had requested. She nodded approvingly and followed me, nimbly swiveling around so her body was facing the wall behind us. Standing on her tip toes, she reached up to full extent of her height and tugged at a protruding root.

After a little pulling and wriggling, she'd managed to lower the thick tendril to a more accessible height. She gripped onto it tightly and placed one foot squarely against the wall, ready to start climbing.

"Alright, Dorothy. We are going to climb to the top. I'll go first to figure out the path. Should we lose our grip, push off from the wall and turn to dive into the water to avoid injury. Got it?" She instructed calmly. Her sudden comfortability and confidence here, in Neverland, made me wonder what kind of reckless adventures Peter and Tip had gotten her mixed up in that scaling a cliff with questionable vines was seemingly no big deal.

I nodded somberly, the debilitating dizziness rolling through my mind a moment before disappearing as fast as it had appeared. Wendy smiled encouragingly at me and I had little choice but grit my teeth and get through it.

"Why don't you tell me about yourself a little while we go?" She called down to me as she began the ascent, and I followed shakily after her.

"Didn't I already do that back in Oz?"

"No, I mean the smaller details. What is your favorite color? A favorite dessert? Is there a genre of book you love or detest? That sort of thing. I am quite fond of tales of adventures with wonderfully romantic endings," She prattled on, her voice beginning to strain with the effort of hauling herself upward.

"Oh," I replied blandly. I hadn't put much thought into conversing on those subjects. "I, um, like the color blue, I guess."

"Blue is a lovely color. I'm rather fond of pink, myself. Mother never much cared for me to wear it though on account of my red hair. Then again, Mother would approve of little to nothing to do with anything here in Neverland. It's much too wild and fanciful for her taste."

I could feel a faint burning in my biceps as I worked muscles I didn't typically find myself in need of on the farm. My foot slipped on a crumbling bit of rock and I gasped as I hung freely from the vine for a sickening moment before I found my footing again.

My vision shuttered through waves of shapes and colors for a heartbeat before flickering back to the wall in front me. I gripped harder onto my tether and panted.

"Are you alright, Dorothy?" Wendy had paused her climbing to call down to me.

"Define the meaning of that statement and I'll get back to you," I grumbled shakily, avoiding looking up. I figured it best if I lost track of how far I had to go before I was relatively safe again, but also found it best if I didn't look down to see how much farther I'd gone from the ledge or the water beneath it.

"Well, I just meant— oh, what have we here?" Wendy mumbled curiously to herself, interrupting her explanation.

"Whatever it is, is it going to kill us?" I groaned, daring to crane my neck to look up at Wendy.

Apprehension tingled in my fingers and toes as I spotted a tremor in her arm supporting the entirety of her weight while she used her other hand to brush and pull at the rubble in front of her.

"Be careful up there!" I hissed, wishing this girl would go back to her meek and submissive self for her own safety. "Your arm is shaking, and it's freaking me out."

"I found a door," she called down to me. "Well, a doorknob. It is pretty worn, I'd imagine it's been here for ages. Not that I've ever scaled this cliff before today, but I am surprised no one else ever mentioned it."

"What is so wonderful about a random doorknob?" I sighed, measuring the distance we had left to climb now that I'd looked up. "Can we get a move on before our arms give out on us?"

"You've got to use your imagination, Dorothy!" Wendy lectured happily. "This could be a tunnel out so we don't have to climb the rest of the way. Or maybe it's hiding a long lost treasure."

"Treasure isn't going to keep me alive!" I snapped.

"No, but it sure would be exciting to tell Peter about," Wendy chuckled to herself. "Not to mention, if there is room, we might have a resting point before we climb the rest of the way up."

"Fine, fine. Whatever. Just do what you're going to do before my arms fall off and take me with them." I groused impatiently.

"Watch your eyes! I'll likely disturb the layer of dust and grit when I open it."

I nodded, forgetting she couldn't see me below her. "Hurry up."

Wendy squared her feet against the cliff face to leverage her strength, clasping her delicate hand around the door handle, and giving it a firm tug.

A shower of small pebbles cascading over me, and I felt a fresh layer of dust coat my body. I loosed a dreaded breath to dispel the lingering particles around my mouth before speaking.

"Well? Is it a tunnel?"

"No, it appears to be some sort of room…"

"Good enough, go inside."

"Shouldn't we be cautious?"

"Wendy! I am not an adventurer. I don't climb cliffs, swim with mermaids, or fly with fairies. I need to get off this bluff. I don't care where, but I need it now. So, move it!" I barked, an edge of frantic anxiety creeping into my voice. Sweat was beginning to gather in my palms, and I had no idea how long I could fend off the disorienting dizzy spells before one of them made me fall— if I didn't slip in my own perspiration first.

"Alright, I'm going to climb through." She agreed, a small air of offense in her tone as my shortness.

I resolved myself to apologize for snapping once I had my feet on solid ground again. This girl was very kind and sweet, but she clearly romanticized everything about this world— or land or whatever— and wasn't seeming to pick up on the urgency of our situation. She scarcely seemed aware of her own frail state from being held captive for so long.

It almost made me wish Tip had been my teammate instead. He was cranky and aloof, sure, but out of my contemporaries here, he at least seemed able to read a situation and act logically. Though Peter would have likely been the most useful since he could simply fly us off the cliff… or Alice could have teleported us to safety.

I pursed my lips as I realized I'd been paired up with the weakest link of our group, which wasn't a good thing, because I was the second weakest link. The sooner we found one of the others, the better off we'd be.

"Oh my," Wendy gasped after a series of scuffles and grunts as she clambered through the odd doorway.

"Hold on, I'm coming," I called up to her, gritting my teeth and hauling myself upward as fast as my aching arms would take me.

When I reached the doorway, I frowned. It was a bit to the right of where I was clinging like a burr to one of the root tendrils. I should have watched to see how Wendy had managed it. For all my judgments of her, she was a lot more nimble than me, that was for sure.

"There's a foothold there, and a root to grip just there," Wendy poked her head through the doorway and pointed. "Then I'll take your hand and help you the rest of the way."

I followed her instructions, warily stretching my leg to find my sparkling shoes bumping into a tiny outcrop maybe three inches deep. But, sure enough, it was enough to transition me over the gap to grasp at Wendy's hand.

The final hop into the doorway set all of my nerves on edge, and I was thankful the dizziness hadn't come back to play in this final crucial step as I pulled myself through the small doorway and fell forward.

Still laying flat on the cool ground, my face resting against my arms while I caught my breath, I asked, "Where are we now?"

"I'm not really sure how, but I think we are back where we started."

"No…" I whined, my brain immediately picturing us back on the ledge where we'd been teleported to.

But, then common sense clicked in. I was sprawled out on a marbled floor so I couldn't possibly be on the cliff, which only meant one thing.

We were back in the Wonderland castle.

Three

Peter

One moment, I was in the Red Castle, the next, I was blinking through smothering, dusty darkness. A slit of light split the area like a blade, illuminating floating particles of dust in the stagnant space. I was sitting, and as I tried to rise, I felt a burning sensation of rope restraining my wrists.

"Hmmm." I mused aloud, darting a look around to surmise my whereabouts. "Hello? Anyone home?" I called quietly.

My voice came back to me in an isolated, muffled echo that told me I was most likely unsupervised. Just the way I liked to be. I couldn't help but grin as I felt the material I was sitting on. A wooden chair.

"Clearly, they underestimate my uncanny ability to thwart extended capture." I clucked to myself. "Hey, Shadow? Are you free?"

I looked down, but in the dark room, my magical shadow couldn't properly form. It was a restraint of its own form— really the only way to effectively restrain a shadow at all was to snuff out the light and trap them in their own darkness.

"Alright, then. If you can't untie me, I suppose I shall have to do it myself," I couldn't help but feel a small thrill of excitement race through my veins, surging side by side with the adrenaline of escape. Beneath that were the less pleasant feelings of desperation, concern for my friends' safety, and rage at having been so easily bested by The Wizard. My rancid, monstrous excuse for a father.

He would pay dearly for all he was doing— all he had already done. But, first, I needed to escape whatever binding situation I was currently in, and I would relish every second of breaking free of this little trap of his. My days of avoidance were behind me, and I couldn't play the ignorant little boy anymore. I seemed to have grown up despite myself, and the sudden shouldering of responsibility was enough to bring me to my knees, if I hadn't already been sitting down.

But, it also was blossoming a strange sense of pride, excitement, and protective instinct within me that was somehow both foreign and familiar at the same time. Perhaps those feelings had been there a long while now, and my soul had aged all along, even if my body had remained young. Maybe this was what it was like to transition from boyhood to being an adult. Higher stakes and more weight.

Now, in this moment, I wanted nothing more than to get back to Alice and my friends, and show The Wizard just how much he would fear the man I had become. Not the *boy* he taunted, but the *man* who would face up and destroy him. I was bigger, stronger, and faster than when I had left Oz. That was the trade in for youth. My fists clenched with the surge of righteous wrath that tore through my body.

"But, I'm still mostly a boy, and only a little bit of a man," I reassured myself with an awkward chuckle. "Don't know if I can stomach growing up completely just yet. And boys will be boys afterall…" I mused, gritting my teeth and flexing my muscles against my restraints.

With a quick puff of air, I kicked my legs out and up, somersaulting backwards, and bringing the chair with me. The force of sudden movement made the wood groan just before it snapped and fragmented against the floor under the weight of my propelled body. Like clockwork, the ropes holding me against the arms of the chair yielded and slacked to the ground with the splintered chair.

I rubbed absently at my wrists where the flipping about had made the rope scrape away my skin, leaving small angry and raw friction burns behind. "And boys tend to break things." I smiled at my handiwork, and began to explore the dark room with a cautiously optimistic saunter. After stubbing my toe approximately five times, my optimism faded and was replaced by the desire for a little light.

I headed for the singular slit of illumination, which appeared to be shining through the seam of a door. Feeling around the surface, there was no door handle to be found. Pushing and throwing my shoulder into it, also had little effectiveness.

"Door or not, if light is showing, there has to be some way to break through. If I could only find a damn light in this place." I muttered to myself. *You could always use magic*. A voice whispered in my head. I ran a hand through my hair slowly, trying to think of any possible alternative option.

I had lived a great while without relying on my inherited magical abilities. Magic had been what had ruined The Wizard. It was what had made him torture me and turn me into a test subject for magical-extraction experiments to serve his greed. I plunked myself down by where I had broken the chair and picked up two pieces, rolling one against the other to start a fire. I spun the wood through my hands faster and faster as I contemplated the depth in which magic had poisoned everything around me.

Magic had corrupted all the Wickeds who lived in this world. It had even corrupted Alice and Dorothy, been used against Tip for nefarious purposes, and had taken Wendy's family from her. Magic had scarred us all for life. It had robbed me of both a father and a mother.

Mother.

A spark lit at the end of sticks of wood, and my hands slowed their rapid rotating. Blowing lightly on the spark to keep the ember alive, I ripped off a piece of fabric from my sleeve, tied one end to the other piece of chair and coiled it around to form a base of a torch.

My mother's magic had been born of beauty and Good. Her imagination was so powerful, it created worlds and creatures, and natural phenomena. It was *her* power that coursed through my veins, that my father so envied and desired. It was her magic that had allowed me refuge in Neverland, to fly with fairies, swim with mermaids, and to live in wonder with my Lost Ones.

The frayed edge of the fabric caught fire in a small plume of heat and light, a soft hiss cutting through the absent din of silence. The reach of the glow was small as the flame traveled the short distance up the fabric to my knotted base, then expanded ever so slightly as it bonded with the wood and burned freely.

The Lost Ones had once been able to escape their own strife and the mundane to my fantastic world of Neverland. They had lived wild and free, able to do things they couldn't in a world of rules, proper physics, and responsibility. An infinite youth. And that freedom had technically been born of my magic— the magic my mother had gifted to me in her final moments of life. In a lot of ways, it provided so much of the comfort of my deceased mother I never allowed myself to think much about before now. It allowed me to meet Wendy and Tip and Dorothy. It had brought Alice here to me to be my friend when I needed one the most. It showed me that growing up with her wasn't so bad.

In a world of manipulations, lies, loneliness, and torment, Alice had helped me grow into a better person. She showed me what it was to really love someone other than myself. To finally look ahead towards a future, rather than hiding in an infinite present. And without magic, that would have never happened. I probably ought to share these insights with her when we finally reunited. It seemed like something she'd fancy hearing.

A pang tore through my heart as I weighed the good and the bad that magic had brought into my life. I stared at my hand, now visible in the glow of my makeshift torch, feeling the phantom touch of Alice's hand in mine. I curled my fingers inward, as if to give her hand a squeeze and say everything would be alright, because it always was in the end. Was that optimism a gift from my mother? How much of me was her, or my father, and how much was just me?

My head hung for a moment, thet tips of my auburn hair falling in my eyes, shining red in the glow of fire. With a puff of determination I rose to my feet and held the torch in front of me to assess my holding place. What I saw before me snuffed out any good feelings I had managed to conjure up, and instead replaced them with cold, numbing despair. A lump came to my throat, my mouth felt like cotton, and a cold sweat rippled over my brow. Every happy thought, and familiar face faded from my mind, and all I was instantly submerged in tangible, internal darkness and pain.

"Not here." The light shuddered as my hand trembled before my worst childhood memories.

Contraptions, trinkets, and torture devices littered the room, the remnant pain seeming to echo off each one and roll over me in waves, rooting me to the spot. A child's screams filled my head, and I stumbled backwards, dropping the torch to cover my ears.

Stop that shrieking, Boy. Can't manage to do this one thing for your father?

"No… No. No." I recoiled as The Wizard's past words penetrated my mind, pulling me back into my youngest childhood self.

Disgusting, putrid, creature. What would your mother think if she saw you carrying on like this, Boy. Straighten up and be a man.

"Get out! Get out!" I felt panic clawing at my heart as it raced beyond what I felt it could endure, and a pit yawned open in my stomach, both empty and weightless, as well as heavy and full of dread.

If you ever want to be a wizard, you'll have to learn to handle this pain. Your mother would still be here if you had been able to control yourself then. Never forget for a moment that you were the one who murdered her. It's your fault that she's dead.

I couldn't breathe as the child's screaming and begging sounded once more. *My* screaming and begging from moments I'd left buried in the darkest corners of my mind erupted out in the open. I wheezed and dropped to my knees, as I tried to suck air into my lungs.

I need to escape. I need to get away. I need to escape these feelings. The thoughts raced wildly through my mind. I didn't understand why I was feeling this ghost of memory so viscerally and repetitively as if I was somehow physically back in that moment. I couldn't access the eternal optimism I always leaned on to carry me through, and instead was drowning in internal despair, guilt, and anguish.

"I didn't mean to…" I gasped in tandem with the little boy's sobs.

I didn't mean to. Please forgive me.

Forgiveness won't bring her back, Boy. The best we can do is try to remove the power you stole from her. You're lucky to be alive after killing your own mother, so don't you dare ask for forgiveness on top of sparing your life. Again.

Pain surged through my body at the echoed memories of his commands to restart the mechanisms designed to rip the magic from my body. It felt so real, like it was really sucking me back into that moment as the pain intensified.

You aren't worth forgiving, Boy. You aren't worth loving so no one will ever love you. You aren't worth the effort of knowing. You aren't even worth a second thought. Just give back what you stole from me!

The pain was unbearable, the screaming of the child-me in my head threatened to shatter my mind, and I felt his former pain trying to consume me all over again. I threw my head back and the screeching of the child erupted from my throat. The present me and the memory howled a cacophony of pain and unfathomable loneliness into the dark musty room. Just like then, no one could hear me, and even if they could no one would care. Everything I had run from for so long, and had tried to forget, all those years playing in Neverland with my lost friends, my time with Alice— all of that just to end up back where I had started. Had I ever even left? Perhaps all of it had been a wonderful delusion and I had been broken all along, unable to confront the horrors of my true existence. No one was real. No one cared. Everyone left, but no one ever came…

The agony faded slowly, draining me of all my strength. I fell to my side, thumping against the cold, hard floor. The torch flickered and danced on the ground in front of my face. Tears ran down my cheeks and my throat burned from the screaming. I stared into the rhythmic flames, feeling flat, small and lifeless.

"I didn't mean to." I whispered hoarsely, choking on another sob. "I didn't mean to." I repeated the same sentence over and over, unable to stand, unable to move, unable to stop sinking further into myself. I didn't know how long I stayed there, collapsed and broken on the floor, but when the cloud finally started lifting from the invasive and repetitive thoughts, the torch had nearly burned out completely.

"We should kill him." A hissing voice called out to me from the darkness.

"What?" I croaked out mindlessly.

"We should kill him. The witch too. Kill anyone who ever dared doubt us or abandon us. Wendy and Tip didn't try hard enough to return to us. They didn't want it badly enough. And Alice. Well, we already know what she's going to do."

"We?" I sniffled in confusion, and though I still couldn't pry my body from the floor, I managed to lift my gaze enough to see a dark wispy figure walking towards me.

It knelt down beside me and lifted me up roughly by my shirt, it's strange wraith like fingers curling into the fabric. The touch felt cold as death but left a remnant burning sensation as it brushed my skin.

"Yes, we." The hissing dripped away to leave the sound of my own voice speaking to me, dark and ominous.

As I looked up into the eyes of this shadowy phantom, I saw him now for who he was— my darkest inner thoughts, staring back at me with glowing red eyes full of malice.

"No, no." I spluttered lamely, dragging my hand to paw around at my chest lest I find myself collared with a moral compass like Alice, but there was nothing hanging from my neck. "I don't want any of that." My words were sluggish and weak.

"Really? *Any* of it?" The shadow grinned at me, multiple rows of shining white fangs spreading across his dark face. "You don't want The Wizard to pay? You don't feel angry that Alice is leaving?"

"Well, you've got me there." The familiar pangs of frustration that poked at my heart everytime I thought of Alice leaving palpitated, and the fearful rage at the thought of my father's smug face as he stood there threatening her and my friends thundered to life.

"We could use our power and best The Wizard. Then, his minions. From there. we will be unparalleled in power in this world. We hold all the cards." The Shadow-Me released its hold on my shirt and sat back across from me, still beaming.

"You're forgetting about Alice. She is a feisty one with quite the magical left hook, if you will," I countered, feeling strangely at ease with this darkness, yet also in terrible danger in its presence. But, I couldn't seem to raise my hands to fight, or my feet to flee. All I could do was keep talking.

"She pales to your power. We can make her do or be whatever we like her to." Images of Alice with her arms wrapped around my neck, staring at me with unbridled adoration flickered into my mind's eye. "We can make her stay with us forever. We can make all of them stay with us forever." The shadow folded his arms smugly.

"We wouldn't have to be alone ever again?" I felt my sense dull, and a faint haze creeped into my mind as I looked down at my hand, picturing this unmatched power coursing through my veins. I was so tired from reliving my most dreaded memories, I just wanted to succumb to the darkness and be done with it all. I'd run and fought to remain happy for so long, and now there was nothing left in me but pain and regret. That's all I could feel.

"Never again. No one would dare even try."

Temptation curled around my arms, like a warm embrace of reassurance and control. "No more running from my father?"

"No need to run from a dead man rotting in the ground where he belongs."

"Killing would make us Wicked though…" I faltered, blinking away some of the stupor as I thought of Alice and her being held captive by the title of Wicked witch.

"Ha!" The Shadow laughed hoarsely, the discordant hissing returning to his voice. "What do you think we are now? The strength of your pain runs deep into the darkest of cockerels where only the Wicked can survive. No matter how you run, that essence lives inside of you, just as I do."

"What?" I gasped, cold dread dousing me like I'd submerged

entirely into icy waters. I was waking up from the stupor.

The shadow leaned forward and picked up the dying torch. "Why don't we plummet into the darkness we've been running from for so long? We just have to give in, and let the last of the light go out. Neverland was always just a mask of what could really be. It's as fake as your father's love. So, I'll be here whenever you're ready to descend into your true self, and call yourself what you've always been destined to be— Peter, the All Powerful Wicked Wizard, and king of this world."

"I can't." I breathed out hoarsely, scrambling away. "I never wanted to be Wicked. I won't be like him!"

"You don't have a choice in the matter!" The shadow snarled at me, crouching, ready to spring at me any moment. The sudden change in disposition made my skin crawl, and I was instantly all too aware of what type of deep seeded darkness I was capable of, seeing the monstrous wraith before me. He was everything I had hoped to never turn into, and that was positively terrifying.

"Ah… No. No, thank you. I'll pass on your offer and if you'd be so kind as to go back to where you came from. Maybe show me the way out as you do?" I babbled nervously. I had been so stupid to let myself fall into my own pit of despair and let this monster try to coerce me. Alice would have smacked me over the head if she'd witnessed it. Then, she'd already be three steps into a counterattack.

I wanted Alice to stay because *she* wanted to. I didn't hold any ill will towards Wendy or Tip for their absence. It hadn't been their fault. And yes, I wanted to defeat The Wizard so badly I could practically taste it, but that was going to be a battle of its own means to protect this world from its true villain. I couldn't let that beast tempt me, even if it was part of me. I was Good.

"Peter?" A small feminine voice called out. It sounded distant, but vaguely familiar. All of these mysterious voices ancouncing themselves out of thin air was making me very apprehensive. The wraith before me seemed somehow restrained despite its efforts to lunge for me.

"Yes?" I replied cautiously, scrambling to my feet.

"Peter, please listen to me. You mustn't let the light go out. Please don't let him break you. Don't let him win."

"Who are you?"

"Ida, you loathsome pest, release me!" The shadow bellowed, thrashing its head. I realized whoever this woman was, she was somehow restraining the beast for me.

"Ida…" I whispered the name to myself, closing my eyes and letting it tumble through my memories, searching for why it felt so familiar. Then, like a zap of electricity, a flood of images rushed through my mind as her words sank in. My eyes flew open with recognition, looking around wildly for the witch I'd known in my early childhood. The very one I'd only just told Alice and Dorothy about the night before, and failed to recall her name. "Why are you a disembodied voice?"

"Don't let your light go out, Peter." Ida pleaded. "I can't keep hold of him much longer and you will have to take hold of your own demons, but for now, you need to let your powerful light shine through and tether the other shadows in the room that are feeding off your energy."

"What?" I squawked, looking around to see flickering creatures crawling down the walls, mouths open as if they were indeed drinking away my energy. "Well, that can't be good."

"I'll take this one with me now. But, you must let your power out. It's not a curse, I promise. Ozma chose you to carry her torch. It's time you let it burn freely. Embrace her magic, make it yours, and fight for the world she left to you."

The physical torch snuffed out, plummeting the room into darkness once more, and I saw the Shadow-Peter bare his teeth as he was forcibly enveloped within the darkness, pulled back to wherever he'd come from,by the disembodied voice of Ida. I could see the glowing beady red eyes of the remaining creatures and hear their unsettling growling and gurgling as they plodded towards me, but something was ringing through me like gunfire as I recalled more and more of the forgotten witch called Ida.

She had been the only one to treat me with kindness durring those years. She was gentle, and nurturing. She never condemned me for my mother's death, nor feared or loathed me. She had been the one light in my early childhood. The one kindness amidst endless cruelty and resentment. When she had disappeared, I had implored an answer of her whereabouts, but. of course, no one had listened to me. And that's when I had run away… to Neverland. All of it was real, and I swore at myself for thinking, even for a moment, under the weight of my anguish, that all of my magnificent memories had been false, or that none of it had mattered.

Ida had been the closest thing to a mother I had known. I had run away in search of companionship, love, and freedom. Wendy had once pretended to be our mother, and had emulated all the qualities Ida had once shown me. That's why I had felt so drawn to her, and why she had been the catalyst of the love I had been in search of.

Something ballooned in my chest, filling the emptiness within with new energy and purpose. My optimism was pushing away my inner doom and gloom once more. Ida had warned me not to let the light go out, and I understood now her words had two meanings. But, the physical torch had gone out, and now it was only me left to stand against the remaining darkness threatening to drain me.

I closed my eyes and took a deep breath, strength in hope restoring me. It was time I stopped being the little boy who let his father torture and torment him. I couldn't shake away the touch of that wraith's words entirely, and fear of my own thoughts lingered in my chest, but I could push away his devious temptations for now and face them another day. I wouldn't turn into my father. I wouldn't become the very thing I hated most. If he was the darkness, then I would be the light. He wanted me to give back what I had taken from him, but he had taken so much more from me. He had tainted the gift my mother had given me, and I wouldn't let him control that for me any longer. I wouldn't let him snuff out my light. My *mother's* light within me. The light, even now, Ida had sought to help me protect and unleash.

"No more dark thoughts, Peter," I ordered myself. "We thrive on happy thoughts. That is the source of our power. *Light.*"

My body began to glow as I conjured all the hopeful happy

thoughts I could. Every good memory that had come into my life. *Wendy, The Lost Boys, Tink, Tiger Lily, John, and Michael— all of Neverland. The new friends of Oz and Wonderland. Dorothy, Tip, and Alice.* My heart swelled. Despite The Wizard, I had found friendship, brotherhood, and even someone willing to love me as I was. Friendship and love he had sworn no one would ever show me. No, he wouldn't bind me in fear of my magic anymore. He may be my father, and there was no changing that, but I was also Peter Pan, creator and ruler of Neverland, and Princess Ozma's son. The Wizard wouldn't taint my connection to her one moment more. And I'd be damned if he kept me from fighting for me and my friends now.

I rose to my feet, my magic shimmering around my body, as I let it flow freely from my heart, bathing the tainted room in white light. This was who I was meant to be, I told myself firmly, and pushed the thoughts of the Shadow-Peter and the fear of his version of my destiny away for now.

"I won't let the light go out." I promised, and stood tall to face the remaining shadow creatures.

Four

Wendy

"Damn it! How did we end up back here?" Dorothy whirled around wildly, then threw her head back, grabbing at her face with a groan. "Why doesn't anything make physical sense here?"

"Keep your voice down, unless you want every guard in Wonderland to come after us," I chided in a hushed voice. "It looks like we are in a part of the castle we didn't see before. Do you know where we are?"

Dorothy shrugged and I looked around the hodgepodge room. It looked like perhaps it had been some sort of bedroom that had been converted into a storage room filled with strange Wonderland items and furniture.

Crossing the floor, passing Dorothy, I approached an old wardrobe with two chess knights as the handles.

"Be careful," Dorothy grunted at me, coming to stand to my side. "You don't want to get stuck in a room of reflection or whatever."

"A what?"

"I had a run in with a sort of chess themed mirror-prison out in the maze. This place does nothing but play wacky tricks on you," She replied, frowning as she pulled her braids loose and began combing through her spiraling curls with her fingers.

I pursed my lips in thought for a moment before resolving myself to open the wardrobe. Perhaps it would take us somewhere else entirely, and we would escape the castle unscathed. It certainly seemed plausible with how Dorothy had described this land.

Reaching forward, I curled my fingers around the knobs and gave a single braced yank, pulling the doors open in one rapid movement. I closed my eyes tight, should anything nefarious jump out at us, and felt Dorothy stiffen beside me for a moment, before she relaxed with a sigh.

"It's just clothes."

"Oh," I puffed with relief and opened my eyes. Sure enough, facing us was simply a wardrobe full of various blouses, trousers, and dresses. "Some of these dresses look very elegant. Do you suppose Peter and Alice held sophisticated parties before you got here?" I immediately imagined Alice gliding around a ballroom in one of the decadent gowns, the picture of confidence.

Dorothy snorted. "You really think either of those two could manage anything sophisticated? Alice *might* be able to manage it, if she could keep her cool, but Peter?"

A picture of Peter in a suit with a tophat and monocle, mumbling stuffy words of nonsense with a posh accent to a crowd of faceless onlookers flashed in my mind, with Alice setting the room on fire behind him. I smiled and shook my head. "You're right. Though I wonder why have such pretty gowns if she never wears them…" I pulled at the bodice of a stunning indigo dress with silver accents, curious as to where it was worn last. Had Peter ever seen her look beautiful in it? Had it been some sort of magical evening?

"Maybe they weren't hers. She did take over the place," Dorothy offered, then set to poking about in the more casual outfits.

"Mmm," I mumbled absently, tugging a powder blue silky gown free from the rod, and held it up against my body. I'd been in the nursery still at home, and had stayed with the Lost Boys for such a long time, I'd never really gotten to see myself in any pretty party dresses— or anything so grown up. Would I look beautiful in these dresses too?

"Hey," Dorothy swatted my arms sternly. "Does it really seem like an appropriate time to be playing dress up?"

I shrank back in embarrassment and shoved the dress back into the wardrobe. "Sorry."

"We should both grab some pants to change into and find a way out of here. We need to get Toto out too. It's the second time I've left him behind in this castle. Pick something and try not to space out again. I don't want to get killed because you want to play pretend," Dorothy chided, and retrieved a blouse and set of trousers for herself, jerking her head for me to do the same. Hand clutching at her temple, she swallowed hard. "Hurry up."

"Right, sorry," I babbled, and quickly retrieved my own clothing of choice. A pink blouse and some taupe trousers. It felt somewhat pleasing to shed the dress I had been wearing since I had woken up. I slipped into a pair of sandals last, and wandered around the storage crates while I waited for Dorothy to finish changing into her chosen blue blouse and ebony trousers.

"I wonder if any of these doors go anywhere else," I pondered aloud, gesturing broadly at a stack of doors leaning against the wall next to the window.

"There is a hallway full of doors that go to weird places, so it wouldn't surprise me," Dorothy replied from behind me. I nodded and continued meandering about.

Poking here and there in the crates, I found most of the contents to be oddball books and pages with what appeared to be miscellaneous spells and magical things written on them. My eyes lit up when I discovered a bin with various weapons inside. I might not be the fastest flier, or have any magical abilities to boast, but one thing I had always been good at was weapons play.

In the corner of my eye, as I strapped myself with a few daggers, two swords, and some chained scythe weapon, I saw Dorothy begin to set to work plaiting her hair back into her seemingly signature braids.

"You should leave it down," I commented softly. "It suits you."

"It does?" Dorothy paused her weaving in surprise at my acknowledgment.

"It does. It's freeing and your curls frame your face very nicely."

"Oh."

"Oh, um. Do whatever makes you feel best though. Don't mind me," I prattled awkwardly as I finished securing all my weapons.

"What do you think you're going to do with all of those?" Dorothy asked casually, slipping her hair ribbons into the pocket of her trousers.

"I am actually quite—" I started, but Dorothy brought her finger sharply to her lips to silence me.

"Something is coming."

"Some*thing*?" My eyes widened in alarm.

"Or someone. I don't know," Dorothy clarified impatiently. We huddled together behind a crate and waited in tense silence. I looked sideways at Dorothy, whose deep brown eyes were glued to the main door.

I knew she was tense and surly from all of the antics we'd had to face since our meeting back in the dungeon, but something told me she viewed me more as some sort of child to look after, rather than her contemporary that could help or had any skills of their own. It wasn't that I felt she was being unfriendly, or even that she didn't like me, but more that she was all pragmatism and I was something frivolous that was nice to chat with, but was meant to be someone else's burden to carry. Embarrassment and self-consciousness churned in my stomach.

"Someone is coming. We need to get out of here. You saw how many of those terrible minions Mombi had before. Toto is a smart dog and he will find a hiding place. I'm sure he only came out because he smelled uoi"

"I know I saw the little creature head down this corridor. He must have gotten into one of these extra rooms." The voice, which was now discernable as one of the castle's Card-guards, sounded again as it stopped outside our room.

"Time to go," I chirped and rushed over to the stack of doors.

"Where exactly?" Dorothy hissed, clutching at her head once more, her breathing becoming heavier. "Damn it. Not now."

"Hopefully anywhere but here! Close the door on the floor on your way, and come here. We are going through this one," I instructed briskly, as I shifted the door to lay flush against the ground and with a quick breath tugged it open. To my immediate relief, instead of showing the marbled floor beneath, the open door now led to the inside of some sort of cupboard. Perhaps we'd pop out in the kitchen.

"Guess, that's our only shot," Dorothy sighed and hopped into the door tumbling out to wherever the other side was in a clumsy crash.

"Oh dear," I groaned, hoping the noise hadn't attracted any unwanted attention, before I followed suit.

"Did you hear that?" I heard the guard call out as I tugged the door we'd used closed and waited, suspending on my stomach in the cupboard, my lower half poking out into the open where Dorothy had disappeared, as I held the knob closed with my ear to the door. "Hey, one of the doors fell over."

My stomach dropped, and I held my breath, shifting to reach for a dagger.

"Don't worry about that, we need to find where that dog went," The other guard called out, and I waited until I heard their footsteps fade before I finally released my breath and shimmied out of the cupboard. I knew they must be talking about Dorothy's pet dog, and I sent a silent prayer out to the universe, asking that the pup stay safe until we could get him back.

When my head poked out, I saw I was kneeling in a pile of broken teacups and saucers. Dorothy was inspecting where rushing into the strange portal, into the shards of glass, had nicked up one of her hands and arm, peppering her the deep blue sleeve of her blouse with holes.

"My hair cushioned my face," she announced wryly, before jerking her head at the cupboard. "Are they following?"

I shook my head and rose to my feet. "Where in the world are we now?" Looking around, I took in the cozy and rather eccentric environment of a small house, decorated entirely with tea-themed this and thats. There was a kitchen, where we were currently standing, that was home to a wood burning stove, various tea kettles, and a very tiny table that had been overturned along with all of its contents. The walls were a cheerful yellow, accented with a pattern of white teacups and saucers along the trim pieces.

At the bottom of the pass through from the kitchen into what appeared to be a small seating area for one or two guests, was a tiny door no larger than that of a mouse. Turning around in a full circle, I also spotted a back door, and a staircase that appeared to lead to a washroom and sleeping area— no doubt the proprietor's bedroom.

"We seem to have found our way into that darned Mad Hatter's cottage," Dorothy grumbled, her attention locked on a place where a broken teapot was dripping liquid and splattering on the floor below. She licked her lips, never taking her eyes off the spilling tea.

"Gracious, it looks like quite the scuffle happened here with that poor Hatter fellow. Do you suppose he's alright?" I asked, sharing the sentiment of wanting to keep moving, but stopped and returned the tiny table to an upright position, located a broom, and set to work sweeping the worst of the mess to one side of the room. Should the owners return, I wanted to tidy up any mess contributed to by our sudden arrival in their home.

"Hard to say. They break their own dishes all the time." Dorothy's reply was a little slurred and echoed with an air of distraction.

"I suppose we ought to head outside and see—ah!" I was cut short by a sudden shifting beneath my feet, and I felt the world around me begin to shrink and expand, like a rapidly beating heart. "What's going on?"

"You can feel it moving too?" Dorothy called over to me, a bit too loudly, now clutching either side of her head with both hands, a crazed glint in her eyes. "I thought it was the tea. Mmm. Tea. I'm really very thirsty, and it'd be a shame to let this pot here go to waste…" she babbled between short excited giggles.

"Dorothy, are you quite alright?"

"Drip drop drip drip drop drip," she hummed to herself as she approached the teapot. Her increasing lack of sense and wherewithal felt very unnerving in contrast to her usual sturdy self. "The teacups like to skip with the butter knives from place to place."

"Whatever do you mean? The cottage teleports too? Goodness, who knows where we are now for certain. Come on. We'd better get you out into the fresh air. When we are outside, we can start looking for the others," I spoke calmly as I guided the still reeling Dorothy away from the kitchen and shoved her through the front door.

We were greeted by a cool refreshing breeze and warm wash of afternoon sunlight. It was just the same as our flight over from Oz, and I realized that not much time had actually passed since we'd been stranded on the cliff. I blinked away the glare, adjusting from the rather dim lighting inside the cottage to the natural daylight.

When my eyes adjusted I stared in amazement at a glimmering White Castle before me. It reflected the sun, giving it a sort of ethereal glow. I thought I could almost hear the individual particles twinkling, like specs of magic dancing in the breeze, and it reminded me of the fairies back in Neverland, twirling in their pixie dust and jingling in their own fairy language to one another.

Wendy.

I stiffened, certain I'd heard a faint voice whisper my name from somewhere within the castle. It was so distant and soft, I couldn't make out the owner.

Wendy, come set us free.

A shiver ran down my spine and I took a tentative step towards the palace. Before I managed to take another step, a crackling sounded behind me and the scent of smoke stung my nose. I whirled around, catching a quick glimpse of a dark obsidian castle carved into a row of equally dark mountains, as I turned to see Dorothy with her hands ablaze, twirling about in circles, catching everything around her on fire.

Dark plumes billowed about the tree line and the flames raced through the grass to start crawling up the nearest tree trunks. My eyes widened and I raced towards Dorothy.

"Stop that! You're going to alert everyone that we are here!" I pleaded, darting in at a selective moment when Dorothy had her flames aimed away from me.

"Whoops," she laughed, and to my surprise, just as I was about to grab hold of her, she vanished, popping up again a few feet away from me. "Hopscotch and pollywogs! One, two, three. That's it! Your turn."

"What?" I gasped. She teleported? I was fairly certain that was not a conscious ability of hers or else she would have used it back on the cliff. But the nonsense she was spouting made my heart sink as I realized she must be in another of her so-called insani-tea crazes.

She aimed a fireball my way and I only barely managed to drop to my stomach to avoid it, coughing as more smoke forced its way into my lungs.

"We are going to have to go through the doors and go back to Neverland. Hopefully they don't know about the one hidden in the floor and we can get away quickly," I explained hurriedly aloud to myself to center my thoughts. "I just need to catch Dorothy."

I puffed my cheeks with determination and retrieved the chained scythe from my belt, rushed in once more to try and restrain the mad fire-spewing witch.

"Gumdrops won't take you over the rainbow! You must climb the corn stalks and spot the narwhals," She was shouting at a burning tree, dropping her hands to laugh and clutch at her stomach. I took that as my moment and slipped the chain around her like a rope, hoping she wouldn't teleport again as I began dragging her towards the cottage.

"Please don't set yourself, or this house, on fire…" I begged, pulling her along with all my might, while she quite literally dug her heels into the ground.

"Fancy a dip? It feels a bit warm in this sandwich," She shouted, and I stole a glance to see her body was glowing and the links of my chain were starting to take on an orange hue as they began to steam.

"Halt!" The command of a Card-guard to my left made me groan in frustration.

"Dorothy, you're going to get us all killed. Straighten up!"

To my surprise, Dorothy's body went stiff like a board and she complied with a strange giddy expression on her face, like she was a three year old literally pretending to be a board.

"I said halt!" The card barked again.

"I don't have time to deal with you," I snapped, continuing to yank Dorothy with one hand while I pulled a dagger into the other and flung it at the card's advancing shoulder, pinning him to the ground.

"Ah! Card down! Help," it cried out, and mercifully the rest of his somewhat bumbling suit swarmed to help him, giving me enough time to tug Dorothy back into the cottage, where I toppled her to her side and dragged her through the house until I was at the cupboard.

Retrieving a large candlestick holder, I ran back and jammed it through the door handle to hold off the cards just a few moments longer, so I could shove a now wriggling Dorothy through the cupboard back into the red castle.

Once through, I flung open the door on the floor and reluctantly untied my captive acquaintance so she'd be able to swim when I inevitably pushed her off the cliff in Neverland by going back through.

"Wait!" I squealed frantically as she giggled before jumping into the portal on her own. "No!"

I tumbled in after her, barely managing to close the floor door behind me. Straining to grab hold of the vine rope once back on the cliff face, I dared to look down at the lapping water for signs of Dorothy.

Instead, I saw dark masses swimming below the surface, beady red eyes glinting from under the water. I swallowed hard, fear and insecurity crawling up and down my limbs as I recognized the shapes of mean-spirited mermaids who'd once tried to drown me. But, never had they looked quite so menacing and monstrous. What had happened to Neverland since I'd been gone? Was this why Peter had hidden away in Wonderland with Alice?

There was no sign of Dorothy in the water, and it only was a single puzzling moment before I heard her giggling above me. A glance upward had me breathe a quick sigh of relief as I saw she was safe on top of the cliff's edge, staring down at me. She'd no doubt teleported herself up there.

Dorothy wiggled her sparking fingers at me in a wave before

sauntering away out of view.

"Gah!" I growled, using every ounce of strength I could muster to pull myself swiftly up the cliff face, collapsing a moment to catch my breath when I finally clawed my way over the edge back onto solid ground.

My weakened muscles were screaming in protest, but adrenaline was still pulsing in my veins. That rush was the only thing that gave me enough energy to scan the horizon to see Dorothy belly-crawling on the ground, swatting fire at invisible enemies a few meters ahead with Toto tilting his head inquisitively a little ways to her side.

I pulled one of my swords from my back and lugged my exhausted body towards the poor insane girl, raising my arm.

One swift motion to the back of her head with my hilt and she was out like a light, and I just had to hope she'd be back in her right mind when she came to again.

"You mean to tell me that preening little ice witch orchestrated to give me this blasted thing?" I demanded in a heated fury. "When Peter looked at it, he gave me some full spiel about *Wonderland* trinkets. He told me there were all kinds of compasses there."

"Mombi has been here for a while. Plenty of time to entangle her conniving self into your life here. I *know* that it is one of her trinkets. I recognize its entire make, *Witch.*" Tip's blunt and unyielding reply was laced with a hidden accusation that I could possibly be in league with our nemesis, and that alone was enough to make my skin prickle with indignation.

But, I thought back to images I had seen within the magic bubbles in Glinda's castle, and recalled my first sighting of Mombi in the projection of Avrilia's banishment. That had been well before I had arrived in Wonderland. Plus, Peter actually knew little of Wonderland when he met me, so it was entirely possible he pretended to be more knowledgeable about the histories just to make himself look good.

One moment I'd been filled with a sense of hopeful calm, having survived a near death experience back in the caves, but unlike surviving with Peter, there was no cloud watching or relaxing with Tip. Not that I'd want to be with him anyway.

"Are you going to spark off again, Witch?" The Lost Boy sighed at me, hanging his head, a clear sign he regretted asking me about the compass and revealing Mombi as its original owner. It was clear he'd resolved himself to work with me, but I could tell he didn't trust me, nor did he care for my company.

We were slowly trudging our way away from the beach, and towards a forest. I puckered my face into a deeper scowl and clutched angrily at my compass, heat building in my body.

"I just don't understand how she would have gotten into Wonderland to give it to the Tweedles to give it to me in the first place. And that nightmare I had too, I'll bet she had something to do with that and—" I stopped short on my rant as I realized with a nauseating jolt that I had been wrong to have blamed Avrilia all this time for being the catalyst of my Wickedness.

I recalled the terrible nightmare which had really activated my compass. The pale hand reaching forwards, the brief moments of icy cold washing over me, and the phantom wisps of purple, showing me images of Peter's death at my hands, and my sister's loneliness as my fault. It had all been Mombi. I felt a strong rage boiling within me, slow and burning. At Tip's unspoken accusations, the manipulations, the compass. *Everything.*

I reached up and rubbed the spot on my neck where Mombi had grabbed onto the necklace, the authority in the gesture so much more meaningful now. She had been claiming me, like a dog in a collar.

A pawn. From the very moment I'd arrived in this strange and wondrous world, I had been collared and steered. I stared down at my one hand, the other returning to grasp feverishly at the compass once more, flickering images of blood stains appearing before my eyes. I could hear the remnant echoing of the crunch of my knife sliding into Glinda's chest, the gurgling of blood in the Jaberwock's throat after I'd cut it open, the shrieks of pain as Avrilia was torn apart by her flying monkey minions. Every crossroads between light and dark, where the compass had willed me to choose Wicked, flashed before my eyes, I could feel sweat gathering on my brow, and pain began searing through my veins.

"Hey," Tip paused our walk and pointed to my hand gripping the necklace. His eyebrows were raised, concerned. "Are you cracking?"

"What?" I managed to gasp, dropping the compass, and returning to the waking moment. As soon as I released the trinket, the source of pain stopped, leaving a sensitive and raw soreness lingering beneath my skin.

I inspected my hand to see a plethora of fissures running from my nail beds all the way up my arm to my shoulder. I *did* look like I was cracking.

"What in the world?" I pondered, reaching for my compass to see it too now had more little cracks in its silver casing along with the new dent and deeper scratches of the shadow demon.

"It looks like you were damaging it while you were holding it," Tip assessed calmly. "Destroying it will kill the destroyer though, so unless you have a weird masochistic thing or a death wish, I'd avoid doing that."

"I know that!" I snapped, though my frustration had more to do with the fear that my power. for the first time, had managed to cause direct damage to the compass, than actually being upset with Tip for reminding me of the rules.

"Alright, Witch. You do you. But, let's pick up the pace, alright? We need to try to find somewhere safe to hang out for the night and then hopefully tomorrow we will find the others." He waved me forward, shoving his hands in his pockets with an ambivalent shrug.

We proceeded a while in silence as the sun moved slowly through the sky towards the western horizon. The forest we were traversing in seemed relatively normal, and nothing particularly wondrous compared to the varying hues of foliage in Wonderland's woods. But, there was something rather at home about the trees, like they were somehow part of marvelous childhood memories I knew I had never experienced, with friends I knew I hadn't had.

"Seems rather empty here. I expected things to be a bit more… lively. With how Peter described things and all," I commented as I inspected the red cracks along my arm, my voice sounding loud and harsh as it dispelled the cloud of quiet.

"Yeah, I had expected to run into someone or something by now." Tip nodded, his gray-green eyes narrowing suspiciously.

"Where are we anyways? I know your memory probably isn't the best after all this time so we might be somewhere less populated." I waved my hand dismissively, offering a solution that didn't set my skin on pins and needles thinking about.

"No, I know exactly where we are. We are near the Neverbird Nest by this point. You can see the top of it through those branches," Tip replied curtly, pointing to a section of branches to our left that allowed a window of the Western coast.

"Goodness, that tree is huge!" I gawked at the girth of the trunk, and the height it must have to even be seen towering in the sky at this distance. "Hmm."

I approached the base of the nearest tree, and started scrambling up the trunk, noting that it seemed every tree here was perfect for climbing—no doubt part of Peter's design.

"What are you doing?" Tip's longsuffering voice filtered up to me and I ground my teeth at his ever surly tone.

"What does it look like? I'm getting a better look around to see where we are."

"I just told you where we are, Witch. You're going to fall and break your neck."

"Oh, stop complaining. How did Peter ever manage to have any fun with you being such a wet blanket?" I clipped back, continuing my ascent until I was just about to break through the top of the foliage. "Besides, if I fall, I can teleport to the ground."

"Why not just teleport up there then?"

"Maybe I *enjoy* climbing trees!" I snapped back, though in the back of my mind I knew the truth was that I had forgotten I could have saved myself the effort by doing that. But, I couldn't let him know that.

"Whatever, Witch."

"I have a name," I grumbled, my nerves growing weary. I was missing Peter's more pleasant company more and more by the moment. Why did I have to be partnered with this judgmental, cantankerous rain cloud of a man. I'd have taken any of the others as my teammate over him.

Even Wendy.

"Yup. And I call you Witch."

As I looked away sulkily, my eyes caught sight of something dragging something else in the growing gloom of sunset at the base of several trees over and I loosed a warning hiss at Tip below.

"What is it?" He whispered back as loudly as he could, body going rigid with alarm.

I shrugged and scrambled down a few branches before teleporting myself tree by tree towards the mysterious blobs.

"Wait! Don't just go head first— Gah." Tip's quiet cry for hesitation ended in a growl of annoyance and my skin prickled with satisfaction at having vexed him as I whisked myself away.

Finally over my target, I hopped down from branch to branch, silently like a creeping cat. The sky had ebbed from scarlet to a twilight purple, the tall trees casting deep shadows onto the ground below. The dragging creatures had stopped and were directly beneath me.

Taking a deep breath, I switched from a crouched stance to a seated position, hooking my calves around the branch and gripping hard with the back of my knees.

I lit my uncracked hand ablaze, unsure of if the fire would further aggravate the fissures in my skin, and swung myself down to hang upside down suddenly in a surprise attack position.

"Got you!" I barked.

"Ah!" Came the startled shriek and I sagged, rescinding my flame attack to a dull glow as I looked, face to face, at Wendy.

"Oh, it's you," I puffed lamely, flipping off the branch with ease to stand beside her and what appeared to be an unconscious Dorothy.

"Thank goodness! Are you with Peter?" Wendy beamed hopefully, but I shook my head and jerked a thumb over my shoulder in Tip's direction as he approached cautiously.

"No, unfortunately, I was paired with this wet blanket."

"What happened to Dorothy?" Tip asked as he came into the immediate area illuminated by my fire.

"I, um, had to knock her out," Wendy replied awkwardly.

"Wendy, you could seriously hurt someone by doing that!" Tip chided, crouching down beside the comatose girl to check her.

"I didn't have a choice! She was acting positively insane and we barely escaped with our lives," Wendy blustered. "I had hoped when she woke up that she would be herself again, but it was getting dark so I was trying to look for somewhere to camp."

As if on cue, a befuddled groan escaped from Dorothy's lips as she started to come to.

"Dorothy? Are you alright?" Tip asked, shaking her gently at the shoulder.

Dorothy's big brown eyes fluttered open and she must have been startled to see Tip hovering over her because she gasped and punched him square in the nose before scrambling to a sitting position and skittering backwards.

"Why?" Tip squawked in dismay, his voice muffled as he grabbed onto his assaulted nose.

I couldn't help but laugh and even Wendy smirked a little behind her hand before checking to see if her friend was alright.

"Oh, it's you guys. What happened? And why do I feel like I have been hit in the head by a train?"

"I feel the same way," Tip remarked tartly, glowering at Dorothy.

"Sorry," She apologized, and Tip acknowledged it with a nod, still holding his nose. It seemed that Wendy's theory had been right and Dorothy was no longer under the spell of insanity. "Weren't we just in the Hatter's cottage?"

"Is that where The Wizard sent you?" I asked, gesturing to myself and the Lost Boy. "We got out of some haunted cave."

"Don't tell me there are ghosts here too?" Dorothy all but wailed, clutching her head. "I don't want to mess around with any more supernatural business."

"No, there aren't any ghosts," Tip chuckled softly, and I rolled my eyes at the first smile I'd seen him crack since the dungeons. "We were in

Echo's Cave but he'd been turned into a monster that attacked us and this one here nearly drowned us." He jerked his chin at me.

"A monster is just as bad as a ghost so don't laugh at me like I'm crazy, you rude beanpole!" Dorothy snapped indignantly, to which Tip raised his eyebrows, bemused at her chosen insult.

He looked at Wendy. "Am I a beanpole?"

Wendy shrugged apologetically. "I'm afraid I don't know what that is. Sorry."

"Huh." He frowned thoughtfully, settling into a seated position. He was much more personable now that there were others around.

"To answer your question though, Alice," Wendy continued. "We were stranded on a cliff here in Neverland below the Neverbird tree. We found an old door in the cliff that led to a room in the red castle. Sorry, but I think we borrowed some of your clothing."

I recognized the trousers and blouses each girl was wearing as mine, noting that Dorothy had already torn up the sleeves on her chosen attire.

"We heard them searching for Toto, and then we had to go through this other door that took us to Mr. Hatter's rather disheveled cottage. Then that teleported us somewhere else outside a big white castle and Dorothy started setting things on fire so we came back through, and, here we are."

I bristled at her explanation. "There was a door that went to Neverland *in* the Red Castle?"

"Yes," Wendy shrunk a little at my angry tone. "It looked like it hadn't been used in ages though. It came out of the floor in some storage room with a wardrobe and a bunch of crates."

"Bloody hell," I swore to myself. "The little gnat probably knew about it all along. When I get my hands on him…"

"Calm down, Witch. Wendy just said it hadn't been used in a long time. Peter probably knew nothing about it, for whatever reason that matters. I highly doubt he was using it for midnight rendezvous with Tiger Lily."

"Who is Tiger Lily?" I demanded, incredulous.

“Oh. Hmm.” Tip clamped his jaw shut. “Never mind.”

“No, I’d like to know!” I shouted, the flame in my hand increasing.

“Well I’d like to not explain!” Tip shouted back, folding his arms. “Let Peter clean up that mess on his own.”

“You irritating little—“ I readied a fireball in my hand, finally at my wits end with the disagreeable Lost Boy, but Dorothy gripped onto my wrist.

“Come on, Alice. Don’t hurt him, he’s on our side,” She said firmly, and I knew she was right so I let the fire dissipate back to a calm, illuminating glow.

Tip squinted at Dorothy with a curious expression, then looked away and pushed himself to his feet.

“We need to camp for the night and now that there are four of us together, we can look for Peter in the daylight. I don’t want to run into any other unexpected adversaries tonight,” He declared.

“You said Echo was the monster that attacked you? How can that be?” Wendy queried as we all got to our feet and traipsed along after Tip.

“Echo apparently is some voice that repeats nonsense back at you,” I explained to Dorothy who had fallen into pace beside me.

“And I thought we’d left Wonderland behind,” She snorted,and I cracked a smile.

“I would say it wasn’t my fault, but Mr. Cranky Face up there seems to think everything I do is wrong.”

“He’s just got that standoffish way about him. We butted heads too when he found out I was Wicked or whatever. I think I might have painted a bad picture of you at the castle when I was explaining things to him. He just doesn’t like us I don’t think. So whatever,” She sighed with a shrug of ambivalence.

“No, he seems to have settled on a good opinion of you. It’s just me he’s got a bone to pick with. But you apparently get a passing mark.” I rolled my eyes, but something in my chest felt like an ember of happiness rekindling to life as I talked to Dorothy as if she and I were friends. Perhaps we were now.

“I do? Weird,” She mused, narrowing her eyes at Tip’s tall form in front of us. “I’m sure it’ll be short lived till the next time I screw things up.”

“Maybe,” I agreed and we fell silent, catching the end of Tip’s explanation of our encounter with Echo to Wendy as we trudged onward.

“Something is definitely wrong with Neverland,” He said ominously.

“I caught a glimpse of the mermaids by the cliff and even they looked particularly darker than I remember.” Wendy nodded along.

“I have to wonder,” Tip sighed, pausing to look us all over. “If this strange dark shadow business is why Peter ran away from Neverland.”

And the surrounding nightfall suddenly felt like cold, eerie palpable darkness creeping in around us.

Six

Dorothy

Tip led us as far into the forest as he could before finally having to call it quits and camp for the night. None of us slept very well, since whether we admitted it or not, we were each looking over our shoulders for ominous shadow creatures to come crawling out of the night.

I had finally lulled my throbbing head into a tentative sleep once the first light of dawn began to illuminate the immediate area, despite the ambient glow of the small campfire Alice started. I had to suppress a small rush of embarrassment of being afraid of the dark at my age. If I ever had any children of my own, I wouldn't be able in good conscience to tell them monsters of the night weren't real.

Dreaming of wandering through a corn maze and eating apples with my Uncle Henry and Aunt Em, I threw my arm over my head and groaned when someone shook my shoulder to wake me up. "Go away."

"Now who's the rude one?" I heard Tip snort, and I curled into a tighter ball.

"Still you. Go away."

"She's not exactly a very chipper early riser. I found that one out back in Oz," Alice chimed in from somewhere to my right.

"And I recall you stealing my blanket from me too. The most Wicked thing anyone could do."

"That's your idea of Wicked?" Tip scoffed and my eyes fluttered open in annoyance. Clearly everyone was awake and I wasn't going to be permitted to sleep any longer.

"Yes," I replied flatly, rubbing crankily at my eyes. When the blearines had cleared I saw it was Wendy who had been trying to rouse me.

She blinked warmly at me. "We are going to head to the Pixie Village today. But, um, you seem to have done a little gardening in your sleep," Wendy chuckled and pointed behind me.

"What are you talking about? I didn't do any gardening." I turned and gawked as I took in the entrance to a corn maze snaking through the forest, with some of the original trees being replaced with heavily laden apple trees.

"Neverland responds to imagination. You must have been drawing on some powerful imagination in your dreams," Wendy explained.

I ducked my head. "I don't have much of an imagination."

"Obviously you have some tucked away somewhere," Tip shrugged. "Why were you dreaming about corn?"

"I'm from Kansas. It's what I'm used to." I looked away grumpily.

Alice approached the nearest apple tree, and plucked one of the scarlet fruits, biting into it emphatically. "It's a nice morning snack anyway." She took another bite, and gestured with her other hand— which I noticed had a bunch of shallow cuts all over it— at Tip and Wendy. "Why are we going to the pixies?"

"They might know what's been happening in Neverland," Tip started, and Wendy jumped in.

"Plus, they can fly around and check Neverland for any signs of Peter."

"And, if we ask real nicely, they can give us some pixie dust so we can get an aerial advantage on this game to get it over with," Tip finished, while Alice nodded along, something shining in her eyes.

"I'd finally get some of my own…" She mumbled to herself, her expression miles away.

"Right," I drawled awkwardly. "Hey, Alice, can you make me a knife so I can cut up an apple?"

"No."

"No?"

"No."

"Oh, here Dorothy, you can use one of my knives—" Wendy started to reach for one of her weapons, but Alice waved her hand with the command of a queen.

"She can make one herself," She said, fixing me with a stern look. Apparently she had gotten up on the wrong side of the ground, and her more easy-going demeanor from last night was gone.

"No, I can't," I groaned. "I don't know how to do anything besides the crazy fire-hands."

"You turned Peter into a leopard the other night," She countered, refusing to back down. "All you have to do is clasp your hands together, envision the knife and pull your hands apart. It's much simpler than transformations."

"You did what?" Wendy gasped, and I waved her off.

"It was an accident and I turned him back. He's fine." I scowled at Alice. "You're really not going to let me have a knife to slice up an apple? You know I can just eat it as is, right? I don't actually *have* to have a knife."

"I told you before that you need to get a hold on your magic. It's not just for your sake, but for all of our safety when we are around you."

"I don't want to learn how to use magic. Magic doesn't exist where we are from, so I don't need it," I bit back tersely.

"You need it here! Maybe if you had some semblance of control over your power we could skip this little charade with The Wizard and be home by now. Or maybe when you lose your wits, you wouldn't burn down everything in sight. Do you really want any of us to get hurt because you refused to even try?" Alice snapped back, folding her arms across her chest defiantly. I had no idea what had caused her to wake up so on edge and confrontational.

Her words stung, and a chasm of guilt yawned open in my chest as I remembered the poor munchkins I had harmed and endangered. I got abruptly to my feet, unsure of what to do with the discomfort swirling in my stomach at this conflict. She had a point, and I didn't want anyone to get hurt, but I didn't want to lose control while trying to be in control either. I didn't expect the seasoned witch to understand that kind of turmoil though, so I balled my hands in fists and spun on my heel towards the maze entrance.

"Of course I don't want to hurt anyone. I never wanted any of this," I hissed, blinking back tears as I walked away. The only thing I knew best was how to be alone. Attachments only led to pain.

"Where are you going?" Wendy called fretfully after me.

"I'm going for a walk. I'll catch up later."

"Um, come back safely!" She conceded softly, and I was thankful for her caring nature, so I could take a moment to myself. I waved a hand in a sharp gesture of thanks, and continued without turning around.

"We don't have time for this," Alice bit impatiently.

"Do you have to be so disagreeable, Witch?" Tip's clipped wordsat Alice faded as the distance grew between me and the rest of the group. "Don't wander off, Dorothy!"

My heart pounded and my head felt airy as I muddled through the cornstalks and kept a mental track of how to return to the others. I wouldn't be gone long, I just needed to collect myself. I didn't want to have an emotional breakdown in front of any of them. I'd spent so long keeping to myself and my immediate family, avoiding my peers, I hardly had any resolve for all of these interactions— especially as the outsider when everyone else had at least one long term friend in the group.

I didn't want to be part of their group anyways. This was all just a means to an end to get back home, and they could all battle it out amongst themselves for all I cared. A sigh escaped my lips as I reminded myself that that sentiment wasn't entirely true. If it had been true, I wouldn't have wanted to rescue Tip, Wendy, and the others from the dungeon. Nor would I have stopped to save a random mouse in a foreign land. And, I wouldn't have grieved so over the munchkin debacle, or been genuinely concerned when Alice fainted back in Wonderland before The Wizard turned everything upside down on us.

I hung my head, stopping my walking, and rubbed rhythmically at my temples. I couldn't walk too far or I wouldn't be able to find my way back, or be able to receive help should I find myself face to face with one of those Shadow Beasts… Or be able to help if they needed it. I knew I did care at least a little, and the idea of actually having some friends felt both terrifying as well as a little wonderful. Perhaps it was time for me to try a little harder to let someone be my friend. Lion and Tiger had been easy to connect with, but then again, I always connected well with animals. That was why my friendship with Toto was so strong and important to me. I loved him. Was it really possible to feel like that with people that weren't already family?

Biting my lip, I oscillated internally. Once I made it home, I wasn't going to see any of these people ever again, so what was the point in trying to force connections? I just needed to survive.

"But, after storming off like an infant, I now have to go back and face them…" I grumbled to myself aloud. The corn stalks swayed and rustled in a light breeze, and I hugged my arms around my chest, closing my eyes to drink in the familiarity the sound brought me.

Heavy footsteps behind me alerted me to a pair of boots that had tromped along to fetch me back. Boots meant either Alice or Tip, and I braced myself for the lecture I'd get from either one for running off as I turned around.

"Going off alone in dangerous territory seems to be a pattern of yours," Tip prompted, to which I shrugged and looked away, my lips forming a terse line. "Are you okay?"

"Following me seems to be a pattern of yours."

"Yeah, and I think I should probably stop. Last time I followed you I wound up in a dungeon while you spent the night in a castle." The words in his response were short, but held a lightness to them that surprised me.

I flicked my eyes up to squint at the Lost Boy. Was he trying to crack a joke with me? A smile started working at the corner of my lips as I let the silence stretch on and watched him grow visibly more awkward the longer I stayed silent.

He cleared his throat. "Er, anyways, we should get back to the others. Wendy and the Witch have already started towards the pixies. I just hope Wendy doesn't go mysteriously missing while they are unsupervised."

"I wasn't trying to be difficult," I said after a few more moments of tense silence.

"I know."

"And I only walked a little ways to be alone for a second to collect my thoughts, so I didn't accidentally say or do something rash," I continued, defending my haughty actions.

"I understand."

"You do?"

"Sure." Tip shrugged, and worked up a half smile, which looked like it meant to be encouraging or reassuring or something.

"Oh." I was taken aback by his sudden agreeableness. Moreover, I was surprised he seemed to sincerely understand where I was coming from. I had expected to get a very irritating lecture from him. "Okay, well so long as you understand."

"I do."

"Alright, then we can go back." I nodded awkwardly.

"You lead, I'll follow," He quipped, gesturing behind him.

This time a small laugh escaped me. "Very funny." I pushed past him and stared at my shoes as we started making our way back to the little makeshift camp.

We had only made it a few paces before I stopped and groaned. "There wasn't a wall of corn here when I first came this way."

"Looks like you imagined a shifting maze."

"I blame Wonderland. They have one of those, and I got stuck in it. That's probably why I even dreamed up a maze in the first place."

"Is it random or does it follow a pattern?" Tip asked, trying to push through the stalks but was repelled back.

"How should I know?" I threw my hands up in defeat.

"Um, *you* imagined it," Tip replied, furrowing his brows quizzically.

"Stop leering at me, I don't know what I imagined."

"I'm not leering. I think that's just my face," Tip's expression looked vaguely forlorn at my unintentional insult, and I couldn't help but snicker at it.

"Maybe we can try to just go through the maze towards the village?" I offered, gesturing to where we had just come from.

Tip frowned. "We might get even more lost. Maybe we should just wait here for a bit and see if it opens up again. Unless you think you can either control the maze or burn it down or something."

"I thought you didn't like all the Wicked magic stuff."

"I don't, but in this case, it's not hurting me and is a means to an end."

"You realize you're literally asking to play with fire with that statement right?" I asked, tilting my head. This time it was Tip's turn to snicker at my joke.

"Very clever." He grinned and nodded approvingly.

"In any case, I don't want the fire to go out of control since we are in the woods and corn fields and trees are known to be fire spreaders on account of being extremely flammable. Plus, believe it or not, I don't want to burn you to a crisp," I prattled, reaching forward to inspect the dense fall of corn stalks in front of me.

Tip was quiet for a moment, an amalgamation of emotions twirling in his eyes. What had I said?

"You really don't want to hurt anyone, do you?" He asked quietly, his gaze piercing.

I shrank under the imposing weight of the stare. "Of course not!"

"Why? You have the power to do it. Why haven't you killed any of us? Why don't you burn us all down?" He pressed, and I blustered a bit.

"I don't really think I need an explanation for why I don't try to kill people or burn them or whatever. It's wrong, and terrible, and I just don't want to do it. Pain isn't something to inflict on someone else just because you can." I waved a hand at him. "I know you grew up away from normal civilization, but I'd think you'd still have learned that basic lesson."

"Oh, I have." Tip's tone was dark and ominous, and I wondered if whatever reason he was probing my morality had anything to do with whatever had made him hate witches so much. I recalled him describing Mombi as someone who sounded truly evil, who would terrorize him however she could, and my own personal impression of her made me agree with that description.

"Good. I am a bit of a loner and, don't get me wrong, I think some people have earned a good sock in the teeth," I balled up my fist and punched my hand emphatically. "But, they've earned the fight. I don't wish to harm or bully anyone just minding their business… Someone just trying to appease their bossy aunt by attending a festival only to get shoved in a bush and carried away by a crazy magical tornado," I grumbled, trailing off into my own rant as images of my homeworld nemesis, Felicity Arroyo, popped into my head. I wouldn't mind knocking her down a peg one bit. I'd like to see her survive anything I'd been put through in this crazy world. She would have burst in tears from the first blood splatter on her precious pink dress. I guess I had kind of done that too, though.

"What?" Tip looked confused and I scuffed my foot irritably.

"Nevermind."

"You're very odd." He shook his head slowly.

I glowered at him. "And you're *still* very *rude.*"

"I'm just being honest."

"See, that's what rude people say to try to cover up their rudeness, but there is such a thing as tact, you know!" I argued with a light hearted eye roll.

"Alright, with all the tact I can muster, I still think you're very odd."

"You've known me all of five minutes, and we've held a handful of conversations, yet you think you've got me all figured out, Lost Boy?" I challenged folding my arms across my chest.

"I've seen enough to have made up my mind on a general consensus, I think."

"Wow," I scoffed, opening my mouth to reply but was cut off by a new voice that felt wispy against my ears. "Well—"

"Hi, there! I'm so glad I found you."

My gaze roved around wildly, until they landed on a pair of glowing red eyes peering out from within the dense stocks of corn. I was instantly back on edge, and that increasingly familiar sense of foreboding doom gripped me like cold talons.

A physically rattling shiver ran through Tip, and he bristled, shoving me behind him. "Get behind me now!"

"Please, I need some help. No, no! There is no time for you to get more help. I need you to come with me now. It's life or death." The eyes squinted in a grin, and a shadowy wraith about the size of a young girl hopped to the ground. She twirled and dithered about, then she opened her mouth, revealing a row of pearly sharp teeth and a long snake-like tongue. "My name is Mombi and I got lost exploring. There is this creature though, and it's in danger, but I am not strong enough or tall enough to help it. Hurry!"

"Pardon?" I frowned, and looked sharply from the wraith to Tip, Sweat was gathered on his brow, his knuckles white as he clenched his fist.

"Dorothy, run." He swallowed hard, grasping for a phantom knife that wasn't in its usual place at his hip.

"I'm sorry, did she just say her name was Mombi?" I demanded of Tip, and he grimaced before nodding, and shoving me forward. "Is she a shadow monster too?"

"Into the maze, let's go. Move!"

Seven

Peter

The hissing shadows shrank away from the light emanating from my body, and I smiled.

"Shadow, buddy? Are you there?" I called out to my old shadow friend, and this time he was able to form beneath me, giving me a thumbs up. "Say, if those other shadows can talk, why have you never entertained me with your verbal wit? You've been holding out on me, haven't you?" I demanded.

Shadow shrugged and hung his head in an exasperated motion before pointing frantically at the other shadow creatures, reminding me that I needed to get rid of them still. He mimed out some gestures, and I took it as him trying to tell me to make those motions. Clearly he had some idea of what to do so I complied with his instructions without a second thought.

Throwing my arms out to either side, I spread my fingers out wide. Shadow mirror my motions, and to my surprise, he rapidly grew larger in form, stretching out across the room. What normally was an indiscernible dark blob for a face, lit up with two shimmering silver orbs for eyes. Most interesting though, was that his fingers continued to elongate and slither through the space until it had made contact with every shadow in the room. Instantly, as my shadow connected with the beasts, I felt a sensation like tiny invisible strings running from my own fingers pulled taught.

"Ah!" I cheered. "This is what she meant about tethering them."

Shadow nodded rapidly, and I realized he was telling me to do the next motion.

"Oh, right. Sorry, Mate," I yanked my arms towards my chest in a swift motion to form a cross.

The tethers followed suit, pulling all of the smaller shadows into mine, where he engulfed them and puttered out of sight once more.

"Ah," I gasped, a torrent of chaotic emotions crashing through my body from head to toe, forcing me to my knees with physical pain. My glow started to flicker, and with each dip in light, I saw the shadow monster version of myself come into view in a shutter.

Despair, rage, loneliness, regret, and guilt. All the negative feelings tore through me, trying to grip onto me to pull me back into the darkness like an undertow.

But, staring at the monsters I feared lurked within myself, I knew I had to fight through it, and it would pass. I forced my mind to think of things I was grateful for, and slowly the painful wave ebbed, my glow increasing once more.

The beast was gone, and I pressed my fist into the floor, trying to catch my breath as my chest heaved like I had run all the way from the Obsidian Mountains to the Emerald City.

Shadow slipped back into the light where my feet met the stone beneath them, and mimed a cheering motion, cupping his hands together and jostling them back and forth on either side of his head in a sign of victory.

"You absorbed them, didn't you? Rather, *we* absorbed them?" I asked, my words coming out shakier than I would have liked.

Shadow nodded.

"And they were nasty feelings embodied as shadows?"

Shadow nodded again, then paused and pointed from me to him.

"Oh, I see. They were *my* nasty feelings. I guess if you avoid those pesky things too long they really do turn into demons," I snorted, my eyes stretching wide in amazement. "You aren't part of that big scary one that looks like us but all monster-y, are you?"

Shadow jolted and folded his arms shaking his head adamantly.

"What does that make you then?"

Shadow shrugged and then did a little jig, as if that were all the answer I needed to know he was on my side. And, strangely enough, it was.

"At least that was all of them. Alright, how about we get out of here and find our friends?" No sooner had I spoken then Shadow started tugging me towards the door. I spotted a bottle of red powder tipped over on the counter and grabbed it as we passed. Once close enough, he disappeared through the slit, and one *click* later the door creaked open.

Relief shot through me like a bullet of pure energy, and I erupted from the dark torture chamber, flying away from it as fast as I could manage. The room had mercifully been part of an annex in the Emerald City, so as not to attract any unwanted attention to the cruel suffering of a child, lest The Wizard's dutiful subjects think he was anything less than wonderful.

However, due to its more private location, I was able to buzz up to the guards stationed without drawing their notice, dumping what I knew was the poppy sleeping powder from the bottle I'd taken, overhead. The scarlet particles settled over their bodies, and within heartbeats, they sagged in a deep slumber, allowing me the remaining freedom to escape the city.

I was in the southern side of The Emerald City already, so I thought about cutting down to Quadling Country to cross over more easily to Neverland to check for my lost friends. I had a feeling that The Wizard wasn't going to hide anyone in the main city, because that'd be the first obvious place to check, so likely the others were tucked in odd places in each direction. But, as I blinked in the late afternoon sunlight, I spotted smoke coming from Wonderland.

"Where there's smoke, there seems to be a Dorothy these days," I mused, trying to calibrate if I had enough pixie dust left to make it there to check it out. "Could also be a wild Alice in her native ill-temper."

I tried to joke with myself, but concern clawed at my throat, making it hard to even swallow let alone laugh. Fire could mean a fight, and much as I admired Alice's fighting spirit, I didn't think she knew what she was up against with my father. Dorothy hardly know what she was doing at all, so she would likely fare much worse.

Puffing my cheeks dejectedly, I resolved myself to head for the pillar of smoke first, then I would go from there.

~*~

Unfortunately, none of my missing friends were at the site of the fire outside the White Castle. Even more unfortunate was that I used up the remaining dust I had on me to get there, so I was stuck sneaking about on foot— Something my poor spoiled feet wouldn't thank me kindly for later.

On a more positive note, I did overhear a guard with a knife in his shoulder say that there was no sign of the *two girls* anywhere in Wonderland.

Two girls, with a mention of a non-lethal knife wound, told me that Wendy was with either Dorothy or Alice, and they had apparently been here and managed to escape.

The sun had set and I'd managed to walk until my feet hurt, grabbed a couple of size altering mushrooms, and shrank myself down to rest inconspicuously once I had safely climbed a tree.

"You can try to be as optimistic as you want, but you know you want to storm that castle and take it back for Alice." Most unfortunate yet, was that I seemed to have found myself still being haunted by the Shadow-Monster-Me from Oz. Though, he seemed unable to materialize fully enough to harm me now, and instead, he was popping up, both in my mind and physically, intermittently, to try and be a bad influence.

"Go away, Evil-Peter," I muttered, rolling my tiny body over on the branch.

"I can't. I am part of you. I am your wasted potential, you just have yet to realize it."

"No, you're just a bad dream that doesn't know when I'm awake."

"You're trying to sleep now," It hissed.

I scowled. "Take your logic elsewhere! I have no use for it. I'm going to go to sleep, and I'm going to wake up and find all of my friends in the morning."

"And kill them? Torture them? Punish them for their weakness?" The wraith growled, the hunger in his words dripping from his fangs.

"No! Bloody-hell. I'm going to find them and have nothing but happy thoughts."

"Of Alice?" The shadow purred in my ear, and I didn't care much for its tone. "Like pinning her down?"

"Maybe with a hug?"

"You have the power to make her do anything you want."

"Nothing against her will. I'd never do that."

"Is that why you deceived her? Lied to her, and sabotaged her wishes?"

"I—" I started to bluster but the Evil-Peter kept going.

"You're slipping out of the facade you've made for yourself. Lying and tricking for your own gain is just the start of taking control of the world around you."

"No," I insisted, throwing my arm over my head to tune the shadow out.

"She will never trust you again. That's why you have to make her submit to you. How else can she ever truly love you?"

"That's not true. She does trust me." I pondered whether I could shove the mushrooms into my ears to shrink them and tune the blasted pest out.

"But, she doesn't love you," The shadow countered, the words jabbing my nerves.

"I don't know that."

"But, *I* know that," It whispered emphatically.

"No, you don't! You don't know anything of the sort, you bloody brute."

"How can you be certain? You let her walk all over you, boss you around, and you do whatever she tells you. You're nothing more than her obedient pet. You refuse to assert yourself, so how could she possibly think anything else of a pitiful weakling like you?"

I jerked up, and threw my fist at the glowing red eyes above my head, seething as the shadow laughed and dissipated, its chuckle echoing menacingly into the night. It had gotten what it wanted by successfully riling me up and making me lose my temper.

My heart thundered in my chest, and I felt a wave of such intense frustration, for a moment, all I wished to do was to rend things in two with my bare hands. The air crackled with static as storm clouds began to form overhead, and I cursed myself for losing my temper. A storm in Wonderland would be as big a beacon to me as a tower of smoke was to Dorothy's whereabouts.

I closed my eyes and took a few steading deep breaths, reminding myself that nothing that the Evil-Peter was saying had any merit and that his only goal had been to upset me. If I was so concerned over Alice, I'd just have to toughen up and talk to her directly— which admittedly wasn't really my style, but if I wanted to squash the nagging doubt in my mind, despite the affectionate display we had shared back in Oz, it had to be done.

I curled my lip and groaned as the clouds quickly dispersed, dreading the inevitable awkward exchange. I was undoubtedly charming and a very fun fellow, but even I couldn't remove the tension from *every* situation. Maybe I could turn it into a joke if things went south, and I'd need to get pixie dust so I could fly away too— Like when I had blurted out that I thought she was pretty when we first met. It seemed like the entire world was working against me, forcing me to confront things I didn't feel like confronting, and I was finding it terribly annoying. It was so much nicer to keep things light and pleasant.

Putting all stressful thoughts out of my mind, I envisioned laying on my back watching fluffy white clouds dotting the clear blue sky until I drifted off to sleep.

My dreams took me to a wasteland of Neverland, where the trees were bare, and all the plant life had withered. The sea was a tumbling mass of darkness as it crashed into the shore, bones and broken pieces of pirate ships left rolling in the infinite ebb and flow against the pitted sand.

Trepidation and sorrow sitting like a brick in my stomach, I walked slowly through my parishing paradise with tears pricking my eyes. What had happened? I had had similar nightmares before, when I felt a nagging feeling in my gut that something wasn't right in Neverland, but was always at a loss of how to fix it when everything already seemed lost.

Snarling tickled my ears in the eerie silence and I scanned my immediate surroundings, taking in the plethora of beady red eyes boring into me from all sides and shadow wraiths began pouring out of every nook and cranny. Demons in my safest haven.

This was a new development to the dream, and I stood paralyzed in agonizing despair as they descended upon me. Their fangs tore into my flesh and I felt a surge of grief choke my throat. Talons cold as death cut to the bone, and a chasm of infinite loneliness stung every fiber of my being.

I lay motionless, gasping as the beasts devoured me whole, my blood turning from crimson to black as it beaded from my wounds onto the ground. When enough had pooled around my shredded body, creating a puddle of darkness beneath me, the shadows began pulling me through the ground into a place of total stifling nothingness.

As the terrible emotional wounds held me captive and barely conscious, I blinked bleary at the bleak emptiness awaiting me. If I died in this dream, would I die in the waking world?

A deep bellowing chuckle pulsed through the smothering air, and I saw the Shadow-Peter, now massive in size, grin at me, spreading his arms wide to receive me.

I tried to think of happy thoughts, but only destruction and desperation prowled through my mind.

"Neverland has died. Give in and take your true form Peter Pan. Lay waste to the rest of the world, and steal its power for your new paradise. Become the darkness they all threw you into since you were born." The Evil-Peter's voice rattled my bones and I closed my eyes as his enormous jaws parted.

A sudden warm tingling in my fingers, made them pop open in

surprise at the pleasant sensation. Golden specs began collecting on the blood coating my body. The feeling of warmth spread through me from head to toe, and the energy that had been leached away from me started returning.

Slowly, the golden dust dulled the pain of my wounds enough for me to move and I scrambled out of the shadows, grasp, paddling through the dark towards the hole they'd pulled me through, like I was swimming through a thick sea to the surface.

The dust swirled and danced in front of my face, showing me impressions of happy memories and faces I had come to cherish. It shimmered around my ears and I heard the laughter of children echo loudly, pushing away the crushing sound of emptiness.

The giant evil Shadow-Peter snarled and lunged for me. I scrambled through the hole back into the withered Neverland, and the golden specs poured from my body over the bloody hole until they swallowed it up with beaming light.

I sat on my knees panting hard from the terrifying and hopeless experience. Those pesky nasty thoughts had almost won and made me forget who I was. I needed to be more careful about getting drawn in from now on. I had to keep the light within me shining. There was still hope to cling to.

My eyes panned once more around my suffering Neverland, and I wished so desperately to heal it. Then, something marvelous happened, filling my soul with delight.

Through the dense barren woodlands, deep in the Never Woods, I saw more golden light twirling, and something new was starting to take shape. Squinting my eyes, I tried to peer in the distance to discern what was forming— whatever it was, it was quite large— but the brilliance of the light was too much to take in.

I felt pure splendor surge through me and my eyes opened in the waking world once more. It was still night, but I leapt to my feet, stuffed the other mushroom in my mouth to return to my normal height, and scrambled down the tree as fast as I could. Wonderland was sleeping around me, so I didn't bother with stealth while under the cover of nightfall.

I had to get to the South as soon as possible. Pelting through Wonderland, I laughed blissfully to myself.

"Someone is imagining in Neverland!"

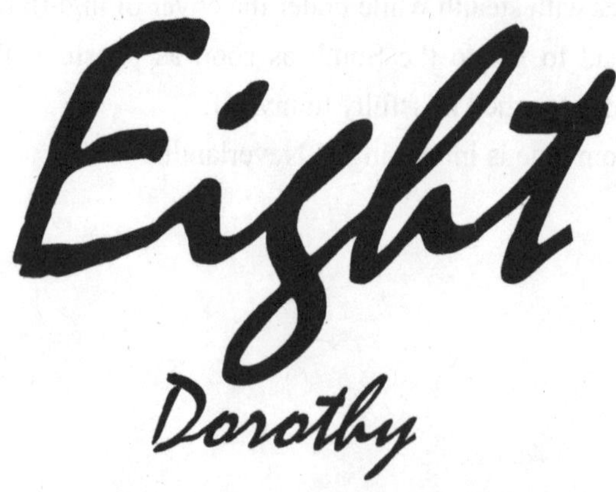

Eight

Dorothy

Corn stalks whipped past my face as Tip and I tore through the maze and I cursed myself for even storming off in the first place. I was smarter than that. Was running away the only thing I was capable of?

"I think you know something I don't, and you owe me an explanation!" I shouted at Tip, my sides heaving as I tried to will away a mounting side ache.

Tip's gaze was fixed straight ahead, his lips forming a thin line. There was a small shine to his forehead which made me realize he was still sweating a bit, though it didn't seem to be from the exertion as he was in decent physical shape.

"Are you okay?" I tried instead when my previous question was left unanswered.

"I'm fine."

"But you look like—"

"I said I'm *fine,"* He barked impatiently and I scowled at him.

"Fine!" I snapped back.

"Why does she seem to show up every time you go off alone, Dorothy?" Tip demanded, turning his eyes lit by fire to stare at me accusingly. "Are you doing this?"

"Am I doing *what?* I don't even know what the hell is happening. How do I know *you're* not the one bringing her around?" I scoffed, daring to look over my shoulder and instantly regretting it as I saw the eerie wraith was still hot on our heels with spindling claws outstretched for the kill.

"Do you really think I'd do that?" Tip's eyes stretched wide in disbelief and I once again kicked myself for saying something insensitive to him in the heat of the moment, but I was also feeling a well of desperate frustration boiling over.

"I don't know! I don't know you," I bit, looking away to watch the path in front of me, my resolve ebbing with fatigue. "But, I didn't do it either. Believe what you want, I know I'm innocent. I'm just getting so tired of running."

"Well, then I hope you're ready to swim!" Tip looked contemplative for a moment, his eyes flicking around our path, recognition shining through.

"What?" I squeaked, but Tip grabbed hold of my wrist and whipped us around a corner of the stalks where the ground suddenly dipped a few feet before dropping off into a body of water.

"Take a deep breath!" He called to me and propelled me into the water.

"No!" I shrieked, flailing wildly as I tumbled below the surface.

Murky water bubbled around my face and I was suddenly eight years old again, trapped in the lake with my parents.

My heart rate quickened with icy panic and images of blood twisting through the water flickered in and out of my pulsating vision. Disoriented, I lost track of the surface, and looked around desperately, my lungs screaming for air.

Seaweed danced around me while I twirled frantically, and as my head started stretching and dipping, I swore I saw my parents lifeless bodies bobbing amongst the underwater flora.

The water around me shattered like broken glass as I screeched bloody murder, sending an aftershock of sound in pulsing rings through the dense liquid. Instinct took over as I clawed feverishly towards the flickering shapes.

Maybe its not too late. Maybe, if I can just get to them, I can save them this time. Maybe nothing ever happened and everything is fine. I can save them. Everything will be fine if I can just grab Mom's hand again...

My head was pounding as I pushed myself deeper through the water, following the trail of blood like the Yellow Brick Road. But, no matter how far I went, they remained out of reached.

Black was ebbing into my vision, and I felt something grip around my hand and yank me upward toward a flickering light I realized must be the surface. It was a large calloused hand intertwined in mine.

Dad? Did I save you? Where's Mom?

When my head broke the surface I floundered wildly, my swimming weak on account of avoiding it since that fateful day.

"Why didn't you say anything when I was calling for you? And why were you swimming to the bottom of the lake? Were you *trying* to drown?" It wasn't my father's voice that hit my ear, and as I caught sight of my reflection on the surface of the lake, all at once, my strange suspension of time snapped back like a whip of pure electricity, and the weight of my world bared down on me once more.

Feeling completely separate from my own body, I stared into the girl in water's face, paddling weakly, barely staying afloat. Her eyes were wide as the moon, glossy with phantom memories and terror, her teeth chattering in a pithy line uncontrollably.

That's me? I'm all grown up, which means...

"Whoa, are you okay, Dorothy?" I vaguely recognized Tip swimming beside me, as my mind slowly slipped back into my body, and connected me to the moment.

I didn't save them. They are still dead. And I'm still lost.

"Hey, it's gonna be alright..." Tip spoke gently, and placed a hand on my shoulder. His voice felt like an anchor tethering me from going completely adrift in a sea of resurfaced grief. My face crumpled like a child, and forgetting all sense of awkwardness or pride, I just sought comfort, and turned to cling around his shoulder and sob.

He looked a little flustered and unsure as he caught my eye, but nodded to indicate he understood, and wrapped one sturdy arm around me while using the other one to coax us to the shore of the lake until he could help me out of the water.

Somehow my breath both quickened and stuck in my chest, and I stopped abruptly, my hands flying instinctively to my chest and throat to claw for fresh air.

"Dorothy?" Tip, who had made it only a few steps ahead of me, turned and looked at me in concern.

"I… I can't breathe!" I gasped. My heart was racing at light speed, causing the blood vessels in my ear to thunder.

"Hey, hey. Calm down. You're panicking," Tip spoke calmly, and stiffly, yet gently, guided me over to a boulder to sit on.

I shook my head frantically. "No, I'm not get… getting… enough air," I gulped, fresh waves of fear were skewering my nerves— which at this point I didn't know if they could take another beating so soon. The pounding in my ears continued and my vision began to bob and weave. Was the insani-tea kicking in again already?

"There is plenty of air, Dorothy. You just need to slow yourself down." Tip remained composed and stoic as he spoke, squatting down in front of me to look me in the eye.

"You'd better get away from me," I warned and tried to get up to attempt to stumble away. If I set this place on fire, then what would become of us? We'd be trapped in the burning maze. *Oh, God. I'm going to kill us both!* I wailed inwardly.

But, before I could manage it, Tip grabbed onto my wrist and sat me back down. "If you need to pace around to work off the nerves, that's fine, but I don't think you need to go off alone again right now."

"But—"

"I'm not going anywhere until you've calmed down. Like I said, you just need to calm yourself down first and foremost," Tip insisted, his face a wall of adamance. "Can you try to slow your breathing if I count it out for you?"

"Count it out?" I furrowed my brows in confusion. "What does that mean?"

"I'm going to count to three and while I do, you're going to inhale for those three seconds. Ready? One, two, three. Good. Now hold that air, four, five, six. And breathe out at seven, eight, nine, ten." He ran through the counting rhythmically three times, and I complied with his instructions. I was amazed to find that my heart was settling down, and my airways felt less constricted.

Seeing me start to regain composure, Tip rose to a standing position again, and leaned against the side of the rock. We sat in silence for a few minutes until I finally found my voice again.

"Thank you."

"Don't mention it." Tip had a small smile of acknowledgement on his lips, but his grayish green eyes seemed to be blinking away relief.

I sat and stared blankly at my shoes, sniffling back tears intermittently while he got up and started walking around the immediate area to give me a little space now that I'd regained my composure for the most part.

My eyes scanned the water in front of me. It had been a chasm of hellish hopeless memories moments ago, but now everything felt so calm and peaceful. The sun was shining, birds twittered in the distance, and a gentle breeze tickled my nose.

What happened? Why did I go back? Why did I think I could go back? How is it that this weird magical world has all been real but somehow my parents are still dead? I haven't thought too hard about that day in years. Why now?

"Care to relax here for a bit?" Tip's voice coiled through my consciousness, dismissing the mental fog I was walking in. I felt weak, vulnerable, embarrassed, and terribly devastated. I hadn't expected that falling in the lake would completely resurrect the night of my parents death to play before my eyes like a movie.

"With you?" I asked in surprise, turning around to stare at him blankly.

"Why not?" Tip shrugged, and sat on the ground next to me. "The shadow is gone now, and I'm the only one around. We really shouldn't split up again so we can talk or not talk. Whatever."

I squinted at him. "You're being nice."

He squinted back. "I'm a nice guy."

"Are you? Could have fooled me…" I muttered under my breath, even though I knew it was clear that Tip wasn't a bad guy, despite him pushing me into the lake after accusing me of being in league with our mortal enemy. He was just guarded and untrusting. It was probably my lingering embarrassment from crying on his shoulder in the water and needing to be calmed down like a child that was making me curt, so I nodded my agreement. "Don't we need to go find the others?"

"It can wait till you're up for it." Tip shrugged. "We can walk if you think that'll make you feel better?"

He was being so conscientious, not snapping or being sardonic in the slightest, and I didn't know what to make of it. Perhaps I had really misjudged him from our rocky first impressions of each other. He had his own issues, just like I did, and realistically, I wasn't always the friendliest when I felt uncomfortable either. Maybe what I'd thought was a disagreeable attitude was actually mutual awkwardness coming out as grumpy sternness? He'd been more agreeable with me and Wendy the night before, and he kept showing up to help. Clearly, he was trying to reach out in the ways he felt he could. It was just rough around the edges.

I supposed I could understand that, and he had shown me a great kindness… Not unlike my Uncle Henry once had when I'd been lost in grief and guilt as a child. So, I worked up a smile and rose to my feet. "Let's keep going."

"You lead, and I'll follow. One of these times, it won't end in trouble." Tip pushed off the rock and rejoined me, returning my smile.

We walked quietly for a little while, the sound of water lapping against pebbles echoing through my head. I made a point to look the other direction, past Tip next to me, at the forest bordering the lake within my corn maze.

"The corn and apple trees were pretty random," Tip laughed softly as he followed my gaze, pointing to the stocks.

"Well, like I said, I am from Kansas. What do you expect me to dream up?" I retorted, but smiled all the same.

"Think it's ready to eat? We could pick some apples too," He suggested, gesturing to the smattering of edible plants. "Seems like you must have had food on the brain last night."

"I haven't eaten since Peter and I swiped the food at the Emerald Castle."

"A very Peter thing to do," Tip nodded along, bemused. "Well, I could eat. Let's check it out." He left the shallow shore line and began venturing to the nearest apple tree.

I hesitated, then puffed a sigh and followed him over. "What do you think the odds are that I subconsciously dreamed up a butter tree for the corn?"

Tip chuckled, stretching to his full height— which was quite tall— to reach some picture-perfect crisp red apples. "I'm going to think it's probably a slim shot. Though, I do wish I had a knife. I meant to get one from Wendy earlier. But, things sort of got out of hand when you asked for one

"I shouldn't have let Alice get under my skin like that. I just... well, it's hard to explain."

"She can be pretty grating," Tip snorted. "And you're scared of your magic because you don't have control and don't want any collateral damage on your conscience."

"Whoa," I puffed, impressed that he'd hit it on the head. "Get out of my brain, please."

"Like I said, I've got a good read on you."

"I'm not sure if I like that..."

"I can stop," He offered, a bit flustered.

"Er," I stammered awkwardly. "Never mind. It's just nice to have someone with more maturity than a spoonful of molasses around."

"I bet. Wendy is more than meets the eye though. Don't count her out on account of her big doe eyes, and more fanciful ideals. We've lived those wild dreams and fairytales, remember. They are real to us, and I have a feeling you'll come around to it too."

"You mean the magic?" I raised an eyebrow. "It just sounds so… childish. Like, 'look at me! I am a powerful witch. Abracadabra. Oh whoops, burned down the forest again.'" I feigned childlike pretending.

Tip twisted the stem of his apple rhythmically and smirked. "You just need more faith and trust."

"Not that again…" I rolled my eyes at the echoed words of Wendy.

"In yourself," Tip finished, pointing to me.

"Pardon?" I queried, baffled at what he was saying.

"You're the only one in control of yourself. So, have a little faith, and trust yourself to stay in control. How else can a self-proclaimed realist adjust to an unrealistic world? Take control of yourself because it's all you can control when things are uncontrollable. The splendor comes afterwards."

I opened my mouth to retort, but despite my better judgment, the Lost Boy was making some kind of sense.

"Fine," I asserted abruptly, feeling slightly challenged, and closed my eyes to concentrate, adding. "I blame you if this kills us horrifically."

"You have my tentative confidence?" Tip replied warily, his voice pitching in an implied question of whether he should offer said confidence.

"Hush," I whispered, and envisioned Alice creating clothing and objects. "I'm going to make a knife for your apple."

"Are you planning to forge it?" Tip asked, and my eyes popped open to see his eyebrows raised in amusement as he pointed to my hands were cloaked in flames.

"No!" I snapped and flapped my hands about to quell the fire. "Stupid fire always coming out willy nilly. I thought I was having an epiphany."

"You probably just need some practice. But, we are still alive. Try again," Tip urged with a wave of his hand.

"Ugh!" I growled as I clasped my hands together in frustration, smothering the flames the rest of the way. At the same moment, an image of a dagger popped into my mind, and I had the sudden sensation of something solid wedged between my palms. "Hmmm?"

I pulled my hands apart and blinked in amazement as the dagger I had pictured appeared. Once I'd pulled my hands apart, and the knife was complete, I flicked it in my hand triumphantly.

"Ah ha! Alice was right!" I cheered.

"Bravo," Tip squinted and leaned forward, plucking the knife from my hands. "I'll take that, before you melt it down."

"Hey! So, rude," I groused with half hearted offense, choosing to bite directly into my apple, rather than slice it up. It was the principle of the thing at this point.

"You made it for me, didn't you?" He countered, plopping down to rest against the trunk as he set to work carving up his apple, peeling away the skin.

"Well, you could say thank you at least," I chided and sat down next to him. "Scoot over so I can lean too. My back hurts, though miraculously my feet aren't aching with all the walking and running I've done since getting here. If my Aunt Em could only hear me complaining about my back, she'd give me an earful about appreciating my youth. You remind me a little of her, actually." I smiled fondly as I thought of my sturdy no-nonsense aunt.

"I remind you of your lecturing aunt?" Tip queried, a touch of amused indignation coloring his tone.

"Yes, exactly." I glanced over at him and nodded confidently, pointing to the apple he was slicing. "She even likes to cut off her apple skins too."

"I'm not sure how I feel about the comparison," Tip grunted, then gestured to my head. "How are you feeling?"

I looked down at my hands, the smile slipping off my face. I felt phantom water rolling against me, icy and paralyzing. I shivered and looked away. "I'll be fine. Just a little waterlogged now. Nothing a tough old farm girl can't handle."

"Want to talk about it?" Tip pressed, though he looked cool as cucumber, munching casually on his apple slices. "I wouldn't have pushed you in the water if I'd known you would be having a particularly rough time of it. Jumping in was our only way to get away from the Shadow, and the other one went in the water with the Witch, so I didn't even know if it would work. But, it's all I had for ideas, and thankfully, it seemed to work once I went looking for you. The shadow vanished when we came up."

"Oh, what was up with that Shadow-Mombi?" I asked, reminded of the familiar wraith.

"It wasn't the real one and it's gone now, so I guess don't worry about it." Tip looked away sharply, and redirected the conversation back to me. "Sorry, did you say you wanted to talk about what happened in the water? I think I started chattering before you could answer me."

I bit down on my tongue and debated whether I felt like divulging my most terrible memory to this brazen and edgy young man with a hazy soft side I'd only just met. Then again, he had followed me to make sure I'd stayed safe with the whole Mouse Queen thing back in Oz, helped out in Wonderland with Alice's ailment, been ready to help fight The Wizard, saved and comforted me despite not being entirely convinced of my loyalty, and chosen to keep me company now instead of making me feel stupid or rushing us along. Plus, I knew there was a softer side to him with how he acted towards his previous odd traveling companions, Saw-horse and Jack… Not unlike how I treated Toto, Lion, and Tiger. Like, well, friends.

Not a half hour ago, I'd been telling myself I didn't need any of these people to be my friends. But something had shifted and suddenly it felt possible that maybe, just maybe, Tip might be a friend to me while I was here after all. That missing click of connection, lost in self isolation, was becoming almost tangible again. I had no idea how he'd managed the impossible of making me feel comfortable talking to him, and yet there I was, feeling comfortable talking to him. It had to be what the allusive sensation of friendship felt like.

"Well, I guess we are kind of friends now…" I mused aloud, tossing my remaining apple core over my shoulder.

Tip began snickering next to me at my chosen phrasing. "How generous of you. I'm honored."

"Oh, hush. I just mean that I told Alice and Peter about it, sort of, and they still were on very precarious terms with me at the time. So, I figure, if you and I are actually friends now, then I guess it'd be alright to tell you too. I've never really had friends before, other than Toto, so I am not sure what qualifies," I rambled defensively, heat coloring my cheeks. Maybe I'd miscalculated and he didn't want to be friends.

"I think we qualify as friends, at least, on my end. You're tolerable enough to pal around with, so, I'm all ears. If nothing else, beats listening to the Witch."

"I think I might be offended," I teased lightly, though I agreed with the sentiment regarding Alice. "She is pretty intense. But, I think we all have our own demons to weather from the past, right?"

"So it would seem…" Tip muttered ominously, his eyes a million miles away before clearing and glinting back at me as he popped another slice of apple into his mouth. "Well, tell me your tale of woe then, *friend*."

"My parents drowned and I survived. I was eight years old and we went off the road and crashed into the water. I don't even remember why it happened. My father was the one driving, not that it makes much of a difference, but I think I remember him being a safe driver. The car was filling up with water from where the windshield had broken and the seatbelts weren't working very well. My mother got mine undone and got me out. She got me out rather than saving herself and promised me they'd be right behind me."

"Mothers can have that way about them, I've heard." Tip nodded along intently, his face serious, contemplative and engaged in what I was saying. I didn't know why but I had expected him to be bored talking about me.

"My father was knocked out, or maybe he was already—" I swallowed down a lump of bile in my throat. "I remember blood. This bright crimson snaking through the water in these big beautiful, deadly wisps. And, bubbles following me to the surface, I guess some of them might have been my mother's last bit of air."

"Well, that's a little morbid," Tip clicked his tongue and start twirling the knife methodically through his fingers with surprising dexterity.

"Yeah, you're probably right. I got to the shore and waited for a long time. I just stared at the water for ages, like somehow they were going to pop up at any time, but of course, they never did. Someone must have come along and seen the damage to the railing and me sitting there or something, because the ambulance and police came and took me away. I mostly remember being so terribly cold from the water."

"Shock too. Shock will make you shiver," Tip commented absently as he concentrated on his blade.

"You know the worst part of this whole story?"

"What's that?"

"It was only eight years ago that they died, but I can't remember their faces very clearly anymore."

"You feel guilty about that?"

"A bit," I admitted.

"Don't. Our minds are fickle things, and as much as we like to think we have a handle on them, we can barely scratch the surface of what they are capable of on their own." Tip paused his knife twirling and tapped the hilt of the dagger against his temple.

"It still feels wrong to have blocked them out. They were good people. When I hit the water, it was so strange, because I was back in that moment— getting out of the car and leaving my parents to drown below me. The cold was even the same. And I thought," my voice wavered, and I cleared my throat to steady it. "I thought I saw them down there and my brain tricked me into thinking I could save them. That I really was back in the moment and if I could only reach them, I'd undo everything."

"A second chance."

"When you grabbed my hand, I thought I'd reached them."

"Oh, um. Sorry, but you were drowning yourself so I had to get you."

"I suppose that's kind of silly to have thought I could have saved them. It's been almost a decade."

"I don't think so. Neverland is a sanctuary that has meant a lot to us Lost Ones. It offers us hope of an infinite future beyond our wildest dreams. So, I don't find it silly that you thought of getting a second chance. Crazier things have happened than rewriting time."

"Wow," I shouldered him playfully. "Was that a rare moment of nonjudgement, from the ever skeptical Tippetarius?"

To my surprise, he returned the gesture, bumping me back with his own shoulder, as firm and sturdy as it had felt around me in the water. "What's the next bit then? From orphan to Wicked Witch of the East."

I hugged my knees to my chest and rested my chin on them. "I went to Aunt Em and Uncle Henry's farm a couple days later. Aunt Em was devastated— she was my father's sister— but she was so strong about the whole thing. She was a rock. And Uncle Henry was so kind. I'm not convinced there is a kinder man out there, if I'm honest. I love them both dearly. They got me Toto for companionship and let me carry on alone, because that's how I always liked it. I was going to study hard and when the time was right, I'd leave Kansas and go find a little place in the world for me. It was all in my control so long as I only had me and Toto to worry about. Until stupid Fecility Arroyo got involved."

"Ah, is this a nemesis? Shall we make her walk the plank then?"

I couldn't help but burst out laughing at the nautical reference. "I would absolutely *love* to see her flounder about in that stupid pink dress of hers. She is one of those high society, wealthy, pretty, blonde girls. Or, at least, she would be really pretty if her face wasn't perpetually pinched into a scowl."

"My, how petty of you."

"No, trust me. You'd hate her. She's mean and nasty and she made fun of my shoes and then pushed me into a bush."

"Pushed you into a bush? Well, I can understand the urge sometimes..." Tip played along, and I realized this was likely the most lighthearted I had seen him since we had met at the entrance of Gugu's forest.

"Oh hush. I was running away from her when I got sucked up in the tornado and ended up here. You know the rest. I got the shoes, your dear friend Peter tricked me into Wonderland, I had some tea, got stuck in a chessboard, talked to a giant butterfly, had a lovely first impression with Alice… Flew to Oz, became Wicked, met The Wizard, had a lovely gentleman named Henry help me escape by slowing down time… Lion and Tiger found me, and then we met not long after. That is my full tale of woe."

"How did you manage to get stuck in a chessboard? *That* seems silly."

"Well, it makes more sense when you've wandered through Wonderland. Trust me."

"You sound very unlucky."

"I guess I was lucky to have landed somewhere safely after the tornado. I was lucky Alice didn't kill me, and that Peter helped me escape. It was lucky that I saw Wendy and was able to tell Peter she was alive. Meeting Lion and Tiger and Henry too."

"And saving the Mouse Queen," Tip added. "Even if it was obnoxious in the moment, I guess it was sweet of you to care, and it helped later on."

"Saved me from putting my foot further in my mouth about Mombi, at least. Sorry for that. I was feeling insecure about being newly Wicked."

"Don't worry about it." Tip waved me off.

"I should have been kinder. I kicked myself for it immediately after you know. I mean, poor sweet Henry had just told me earlier about how he had been kidnapped and enslaved, and how he had been living under his captor's nose. I was sympathetic for him, so I should have been for you too. If Henry hadn't take that risk to trust me and help me… Ah, that's another thing I was lucky about. Henry knew a lot of stuff about Wonderland and Neverland so he knew the truth of things. Sorry," I paused for breath. "I must still be a bit nervous. I never talk this much. To anyone. I didn't even know I was physically capable of rambling." Now that I'd ever so slightly opened my mind to the idea of having a friend, it was as if years of repressed conversation was spilling out of me like a waterfall of words. I was actually holding a lengthy conversation with someone, and was enjoying it. I beamed inwardly at my socialization breakthrough.

But, Tip was staring at me with a hard gaze of contemplation. "You said the man's name was Henry? He'd been kidnapped and knew about the other directions? Even Neverland?"

I furrowed my brows and thought back to Henry's commentary when he'd saved me. "Yeah, that's how he knew the lies The Wizard was trying to spin."

"How old was he?" Tip pressed, and was now gripping the hilt of the dagger firmly in his hand.

I couldn't help but feel a little pool of dread and disappointment at the sudden change in Tip's demeanor as he flipped from casual and good natured back to focused and intense. It had been so nice to just spend a little calm downtime with him— my first non-animal friend— so easy and normal despite sharing some heavy experiences. I was reluctant to go back to the reality where we were playing a homicidal game of hide and seek with a magical egocentric maniac and his icy mistress. We were on the losing side currently too, with no clear idea of how to proceed, so avoiding it in this little bubble seemed perfectly reasonable to me.

"He was an adult, older than you for sure," I replied slowly. "Why?"

"I think… but it might be a stretch." Tip rose to his feet and began pacing back and forth in front where I was still slumped against the tree. His thick boots trampled the grass sprigs beneath them, churning up earth scents as they squished with the remaining logged lake water from our impromptu swim.

"What is?"

"But if it is true, then we need to find Peter and tell him and Wendy right away!"

"Hello? Remember me down here? Yeah, I'm the one who isn't inside that thick skull of yours and has no idea what you're talking about. Care to fill me in on this odd moment of revelation you're having?" I grumbled, pushing myself to a standing position. I arched my back to relieve some of the tenseness, and stretched my arms, hoping to make my muscles a little less cross with me.

"Come on, let's get back to the others and we can tell them our discovery."

"I appreciate you sharing the credit, but I still am not privy to this discovery," I muttered sourly. I was back to being the odd one out again.

"We used to have a Lost Boy called Henry. He was already a little older than me, even before all the weird age altering stuff. He was brilliantly kindhearted and selfless, and we thought he left us to go back home a bit before I was taken. So, I'm thinking the Henry that was kidnapped and saved you, was a former Lost Boy."

The correlation slapped my brain with an additional connection. I turned and smiled broadly at Tip, the reflecting sunlight casting beams of white light in stark contrast against his ebony hair,

"Do you remember what The Wizard said to us?" I gasped, savoring that increasingly rare feeling of an idea clicking into place— a small click like a puzzle piece connecting, that suddenly took something tangled and turned it into perfect sense. Such a rare occurrence in this world of nonsense.

"I try not to recall too much of what that bastard says, actually."

"The game, Tip! He said we needed to find all the *Lost* friends to be able to beat him. He didn't mean just us five. If my Henry is also your Henry and is a *Lost* Boy, then I think we need to find him too."

"Dorothy, you're brilliant! Let's get back and tell the others. I just thought it would be good news to know Henry was alive and well, but you've cracked the case. Good talk. Come on." Tip's words were a tumbleweed of excitement, one statement blurring into the next. He spun on his heel and started marching towards the direction we'd deemed would lead us towards the Pixie Village where we would meet up with Wendy and Alice.

Good talk. I smiled at the strange enigma of a man with a small shake of my head, and scrambled after him. If I was odd, he was downright strange, but, at least it was relatively entertaining when he wasn't being difficult and grumpy.

"Wait for me!" I bumbled, catching up to him. His face was scrunched in deep thought, making worry ping through me. "What is it?"

"I have a question, and don't laugh at me…" He started.

"No promises. Go on, ask it."

"What is a *windshield* or *seatbelt*? And what did you mean by driving a *car*? Like a car on a train? Also, what is an *ambulance*, and why did it come to you?"

I balked for a heartbeat, having forgotten that Tip was from the same world as me, but from much earlier— apparently before cars had even been invented. This big revelation about our fate with the big bad enemy of this world, and he'd gone back to pondering words he didn't know from my story. My lips twitched and I couldn't help myself.

I laughed.

Nine

Wendy

"She just had to go wander off alone," Alice was grumbling as we picked our way through the forest. "And she had to make that eyesore of a maze. And Mr. Difficult *had* to go after her… I say let her face one of those beasts on her own to teach her a thing or two."

Dorothy's addition to Neverland, like most Lost Ones eventually contributed during their stay on Neverland soil, had come in the form of a giant corn maze. I had thought it wouldn't impede our trajectory towards the Pixie Village, but alas, we couldn't part the wall of corn that stood in our way, and had to take a longer route based entirely on my memory from years prior.

"Do you think maybe you were a bit hard on her?" I ventured softly, twirling the base of my braid anxiously around my fingers. "She had just woken up."

Alice flashed me a glare that looked like it could have seared straight through my face, her lips forming a tight line of annoyance.

I looked away sharply and ducked my head. "Sorry."

"She needs to get more comfortable with her abilities for all our sakes. You're lucky she didn't kill you when she lost her head this last time. Do you know what she did to my guards and monkeys I sent after her?" Alice demanded stopping to face me, standing tall and imposing.

I did my best not to flinch. "No… not specifically. But, I don't think I really want to—"

"She tore them to shreds with her bare hands. They were pieces of pulp when I found them." Alice launched into the explanation, ignoring my bleating protest. "She also killed some of the munchkins in the village that, before then, hailed her as a Good witch and savior. Then, lit the place on fire, and when she *couldn't control herself*, even in her right mind, she left them there to die. Tell me, do you think that is acceptable behavior towards anyone, let alone one of us?"

I shrank further into myself, embarrassed. "No, of course not. But, she didn't mean to…"

"If she doesn't at least *try* to make a stable connection with her powers— even for basic things— then her next unintentional victim could be Peter, or me, or you, or Tip. It could even be her dog. I can't just let that happen. So, I'll push when I need to and she can throw all the fits she wants to, but like it or not, we are in this game of survival together and we are in dire need of an advantage." Alice's body was a rigid wall of adamance, her scratched up hand clasping around her necklace, knuckles white.

For a Wicked witch, she certainly seemed to care a lot about the lives of others. She was strong and assertive in what she wished to accomplish. Perhaps that's what Peter liked about her.

"Come on," She pursed her lips and sighed, her stance returning to normal before turning to continue our trek.

I felt the uncomfortable silence prickle my skin like needle tips and racked my brain for a different passing conversation to take the tension out of the air.

What could I possibly talk about that interests the both of us, that doesn't make her angry?

"Um," I cleared my throat awkwardly. "When we were in the castle changing our clothes, there were a few lovely dresses and gowns in the wardrobe."

"Yes, there were," She replied flatly.

"There was one that I found particularly pretty and I wondered what special occasion you'd worn it to." I continued, a small bud of hope at a peaceful interaction blooming in my chest.

"Which dress?" Alice tilted her head curiously.

Good job, Wendy! You found a safe topic.

"It was a dark indigo blue with sparkling silver accents. For which occasion was that dress worn?" I blinked warmly, expecting details of some peculiar party.

But Alice's eyes sparked and she clicked her tongue. "Murdering a witch in her castle after she gave it to me. Peter liked the dress too, if I recall."

Oh no. Abort mission, Wendy! What a stupid question to ask. What were you thinking, poking about in her past like that?

"Oh!" I spluttered lamely, my heart instantly sinking.

"It was my predecessor, the former Wicked Witch of the West. She broke my compass to cut the ties of control over my morality for the compass' owner— whom I recently learned was Mombi. Unfortunately, the instability of the compass toggling on my morality led to me taking control of her minion monkeys and having them rip her apart. Magic does wonders to get blood stains out of clothing, by the way. Since that day, to the best of my ability, I have fought for control of myself again. I will be no one's plaything."

"Goodness," I couldn't find any more words to contribute, and I bit my lip self-consciously. I'd really stepped in it with that conversation attempt. I hoped I hadn't offended her, but her face remained neutral as if she had just told me about the weather.

Both of these new girls were very twisted and I couldn't wrap my head around having that kind of driving evil lurking within to harm others at any given moment. Would I be capable of such an evil if I'd had a cursed compass or drank poisonous tea? Somehow, I felt like the answer was no and I'd sooner die myself than kill another being.

"What is that?" Alice stopped abruptly and pointed in front of us. I followed her finger to gaze upon a mass of tangled thorny tendrils, seeping black wisps. "Looks awfully ominous."

"Oh, those are the Shadow Thorns," I explained, recognizing the shadows as a long time landmark of Neverland. "We always assumed that was likely where Peter's Shadow had come from. But, no one wanted to crawl around in a clump of brambles so we never investigated too thoroughly."

Help!

My spine went rigid as another faint voice pressed into my ear just like it had outside the shimmering white castle in Wonderland.

"Did you hear that?" I whispered, shooting Alice a nervous glance. She returned it with an expression of confusion.

"Hear what?" Her brows furrowed and she leaned her neck forward straining to listen.

"It's the second time I've heard a strange voice… it was asking to be helped."

"That sounds suspicious… and you didn't have any tea?"

"No, I was warned to leave well enough alone from the tea by Dorothy," I continued, absently twirling my hair in a nervous spiral. "I suppose maybe I'm just a bit on edge. Forget I said anything."

"Well, hold on." Alice rested a hand on her hip. "Just because I don't hear it doesn't mean it's not real."

"Oh."

"Oh? Why did you bring it up if you're surprised to be listened to?" She narrowed her eyes at me.

"I don't know," I blustered, insecurity churning in my stomach. This girl was so dreadfully intimidating, I couldn't make heads or tails of how I was supposed to act or what I was supposed to say.

Alice sighed and shook her head. "Are you afraid of me? Is that it? You pulled the short end of the stick by getting stuck with me, the big bad scary witch? Your friend certainly seems to feel that way."

"No!" I blanched. Somehow not saying anything had offended her as much as saying something foolish would have. I froze, unsure of what to do next.

"I'm not going to intentionally kill you, so go find where you left your spine behind and reassemble yourself. I'll wait." She folded her arms and raised an eyebrow.

"Sorry," I bleated, then gave myself a good mental shake in an attempt to dislodge my insecurities.

Alice puffed another sigh and rubbed her temples rhythmically. "No, I'm sorry. My surliness is coming in spades today, and Peter would give me an earful if he heard me speaking to you that way— as bothersome as that is. This isn't productive, and I just want to be through with it all as soon as possible before something terrible happens."

To my surprise, there was the smallest wobble of trepidation in her voice, and at the slightest sign of vulnerability in the young witch, I steadied myself. *This is no time to be a mouse, Wendy!* I chided myself, and nodded resolutely.

"I heard something outside the castle in Wonderland. It was asking me to come set it free. And just now, I heard another voice calling for help."

"Curious," Alice pursed her lips thoughtfully. "And you don't recognize the voices?"

"They are a bit too faint to discern, I'm afraid. But," I paused and fished for a sentiment to describe them. "They seem sincere, and not hostile."

"Could it be some sort of Lost Boy? Shouldn't they be about?" She ventured, peering through the woods around us, like she expected to be greeted by a throng of children at any moment.

"Didn't Peter tell you?" I queried, then immediately kicked myself for it as her head snapped stiffly back to me.

"Didn't Peter tell me *what,* Little Bird?" Her tone was lilting but the words were being pressed through gritted teeth, and I could see her muscles clenching with a struggle of self control. I really wished Tip and Dorothy would hurry and catch up to us again.

"There aren't any Lost Ones here anymore… Um, Tip and I are the only ones left."

Alice's jaw set and she clicked her tongue in annoyance once more. "No, that bit didn't make it into the briefing. That devilish little gnat never tells me anything. I ought to turn him into a toad again and hang him by his toes until he tells me *all* the pertinent information. Ah!" She jolted, her hand that had been balled around her compass releasing with more fresh fissures running up her skin. "Bloody thing."

"Peter only told us back when we were on our way to meet you in Wonderland. I'm sure he would have told you. I think he was ashamed. He's very prideful when it comes to Neverland."

"Don't you think I already know that?" She bit at me and I took a physical step backwards. She closed her eyes and took a few slow breaths to compose herself. "Aren't we needing to get to that Pixie Village?"

"What about the voice asking for help?"

"Not our problem right now. If we can find Peter, maybe he will have an explanation." Her tone was tight with little to no room for arguing, so I nodded slowly.

Wendy, don't go!

The voice pleaded, and an instant pang rang through my heart. I knew that voice from somewhere. I turned away from Alice and drew my sword, slowly approaching the Shadow Thorns.

"What are you doing?" Alice groaned. "I thought those shadows were harmless?"

"The voice. It's coming from inside."

The familiar spark of curiosity pinged through me as Wendy and I stared at the dense, twirling black mist.

"You hear the voice coming from inside? Why can't I hear it?" I squinted and squatted down to look from a new angle. "Oh, there looks to be an entrance. Should we go inside?"

Wendy's brows rose then furrowed. "You mean you want to go into a strange opening of thorns and shadows?"

I shrugged. "The others haven't caught up to us yet anyways, so I don't see the harm in taking a small look while we wait. Could be an adventure waiting to happen, after all. Although we might have to put a pin in to circle back after all this nonsense is over."

Wendy's expression melted into something terribly wistful. "I see. That must be it," She murmured softly, her arms wrapping around herself self-consciously. Her voice dropped to hardly more than a whisper. "I'm sure he loves that."

"Pardon?" I quirked an eyebrow skeptically. "Who are you talking about? Who are you talking *to,* for that matter. I can barely hear you." It took everything in me not to roll my eyes. This girl was meeker than a mouse a good share of the time, and her perpetual essence of hesitation in my presence set my impatience boiling.

"Nothing! Sorry, I didn't mean… I didn't realize I was talking out loud, er— Oh dear," Wendy spluttered, her face blushing deep red. "Never mind."

"Right..." I trailed away. As I stared at the tendrils, cloaked in shadows to form an entrance to an infinitely dark hole, my compass started ticking. Then, my whole body began to throb, and I felt compelled to go inside the mysterious entrance.

Common sense told me not to listen to the urge to indulge in my insatiable and detrimental curiosity, but I was struggling to will myself to heed its warning. We should honestly stay in one place until Tip and Dorothy found us. Wandering further, or going into a questionable hole would only delay our progress, and I didn't *need* to know what the mysterious voice Wendy was hearing. I didn't *need* to know what was on the other side of the hole. For all I knew, it was just another Shadow Beast. Going into a suspicious shadowy hole after nearly getting killed by a shadow monster, was the opposite of what we should be doing. No, it was most sensible to avoid the whole thing.

But, I found myself giving in a heartbeat later. "Well, come on then. Let's have a look. Best be careful though. Crawling into a strange hole was how I found myself lost in this world to begin with, and I would be most annoyed if I somehow fell into a world within a world. So, we shouldn't go far, and one of us keep at least part of our bodies on this side of the hole."

"That's good advice." Wendy nodded amicably, fidgeting madly with the tip of her ginger braid.

"I give myself very good advice, but I very seldom follow it," I hummed one of my favorite turn of phrases. That one usually came up everytime I did something I knew better than to do.

"I am a bit curious to know what this place is. The only one who ever even came close to crawling in here was a Lost Boy named Lionel, and I think it's because he's the one who contributed to this part of Neverland."

"Curious." My mind was twirling in all the infinite possibilities imagination as a source of magical creation could yield, but I shook it away. "Well, if we have a foe lurking in there, better get the reveal over with and out of the way. Are you going to be able to handle yourself if we have to fight?"

I didn't expect much out of the prim Lost Girl, given her demure nature, but I'd never hear the end of it if she died on my watch. My compass ticked impatiently, urging me towards the shadows. It didn't give two figs about Wendy, and it was only the tiniest shred of humanity in me that made me feel the slightest bit conscientious.

She nodded and tapped the sword strapped to her back. "I'm good to go!"

I refrained from warning her not to stab either of us while waving it around, but figured she had enough common sense to spare her the condescension.

I grunted my acknowledgment, and started forward towards the void. I should have felt afraid, I think, but instead, I only felt a strange sense of peace— the kind of peace only a demon might feel in an abyss of absolute darkness. The touch of the flickering shadow wisps was cool and soothing as they kissed my skin. I felt so oddly at home, like I could just forget everything I had ever cared about and dive into their full embrace to feel the extent of my true self— and of the true power that it would awaken if I submerged within them.

"I'm right behind you, Alice," Wendy's gentle voice sounded behind me, and the wisps hissed softly. "Ouch, I didn't expect them to be so hot!"

Hot? They feel so cool and refreshing to me. I suppose only a Wicked witch would feel soothed by the kisses of a demon's black hellfire. I mused, letting one of the twirling tendrils dance around my hand without any trace of heat. All of my Wickedness always burned, but here it was like fresh spring water. I hadn't even permeated the entrance yet. Its touch wasbeckoning me onward. So, I complied, and kept crawling until I had successfully poked my head inside the hole.

"Oh!" I gasped in surprise. Beyond me was an entire mirroring forest, bathed completely in black fog. It was a world of shadows.

"What is it? Ouch! Cursed thorns," Wendy squeaked from behind me. Another misfortune that had failed to harm me. Was this place welcoming me?

"There is a forest in here!" I chirped, my curiosity getting the better of me. Without hesitation, I launched myself completely into the strange shadow space. And the ticking of my compass deadened. I felt... *free.*

Elation flowed through my body from head to toe with such fervor I couldn't contain my rush of energy for fear I might burst. To even my own surprise, a small squeal of excitement pushed through my lips and I broke into a sprint deeper into the world, nothing but euphoria in my mind.

"Wait, what?" Wendy shouted. "Alice, where are you— ow— where are you going? What happened to keeping part of our body on this side of hole? You can't just go running... oh, blast it all!" She muttered and I could only faintly hear her charging in after me.

I couldn't help myself. I never knew peace could feel so invigorating. There was no pull between right or wrong raging in my chest. There was just me— the me I was when I first came to Wonderland and started my adventures with Peter.

I stopped running and spun in circles, head thrown back, arms spread wide, the darkness coiling in tandem with my rotating body.

The labored breathing of Wendy sounded beside me, and there were beads of sweat on her brow as she scowled at me.

"That was so reckless! We need to go back right away." Her voice was faint, hardly more than a whisper despite her standing right next to me.

"Relax, Little Bird!" I sighed, and impulsively grabbed her hand in mine. "We just stumbled into some Shadow World within our own world. How can you not be marveling at it? It's so refreshing." My voice also sounded muted even though I was speaking at normal volume.

"Refreshing? It's boiling in here! We need to go back to the entrance before we get stuck," Wendy sniffed, wiping her forehead with the back of her free hand. What was clearly conveyed in a hissing volume, boomed through the gloom.

"Is sound inverted here?" I whispered, and sure enough my voice thundered in volume. I shouted my next words, enthralled when they came out as whispers. "How interesting! I guess there is something be said of no one hearing you screaming in an abyss of darkness"

"Wendy, help me!"

"I'm hearing the voice again," Wendy stiffened, adjusting her speaking to conform to the strange sound rules of this place. "And please stop saying such unsettling things."

"I heard it that time too." I perked up, turning to discern where the voice had called from. "And it seems it knows you by name. It sounds like a man."

"I don't know any men here other than the pirates, but that certainly isn't one of them." Wendy cowered nervously.

"I suppose we better look into it."

"That sounds risky."

"What if they need help?" I countered.

Wendy opened her mouth then snapped it closed again, confliction creasing her expression. She pursed her lips and then nodded in resignation.

"Hello! Where are you?" I whispered as quietly as I could, allowing my actual words to bellow into the dark woods.

"Help! I'm in a hole."

"Well, yes we've gotten that far," I whisper-shouted back.

"No, I'm in a hole in the Shadow Woods. In a cage at the bottom. Please get me out!"

"Who are you?" Wendy held at her arm to give me pause before I managed to start off towards the voice. It was probably a good thing she followed me in here. I couldn't manage to feel a shred of fear, negativity, or hesitation.

There was a pause before the man replied, "I knew it was you, Mother Wendy. It's me, Lionel."

Wendy's entire body went rigid for a single heartbeat, and her face looked like someone had slapped her. The next heartbeat and she was gone, propelled by sheer force of instinct to protect something precious.

My brows rose as she adeptly pulled her swords from her back, never once breaking her stride. A gentle doe turned ferocious lion in an instant.

I followed along behind her, the shadowy foliage whipping past my body as I ran, the sensation reminding me of cool water droplets misting me on rainy winter mornings back home. It was a strange comfort.

Wendy, intent on her mission, locked eyes on the hole the man calling himself Lionel had mentioned, and to my immediate surprise, she leapt fearlessly into it without a single air of hesitation.

This Lionel must really mean something to her, I realized as I hurtled after her. Hearing his cry for help and knowing who was pleading had given her sudden invincible courage, and I was vaguely impressed by it.

A brief flashback of floating down the rabbit hole encompassed me as I plummeted into the pit. Somehow, the darkness felt darker here, and much less welcoming than it felt above. My skin prickled with the first feeling of dread since entering the space.

I landed softly, bending my knees to absorb the impact. I had to squint to peer through the dense darkness, much like back in Echo's Cave, to make out the form of Wendy next to a large cage with bars of pure black, with spiraling cinder colored clouds wrapped around each one. It was a cage of shadows, and within was a thin, pale, man with blonde shoulder-length hair.

"Quick, give me your sword," He was commanding the shaken Lost Girl. As I drew closer, and my eyes adjusted little by little, I could see her cheeks were glistening with tears while she obliged his request.

"I can't believe you're here," she breathed, the words booming around the pit. "It's really you, Lionel."

Lionel grunted and started swinging the gifted sword madly at the bars, trying to break through them. Instead, after several slugs, the steel of the sword itself cracked and broke in two.

"Blast!" He shouted in frustration, though it came out in a whisper. "We need something stronger."

I could feel the frantic agitation palpitating through the air, and with each pulse of despairing emotion I felt like the darkness was getting denser.

"Let's shed a little light here and see what we are working with."

"You'll never be able to get a fire going with the wood in this place," Lionel shook his head.

"I'll accept that challenge," I quipped and waved my hand to summon a flame.

Lionel flinched from the sudden swell of light in the dark space, Wendy's eyes widened in wonder, and I simply gawked at my hand. The flame was a silvery white and shimmered brilliantly. It looked like the flame of a falling star, and I'd never conjured anything like it before.

Instantly, the surrounding black fog hissed and shrank away, and the feeling of cool calm evaporated into a furious heat. The hissing grew into snarls and no one needed to say a word for me to know I had angered the shadows of this world with my light.

"How'd you do that? Are you a fairy?" Lionel gasped, cowering from the light.

"No, I'm a witch and usually a Wicked one, but this feels so… not that." I was transfixed by the ethereal glow I was creating. Why did this magic feel intrinsically *Good?*

"Alice, look! The bars are cracking. Hit them with your fire. Lionel, stand back." Wendy shoved me towards the cage, breaking my stupor. "We've got some company."

Sure enough, a plethora of small beady scarlet eyes surrounded the pit, spitting and hissing as they started crawling down the walls towards us.

I aimed my fire at the cage and unleashed, shattering the bars with a single blast. Wendy helped Lionel to his feet and led him along behind me, while I turned my silver flames on the wraiths to clear a path.

"Give me your hand," I barked, grasping for Wendy. I was panting in the suffocating heat, the intensity of it draining my energy. "I'm weakening in the heat but I can get us out of the pit. Then we have to run for it!"

In a blink we went from the base of the pit to the forest floor, and without missing a beat we tore through the woods in the direction of the exit, while a swarm of wraiths descended upon us. Wendy was jabbing and slashing expertly at the advancing enemy as she ran, while I continued blasting with my fire. Managing a small moment of reprieve I flashed up a swatch of fabric and handed it to the Lost Boy.

"Cover your eyes. The light will be a shock to you after being in here for so long," I instructed, remembering the pain I'd felt in my eyes when we'd left the caves. I could only imagine the shock of having gone years without light, and his reaction to the glow of my flames had told me it would be a transition. "You can adjust a bit more gradually once we are out."

He grunted his thanks and fastened the cloth to his head, trusting Wendy implicitly to lead him to safety.

"We are almost there! I see the opening ahead," Wendy cheered. I felt my chest swell with relief only to gasp as something caught hold of my foot and tripped me.

"You can't abandon me. Stay here in the dark. Couldn't you see how wonderful the darkness made you feel? How it welcomed you kindly into it? You're meant for it. Explore with me, and we can test our boundaries. Give in, Alice and together we will be unparalleled, forever," Someone rumbled in my ear, and a million knives tore through my nerves as the voice mirrored Peter's, though it sounded huskier and seductive in a way I'd never heard him speak before.

"No!" I shrieked and blasted the hand, now trying to pin me down, with fire.

"Damn, witch! You will submit to me and be mine," It growled, the tone dipping into garbled monstrous sounds, no longer sounding like Peter at all.

"You won't ever take him over!" A second Peter-voice challenged the first, sounding lighter yet not quite tangible. Scrambling to my feet, I turned to see two shadows facing each other, one the familiar shape of the enchanted Shadow that followed my Peter around, the other imposing with beady red eyes.

A woman cloaked in teaming shadows appeared beside the normal

Peter-shadow, and slipped between me and the evil wraith.

"Ida, cease your meddling! You can't change what he was meant to be."

"He was always meant to be Good. And you won't steal his inner light, or trap this girl here with you, no matter your twisted delusions of grandeur," The woman called Ida stated firmly. "Ozma and I will never stop protecting him or what he holds dear. Now, run dear child, before this devil makes a liar out of me and traps you here for good."

The last of her words were directed at me but I was completely stupefied by what I was seeing. Who were all these Peters? And this mystery woman protecting him along with his deceased mother? Her presence was cool and serene unlike the heated touch of the other malicious shadows, and she looked mostly tangible and not at all like the evil wraiths.

Together, her and Shadow lunged for the demon masquerading as Peter, driving him back further into the woods.

"You can't escape the darkness, Alice, no more than your precious Peter can." His ominous growl faded with distance, and I held my breath.

"Alice, come on!" Wendy grabbed my wrist and yanked me forward through the hole back into a Neverland.

We exploded into the fresh air and fell to our knees in a breathless heap. The compass started ticking slowly and felt as heavy as a boulder around my neck. The feeling of being shackled to my Wickedness had returned.

"What was that…" I puffed shakily, wondering what that demon Peter had been and how he factored into whatever was wrong with Neverland.

"Wendy give me a knife, quick," Lionel barked, drawing my attention back, as an unfamiliar single wraith emerged from the hole behind us. "You can't harm this one," He added when I summoned a fire, blinking in confusion as this time it was back to its typical red and orange hue.

Wendy complied and looked on with big round eyes as her childhood friend impaled the beast, ignoring the screams of agony. His body convulsed a few times and I started when I saw a lingering shadow wisp where his left hand should have been.

"Your hand!" I gasped but Lionel turned and plunged the knife into his hand, dispelling the shadow, leaving only his wounded flesh behind.

"Lionel! What in the world?" Wendy squealed in dismay and ripped a part of her shirt to quickly set to work bandaging the man's hand.

He turned, his breathing labored from whatever had just transpired, and looked at us from behind his blindfold, face entirely stoic.

"These shadows are inner demons and we all have one that haunts us. The only way to beat those ones is to kill it yourself and absorb the darkness you poured into it to give it its life"

"What?" Wendy and I blustered in unison.

"No mercy. No remorse," He rasped. "Kill it at all costs or it will kill you and take you over."

Eleven

Peter

"No sign of any forest fires, so no Dorothy." My feet were dragging, and my burst of enthused energy from the previous night was waning with each step I took.

Step. Because I'd run plum out of pixie dust and needed to get back to the village to get more. My eyes were bleary with fatigue from my impulsive decision to forgo sleep and go for a run, and I felt the slightest bit of dread about returning to the Pixie Village.

The last time I had been there, I'd gotten an earful for my negligence of Neverland, so I took enough to keep me well stocked for a while to avoid coming back for another lecture. But, with all the excess flying and extra flyers, I'd run out sooner than anticipated.

I trudged onward through the Never Woods, pausing to drag my hand across the trunk of one of the towering oaks. Memories danced through my mind of the Lost Ones racing to climb it, the winner getting to choose who would be banished to the Prison of Solitude and who would get to choose the next adventure.

Gazing around me, everything about the splendorous land looked the same to the naked eye, but in my heart it felt too quiet, like it was cloaked in some invisible loneliness. No, to me, without the Lost Ones, it might as well be the same bleak wasteland as my nightmares.

Maybe bringing Alice here would have brightened it up. She had brightened my life in general, but I knew deep down, I feared that if I brought her to Neverland, and it wasn't better, it would tarnish the light she had given back to me.

Thrumming my fingers against the bark, I thought of those bright blue eyes that forever existed in curiosity. Then came the painful reminder that even once I found her, she still planned on going back to her world at the end of all this, and I didn't know how to handle that— so I simply hadn't.

She would have loved Neverland, and I probably could have spared her a lot of heartache if she hadn't gone to Wonderland. But, there was also the added layer that everyone who came to Neverland had always wound up leaving me.

Maybe it was a hidden curse of this place. Nothing could remain so magnificent and carefree forever. So, if I brought her to Neverland, would it be the kiss of death and she'd leave me like all the others? Would what I had to offer ever be good enough to make someone stay for good? I cared too deeply for her, so I never could stomach the risk.

And sadly, even keeping her from Neverland hadn't kept her from wanting to leave. I still wasn't enough, and I didn't know how to be more than I was. What did I need to do to convince her?

"Maybe that's what I need to ask her," I mumbled thoughtfully to myself. "Though I suppose if I had spared her the horrors she had suffered and kept her innocence kindled, maybe she would have found it enough for her and we could have been happy together…"

I trailed off, a strange sadness working its way in circles from my heart to my stomach and back again. It was different than the overwhelming despair that seemingly summoned my evil shadow self though. A stinging pricked my eyes, as I allowed myself to be wistful and a flood of new thoughts and desires swirled to life.

I wanted there to be children running in this forest again. I wanted to keep searching for broken spirits and bringing them back from the brink of darkness into a world of light. I wanted to soar through the sky with Alice at my side for all of it forever. I wanted to free her from her internal torments so she could live freely again. I wanted Tip to recover from the horrors he'd been forced to endure after being stolen away under my watch. I wanted to give Wendy answers to what became of her brothers, and reawaken the brilliant spirit within her. I wanted to show Dorothy what it meant to be connected with kindred spirits. I wanted Oz to be free, and Wonderland to be restored. I wanted to be someone my mother would have been proud to call her son. I wanted to fix it all and protect everyone from any more pain.

I clutched at my chest, the intensity of my desire rushing in rapid palpitations. I wanted it all so badly, but I had no idea how to go about it. What it all boiled down to was changing the world and the lives of everyone in it. That was a task too big for any boy to shoulder…

"But, maybe a man could shoulder it," I reminded myself of my revelation back in Oz.

I wasn't truly a boy anymore, and hadn't been for a long while now, no matter how I tried to convince myself otherwise. I'd stopped being a child the day I lost Wendy and her brothers. I was older, faster, and stronger than I was back then. And once I had my friends back beside me, we wouldn't fail. With them here, I was responsible for them, and I wouldn't let any more of their lights go out.

I sniffled and rubbed my face to center myself. "Ah, buck up, Mate. You're just overtired. There is someone in Neverland imagining. It isn't dead, and it's time to fix things."

I squared my shoulders and resolved myself to keep trekking forward, when a soft whistling sounded past my ear. With a squawk of surprise, I jumped out of the way of a whizzing knife headed straight for my hand.

Unceremoniously losing my balance and tumbling to the ground, I spat out a mouthful of leaves and dirt and lifted my head to look for my assailants.

"You look confused, Pan." Her voice was silky smooth, pitched with mockery. "Did you forget about me?"

"Uh, ha," I laughed nervously. "Lily, is that you? It's been a while hasn't it?" This time I only just managed to barrel roll out of the way of another knife.

"You codfish!" She barked and emerged from the shadows while I scrambled hastily back to my feet.

"Are you angry? Because you seem a little angry. How about we put the pointy objects down and have a chat?" My eyebrows shot up as I stared at who faced me.

The teenage girl staring coldly back at me was positively breathtaking. She was dressed in black pirate garb, complete with a feathered hat lined with red.

"Whoa," I breathed, running a hand through my hair awkwardly. "Tiger Lily, you grew *up*. But why are you dressed like a pirate?"

"Shut up!" She snapped, reaching for her bow and arrows strapped to her back.

"Cranky. How are things? How's your father?" I prattled on, like an old friend of mine wasn't getting ready to try to murder me.

But Tiger Lily froze and looked at me with fury blazing in deep golden brown eyes. "He's dead. I had to kill him."

It was my turn to freeze. "Wait *what?*" I spluttered. "The Chief is dead? What do you mean *you* killed him? And I still need an answer on the pirate attire, please and thank you."

"He was taken over by a shadow and was trying to kill me. He wasn't human anymore."

"A shadow?" Cool dread pooled in my chest, and my brain flickered to the unnerving images of the wraiths I'd defeated in Oz. "There are more in Neverland?

"Where were you?" She hissed, aiming her arrow for my chest. "Why did you let this evil into Neverland and leave us all to die?"

I was at a loss for words. I could see tears brimming in her wrathful gaze, and I felt shame burn in my stomach. Tiger Lily was part of Neverland, conjured like the rest of it, but it hadn't truly occurred to me the depth of pain my old imaginary friends could feel in my absence. I had left Neverland to spend time with Alice because I didn't value the Imagineds as *real* company.

But, now, after everything I'd been through I felt like an absolute villain for being so careless with their lives, just leaving them here to do their thing despite knowing there was something not quite right brewing in Neverland. I had only been concerned about convincing Alice to stay in this world and making *Wonderland* the best possible adventure for her.

And I had failed. I had failed Alice. She was Wicked because I was too much of a coward to bring her to Neverland. I had failed Tiger Lily and The Chief, who had paid with his life, because I had played fast and loose with their importance. I had failed Wendy and Tip and John and Michael. All of Oz. All of Wonderland. And even now, I was probably failing Dorothy somehow. I thought I had been keeping things light, but had I been dancing with the darkness all along?

Subjects of *mine* were dead. Lost Ones were likely dead. Those who weren't dead, or gone, were tortured and imprisoned. Alice was corrupted and scarred for life. Directions had been seized. I did nothing to stop it. I only cared about saving myself.

"I'm… already turning into *him*," I didn't even try to move from Tiger Lily's aim. If she shot true and ran me clean through, I'd deserve it.

"What?" Her lip quivered beneath her wall of defiance.

"I failed you all." My eyes widened and I felt my entire being crushed under the weight of it.

"Yes, you're finally seeing what I've been trying to tell you. Your true self is coming into view at last. Embrace it. Let us take our rightful place at the top of this world. You were destined for darkness the moment your mother died and your father smothered her light," The familiar voice of the Shadow-Peter purred in my ear, my latest revelation likely allowing him to appear. Before, I could try and counteract the negative spiral I was in, his cold talon-like hands curled around my throat and pressed in, finger by finger, like he was enjoying his sudden upper hand.

Tiger Lily gasped and loosed an arrow, not at me, but at the wraith. With a startled snarl, I was released and the creature locked eyes on the girl, running his tongue slowly across his carnivorous fangs.

"Lily, run!" I coughed, scrambling away to collect myself.

"Shadow, help me out here."

My trusted old shadow mimed frantically at me, trying to tell me I'd better start glowing and fast.

"The light. The light. Don't let the light go out," I murmured to myself shakily. *But, everyone is still missing and I don't know what I'm doing. I'm going to fail all over again.* I wailed inwardly, trying my hardest to force the intrusive thoughts away. "The light. I need more light."

Come on, Neverland. I promise I'll make it up to you, just please give me some light! I closed my eyes and tried to call out to my haven, as Tiger Lily refused to cease firing arrows at the wraith, each one sailing right through it. The beast chuckled, low and cruel as it prowled forward unscathed. Tiger Lily's eyes widened then narrowed with vehement adamance, still not budging even an inch. *Please, I need a little light.*

"Peter!" A single voice shouted and my eyes popped open, head instantly cleared.

Alice. She had found me.

My head whipped to my right and, sure enough, I saw her pelting through the woods, determination and unwavering resolve fixed on her face.

Thank you, Neverland. I sighed in relief, and looked at Alice as she leapt at the wraith, fire blazing in both hands. Positively insane. But just seeing her alive and well, was enough to ignite hope within me once more. I flooded with it until it seeped from my pores and illuminated the area.

The wraith hissed and shrank from the mutual light of Alice's fire and my glow. It glared at Alice with a smug and knowing gaze.

"You again!" Alice bellowed. "You can't take him, I won't let you. I might not be able to kill you, but I know you don't like fire and light!"

"Come again, Love?" I piped up, tilting my head, unsure of how Alice possibly was familiar with this demon.

"You couldn't stay away from me, now could you?" The shadow cooed, in a gnarled playful tone, that made my lip start to curl in indignant disgust. Was my Evil Self trying to move in on my girl? That was something to process later.

Alice looked less than impressed and she jerked her head at me. "Kill him, Peter. You're the only one who can."

"But Lily's arrows went right through it!" I countered, looking around for my old friend but she was nowhere to be seen.

"So there is a Tiger Lily!" Alice crowed, her face pinched in a scowl, and I could see her internally trying to refrain from turning her fire on me. "No matter. He's *your* Shadow Beast. You have to kill it."

"Looks like the Lost Boy was awfully chatty on the way over here," the Wraith folded its arms across its chest.

I perked up, more light beaming through. "Tip's with you?"

"No, Wendy is."

"You didn't—"

"She's fine!" Alice snapped impatiently.

"I'll take my leave for now. But just remember, whenever you falter, I'll be waiting. This," he gestured to Alice with a cruel grin. "Will just make the pain more delicious as it eats you alive. And her all the more delectable when she's at *my* side."

"No!" I shouted and reached my hands out to tether the beast, but Shadow's fingers weren't fast enough and the wraith flickered into nothingness, leaving just me and Alice alone. Why did every evil entity in this world want her to be theirs? She seemed to attract a type and I wasn't sure what that said about me.

We stayed poised for battle a moment longer, before slowly, I dimmed the glow to nothing and Alice let her fire putter out. She turned and faced me, the heat of conflict still dying away in her brilliant blue eyes, and I watched her spinning arrow of her compass coming to a halt.

"You're okay," she whispered, then lunged for me, embracing me with such an impact I nearly fell to the ground.

"And you're okay," I echoed, returning the hug with equal fervor, and rested my chin on her head affectionately. "I'm so sorry."

"What for? I mean, I know what *I* have a bone to pick with you about, but I'll let you tell me in case I've left something out," She joked softly, burying her face in my chest.

"Um, I'll put a pin in that trap for later," I laughed. I wanted nothing more than to melt to the ground, hold Alice close and watch the clouds roll by like we didn't have a care in the world now that we were together. But, I had made a promise to Neverland. It gave me Alice back to be my light, so I needed to see my end through. "You mentioned Wendy… alive and well? Where is she?"

"Oh, yeah." Alice ducked her head and tucked her hair behind her ear as we separated from our embrace. "Um, she was catching up with Tip and Dorothy where we saw them leaving the corn maze. I sort of ran off and left them without saying anything when I had this sort of feeling of where you were."

"A very Alice thing to do," I nodded along. "So, there's a corn maze now? Wait, we are all together again! We just rejoin them and then game over, right?" I chirped, but Alice shook her head slowly.

"Afraid it's not that simple…"

"Oh, no," I groaned. "Why not? That was the rule of the game , right? All of us together and we have the power to defeat him. Well, we are all together. I've gotten all my lost friends."

"Not quite. I'll tell you but you're going to want to brace yourself."

I squared my shoulders and grinned. "Hit me with it, Love."

"No, I mean really brace yourself. I don't want that *thing* getting a hold of you if you react poorly. I know all too well what that's like." She gestured to her compass.

"Oh yeah, how are you two acquainted by the way?"

"Who's Tiger Lily?" Alice glowered at me, and I clicked my tongue.

"Nothing to worry your pretty head over just now, but I see your point. Social relations can be discussed later. Now come on, out with it! You know suspense is only fun when I'm the one with the news."

Alice rolled her eyes and took my hand in hers. I noticed a bunch of markings running up her arm that looked inflamed and painful.

"I'm fine," she started, seeing my worried gaze. "But, I was attacked by a different Shadow Beast when I was sent with Tip to Echo's Cave."

"I thought you were with Wendy, and Dorothy was with Tip?" I interrupted.

"Hush. This will go faster the less you talk," She snipped, poking me in the chest. "The thing scratched my compass and then a rock, from a blast of mine damaged, it more. Now, my arm has decided it wants to be in solidarity with the bloody thing."

"Are you… *breaking*?" My heart dropped to my feet. "Like, how the destroyer of the compass dies. Are you trying to tell me it's killing you?" I demanded. I felt light headed. Death was far worse than going back to her world.

"No. Well, I don't know. But, I am fine for right now so let's leave that alone. I need to tell you about the game."

"You dying, or possibly dying, isn't what I needed to brace for?" I swayed a little, anxiety churning in my stomach, making me nauseous.

"I'm not dying, calm down." Alice waved me off. "Tip and I found Dorothy and Wendy last night and then Dorothy threw herself a pity party and wandered off in the corn maze she apparently imagined in her sleep."

"Ah! That was *Dorothy*. I felt it. I felt Neverland surge with fresh imagination and I rushed here from Wonderland." I perked back up. "A corn maze, eh? That could be fun."

"Tip went to get her and they took their sweet time, so Wendy and I started heading to this Pixie Village we were all supposed to go to, figuring the other two would catch up. Then, Wendy started hearing voices coming from these thorns…"

"Wendy is hearing voices? That doesn't sound promising for her sanity."

"There was an opening in the thorns."

I raised an eyebrow. "You went through it, didn't you?"

"I went through it." Alice nodded with an honest shrug. "Turns out it leads to a Shadow World!"

"Whoa. I didn't put another world in Neverland. Are you sure that's what it was?" I could hardly believe there would be a hidden world in Neverland that I didn't know about.

"Positive. I ventured into it."

"Of course you did, Love. Your curiosity is a curse."

"I haven't heard you complain about it before now!" Alice quipped back. "Now, hush. This is the important bit. Once inside, I heard the voice too. And it seems there was a Lost One stuck in there all this time."

There it was. That was the gut punch I had been warned to brace myself for.

"What do you mean a Lost One was *stuck* there?" I spoke very slowly, trying to keep calm.

"He was in a cage at the bottom of a pit."

"Well, we have to go help him!" I made to leap into the air, faltering when I remembered I still needed more pixie dust. "Blasted lack of pixie dust!"

"Peter, calm down. We already got him out." Alice turned me to face her. "He's out. He's with Wendy and the others now. And he's the one who told us about the individual shadows that all the Lost Ones, left in this world, need to defeat to restore Neverland and to also give us the power we need to beat The Wizard. I don't think he counted on us finding that out, so he stacked the deck against us. There are shadows born of the pain of each Lost One here who has made something in Neverland and while there are lesser shadows that can be brought down by anyone, the individually linked ones can only be killed by their creator."

"So, that thing is my shadow? And there's one for Tip and Wendy too?"

Alice nodded somberly. "And for five others."

"What?" I felt like the ground had been pulled from beneath my feet.

"Excluding this guy we found in the pit, there are four other Lost Ones held captive in this world that we need to find. So, The Wizard's game won't be finished until we find *all your Lost friends*. And, your Neverland won't be healthy again until those lost friends defeat their shadows. Thankfully, we found this fellow first, because since he was in the Shadow World, he's been connected, sort of, to the others through the shadows. If I understand correctly."

"I can't believe it. There are others here that I didn't know about? I just let them rot."

"You did nothing of the sort so straighten up. Beating yourself up now isn't going to rescue them. Stick up your chin and look sharp. We are going to save them now." Alice shook my shoulders with conviction burning in her beautiful face. I envied her sense of unbridled resolve. "The others should be here any second now, I'm sure, and we can go from there."

My eyes stung and I steadied my breath as I thought of facing another Lost One I didn't know was trapped in this world, waiting for me to save them. First Tip, then Wendy, and now who else? "Who was it that you found?"

"Why don't you look for yourself?" She smiled softly and turned me around to see Tip, Wendy, and Dorothy standing all together behind me. And beside them stood a thin young man with bright blue eyes and long, messy blonde hair.

"Hello, Peter. It's good to see you, my friend." He smiled sincerely at me and stepped forward to embrace me like a brother. My breath caught in my throat.

"Lionel."

Twelve

Dorothy

Shock was plastered across Peter's face as he hugged his old friend.

"Seems to be a lot of you popping out of the woodwork," I murmured to Tip. "What's the deal here?"

"We haven't even told him what you've learned about Henry yet," Wendy whispered on the other side of me. "Do you think he can take it?"

"The Witch told him there were four left. I'm sure he's prepared," Tip threw in. "I'll bet he's chomping at the bit to know who the others are that are left here."

Lionel and Peter parted, and Peter rested his hands on the man's shoulders. "Who else is still here?"

"See?" Tip snapped his fingers victoriously, rocking back and forth with a satisfied bounce.

"My, such enthusiasm," I snickered, and Tip immediately sobered.

"Oh, hush. Don't make me throw you in the lake again," He joked, then immediately blanched. "I mean uh, I wouldn't actually… you know that I know…" he gestured awkwardly as he grappled with forming a full sentence.

Wendy and I exchanged an amused look.

"Are you quite alright, Tip? You seem a little flustered there. Did you throw Dorothy into a lake while you two went galavanting through that maze? That's not how you flirt with a girl, you know," She laughed. I couldn't help but snort at her accusation's obvious absurdity.

"Running for our lives was hardly what I would call gallivanting," Tip grumbled and folded his arms, heat coloring his cheeks. "And I was *not* flirting."

"Whatever you say, Tip Dear," Wendy chirped.

"I'm older than you, you know."

"Well, of course. You were always a bit older than me." Wendy tilted her head, and I also wondered what had crawled up Tip's pants to make him so suddenly cross with Wendy.

"We aren't kids anymore. I'm all grown up. You don't need to do all the Mother-Wendy fussing nonsense with me." He shrugged uncomfortably.

Wendy looked instantly crestfallen, and she swallowed hard before forcing a smile. "Right. Sorry, all the reunions must have made me sentimental. Please, excuse me." She ducked her head and walked away to join the other group, though she stood a little to the side and remained quiet.

I turned to Tip and raised my eyebrows accusingly. "What was that for?"

"I don't know. She was rubbing me the wrong way." He looked away.

I understood getting annoyed and I understood saying things without thinking them through, but considering their long-standing friendship, it surprised me that he shut her down so coldly. What was the point of feeling close to someone if they knew all your vital points to hurt you?

I stepped in front of the surly Lost Boy and lifted my chin. "She didn't mean anything by teasing you. I was doing it too. You want to take a stab at me now also?" I challenged, surprising myself at my directness. Was I feeling protective of Wendy now? Why would that be?

"No! Wendy and I don't actually really know each other anymore since we've grown up. Rather I grew up, and she's still clinging onto a past that doesn't exist anymore. She was locked up with nothing to do but pine over Peter. I didn't have that luxury."

"That's pretty cold." I was taken aback by the fire in Tip's eyes.

"I didn't mean to be," Tip sighed. "I overreacted. She, unfortunately, just managed to hit a nerve," He admitted. "I do care about Wendy. I didn't mean to hurt her feelings."

I looked him over, assessing his sincerity. "I know you didn't. Sorry the idea of gallivanting with me got you so upset."

"It didn't... I should apologize to her."

"Probably. Especially since *you* flirting with me is the most absurd thing I think I have yet to hear since getting stuck in this wacky world—And I've gone insane twice now," I chuckled at my own joke. Well, it was true, but it was still funny. "So, it was so clearly a joke. You need to lighten up, and that's coming from me."

Tip looked perplexed. "Why do you think that's so absurd and laughable?"

"What?" I choked on my laughter and died a little inside at the unattractive hacking sound I made in the process. "Because it is absurd. Isn't it?"

"I just mean that I could if I wanted to, in theory."

"Which you absolutely don't," I interjected awkwardly, wanting nothing more than for this painfully uncomfortable exchange to be over.

"I know *how* to... it's not so absurd for the idea of me being able to convey... not to anyone in particular, but in general..." Tip fished once more for a full, coherent sentence.

"What in the world are you babbling about?" I sighed, completely lost at this point. "I feel like I'm talking to the Hatter and the Hare again."

"I'm not saying anything at all," He puffed in sulky defeat, turning abruptly. "I'm going to apologize to Wendy now."

I furrowed my brows in confusion, unsure of what had just transpired. Tip was so strange, I didn't understand him at all. "Whatever, sure. I'm actually going to pay attention to what they are talking about before they choose to throw us into a volcano or something."

"A volcano? Why would they do that?"

"I don't know! Why do those two do anything they do?" I gestured to Peter and Alice who were deep in conversation with Lionel.

Tip frowned thoughtfully. "That's fair. Come on then." He smiled, seeming a little less on edge, and leaned forward, brushing past me as he went to join the others. The touch— graze, more accurately— caused a faint flutter in my chest and I jolted.

It was probably the tea. I shook my head and followed behind him.

"So it's that last generation of Lost Ones then?" Alice was saying, wheels turning behind her eyes. "The ones Peter didn't take home personally?"

Lionel nodded. "That would be the sum of it, I think. I'm not entirely sure who all was still there after I got grabbed."

"Henry is in Oz," I piped up, causing everyone to whip their heads to look at me. I took a step back. "Um, Tip and I gathered that the nice man who helped me escape the Emerald City was a Lost Boy called Henry."

"Oh, dear Henry," Wendy clasped her hands together happily and dropped them self-consciously, causing me to shoot Tip a look. He clicked his tongue and repositioned to stand beside the Lost Girl, ready to apologize.

I smiled approvingly. Friends should be nice to each other, I thought. That's what I would want.

"So, we need to get him out of the Emerald City," Peter declared, jumping and frowning as he seemed to realize he still couldn't fly.

I opened my mouth to suggest we go get him some more pixie dust first, when I heard Wendy gasp, and Tip jolted for his knife before everything went dark.

~*~

My head pounded and the world swayed around me, slow and sluggish.

"Oh no," I groaned, assuming I was waking up from another spontaneous craze following those weird butterflies in my chest. "What did I burn down this time?"

Then I realized I could hear sloshing water, and that it was the cause of my lack of equilibrium. Was I on a boat? What kind of insane act caused me to board a boat?

I tried to move my arms and legs but I was tightly bound, the rope rubbing painfully against my skin. So I was a hostage on a boat. Daring to open my eyes, I blinked rapidly, taking in the dark, aged mahogany walls around me. Then my gaze slowly landed on each companion I'd been with before blacking out.

Tip, Lionel, and Peter were bound back to back on old splintering chairs, while Wendy was chained to a mast. I gasped in surprise when I saw Alice, who was chained up as well, and her entire body from the head down was suspended in water. It was some sort of tub compartment built into the ship to hold water without actually putting a hole in the floor. Quite clever if you thought about it on the captor's end.

"Hey!" I hissed, trying to draw the attention of any of the others. Peter and Tip groaned acknowledging they too were awake and equally miserable.

"Ambush," Tip hiccuped. "Pirates."

"Are you alright?"

"He gets seasick. He is basically useless on a ship without pixie dust to keep him floating," Peter explained, his head still slumped.

"Oh, good you're awake," Someone new spoke.

"Not another ominous disembodied voice, I beg you," I grumbled in defiance to the reoccurring cliche of this world. "You all just skulk in the shadows until you find a good time to announce yourself, and it's stupid."

"Down, Sparky," Tip managed to croak out, lamely referencing my easily aggravated fire-hands.

No sooner had he gotten the words out when I felt cold clammy hands grip my cheeks roughly, turning my head forcefully to look at my latest captor.

He was tall and broad-shouldered, raven-haired, with brown eyes, and a shadow of a beard studded his chin. He wore typical pirate attire, sans hat, but had opted for a long leather coat, covered in various knives. He had to be no more than in his early-twenties, and had a smirk smeared on his face. So far, I realized The Hatter was probably the oldest person I had come across in this place. No one seemed to make it past their twenties here.

Just beyond him, I spotted a stunning girl unlike anyone I had ever seen before, her blatant beauty making me instantly shrink with insecurity. Warm bronze skin set over striking cheekbones, glittering golden brown eyes and crimson lips, framed by long rich black hair that seemed to simultaneously hold every hue of dark brown within each strand. She, too, was wearing typical pirate garb.

"Well, aren't you spirited, Lass?" The man purred in a husky Scottish lilt. I saw something at the end of his other sleeve glinting in the firelight, and realized after a moment of staring, that it was a hook in place of his hand.

The girl folded her arms and looked at Peter expectantly. "You owe us some answers."

"Do I look like I have answers, Tiger Lily? I just woke up and I have no idea what's happening," Peter all but whined, squinting at our latest adversaries. "I guess this explains the new outfit. Sort of. Why is Alice underwater? Is she alright?" His eyes flicked over to the still-unconscious girl's bobbing body.

"I was warned she wields powerful fire magic, and I didn't fancy her burning my ship down," Hook rasped lazily. "But, I think you were asked a question by Lily, here."

"My entire family is *dead*, Pan. Because of the shadows you let terrorize us. I couldn't hurt that one attacking you, which means it's one of those extra violent ones that can't be killed," Tiger Lily asserted, stepping forward to stand directly in front of Peter. "Only I guess *you* can kill it. So, not only did you allow the shadows to exist here, you could have killed them and instead let them slowly slaughter us!" Her voice pitched with an irate edge, and she expertly flicked a knife into her hand to hold at Peter's throat.

"Tiger Lily? Is that you?" Wendy croaked, and smiled kindly despite obviously still coming to her senses. "How wonderful to see you again."

Tiger Lily frowned and faltered on her threat to Peter, opting to put the knife away. "I thought you died," was all she said in response, and the smile slowly fell from Wendy's face.

"I was held prisoner all this time, actually." She cleared her throat.

"Look, I don't know what history you all have with each other, and frankly I don't care," I snapped, feeling at my wits end after little to no sleep, running from a monster, and the traumatic swim. I didn't feel like minding my manners or playing their little games. "Lost Ones are being held captive in various places in this world— seemingly by Peter's psychotic father— and they each have managed to create an inner demon of a shadow monster that wants to kill everything or whatever. Those ones have to be dealt with by whoever created it and no one else."

"You aren't supposed to just cooperate with their demands," Peter groused, like this was still somehow a big game of pretend.

I concentrated everything I had left in me on my shoes, grasping for control like Lion and Tiger and Alice had all told me to do. Despite our argument earlier, Alice was right about my magic being a tool that could make or break a situation. Though part of me was still afraid since my second insani-tea stupor, that I would lose control and harm everyone around me, I reminded myself that I had made the fireballs in the dungeons, and had managed to hold off Mombi in the Ozian woods. This wasn't the Munchkin Village. I could do this.

My hands went ablaze, and I cheered inwardly as the flames instantly incinerated the ropes binding them. I swiped them at my feet in a single fluid motion, and rose defiantly, fire flickering in my palms.

"Unfortunately for you, you have more than one fire starter on your hands. Now, let the others go, or I will burn this ship down." I lifted my chin to sell my threat, and felt remarkably tough doing so. I hoped the others who were conscious were getting a good view of this, because for once, *I* was the one saving the day. Maybe this was how Alice got to be so confident. However, despite my elation, I knew more than anything, I had no desire to end up back in the water, so I really hoped my bluff worked.

"You light the ship up, and you and your friends are burning down with it, Lass," Hook drawled, running his hooked hand slowly across a sword he pulled when I stood up. "And you're too cocky. With a threat like that, me and my crew could have twelve swords and ten bullets in your chest before you managed to burn a single spark. So why don't you sit back down and keep telling us what we want to know."

"Hook, leave her alone," Tip wheezed.

I hesitated, my moment of triumph ebbing, though frustration still raged inwardly. A cursory eye flit about the room and I could see several unnerving looking degenerate men peppering the walls. Each one had gnarled scars, sneering faces, and adorned multiple weapons. This Hook wasn't bluffing like I was. I believed they would kill me before I could do any real damage.

"I already answered your questions." I left my hands burning on the off chance it bettered our standing to have me primed and ready.

"Where are the alleged Lost Ones?"

"I don't know. I already told you they are being held captive."

"Then what, pray tell, are you lot planning to do about it? From what Tiger Lily told me, the lad didn't have much fight in him against the beast. And capturing you was more than an easy task."

"The monsters are much less sneaky. They don't knock out young women and tie them up like you bunch of creeps." I gritted my teeth. "We were trying to figure out the rest when you ambushed us."

"Make her walk the plank, Captain Sir!" One of the henchmen bellowed. But Hook merely smirked and shook his head.

"I like your spirit," he admitted, dipping his head. "It's quite…" he paused and dropped his eyes emphatically to my hands. "Fiery."

I furrowed my brows, unsure of how much to trust the compliment. "Thank you?"

"We will cut you loose," he began.

"But—" Tiger Lily protested but Hook raised his hand to silence her, never taking his eyes from me.

"I don't want to keep losing my crew every other day, so if aligning with your bumbling group is the only lead on how to remedy the issue, I'm going to take it."

"We are not bumbling," I bristled at the insult. "Last I checked you needed our help, so I'd lay off the condescending comments there, Pirate Boy."

"That's Captain Pirate Boy to you," Hook clicked his tongue and grinned at me. I didn't respond.

"We found one Lost Boy, and he killed his shadow already," Wendy broke the silence, her restraints *clinking* loudly as she shifted. "We know there is one more Lost One in Oz."

"Let her go." I jerked my chin at Wendy.

"Captain." Hook rolled his shoulders back, still grinning at me.

"What?"

"Let her go, *Captain.*"

I rolled my eyes. "Are you serious?"

"You're on my ship."

"You put me on it."

"The least you can do is be gracious to your host."

"Hook…" Tip growled. "Stop screwing with her. Let us go."

"Yeah, what he said, you old codfish!" Peter echoed. "If Alice wakes up like that she will blow her top. I hate to tell you, but she can do damage with more than just fire. Heads will roll. All that stuff."

"Let them go, *Captain,*" I conceded, spitting the words out, when Hook refused to budge.

"That wasn't so hard, Lass." He crossed the floor and released Wendy personally, the tip of his Hook acting as a key to the shackles. He gestured to the others. "Go ahead."

"Peter, stop playing possum and get yourself out," I snapped, reluctantly letting my flames dissolve before I stopped to untie Tip's restraints.

"Oh yeah. I forgot about that again," Peter chuckled. "Ah ha! Bet you weren't expecting that!" As he magically broke through the ropes, he preened a little.

"We already know you have power, you idiot," Tiger Lily spat. "We are from your mind."

"Like Lion and Tiger," I acknowledged, shoving Peter towards Alice once I had Tip free. "You go defuse that bomb."

"Defuse?" Peter wrinkled his nose in confusion.

I sighed. "You people need less magic and more electricity and technological advancements here. I can only imagine what you'd make of a television. Go release your girlfriend. You're the only one she won't kill if she wakes up."

"Fair enough," Peter shrugged and sauntered towards the weird pit of water where Alice was suspended.

"Ugh," Tip groaned and I crouched to check on him.

"Here, let me see your wrists," I commanded.

"Why?" Tip asked dubiously.

"Oh, just cooperate." I snatched his wrists and felt his whole body jolt, then follow with another miserable groan. "I know a pressure point to help with the motion sickness. I used to feel sick in the car— you know the ones I told you about earlier— for a while after the accident. My Aunt Em taught me this trick and it helps."

I pressed my thumbs with light pressure into the Lost Boy's wrist. It took several heartbeats, but I felt his rising pulse gradually slow, and his rigid stance slacked ever so slightly.

"It's no counting to ten, but it usually does the trick well enough." I caught Tip's eye and smiled.

"Thank you." Though puny, he did his best to return the smile. "I hate that I get so sick. I'm useless."

"Only on the water. You did alright in it," I joked.

"Very clever." He smirked.

The sound of heavy boots drew my attention and I looked up to see the captain standing over us. He had removed his weapon studded coat, and was now in a weapon studded vest over a white tunic. The sleeves were pushed up to his elbows, and there was a leather guard around his forearm where the hook was fastened.

"Poor Tippy still has trouble with his sea legs, eh?"

"Don't call me Tippy," Tip groaned in such a way that told me that nickname had been the source of a longstanding argument.

"What do I call you?" Hook addressed me.

"Dorothy," I replied flatly.

"Well, Dorothy, I like you and your *fiery* spirit," Hook said smoothly and I instantly wanted to shrink inside myself. Tip snorted and Hook paid him no mind. "I have a feeling you're going to be the most tolerable one to deal with, so you're the only one I'm willing to deal with. Captain to captain, so to speak."

"I'm not a captain of anything. Even when we'd play kickball with my cousins on the farm, I never was captain," I blustered lamely.

"Haven't got the slightest idea what you mean, my dear," Hook laughed. "But what I'm saying is, you've gotten my interest and my respect. So, if you would be so kind as to come with me, I'd like to feel out this shadow business with Pan and you a little more thoroughly. Seems like you're the one with a sensible head."

"I don't know if I trust going with you," I replied bluntly.

"But my surrender was so easy."

"I don't trust easy anymore," I doubled down on my mistrust.

"I let your friends go, didn't I?"

I fished for an argument but couldn't think of one so I scowled and dropped my hold on Tip's wrists to follow the hooked man.

"Wait…" Tip reached pitifully after me. "I think it was helping."

"I think you can grip it yourself, Tippy. Dorothy has better things to be doing." Hook narrowed his eyes and winked at Tip, who's eyes widened with some revelation of a hidden insinuation in the pirate's words, and his face flushed. "That's what I thought."

"You're an ass," I sniffed.

"That I am. Come on." Hook beckoned me and Peter to the follow up to the main deck.

I blinked in the bright sunlight, once more tasting salt on my lips as I was greeted by the Sea mist spray of the ocean. Thankfully this time I wasn't scaling a cliff.

I don't know what I expected, but referring to what we were on as a *boat* wasn't an accurate description of the ship we were on. Thick masts towered into the sky overhead, weather-worn sails whipping in the buffeting wind. Several shirtless men were at work tending ropes. The room we had been in was clearly only one of many, and I considered the fact that this ship might have more working space to it than my entire farmhouse.

Hook followed my gaze and leaned towards me. "Those there are called riggers. They operate the intricate rope system aboard a ship as magnificent as the Jolly Roger."

"Where is Smee?" Peter asked, peering around the ship as he popped out behind us.

"Excuse me, Lass." Hook dipped his head and strode over to Peter.

"Dead," He answered, his voice low and menacing. Before I knew what was happening, Hook balled his fist and swung at Peter, knuckles connecting to his jaw with a crack.

Peter reeled and fell to the ground. "Bloody hell!" He spat blood from his split lip and rubbed at his assaulted jaw.

"Hey!" I shouted, and rushed over to help Peter up. "What the hell was that?"

"That, Dorothy, was a little payback from every Imagined who this bottom feeder left to fend for themselves. The ones who didn't make it. The ones who have fallen while he was off doing who knows what who knows who!" Hook explained, an acidic edge undercutting every sentence.

"The shadows aren't his fault!" I snapped, and once more surprised myself at the strange feeling of protective instinct breeding assertiveness. "I knew I shouldn't have trusted you."

"No, Lass. If you couldn't trust me, I would have used my other hand." The Captain raised the hook for emphasis.

"You sucker punched him! He's not who you should be angry at.

You can take that *other* hand and shove it up—"

"No, Love," Peter interrupted me.

"Don't call me that," I bit. "'Love,' 'Lass,' 'Witch,' 'Wicked Witch of the East'— I have a name!"

"I earned that hit. He's right."

"What?"

"I said I earned it." Peter rubbed the blood running down his chin away with the back of his hand and dusted himself off as he got to his feet. "The shadows are my fault. At least some of them are. So, anyone who has died by one, their death is on my hands."

"What are you talking about?"

"Neverland is of my mind. These Imagineds are too. But, it seems like this rotten noggin of mine," Peter tapped his temple. "Well, it pushed some nasty feelings away until they sprouted legs and teeth and claws and took on a life of their own. And, it would seem, my poor forsaken friends have pushed their own nasty feelings down, until they sprouted claws too and now are haunting their contributions to Neverland because those pieces are of *their* minds."

I squinted, trying to make sure I understood what Peter was explaining to me. Hook folded his arms across his broad chest and listened intently.

"Like, the corn maze I made?" I clarified slowly. I thought back to the strange Mombi monster, and wondered if that had been there to haunt me. But, she was a little girl, and Tip seemed to know more about that whole situation that he had let on. Perhaps not all shadows were confined to their contributions.

"Like the corn maze— which I will be challenging you to a race in when all this dark business is finished by the way." Peter grinned at me.

"Everything alright out here?" Tip exited the hull and joined us with green pallor and shaky legs. The guy was loyal, I'd give him that.

"Tip top," Hook answered, placing heavy emphasis on the p's to make them pop on his lips.

"Why…" Tip hiccuped. "Why is Peter bleeding?"

"I'm fine, Mate. However, you look like you need to get back to solid ground."

"Yeah, we should go to shore." I went to the edge of the ship and rested my arms on the railing to peer towards the beach. "There is a Lost One called Henry who is in Oz. We can start with him. When the new guy wakes up, we can try and figure out the rest."

"Lionel's awake and so is the Witch, so watch out. She probably will burst out here, guns blazing, any time now," Tip grunted as he slumped over the railing beside me.

"You left her down there with Tiger Lily and Wendy?" Peter asked, slight nervousness entering his voice.

"Your mess, Buddy. Not mine," Tip clipped.

"Okay—" I started to redirect the conversation back to planning but stopped as the ship creaked and lurched beneath me. "Oh, Hell. What now?"

"Men! Man your stations and ready the cannons!" Hook's casual too-cool-for-school demeanor shifted in an instant to commanding captain of battle-worthy pirates. A sword was back in his hand so fast I missed it happening.

"Which is it, Captain?" Tiger Lily's voice boomed as she too appeared on the deck in a flurry.

"Is something attacking the ship?" Alice was right behind her, Lionel next, and Wendy brought up the rear.

"Tentis, I'd wager," Hook answered ominously.

"I don't like the sound of that…" I groaned, turning my back to the railing and as another hit buffeted the ship.

"I said to *man the damn cannons*!" Hooked bellowed again, heading towards the hull.

Another hit shook the ship, making it shudder and creak alarmingly. I reached for the railing to steady myself, but my hands grasped blindly in the air.

Another hit. Another rock. And as I lurched backward, I had the same sickening sensation as when my house lifted into the tornado. My eyes stretched so wide in fear I thought they might pop out of their sockets, and the most ear splitting scream of terror tore through my throat as I tipped overboard and plummeted towards the ocean.

The ocean with some unidentified Tentis-creature in it. The ocean where I couldn't swim well. The ocean that, plain and simple, was water to be submerged in.

"Dorothy! Not again…" Tip shouted, and to my surprise, I saw him climb onto the railing and dive in after me, just before my back slammed into the water and I sank like a stone.

Thirteen

Alice

Something terrifying was lurking beneath the water's surface, and I could feel evil radiating from it.

"What is a Tentis?" I stopped a bustling pirate and demanded an answer.

"Tentis is the kraken that lives in the whirlpool off the coast of the Hollow Woods," He answered before lumbering off, as fast as his pegged leg would take him, to help the rest of the swarming crew.

"Are we near the Hollow Woods?" I turned to Wendy, who was busy restrapping her weapons to her person.

"We aren't at the whirlpool, but I think we must be close to the Prison of Solitude."

"Who came up with these names?" I sniffed, thinking that *The Prison of Solitude* sounded like a dreadful place.

"Tip made the Hollow Woods," She answered, coiling her chained scythe in her hand, ready to snap it at any foe who approached her.

"So is this horrible thing his?"

"No," Wendy's eyes shone with mixed emotions. "My brother, John, contributed to Tentis' Whirlpool."

"I thought he died? Can someone still have a Shadow Beast if they are dead? How does that factor into this blasted game of hide and seek?" I rambled aloud in frustration.

Wendy paled, every muscle in her body tensing each time I

mentioned the possibility of death, and I swallowed. I was trying to come up with a way to briskly backtrack my insensitive statement— as based in reality as it likely was— when a scream from Dorothy split the air.

"Dorothy! Not again…" Tip gasped before clambering onto the railing to dive in after her. If they died in the water, I would once again be faced with the question of how shadows fared for the dead. Then there was still the matter of Dorothy's shoes, but at that point, that was a secondary concern.

"Tip, what are you doing?" Peter raced to the side of the boat, looking desperately for his friend. "Gah!"

Flipping around, he approached the nearest mast and began hauling himself up by the rigging until he crawled successfully into the crowsnest.

"Peter, what in the world are you doing?" I demanded, my eyes flitting from him to where the other two had gone overboard.

He ignored me and cupped his hands around his mouth. With all the volume he could muster he crowed into the sky towards the shore.

"He's trying to call Tink," Wendy whispered.

"Who is Tink?"

"She's Peter's fairy."

"Peter has a fairy? Like, what? A pet?" I crinkled my nose. I was becoming more and more anxious about where Tip and Dorothy had vanished in the water with each passing second.

"No, she is his friend. And usually the one who'd give him pixie dust."

"Tink! Come on, I need you!" Peter shouted at the top of his lungs.

"Peter, look!" Wendy gasped and pointed with delight in the distance. I squinted but could very faintly see a tiny ball of glowing white and gold light zooming straight for us. "She's coming!"

"She will give him more dust?" I asked quickly, taking one step towards the railing. "So he will be able to fly again, right?"

"Hopefully. She um, isn't always cooperative or in the best of moods. And she might be cross with Peter like Tiger Lily is."

"Good enough," I chirped before rushing to the side of the ship and heaving myself onto the railing. I might be able to telekinetically left one of them out of the water, or use my magic to knock back the creature's tentacles. I just knew I needed to make sure they were going to survive. "Peter, I'm going in after them!" I called up to Peter, who whipped his head down.

"What? Are you mad? Don't you dare jump, Love. I swear—Alice!"

"Too late," I called apologetically, as I bunched my muscles and dove towards the sea below. Fear coursed through as I saw thick dark tendrils coiling below the surface, and knew they must belong to the kraken-like creature.

Half of me was concerned about Dorothy dying and losing the shoes. We still needed them to get back home. But, underneath my selfish inclination, there was something else. I didn't know Dorothy very well, and I knew—and liked— Tip even less. However, I knew I didn't want either of them to die. Rocky as it was, they were now my friends, and friends didn't let other friends drown or get eaten by sea monsters.

My body sliced through the water, and it was cold enough to paralyze my body for several heartbeats. Cacophonous bubbles raced past my face, and I opened my eyes against the salt water to see rippling images of fire flashing, disturbances of the surface from severed pieces of the ship falling into the water, and a mass of coiling darkness biting and lunging around the ship like a rabid animal. It was breaking the Jolly Roger apart.

My ears echoed the thundering chaos above me, and for a moment I recalled falling into Nonsense Falls, when everything went truly awry. I couldn't let anything bad happen if I could do something about it. I was still weaker than I cared to admit from the compass damage earlier, along with my various injuries— and getting knocked out both by potion, and by force, twice on top of that— and a part of me feared using any form of powerful magic for risk of setting off the cracking in my arm again.

I thought briefly of the strange ethereal fire I conjured in the Shadow World, and how I had wanted to ask Tip some questions about the function of the moral compass. While in that world, the ticking had stopped, and the weight of Wickedness had lifted. I had felt *Good,* and I wondered, if somehow, my compass had found its way to the northern polarity and randomly accessed some store of Good magic within me. I didn't know if such a thing was possible, but I felt like maybe Tip would have the answer— so long as he didn't die.

I swam to the surface, trying to look around for any signs of the other two, but all I could make out were long scaly tentacles slithering in front of me. I needed to do something to get it to stop tearing the ship apart. I was powerful, I should be able to do something. But again, doubt clawed at my stomach as I thought of using my magic. Something that powerful would likely require me to rely on the compass, and the Wicked magic seemed unstable at the moment. But, what if I was too far gone and couldn't manage Good things anymore, only Wicked?

I broke the surface and gulped in as much air as I could manage, before finding a bit of debris to cling to as the sea rolled in escalating agitation. Scanning my surroundings, I saw Peter floating in the air next to where Hook was still standing on his sinking ship. The distant ball of light was now glimmering and flitting around him. Since he was floating, I guessed he was successful at getting more dust from her. Wendy was nearby, still on the broken deck as well, a chained scythe in one hand and a sword in the other. Her braided red hair waved in the absent force of the beast's advances, and she had a determined look on her face. A different side entirely now that she had a weapon in her hands, appearing again, just like it had in the Shadow World. A far cry from the scared little thing jumping behind Peter for protection from me in the dungeons of Oz.

"Hey, Witch!" Tips gurgling voice shouted over the din of intermittent battle in front of me. I turned to see him swimming confidently towards me and my piece of broken planking.

I breathed a sigh of relief to see him alive and well, but frowned when I saw he was alone.

"Have you seen Dorothy?" He asked, concern creasing his face, as he reached me and grabbed onto the opposite side of the board. "I lost track of her when one of those damn tentacles got in my way."

"You mean she was close to that thing? That doesn't sound promising at all," I gasped, dread settling like a stone in my stomach. I thought of the story she had shared with Peter and me back in the Emerald Castle about how her parents had died. If falling in the water had been enough to remind me of Nonsense Falls, I could only imagine her dreadful memories being stirred. I didn't know a lot about America, but I knew Kansas was landlocked in the middle of the country, and something told me Dorothy wasn't a frequent swimmer.

I bit the inside of my cheek in frustration, trying to figure out how best to find her. She wasn't going to die by drowning. Not after what happened to her in her past. It was too cruel, too unfair, even for a world like this. The intensity of my resolve was startling, but felt warm, and I reminded myself again that this was because I really did see her as a friend now.

"What is it?" Tip asked, my own growing concern mirrored on his face.

"Dorothy!" I called out, breaking away from the board to swim around the floating debris. "Dorothy, where are you?"

"You should paddle with the board. What do you expect to do if you find her?"

"You don't understand! She is probably terribly frightened right now."

"I know that!" He snapped. "I was with her in a lake earlier and she had a total meltdown about her parents underwater and nearly drowned herself while in some delusion that she was looking for her folks."

"Go help Peter and Wendy over there and I'll look for Dorothy," I bit, begrudgingly sprawling my torso across another broken bit of ship to paddle with.

"We all are in a bind, Witch, so we need to think rationally for everyone's sake, and not just about the future of those stupid shoes," Tip warned with an edge to his voice. Another accusation. Perhaps Tip wasn't quite on a friend level with me. He was more firmly established as a reluctant and irritating ally.

"That's not what I'm worried about. I am, however, concerned about Peter fighting that creature so, maybe it would be best if one of us did go help." I jerked my head towards the ship, where Peter was clearly trying his best to use his rusty magical abilities to drive the beast away.

"You have magic, so you go help them. Your spontaneous combustions might come in handy. Use some of the flashy stuff to drive the darkness back. I'll keep looking for Dorothy," Tip conceded with a curt nod, determination glittering in his eyes. "I *will* find her."

Something told me, he refused to let her die by drowning just as much as I did, so I nodded back and turned to swim back towards the ship. I felt anxiety twirl wildly in my stomach again at the idea of using magic strong enough to fight a monster without leaning into the pull of the compass for fuel

I could see clearly now that the fire was from the failing cannons and gunpowder igniting. Where the ship was burning, it was splintering under the weight of the egregiously large dark tentacles coiling around it. I'd used fire on the smaller shadows. I didn't need to kill this massive beast, I just needed to help drive it back. At the very least, maybe I could teleport others to safety. I needed to remember I could jump short distances now.

"Got her!" Tip called over to me, and I paused my paddling to turn and squint to see him approaching a waterlogged Dorothy over to the far left. She was wildeyed and chattering, but thankfully, alive. "It's gonna be alright, Dorothy. You're safe now." I barely heard Tip's gentle, comforting words at the sound of a thunderclap over head.

Storm clouds were rolling in and when I turned back to face Peter again, I could see static charge and tiny tendrils of lightning sparking around him, while a strong wind cut through the air. Something told me this power was brewing from a place of desperation and frustration. I realized every time I had seen a storm in this world, it had been a moment of stress for Peter, and, typically, a moment of potential peril for me. I needed to help him.

"Alice, look out!" Lost in my own inner thoughts, I was ripped back to the moment at Wendy's voice shouting a warning at me. Peter was now glowing in the air, facing the beast, casting his own shadow forward with glowing eyes to tether the creature— no doubt a fancy new magical trick of his. But, that wasn't what Wendy had been alerting me to.

I snapped my attention directly forward to see the main mast, fully aflame, crashing towards where I was floating.

"Oh, bloody hell," I swore, before taking a breath and diving as deep as I could go beneath the water. I tried to angle myself away, but the pull of current from the mast sinking through the water dragged me even further down with it.

I spiraled into the depths of the Neverland Sea, where it was growing darker and darker, the further away from the surface I sunk. I reached a frantic hand, willing myself upward, and wishing now more than ever that I had Mombi's blasted water magic.

My vision was going bleary and I blinked sluggishly through the water, no longer able to hold my breath. I saw a figure swimming rapidly towards me. No doubt one of those dreadful mermaids came to drown me for certain this time. I was almost certain I was going to die. Fire and lightning would do me no good under water, and the suction was too strong for me to swim against. This was it. After everything, this was it.

A flurry of my most important memories flashed through my mind in an instant, and my heart thundered with clarity. It wasn't home or my family I was thinking of. Only one thing came to mind at that moment.

I'm sorry, Peter. I thought as my consciousness ebbed. *I wasn't careful enough. My wandering mind really was the death of me. Please, don't let this destroy you. I love you.*

Fourteen

Peter

"Alice! Where did she go?" I called out, scrambling as quickly as I could from the crowsnest.

"Peter, look!" Wendy alerted me, pointing towards the shore gleefully. "She's coming!"

Tinkerbell. You never fail me. I breathed a sigh of relief.

"Oh!" Wendy squawked as the tiny ball of shimmering light whizzed past me to dive bomb her.

"Bloody hell," I swore as Wendy threw both arms over her head and was starting to curl herself into a protected ball. The light swooped and grabbed hold of her russet braid, yanking her backward.

"Peter!" She yelped, flailing blindly at the back of her head.

"Ah ha!" I lunged at the end of Wendy's braid, cupping my hands around the light, finally catching it. "Ow! She bit me!"

"She certainly has some pent up anger," Wendy sniffed woefully, rubbing at the back of her head.

"Tink, you little pest, now isn't the time!" I declared, pinching at the captive light in my hand and dangling it in front of my face. It was a small woman, dressed in leaf-made clothing, with beautiful shimmering wings that I was using to suspend her. She scowled until her face was flushing a cherry red, and she punched and kicked the air violently. I smiled at the spirited little creature. "I've missed you, Tink. I've gone and run out of dust and gotten myself in a jam again, I'm afraid. Do you think you can give me some more if I let you pull Wendy's hair when we are out of this bind?

"Peter!" Wendy cried in dismay.

The tiny fairy stopped her blind thrashing and blinked at me, the scarlet falling from her cheeks. Her large golden eyes seemed to be contemplating me, and a sly smile curled around her lips before she gave me a definitive nod of approval.

"That's the Tink I know and love." I grinned and released my hold on her wings. True to her word, she flew around me, golden sparkle cascading down and coating my skin. Feeling whole again, I hopped into the air and hovered. "Thanks, Tink."

I buzzed over to the edge of the ship, dodging tentacles as I looked for Alice. Another hit from Tentis tore a large chunk of the hull asunder, and the splintering debris fell into the water below. The shift in the equilibrium of the ship knocked a pirate's torch out of his hand, unfortunately igniting the gunpowder kegs being used to fire the cannon he was manning. The ship erupted in flames.

"Oy! Care to lend the rest of us a hand?" Hook shouted at me, and my eyes briefly caught sight of Alice's blonde hair breaking the surface, along with Tip's bobbing head paddling over to her. They were safe for now.

I flitted back to the pirate, looking over my shoulder at where my friends were in the water with the bulk of the monster. Perhaps I ought to go down there and try driving him away at his center of mass, rather than ticking him off by jabbing his arms.

"You've more important things to worry about," Hook scoffed, impaling a tentacle with the end of his sword. It barely made a scratch. John had done good work in imagining Tentis. He was made of sturdy stock. "She chose to jump overboard. If she drowns, she drowns."

I whipped my head around and glared at the captain, muttering darkly, "Say her life doesn't matter again, I dare you." I didn't even need my Shadow Beast to make good on that threat.

"Her life *doesn't* matter if it means everyone else dies," Hook growled, matching me tone for tone in menace.

Lightning crackled along my body, and angry storm clouds rolled into the sky. I could smite the brute if I wanted to. I knew I had the power, but I forcefully pushed away the righteous anger I was feeling, lest I somehow summon another demon into the fight, and turned my attention towards the shadowy tentacles. As long as the others were safe, I could focus on the task at hand.

"Alright, Shadow. Let's see if we can wrangle the big one." I cracked my knuckles and rolled my shoulders back, not particularly looking forward to what massive amount of negativity I was about to absorb. He mimed something to me that I didn't quite follow, then sagged and gave up on the attempted communication. His eyes glowed and we assumed our mirrored stance as I began to think my happy thoughts and glow outwardly.

"Alice, look out!" Wendy's desperate cry of warning, following a thunderous snap, broke my focus, and I dropped the shadow tethers to whirl around and see what had caused Wendy to call out.

A large flaming mast was plummeting towards the water— right for where Alice was swimming back to the ship. I saw her suck in a breath and try to swim away, but as the heavy object sank into the ocean, it created a sucking current, dragging Alice down with it.

"No!"

"She's as good as gone," Hook bellowed behind me. "You need to take care of this. If her light is out, it's out, and you need to accept it."

"Her light is *my* light," I spat at the pirate. "I can't let it go out."

Ignoring the pirate and Wendy's protests, I zoomed towards the water, crashing into it like a missile. Alice was below me, being swallowed up by the dark depths of the sea. I reached my hand towards her, hoping somehow she could find the fight in her to meet me halfway, but her body was limp, and I knew she was unconscious.

Water magic. I think I have that. It isn't strong but I might be able to... I willed the current of the water to switch, and had to stop myself from physically gasping in relief and drowning myself in the process, when the water obeyed my command.

The current shifted and lifted Alice's body to me. Wrapping my arms tightly around her, I kicked as hard as I could back towards the surface. Once, my head broke, I lifted directly into the air, carrying Alice's waterlogged body with me.

I stared at the shadowy tentacles coiling into a death grip around the remainder of the ship, and thought about the fact that Tentis had been John's creation, and not mine. Whether John was dead or alive, I didn't know if I could destroy his beast entirely whether I wanted to or not. "Shadow, is that shadow one I can absorb?" I asked my shadow quietly, his form rippling on the surface of the water.

He shook his head slowly, and I understood that he had merely been trying to help me use the tethers to restrain it. This wasn't a fight we were going to win.

"Tip, Wendy, Tink! Gather who you can and head for the shore," I commanded as I hovered a moment over the sinking ship, my eyes locking on the blazing gaze of Hook. "The Jolly Roger is done for."

-*-

"Alice, come on now." I pleaded, hovering over her, tapping gently at her face. I nearly jumped out of my skin when she groaned and her eyelids twitched. "She's coming to!"

"For goodness sakes, both of you need to give her a little space. Crowding her isn't going to do anything," Wendy chided both me and Tip, who had assisted in both Alice's revival and Dorothy's rescue. Our witches were in sorry shape.

"What are you doing?" Alice croaked, her eyes fluttering open to a squint.

"Ah, thank goodness, Love. You gave us all quite a scare!" I cheered, and reached out a hand to give hers a tight squeeze. I wanted nothing more than to kiss her in relief at that moment, but the surrounding onlookers held me at bay. Plus, she seemed a bit cranky post-near-drowning.

"What are *you* looking at?" She asked sourly, pointing to Tip, who was now stepping away from us. Wendy was still hovering nearby with Tiger Lily too.

"Tip was the only one who knew how to help with reviving you. He did chest compressions and some sort of arm lifting thing… I'm not really sure, but it seemed to help," I answered briskly on Tip's behalf.

Alice sat up in a seated position and grabbed onto her head. "I'm surprised he saved the terrible Wicked Witch of the West," she commented wryly.

Tip merely shrugged in response and looked away in his noncommittal, monotonous manner when he didn't care to deal with something.

"Well, thank you. I guess," She nodded to Tip, and tried to force a smile.

"Don't worry about it," He shrugged again. "I'm going to check on how Dorothy is feeling. Lionel too. We really need to make ourselves a proper camp. Maybe we should think about going to the old hideout."

I hadn't been there in a long while now. With everyone gone, it stopped feeling like home. A small part of me almost felt guilty at the idea of returning there without the full group reunited once more.

"What happened and where are we?" Alice looked around, but didn't get to her feet just yet. Instead, she splayed her fingers across either side of her temple, and I knew after being knocked unconscious twice in such a short amount of time— three times, if we included the time with The Wizard the other day— her head had to be killing her. She'd complained of headaches before, so I knew she was more prone to them in the first place.

"Peter was trying to control the beast with his shadow puppet magic, but when he saw the mast fall towards you he left his post and interrupted the whole thing," Wendy jumped in to explain, her doe eyes darting around the small assembly of people. "He got you and told us all to head for shore. That's where we are now."

"And the Jolly Roger?" Alice inquired, turning to peer at the ocean, like she expected some miraculous recovery for the sinking she's last seen.

"Dead as a doornail," Hook groused, and we all turned to acknowledge his presence. "The lad here decided that your life was more important than anyone on the ship, or getting rid of the beast."

"I already told you," I sniffed impatiently. "That wasn't a shadow I could absorb. The best I could hope for was holding it at bay to escape—which is what we did."

"These shadow rules of yours seem awfully fast and loose and entirely too convenient." His eyes gleamed.

"What are you trying to say, Codfish?" I challenged, dropping Alice's hand and standing to square up with the Captain. I felt a little flicker of pride when I realized I had grown a lot since the last time I had confronted him head on. We were about the same size now, though his build was a bit brawnier than mine. In fact, I was quite certain I was even a little taller than him. Another reminder that I was no longer the little boy I'd once been.

"I'm sorry about your ship. I'll replace it," Alice grunted, her fingers now dragging down her face as she leaned forward, then huffed with effort and pushed to her feet, swaying a little.

"How are you going to replace a whole ship?" Hook snorted, causing Alice to glare at him in such a way that conveyed her thinking he must be the dumbest person she'd ever met as clearly as if she had said the words aloud. .

"*Magic.*" She waved her hands and wiggled her fingers emphatically.

"Can you make a ship, Love?" I whispered to her. "That sounds a little out of your wheelhouse considering you once told me you had never been on a ship before."

She waved me away. "I'll figure it out." She looked at the group of people clustering around her, clutching her compass with one hand like she always did when she was feeling insecure. After willingly isolating herself from most Wonderlandians and only really interacting with me for the past year, I had to wager that she must be feeling overwhelmed.

In the moment of calm, I would be lying if I didn't wish for a moment alone with her to discuss my Shadow problem. I'd dreaded broaching the topic on account of having to clarify those pesky romantic notions, but now that we were together, I realized that with something this heavy weighing on me, I wanted nothing more than to share it with her—and her specifically.

"Would you lot mind giving us a moment?" I piped up, clearing my throat of the lump of awkwardness that made my voice crack a little, something it hadn't done in a few years. I must be more nervous than I thought. *This is part of it, you coward.* I consoled myself. *You need to prove that bastard evil-you wrong about at least one thing.* "If you want to go wait with Lionel, Tip, and Dorothy, we will be along shortly and roll up our sleeves to really get serious about this hide and seek business."

The group of onlookers slowly meandered away, with Wendy giving me a long pensive look before a small, sad smile danced on her lips and she shuffled towards the others.

"*You're* getting serious about something?" Alice joked and poked me in the shoulder. "I can hardly believe it."

She and I were the only ones left and I suddenly felt a little self-conscious. We hadn't been fully alone more than a handful of minutes since back in Wonderland, when we had argued before this whole caper even really started with The Wizard. We'd had that moment in the dungeons, but others were still right there—and that had been awkward enough. Everything had been happening too fast since I'd chased after her in Oz.

So much had happened and been said since then. So much had *changed.* We were just now, in the middle of a whole mess of chaos and pain, getting some breathing room to address things properly. But, I knew I needed to silence the doubt gnawing at the back of mind in regards to Alice's intentions towards me. It would be one step closer to quelling that inner demon of mine. Even if she didn't care, at least I'd know and could hopefully move forward, though a small part of me wasn't sure if I would ever recover from such a blow.

I was torn between wanting to melt into her arms for reassurance, comfort, and affection, and wanting to burrow directly into the ground with embarrassment for everything that had openly transpired between us.

I was starting to lean more towards the latter, but Alice broke the ice by slipping her hand into mine, her thumb stroking my fingers reassuringly.

"Are you going tell me what has you so freaked out?" She asked, looking straight at me, while I averted my eyes.

"What?" I feigned ignorance, immediately regretting my desire to confide in her. Vulnerability was positively terrifying.

But, I took a deep breath and told her everything I had experienced since being waved to Oz by The Wizard. I kept it short and to the point, no over-embellishments, and she listened intently, nodding every few statements as she continued to lightly rub her thumb across the top of my hand.

"Goodness, Peter," She breathed when I found a stopping place in my saga. "First of all, thank you for sharing all that with me instead of hiding it, like your many past girlfriends."

"Taking shots at me, are you, Love?" I grinned.

"Only ones you probably deserve," She laughed quietly and shifted slowly to give me a hesitant hug. Her body seemed slightly rigid like she too was feeling a bit uncomfortable and uncertain. "Secondly, I'm so sorry you went through all of that, and on your own too. You really are the bravest person I've ever known."

"Thanks, Love." I felt a rush of affection flood me as I returned the embrace and squeezed tight.

After a moment, Alice pulled away just enough to look me in the eyes, her gaze full of adamance and adoration. "I met that Shadow-Peter. And, I hope you know as well as I do, that he and his entire purpose and existence is a complete and utter *lie*. You are not the desolation you were born into, Peter. You are the light of hope that keeps others from despair in the depths of their own darkness. It's not to say you never feel cross or sad, or upset, just that you never stay in the darkness. It falls away around you. You don't harm, you protect. You don't destory, you save. Not just me. You've saved all of us here at some point or other."

Her voice caught in her throat and her bright blue eyes well with tears. I felt a pricking sensation at the back of my own eyes and the bothersome tingle in my nose that told me I was close to crying myself.

Alice cleared her throat and steadied her voice. "And, I hope you know that that is the *truth.* It would just kill me if you couldn't see what a miracle you are."

I took a sharp intake of breath. The one piece I'd left out of my recount had been about Alice and my relationship — friendship, romantic, or otherwise— and the doubt I felt that she could ever truly love me as I'd come to realize I did her.

But, the way she was gazing at me now, with so much emotion in her eyes, so much affection in her touch, how could I doubt that she cared about me? On whatever level that was, her words gave me the courage to find out.

"There's one more thing…" I began, my heart hammering so hard in my chest, I was certain she could hear it, or feel it through my arms.

"Yes?" She tilted her head imploringly and began to paw self-consciously at her hair. Foggy images of a faint memory flooded my mind— a white shadow leading me to the sign post the day Alice arrived.

"You did that when we met, you know," I laughed and poked her in the arm. "Got all quiet and shy, and started messing with your hair. Some things never change, do they? That's sort of comforting." I was shamelessly stalling now, and was liable to pass out at any moment.

"Well," Alice started with a sly smile. "*Some* things have changed, haven't they?"

"You've got me there, Love. Some things have changed a lot. Is that," I paused and ran my hand through my hair awkwardly— apparently a trait we shared when uncomfortable. I'd accidentally jumped right into the thick of it. Now was my last chance to back paddle with some dignity. "If you want to take anything back I und—"

"No! No, I mean," She stammered, raising her hands and waving them in front of her rapidly. "Unless you…?"

"I wasn't going to, er. That is, I think I like it better now that we are, um, being more… Uh," I faltered, a faint heat creeping into my cheeks as I stumbled over the most basic words. "I *know* I like it better, actually. But I don't want you to feel obligated to—"

"I don't! I mean, I do too."

"Do what?"

"Like it better," She scrunched up her nose and laughed, dragging her hand down her face. "We are truly terrible at this, aren't we?"

I puffed a sigh and threw a look over my shoulder to where Tip, Wendy, and Lionel were clearly watching Alice and I. My entire body burned with embarrassment and I released Alice's hand and started walking away towards a more secluded wooded area out of view of prying eyes, then turned and jerked my head for Alice to follow. "Uncharted territory is tricky to traverse. Especially with an audience."

Alice trailed along behind me and rested her hands on her hips. "Well, what was the other thing you're avoiding telling me about?"

"You always see right through me, Love."

"And you always dance your way around it," She countered with a shake of her head. "Come on now, spit it out. There are important things that need our attention, so best not take all day to ourselves."

"Patient as ever. Okay," I clenched every muscle in my body. *This is it. Living in the protection of the unknown no more. You're directly asking how she feels and will likely have to say how you feel so buck up and do it. Don't be a cowardly codfish!* "The demon thing said something else that kind of got under my skin and I thought maybe it was time I asked you to clear it up for me."

Alice's eyes widened anxiously and her cheeks flushed red. "Um," she stammered, all semblance of confidence gone. "A-alright. I'll try my best. What, um, did he say?"

Spit it out. Spit it out. Spit it out!

I couldn't bring myself to look her in the eyes, so I kept my eyes glued to my feet, and finally got out the words, my voice much more quiet and meek than I cared for. "That you could never trust me again. That I would only ever be a pet to you because you could never love a pitiful weakling like me. And, er, I didn't much fancy the idea of that. So, all those vague conversations and kisses aside, I thought best get the answer once and for all. Be direct for the first time in my bloody life."

Alice was silent. I was certain I was trembling, about to physically burst into a million pieces. I'd put her on the spot. Of course she wouldn't answer. I'd probably just made her mad and was liable to get a fireball to the face any moment now. Panic was setting in. I didn't want the answer. Not if it was negative. I was better off not knowing.

"Er, sorry. I shouldn't have… it was silly. Let's go ahead and get back to the others. You were right about having important things to deal with. Let's just forget about this whole little exchange and never speak of it again? Deal? Deal. Let's go." I couldn't stop the nervous words from tumbling out of my mouth and I was sweating again.

Why? I wanted to wail at the sky. When did I become so fumbly and awkward? I wished to be daring and strapping, and there I was, barely able to string two sensible words together. I could have sworn I'd once been much more charming and smooth.

I made to zip away but Alice caught my arm.

"It's not true."

"It's not true?" I echoed, dazed and confused. I didn't even have the wherewithal to know which part of my rambling she was responding to.

"What your Shadow Beast told you," She clarified quietly. I dared look up at her to see her cheeks burning scarlet. Was that anger? If it was anger I was really in for it. Maybe she would turn me into a toad again, and toss me in the sea with Tentis.

"Okay…" I paused to try and center myself. "Can you elaborate on which part?"

Alice looked up at me with such ferocity I tried to take a step back, but couldn't, as she was still holding onto my arm, her grip getting tighter.

"You're not a pet," She began. *Just that part?*

"I appreciate that. Thanks for clearing it up—"

“I trust you implicitly,” She added, her breath coming out in puffs. She was getting worked up to something. I felt fear ping through me as I realized she was going one point at a time and was about to get to the crucial clarification. The one that would make or break everything.

She was so tense, I was certain I would have bruises when she removed her fingers.

“And?” I promoted quietly, my lips moving of their own accord.

She closed her eyes and took a deep breath.

“I’ve been hopelessly in love with you for years.”

I froze. Did she just say that she loved me? Hopelessly even? I must have misheard her, but I couldn’t repeat it in case I’d suffered some blip in brain function and imagined the whole thing— a cruel but entirely plausible thing to occur on Neverland soil.

“Do you really mean that?” I managed to croak out, placing a shamelessly trembling hand on top of hers.

She swallowed hard, but lifted her chin, full confidence and conviction returned. “I do. I am. I love you, Peter. With every possible fiber of my being, of that, I am completely certain.”

I had asked, and asked again, and now, like a complete idiot, I hadn’t the faintest idea of how to respond.

“I don’t want you to feel like you have to say—” I blurted, but Alice interrupted, smiling as she pulled me close, tilting my chin down.

“That I *have to* love you? No. I *get* to love you. And it will forever be my deepest honor and greatest pleasure. It’s the best thing I’ll ever do.”

I felt ready to burst with pure, unbridled elation I hadn’t known was possible to feel. Had she not been holding me, I likely would have started flying laps around all of Neverland.

“Thank you for clearing that up for me,” I beamed. “Alice Liddel, Queen of Wonderland and Neverland.”

“I’m not the Queen of Neverland,” She scoffed playfully, with an inquisitive tilt of her head.

“I’d like you to be, and I realized you should have been all along,” I whispered, leaning down. “Because I love you, too.With every possible fiber of my being, of that, I am completely certain. You are my everything."

"That shadow can go to hell," Alice laughed before closing the distance between our lips.

"Do you think everything is alright?" I asked, leaning as far as I could without falling over, to try and peer at where Peter and Alice had disappeared.

"I'm sure they are just having a little privacy to be nauseatingly affectionate with each other and make out," Dorothy grumbled from where she was still lying on the ground with a hand over her face to block out the world.

"Glad to see you're back to yourself," Tip quipped, but his lips twitched with a smile. "You'd probably be singing a different tune if it were you. But hey, you're still young. Probably haven't even had your first kiss yet, right?"

"Oh yeah, you're *so* wise and experienced since you're really like a hundred and fifty, right?" Dorothy sniffed, pushing herself up to a seated position, wild curls spindling around her face.

"I am not!" Tip huffed then paused contemplatively. "Wait, what year is it back in that world again?"

"1967."

"Well… I'm not a hundred and fifty. I'm nineteen. I think," Tip huffed indignantly, and started flipping a knife in his hand.

"What is *making out?*" Lionel asked from where he was watching the other two's exchange with great captivation.

Dorothy snorted and Tip tilted his head but didn't answer. When no one else piped up, she sighed. "Kissing. A lot."

"Oh!" The small startled trill of dread escaped me and I shot to my feet. Something heavy and boiling was snaking through my stomach at the thought of those two sharing stolen kisses in the woods… the woods where I had once stolen a kiss from Peter and called it a thimble. I had been so forward and brazen back then. I wanted something and went after it.

I slumped back onto the log I'd been perched on. Jealousy was a Wicked emotion and I did my best to will it away.

"I think we should go ahead and figure out the next step ourselves and fill the other two in when they deign to return to us," Dorothy changed the subject and started playing with the end of one of her curls.

"They will just blow up any plan we make with their impulsiveness, but sure," Tip conceded with a shrug. "Wendy? Are you with us?"

I'd spaced out again, barely listening to their conversation while Ijumped from one memory to the next of my time with Peter and the Lost Ones. Then, I suddenly felt a twinge of embarrassment run through me as I recalled every possible embarrassing thing I had ever done in front of them.

Any of those reasons could be why it was Alice with Peter in the woods now instead of me. If only I had been better somehow, maybe he would have waited for me. I wondered what I could have done differently, then felt frustrated that I couldn't just let it go and instead kept looping over the endless possibilities over and over again.

"Wendy?" Tip tried again. "You're making faces. Are you alright?"

"Oh, sorry. Just got lost in thought." I leaned forward, forcing myself to watch their moving lips to make myself focus. "Go on."

"Shouldn't the goal be to go find Henry?" Dorothy began. "Since we know roughly where he is without all the mumbo jumbo guess work."

"Right, just waltz right into the middle of enemy territory?" Tip scoffed, rolling his eyes. "I'm glad to know he's alright and all, but I'm more interested to know why he hasn't left Oz if he's been free all this time."

"With a fancy time watch," Dorothy nodded along.

"With a fancy time watch," Tip echoed emphatically. "Exactly. If he were in some severe state of peril, I imagine he'd have left by now."

"Do you know where any others are?" I addressed Lionel, who was sitting across from me, his hands folded in contemplation beneath his chin as he rested his elbows on his knees.

"Wonderland, for sure," He replied, his crystal blue eyes glinting. "There are others in Oz, though one has moved to Wonderland recently. But, it sounds to me like both are hostile territory at this point. Wherever we go, we are looking for a fight."

"Are you certain you weren't picking up on Wendy and I going from Oz to Wonderland the other day?" Tip asked, waving a thumb between me and him.

Lionel shook his head. "No, there was another that shifted too. And one that was already there as well."

"Hold on," Dorothy started to count out the list on her fingers. "So, there is Henry. Then, two more are currently in Wonderland. I think that means we will get more bang for our buck to search Wonderland first since Henry will be hard to get to. Any idea who it is we are looking for?"

"They are linked to contributions to Neverland, so I'd wager it's the core group that stayed here the longest. That's Pat, James, Sam, Henry and Lionel. Plus me, Wendy, and her brothers— er," Tip stumbled over his words when he mentioned John and Michael, and my heart instantly felt as heavy as a ton of lead. "Plus me and Wendy."

I glanced out at the ocean in the direction of John's whirlpool. "Don't you suppose there's a chance they are alive if John has a shadow?"

Tip shared a hesitant look with Dorothy and Lionel. "I suppose there could be a chance, right?"

"I hate to tell you this, Mother-Wendy," Lionel shook his head sadly. "But I could only feel the shadow tethers to four others, and you two. If they are alive somewhere, they'd be pretty far away to not register a connection to their beast."

I bit my lip to keep it from trembling. A small heat coiled through my heart that they could so easily discard the possibility that my brothers were alive and in need of rescue.

Even if they don't want to hold out hope for you, I will. I won't ever stop searching for you. I sent the thought into the universe, hoping somehow, it would find its way to my lost brothers wherever they may be. Their big sister wasn't going to leave them behind.

"I heard some voices like Lionel calling out to me when Dorothy and I were by a white castle." I bit down my frustration and offered what pertinent information I could. "They were asking to be set free."

"Is this white castle hard to get to from Neverland?" Lionel asked, looking expectantly at each of us in turn.

"I'm afraid I'm really not certain," I explained apologetically. "Dorothy and I were teleported there from somewhere else entirely."

"I haven't a clue. But that's something the Witch will know when she decides to return." Tip rolled his eyes. "Dorothy got lost in the water too, and you don't see her mooning about."

"Yeah, I don't do that. I avoid boys back home." Dorothy nodded emphatically.

"Is that so?" Tip raised his eyebrows and crinkled his nose playfully. "Afraid we have cooties?"

"No!" Dorothy huffed. "You are all just big dumb idiots, in my experience, with egos the size of Jupiter. Sure, they might play football or something, but it's hardly something to preen about. All the brainless girls go wild for it though. Stupid."

"What is football?" Tip tilted his head.

"Oh, I don't know. A tackling game or something."

"Hey, I think we've played that too." Lionel chirped.

"My, how hard you must be to impress as the only girl around with a brain, and you condemn all boys on account of a game they may or may not play... That you don't entirely understand in the first place, right?" Tip grinned and squinted his eyes in such a way the bespoke knowing he was intentionally riling Dorothy up.

She looked taken aback, then scowled. "I also condemn overly rude boys."

I swatted at Tip's arm rapidly to pull his attention from his flirtatious banter and gestured to where Peter and Alice were headed in our direction… hand in hand.

Stop being so foolish and petulant, Wendy. This is absolutely ridiculous and you are positively wicked for not simply being happy for them. I scolded myself with all the self-depreciating anger I could muster, before finding a smile and rising to greet the pair.

"Oh, good! We were needing some answers from Alice." I clasped my hands together and smiled wider when I saw faint blushes lingering on both their cheeks. Clearly something excitable had happened.

You have no claim on Peter, you idiot girl. I drilled into my brain. *Though if you hadn't have gotten captured, Alice wouldn't have been able to sweep in and turn his head in the first place.*

"About time too!" Tip glared at Peter and Alice both, but squinted even harder at Peter, like he was trying to gauge something.

"Sorry, we had some stuff to get sorted first," Alice lifted her chin defiantly. "We were hardly gone very long. So, what do you have to ask me?"

"Where is thc White Castle located in Wonderland?" Lionel inquired. "How hard is it to reach from here without detection?"

"Oh, goodness. I'd say it would be pretty difficult." She stooped down to draw some markings in the dirt with her finger. "If Neverland's western border is here— I don't know where we are more specifically right now, and you can blame Peter for that one— then the White Castle is roughly over here, and the Red Castle is between the two. Why?"

"Wendy heard voices by the castle so we think we should try there first," Dorothy explained.

"What about Henry? We know where he is," Peter countered. "Also, where did everyone else go? I promised Tink she could pull Wendy's hair in return for helping me."

"If you have been here with the rest of us," Dorothy drawled, "Then you'd know that Henry is in the heart of enemy territory and the least accessible right now."

Tip poked her in the arm. "You suggested the same thing two minutes ago, Miss High and Mighty."

"Hush. I'd like to at least pretend to be in the know about something," She snipped, swatting his hand away.

Alice rolled her eyes. "I take it you want to try Wonderland first then?"

"It seems the lesser of two evils at this point, if you'll forgive the pun." Lionel shrugged.

"I still need to rescue Toto from there too. He's a smart boy and will stay hidden, but don't think I've forgotten him." Dorothy folded her arms.

"What about their beasts?" Alice asked, pointing a dainty finger at me and Tip. "Shouldn't we take care of those first and foremost since we already have you two here? I have no idea if this blight on Neverland has any connection to The Wizard's game, but I say we should cover our bases and fix each direction as we go. I'd hate to imagine these shadows gaining momentum in Wonderland."

"Good point, Love," Peter wagged a finger at her, and my skin tingled at him referring to her by that particular term of endearment—despite being well aware it was a common colloquialism for him. "Tip, you added the Hollow Woods. I say we go sort that bit out."

"What about Wendy?" Alice fixed me with an unreadable stare. "What was your contribution to this marvelous place?"

"Um," I ducked my head, once more intimidated by her brazen demeanor. "The mermaid lagoon."

"Of course, it would be the mermaids," Alice scoffed, making my nerves jump.

"They've tried to drown people for ages. You aren't special there, Love. Sorry," Petter quipped, patting her blonde head patronizingly.

"Yes, they attacked me too, unfortunately. They didn't seem to want to share Peter's attention," I started to laugh but then snapped my mouth closed as I instantly regretted what I had just indirectly admitted. The mermaids were from my mind and were possessive of Peter, which meant I had just told Alice *I* was possessive of Peter. I wanted nothing more than to burrow deep into the ground, and the sudden rush of mortification caused pricking behind my eyes.

Don't you dare cry! I wailed inwardly, and managed to avert my eyes before they could spill tears.

"Well, rest up, Mates." Peter, seemingly oblivious to my blunder grinned broadly and threw his arms around Lionel and Tip's shoulders. "Tomorrow morning, bright and early, we are going to tackle Tip's inner demon in the Hollow Woods. We aren't too far away and, if we make quick work of it, maybe we can move back into the hideout like old times."

Lionel's face brightened at the idea of an adventure with his old friends, while Tip looked less thrilled at the idea. I looked at their unified form and wondered why I hadn't been included in the invitation. I was a Lost One too, after all. Where did I fit in with that trio now?

"I'm sure I could probably just go check it out on my own," Tip sighed.

"Nonsense!" Alice cried. "We barely survived the one in the caves. You'd be lucky to have those two for backup."

"We didn't fare too well with the one in the maze either," Dorothy chimed in. "Which, by the way, I don't think that shadow was mine since it was—"

"Weren't you asking where everyone went? And what are we doing for the rest of the night?" Tip asked Peter loudly, drowning out the end of Dorothy's statement. Dorothy scowled at him for the interruption but didn't pipe up again.

"Yeah, Hook was pretty cross about his ship, and Tiger Lily tried to shoot me earlier," Peter chuckled awkwardly. "I feel like I might need to mend a few bridges there. And who knows what Tink has in store for me now that we are out of danger. I think we should spend tonight catching up and getting ready for a good round of fights tomorrow."

"I think they went further down the shore towards the Valley of Beasts." Tip nodded along to Peter's suggestions.

"That sounds needlessly ominous," Dorothy grunted. "I thought this place was for children."

"Yes, but we weren't *boring* children," Peter huffed. "I'm going to go find them and see what I can do to smooth their feathers. If I don't come back soon, assume Lily put an arrow through me."

"I'll come with you," Tip offered, and Lionel voiced his joining as well. I was about to speak up that I would go with them too, but faltered when the three boys— young men now, really— sauntered away together before I had a chance.

Lionel and Tip were trailing along on foot, laughing and bumping each other as they went while Peter flew in the lead. It was almost like nothing had changed, except everything had. Tip's earlier comment reverberated through my mind. They were all grown up and none of them needed Mother-Wendy anymore. The realization that I no longer fit with the friends I had missed so dearly struck me like a dagger through the heart.

Where do I fit? What value do I have to offer if they don't need me anymore?

"Hey, do you hear that?" Dorthy's alarmed tone cut through my cloud of disconnect, startling me back into the present.

Alice's hands were ablaze in an instant, ready for combat. I could see the tiny arrow in her battered compass twitch and begin to swivel about.

"Come out!" She barked, while Dorothy and I both slipped nervously behind the commanding witch. I stole a glance in the direction of the boys, but it appeared as though they had engaged in some sort of race and were too far away now to hear us without a sizable commotion.

I held my breath and reached for one of my swords, while Dorothy focused hard and materialized flames in her hands as well.

"That's not a very friendly way to speak to someone *lost* in the woods."

"Hey… I know that voice." Dorothy perked up with recognition and Alice relaxed her stance, letting the flames die away.

"Cheshire, how did you get lost in Neverland?" Alice smiled with relief, though her furrowed brows suggested no small amount of confusion.

"Are we lost? I thought I followed my guide rather expertly." The fluffy white and ginger Wonderland cat materialized in front of the line of trees that made up the beginnings of the Never Woods and grinned at us.

"Who is *we*—?" Dorothy started to ask, but was cut short as something small and black shot out from the trees and tackled her at the chest, knocking her backwards from where she had been sitting on a log. "Toto? Toto!"

"That is one of the 'we'" Cheshire purred lazily, flopping down dramatically.

"Only one?" Alice asked, squinting her eyes at the woods.

"No, there is more than one," The cat chuckled and disappeared once more.

"Come on out. Everything is fine," Alice called out directly, forgoing any further attempts at conversing with the riddling feline. There was short pause, before several figures began pouring out from the trees,

Two very round gentlemen bounced into the open, followed by a finely dressed large rabbit, and a flood of small individuals I gathered must be the munchkins from Oz. An absurdly large butterfly with magnificent blue wings fluttered to the edge of the branches and scowled down at the lot of us.

I looked on silently as Alice rushed to greet the twins and hare, while Dorothy's eyes welled with tears at the sight of the munchkins and she set her dog down to begin apologizing profusely for burning down their village. Even a few defecting Card-guards were in the mix, along with a human-sized Lizard carrying a ladder. I once more felt woefully out of place in the hodgepodge group, though I was relieved to see that the innocent Wonderlandians and the displaced munchkins had all managed to find their way to Peter's sanctuary.

Last in the throng of newcomers were two entities I did recognize, and my heart welled with warmth. One was a tall stick figure with a pumpkin for a head, and the other was an animated sawhorse. I was so glad to see that their long journey through the south of the Oz had apparently gone well enough that they had managed to make it here in one piece.

"Jack, and Saw-horse! You made it to Neverland," Dorothy cheered. "Tip will be beside himself to see you. You might even get a smile out of His Grumpiness. He just went down the beach a ways, but we can go find him. How did you know where to find us?"

"Tip had told us plenty about Neverland," Jack, the pumpkin man, explained. "We were trying to find where his old hideout was, but we got lost."

"Luckily for us though, we ran into this group who were coming to find you as well," Saw-horse added softly, still as shy as when we had left him.

"Where is the Hatter?" Dorothy inquired of the Hare, whose ears drooped.

"Captured. The Hatter is the most wisest and bestest and… Captured!" The poor insane creature babbled hysterically.

Dorothy frowned and looked at Alice. "Well, that's not great. We did happen to pass through his house and it looked a total mess— I assumed that was normal, but maybe it was from a scuffle after all. I wonder why they would go out of their way to take him."

"Do you not know of that Hatter's significance to Wonderland?" The lizard, carrying a small ladder, asked, his eyes wide.

"I know nothing about anything, if I'm being honest. But, wait. You all congregated after he was taken then?" Dorothy moved her hands like she was visually trying to connect those scattered dots.

"And how did *you* know where we were? You said you had a guide? *Who* was it?" Alice asked the giant butterfly, placing an odd emphasis on the word *who,* but it was once more the cat who answered, and his response caused Alice's entire body to go rigid with crackling tension, her attention enraptured on nothing else.

"Why, who else but the White Rabbit, of course."

Sixteen

Wendy

I managed to slip away from the gang of new arrivals while Alice attempted to interrogate her mad friends about the mysterious vanishing White Rabbit, and Dorothy tried to mediate. It all made little difference to me since I hadn't the faintest idea of his significance in Alice's story, so I made my way down the beach to see where the boys had wandered off to. I found them, sitting peacefully with Hook, Tiger Lily and the other pirates. Evidently the peace negotiations had gone well. Tink was sitting on Peter's shoulders, just like she had a million times before. Though, it was a bit odd to see the Lost Boys interacting in such a friendly manner with the pirates, who had always been our foes.

"Hey, Wendy! We were just talking about you," Peter called out when he saw and flew over, pushing me into the center of the group, while Tink took the opportunity to yank hard on my braid.

"Ouch! Alright, Tink, you got your reward, now please leave my poor head alone." I rubbed a hand along the back of my stinging scalp, then turned to look at Peter who was snickering at the feisty fairy. "You were talking about me, Peter?" I brightened a little, forgetting that I had meant to tell them about the arrival of the munchkins, Wonderlandians, and Jack and Saw-horse. "What about?"

"About your dueling. Captain Codfish here pointed out that he'd never fought you one on one before. Apparently, I hogged all the fun." Peter was grinning from ear to ear, and he pointed to my sword. "Fancy a duel with my old nemesis? All in good fun, of course."

All eyes swiveled over to me, and I felt a little nugget of pressure and apprehension form in my chest. Was I going to be able to hold my own against the pirate? I squinted at Hook, thinking back to the last time I had dueled on the Jolly Roger. I realized it was true that Peter had always been the one to terrorize— er— fight the captain, so this would be a first for me. I was rusty, to say the least, but I was a bit older and bigger now and I imagined that would help me hold my ground. I definitely wasn't the strongest physically, however, I still knew how to leverage and use my small stature to my advantage. That, and I had gotten some use out of my weapons with the two Shadow Beast attacks, so that gave me a little working practice.

Regardless of any trepidation, I couldn't say no to the happy faces of my old friends as they waited for my response. They all looked so at ease, and I knew in the coming morning things would go back to taking a turn for the dreary. *I really shouldn't quibble and spoil their good fun.* I told myself firmly.

"This lot has really sung your praises, Lass," Hook rose to his feet and walked to the center of open space. He pulled out his sword, then bowed, extending his hooked hand. "I'll admit, it has piqued my interest."

"Alright, sword to sword then?" I accepted the challenge and nodded politely. Now was my chance to remind them that I could be just as ferocious in battle as any witch. "I trust this is just a demonstration and not anything nefarious? No stabs, cuts, or wounding, just going to a standstill, disarming, or surrender."

"You sound like you don't trust me, Lass. We pirates may fight dirty to win, but we do have a code of honor. If I give my word I won't kill, there's a good ninety percent chance I won't."

"How reassuring," I stopped myself from rolling my eyes at the madly grinning captain in front of me.

"Perhaps she should use all her weapons against someone twice her size, wouldn't that be marvelous fun?" Lionel suggested, rubbing his chin thoughtfully. This must all be some surreal salvation for him after so many years in that shadow prison. I had so many questions— how did he eat? Where did he get new clothing from when he had outgrown his boy clothes? How did his ties to the shadows really impact him, and how had he been able to defeat his beast without so much as a second thought?— But, all of those questions seemed impertinent so I bit them down.

"She can use whatever weapon she wants," Hook obliged, his eyes glinting.

"Go on, Wendy. You can take a codfish like him in your sleep. I'm not worried," Tip smiled, taunting Hook with Peter's favorite pet name for him.

"Funny, I don't recall ever dueling you either, Boy," Hook leered at Tip, who seemed to bristle in response.

"That's because I don't *duel*. I brawl, Pirate," Tip quipped, eyes narrowed and alive. It was good to see his old, less surly, spirit returning the longer he was in Neverland and surrounded by friends.

"Gentlemen, it is terribly rude to keep a lady waiting," I scolded lightly, drawing my sword for an emphatic and delicious moment of irony to calling myself a lady while I wielded a weapon.

Tip and Hook snorted and scoffed but didn't bicker any further. I took a moment to look out over the group, and my mind wandered to how launching an attack on Wonderland might play out with our newly reunited allies. Munchkins, short in stature but sturdy and low to the ground. If they were nimble, they could hold their own with close combat. The Wonderland group were all chaotic fighters, as I had witnessed in our escape from Wonderland. Other than the few deserting Card-guards, finding a fighting style for them would be difficult, and likely they would need to find a role on an individual basis.

Obviously, the pirates and Tiger Lily were more suited to fighting, so the Imagineds from Neverland would likely be a good front line and offensive force. Even Tink could play a support role in the right instance.

Caterpillar, as I had learned the butterfly was called, would be a good aerial fighter, and perhaps we could find a way to suit his many hands with bows. That could take down advancing Card-guards, but would have little effect on the magical scarecrows and tinmen. But, if they were flaming arrows, he could at least stand a chance with the scarecrows. The lizard man, Bill, was tall and lanky, but he had tough skin and long limbs. He would likely be good at dodging and darting. The Tweedles, I recalled the names of the twins, were a hard bill to fit.

They could potentially serve as a distraction, and with their bouncing about they could likely disarm foes by knocking them over. Then perhaps Bill could dart in and take their weapons, leaving them at a disadvantage for the other fighters. *Yes, that could work.* Cheshire would be good for distraction and misdirection. The March Hare, I hadn't a clue what to do with.

"Well, are you ready or not, Lass? Daylight is wasting," Hook's rough voice broke through my militant planning. The news of the Imagineds would likely derail the skirmish, so I'd bring it up afterwards when everyone was perfectly primed from the adrenaline rush. I'd always been decent at strategy, and both the impending battle, as well as this duel was no different.

I lifted my chin and raised my sword. I was gentle, timid, and oftentimes a bit easily pushed over. But, with a weapon in my hand I was different— cunning, strong, and resourceful. I was a protector. I could stand my ground.

"Count us in, Tip," I commanded, settling into a fighting stance.

The air seemed to still, and time slowed, while Tip counted backwards from three, while the pirates, Peter, Lionel, and Tiger Lily watched with twinkling eyes. A quick glance at Tiger Lily, and I wondered who my old friend would be rooting for in this duel.

I used the moment of calm to center myself and plan my first move, feeling the usual well of confidence building within me when I curled my fingers around a weapon. With a sword in my hand, I wasn't a damsel anymore. I was ferocious. I was skilled and useful. I was a fighter.

Hook was watching me like a hawk, likely reading every twitch of my muscles to surmise what I would do. I let my body relax a little, subtly shifting my weight into the balls of my feet. On the surface, I made myself look like I would be taking a defensive stance.

But, when Tip hit the final count, I launched forward on the offensive. I brandished my sword at the captain, but he didn't change his stance to defend. Rather he held his weapon at a different point, and with his longer arms, at equal point of impact, I would be struck first.

I let loose a hiss of frustration at Hook's brazen confidence. His face was bemused, and not at all edged with concern, marking the true face of a skilled fighter. In a duel, you gave nothing to your opponent. Wearing your intentions on your sleeve might as well be chaining you to the ground, for it allowed the other fighter to predict your moves. Wearing a mask of steel nerves was the best way to disarm your adversary.

So, I couldn't count myself as the weaker opponent until I ripped that mask of calm from his face to see where I truly stood. I blinked and dispelled my own uncertainties and doubts, shedding them like the scales of a snake, to fuse with my weapon. I was the viper here.

I kept charging at the captain then dropped to a sliding crouch to swing my torso beneath his sword, pivoting my own blade into an aggressive arch. Like a crack in the steel, I saw a heartbeat of surprise flicker in Hook's eyes before he countered my swing.

He certainly had the upper hand when it came to brute strength as his blade collided against mine, driving my heels against the ground. But, I was nimbler and lithe. It would just be a matter of finding his weak point, and pacing my stamina.

"Slippery, Lass," Hook jeered, narrowing his eyes. "Are you trying to emulate a cat or a snake?"

I smiled with demure resolve. "Oh, Captain, we both know how reptiles get under your skin."

A twitch in the jaw at my reference to the crocodile Hook so feared, acted as another crack in the mask. He adjusted in an instant to hold my sword at bay with his hook, positioning his sword to drive me back.

Blast! I swore internally. I should have formulated a strategy against the metal hook, an advantage in a storm of clashing steel. I'd have to be cunning as I went to counter it effectively. I could take the defensive and fallback to analyze his fighting pattern, but that would risk not being to gain traction back against his driving strength.

No, speed was the necessary element here. I'd have to be fast, using my smaller size to outpace him, and look for his openings as I went. More than anything, I needed to not back down. If this was a real battle with lives on the line, as a senior fighter, it would be my duty to be the first line of defense to protect other innocents.

Not to mention my own personal longstanding oath to Peter, to protect him and his inner light. Then, there were Dorothy and Tip to figure in too, though Dorothy had her magic, and Tip was also a skilled fighter. My priority would be guarding the Imagineds so they could execute their dedicated assignments.

I flinched against the rattling impact of Hooks sword slamming against mine, to my surprise, with the broad side of the blade to force me back. I leapt away instinctively.

"Seems like your mind is wandering, Lass. Don't tell me you're not giving me a full fight here." Hook's husky voice scraped against my ears.

"Certainly not, Captain," I narrowed my eyes and kept my tone and breathing even and respectful.

Then we leapt back at it—- a torrent of clashes, blocks, and blows, twisting like willow fronds in the wind, then colliding like a strike of lightning. As it dragged on, I could feel my stamina beginning to pulsate.

I wasn't in the best physical condition, and while this was good endurance training, my own pride refused to be wounded by defeat in the one area I knew I excelled at against all odds.

There was a rhythm to the fighting now, like a dance, where even a shift in tempo or steps didn't disturb the exchange of blows. I realized that even though his hook acted as a sort of shield, in order to use both the length of the sword and the hook, the captain's movements needed room for broader strokes. So, I pressed harder, getting in closer and closer until—

"Got you!" I exhaled as I flicked the pirate's sword out of his hand, bringing my arm back in a fluid snap to point the tip of my blade at his chest.

"And I have you, Lass," Hook growled lightly, and a quick glance down showed that though I had managed to disarm his primary weapon and hold him at point blank, this also freed him up to maneuver his smaller weapon— the hook— to brandish at my throat.

A draw.

"Well, that was an entertaining fight," Tip commented, applauding slowly. "Looks like this duel has ended in a draw."

"That was amazing, Wendy!" Peter cheered, then wiggled his brows smugly at Hook. "And that was her after being out of practice."

"You haven't changed a bit," Lionel added happily, his golden hair swaying around his face as he wriggled with enthusiasm.

Hook and I panted, still staring each other down with our weapons raised.

"Color me surprised, Lass," Hook chortled. "I must say, I did not expect such a display from you. You have a gift for fighting."

"So long as there is something worth fighting for to protect, I will fight." I dipped my head and lowered my sword. As the adrenaline ebbed, my muscles began wailing in protest at the vigorous exertion I had just put them through. "If you'll excuse me."

Hook lowered his weapon as well and gave a small bow, which was somehow both sardonic as well as respectful. Then, he began whistling a slow, almost mournful, shanty as he sauntered off to rejoin his crewmates, leaving me with my old friends. Tiger Lily hesitated a moment, seemingly unsure of which group to join. She ultimately shrugged, but gave me a tentative smile, and followed Hook. Her life was with them now, and it seemed to me that she was keeping an eye on Hook, genuinely concerned for his well being and happiness.

I felt my heart ache with empathy, knowing all the man had lost. Though he'd been imagined to start, he was now a living, breathing, human soul capable of love, pain, laughter, and grief just like the rest of us. He'd lived a full life, with the ship as his home, and his crew as his family—

both now irreparably damaged. How he must be hurting, yet he carried himself with dignity squared in his shoulders. It really was dreadfully sad.

But no, the hollowness blooming in my chest went beyond my sympathy for the pirate captain. Thinking of all *he* had lost only led me to think about what I, myself, had had ripped away from me.

John and Micheal were gone— presumed dead by most. My own time in the world I hailed from was long gone, along with anyone who'd know me. I'd never see my mother and father's faces again. The splendorous land I had grown to love and explore, was on the brink of destruction, with powerful adversaries bent on wiping it away like a smudge on a window. Even Peter, who I'd prayed every day to find me, who I cared for more than anyone else… I'd lost everything else, and spent all that time alone as a prisoner just for him to find me, but his heart belonged to someone else!

I couldn't even fault him for it, as it sometimes seemed fate itself had brought Alice and Peter together. And I knew she loved him as fiercely as I did. Perhaps even more, so I couldn't hate her for it either.

"Is that...? It couldn't be!" Tip exclaimed, peering into the distance behind me. I knew the others must have come to join us, so I started to explain the new development.

"Oh, yes. I meant to tell you that a group of the Imagineds from Wonderland and Oz have made it—" I was cut off as Peter and Tip abruptly raced off to greet the others. Lionel blinked warmly at me before trailing after the others to follow the excitement.

I stood alone, looking all around me. Tip was speaking with the Imagineds, who were grouped together in little friendly units, and Hook and Tiger Lily were smiling amongst their crewmates.

Dorothy was a little to the side, playing with Toto, who was twirling and leaping with joy. Her face bore equal enthusiasm and affection for her dog as she laughed along, and I didn't miss the small smile curve on Tip's lips as he snuck a peek at her while trying to look serious and focused on the munchkins he was now speaking with along with Jack and Saw-horse.

Peter and Alice had launched into a deep conversation— no doubt about the White Rabbit— and Lionel was hanging on their every word.

Seeing everyone interacting, having a place amongst each other, never had I felt so alone and misplaced as I did then. Never had I felt so inexplicably *lost.*

I missed my brothers terribly. Michael would have noticed I was feeling sad and had me hold hands with his prized teddy bear to cheer me up, while John would have found some brilliant way to keep me included in the conversation.

They were dear and thoughtful souls, but without them, I didn't quite fit right anymore, and I had to wonder if I even mattered at all now that my role as nurturer was obsolete. Did my existence have any impact? I'd fallen from grace, plummeting so suddenly into a bit of icy acrid disparity, it sucked all the air from my lungs.

I'd loved and lost. And lost and lost and lost. All was lost. I had no one waiting for me back home, and no one here asking me to stay. I felt viewed as some sort of burden to look after, rather than a capable friend or loved one. I had no one anymore. So, what was I fighting so hard for— a future I no longer belonged in? My life had been stolen from me.

My lip trembled and a lump had lodged itself in my throat. Unable to bear it a moment longer, I turned and fled the crowded area, racing away as if distance would be enough to close these gaping wounds I kept trying desperately to ignore.

I didn't know or care if anyone had noticed me race the area. In the bustle of chaotic enthusiasm, I wouldn't be surprised if they hadn't. Tip's earlier words lingered in my ears, haunting me. He didn't need me. How many of the others didn't or wouldn't need me too? What then? I didn't I could withstand hearing those words come from Peter directly. It would hurt to much. My amicable conversation regarding his affection for Alice back at the Red Castle had already been enough to threaten to tear me in two.

My pain wasn't helpful to those around me, and that's who I was. If I wasn't useful, I'd cease to exist. That blasted moment of stillness was all it had taken to bring it all back up and I couldn't stomach it one moment more.

So, I ran. I didn't know where to, but I ran all the same. I'd return to the others when I'd quelled my emotions. Night was falling and soon I would become invisible, enveloped in a cloak of starry darkness, hoping to find somewhere to breathe where the air was unchoked by the infinitely chasm of loneliness and grief yawning open within me.

Seventeen

Peter

"I'm so frustrated!" Alice growled.

When she and the others had come wandering over to find us, the night before, she'd wasted no time informing me that Cheshire had claimed to have been led here by the illusive White Rabbit that no one had seen in six years since her arrival. Now, she was fit to be tied over the fact he had managed to vanish on her again. Personally, I was more interested in what larger role the Hatter played, but figured I'd have to ask Bill about it at a later time.

"Relax. Love. chasing the rabbit and falling down holes isn't the priority right now." I shook my head with a laugh. "I thought you were going to go about trying to organize the Imagineds about taking Wonderland back while we go look for Tip's beast?"

"I know," Alice pouted, folding her arms. "It's just so—"

"Frustrating?" I finished her sentence with a wiggle of my brows and a devious grin.

"Yes, it is. And so is that. He could have the answers I've been looking for and maybe it could save us all. You know when you look at it like that, it isn't such a small thing to think about," She argued, poking me in the arm.

I tugged her into a hug of farewell. "Well, regardless you need your full head on your shoulders and all the patience you can muster to try to get that group of Wonderlandians on the same page."

"Bill always listens to me," She laughed, returning the hug. "Come back safely, please."

"Tell Bill to keep his ladder to himself because I'll be back before you know it! And no getting into any fights with Tinkerbell. You two hotheads need to play nice or I will be most displeased," I joked back and separated from our embrace, but kept our hands linked a moment longer. I still couldn't believe she had really admitted to loving me. Moreover, I still couldn't believe I had admitted it back. It was marvelous and terrifying and I wasn't entirely sure what I was supposed to do with myself now.

"Will do," Alice promised amicably.

"Have you seen Wendy?" I asked, looking around the group. "I know she went to clear her head last night and didn't come back for a while, but I couldn't find her this morning and I was going to have her come with us to the hideout. It used to be her home too, after all."

Alice shrugged. "I haven't personally seen her this morning. But, I thought I heard Tiger Lily mention that she saw her go off in the woods nearby again. I guess she needed some more alone time. It's been a lot the past few days so I can't really blame her."

"Maybe I ought to go look for her…"

"Hey, Peter. It's now or never," Tip called over to me. "Or, I'll be heading out on my own. Which is fine by me, by the way."

I frowned, but Alice squeezed my hand. "Don't worry, I'll go look for her. Be safe, and I'll see you soon." She leaned up and pecked me on the cheek before releasing my hand and walking away.

I smiled after her. "Thanks, Love."

Lionel and Tip were waiting a few paces away, and together we started to make our way to the woods, passing Dorothy and Toto along the way. She was attempting to practice some of her magical abilities.

"Hey, Dorothy?" Tip called to get her attention.

"Yes?" She asked in surprise, seeming startled out of her deep focus.

"Don't burn the place to the ground while we're all away, okay?" He smiled and patted her on the head.

"I won't!" She puffed indignantly. "I really am getting a hold of my magic now, no matter how ridiculous that is to hear coming out of my mouth. It's true, so stop patronizing me, rude boy." She jabbed him in the chest and folded her arms crossly.

"Good. Just testing your resolve." He teased and turned away with a wave, leading our trio into the woods. "See you later!"

"Be careful," She called after him, then blushed ever so slightly, and added in, "both of you! Alice will ring our necks if you don't come back in one piece, Peter. So, Tip, please keep him in line. You too, Lionel"

"I'll do my best," Tip promised, giving me a friendly nod. "You ready, Buddy?"

I watched their exchange, my eyes zipping back and forth between the two with a grin. "Uh huh."

"Then I guess it's time for an adventure."

I whipped around and chuckleld deviously at my friend, having the good decency to wait until we were a good range out of earshot before interrogating him.

"So, what's all that going on with Dorothy?" I asked with an impish grin.

"What are you talking about?" Tip sighed as he trudged through the sand towards the woods.

"You two seem awfully chummy as of late. I'm starting to feel replaced as your favorite compatriot!" I feigned insult, and elbowed Tip in the arm. "Come on, Mate. You can be honest with me."

"Ha!" Lionel guffawed. "I never thought I'd see the day you two would be talking about romance. When I got out of the Shadow World, this was not what I expected in the slightest. But, hey, we are all grown up now, and have some very pretty girls in our ranks, so can't blame you. I never really paid much attention to how pretty Wendy was until I saw her again, but she always had a thing for Peter anyways."

"Oh, yeah. That was a bit awkward when Alice came into the picture. Wendy is great and all, but it never was what had I felt with Alice. From the very beginning, when I saw her on her first day, we clicked.

Wendy and I talked about it back in Wonderland though, so I think she's fine with it and put it behind her. Besides, I think Henry always sort of quietly fancied Wendy."

"Really? Poor, shy, little Henry." Lionel shook his head and scuffed his foot. "I doubt he'd ever have the guts to act on it. Honestly, I think nearly all of us had our first crush on her. She was pretty amazing. Suppose it's too late to let her know that? I wouldn't step on Henry's toes or nothing, especially when we will be getting him soon, but you know. Just let her know she's pretty special."

"It's never too late to compliment a girl. I find they quite like it." I raised a finger, imitating a scholarly stance.

"Oh, good grief. What even is this conversation right now?" Tip groused, discomfort visible in every inch of his slouching body.

Lionel snickered and threw an arm around Tip "Well, go on then, Tip, answer him. Don't leave us in suspense. Are you in love with Dorothy?"

Tip immediately bristled. "Absolutely not! Good grief, man. I've known her for a matter of days."

"So?" I shrugged, wondering why time mattered in whether you had a connection with someone or not.

"You're too naive for your own good, Buddy," Tip sighed, then when I kept grinning at him, he cracked a small smile and groaned. "There's nothing to be smiling about. She just intrigues me," he answered honestly, keeping his eyes fixed straight ahead. "She's interesting. Unique."

"She seems awfully sour, if that's what you mean," I clicked my tongue.

"I don't think I've really interacted with her enough at this point to have an opinion. I like her freckles though. They add character." Lionel frowned in contemplation. He always had been more blunt and open with his thoughts, not having much of a filter between what went on in his head and what came out of his mouth.

"She has some layers. It's fun to rile her up, because she's easily ruffled, but half the time I think I am offending her more than joking with her. Her sarcasm is more a defense mechanism because she's never had friends. And yet, she's kind when she doesn't have to be, even when it's easier to be mean. She's vulnerable but somehow it seems to make her strong enough to endure her demons."

"She told you more about those, I take it?"

"About what happened to her parents and how she felt about it." Tip nodded, then added for Lionel's benefit. "They drowned and she survived. It's why I had to go help her in the water. She completely freezes up in terror."

"Oh yeah, she's an orphan like you." I felt an unsolicited chill envelop me for a moment, then vanish as quickly as it had come. I shook my body, and shrugged it off.

"Being in that shipwreck brought up a lot of old wounds for her about it all," Tip sighed.

"Seems to be an abundance of those as of late," I grunted in agreement. The mission we were on now was in search of inner demons, as it were.

"And, she seems like all the while she's learning more about herself, yet simultaneously is unapologetically true to who she knows herself to be," Tip continued, then wrapped up his comments, seeming to realize he had been speaking more than he usually did, all at once. "It's just... intriguing to spend time around her. It's a bit refreshing to know someone who has been formed away from this world and its dangers. But, that's all."

"I find myself in danger every time I spend extended time around her. Suppose she's just bad luck?"

"I'll wager your own choices are what put you in danger, my impetuous friend," Lionel chuckled.

"Plus, you have a hot-headed witch of questionable morality on your arm, that doesn't help that area either," Tip added.

I opened my mouth to object, but shrugged it off. "Yeah, that's pretty fair, actually."

"Trust me, I know." He rolled his eyes, and I recalled the two had been paired at the beginning of the game, and neither one seemed particularly fond of the other. Tip didn't even refer to her by name.

"All I am saying is that you two have really buddied up and seem to get along real well. You've laughed and cried—" I started to press.

"I have laughed, but I haven't cried," Tip corrected, interrupting my list.

"But you've been an awfully willing shoulder for her to cry on." I wriggled my eyebrows suggestively.

"It's what friends do." Tip shrugged, his shoulders staying slightly raised in defense of his obvious awkwardness.

"I'll be sure to blow my nose on you the next time I feel blue. Are you going to tell her she *intrigues* you?" Lionel laughed, patting Tip on the back. The sight of the Lost Boys, though grown, acting like old brothers again warmed my heart.

"Nope."

I frowned. "Why not? If it isn't love then you should have no problem saying she's interesting. People like to hear those sorts of things. Compliments and stuff, like I was saying before. I say them all the time. Tip, I find your sword skills very *intriguing.* See?"

"Aside from you and your witch, most guys don't go around complimenting girls without it being construed immediately as forward intentions."

"Nah, I think it's just being friendly!" Lionel argued, and I nodded along eagerly.

"Well, you're both hopeless flirts."

"And you need to remember to lighten up some! Smell the wild flowers, flatter a pretty girl, dance a jig, climb a tree— whatever tickles your fancy," I suggested, ticking the items off on my fingers. "The hugs and kisses from a girl aren't half bad either, really."

"Oh, good grief. I don't think those things have anything in common, Bud."

"Sure they do! It's seizing the day," Lionel insisted.

"*Carpe diem.*"

"You're excused."

"No," Tip laughed. "It's a saying in Latin that means *seize the day.*"

"Where is Latin? Gillikin Country?" I scrunched up my nose when Tip shook his head. "No matter. My point being, you need to let go a little, and recall your sense of adventure."

"I still have a sense of adventure!" Tip argued in dismay.

I beamed, and flitted in front of him, flicking pixie dust in his face, making him sneeze.

"Good. Time for a scavenger hunt. And it's timed. First one to find Tip's Shadow Beast wins and gets to make the loser perform a dare of his choosing!" I called out the rules over my shoulder and I zipped away through the Neverland trees, sprinkling a layer of dust on Lionel on the way.

"Cheater!" Tip chided, launching into the air behind me. I saw a brightness return to his face, like his life-force and childlike wonder were being replenished.

"Scoundrel!" Lionel echoed the sentiment and followed suit.

"Never a cheater, always an opportunist!" I crowed, willing myself through the air faster.

"An opportunistic cheater!" Tip heckled, hot on my heels.

"You'll have to do better than that to beat me," My words rang through the air laced with laughter, and I felt light. Happiness and gratitude for racing through the Never Woods with two of my best friends was so uplifting amongst all of the pain and uncertainty of everything else. I hoped it had taken the edge off Tip's apprehension at finding his beast too, providing a needed distraction.

The euphoria was short lived though as Tip darted away from me, dipping and weaving with great speed and nimble precision, towards the heart of the Hollow Woods.

"Blast!" I swore behind a competitive grin. "Me and my happy thoughts lost us the first round."

I veered my trajectory and caught up to my friend who was

floating ambiently in the air, staring at the hollow entrance in a large oak tree that would take us to our old hideout. As Lionel and I hovered beside him, I could see the light of adventure had drained away.

"You think I can absorb one of those things like you do, even without magic?" Tip's face crinkled in deep contemplation.

"It's facing your pain, so yeah. The question is, how do we find your beast specifically?"

"I have a feeling it'll turn up and seek me out once we go inside."

"Better to just get it over with. Remember," Lionel placed a firm hand on Tip's shoulder. "No mercy. The Shadows are evil and if you let them get into your head, they can take you over and make you Wicked. You have to be ready to embrace whatever pain they are born from, and strike them down."

Tip squared his shoulders and flicked his new dagger into his hand with quiet resolve. "I'm ready, just don't judge me for anything you see in there. Unless you just want to stay outside and wait?"

"We all have our demons, Mate. We are merely here to support you brutally slashing up yours. And if there are any other smaller ones lurking about, we will take those ones down. Let's go!" I tried to lighten the mood by overanimating my tone.

Tip sighed and nodded, then the three of us entered the hollow tree one at a time, with Tip taking the lead into the hideout.

The old fort was nestled into a forest of thick trees. Unlike normal trees however, these had their branches embedded in the ground, and their roots twisting into the sky. Furthermore, there were a series of hollows in the trunks that, entered in the right sequence, teleported us to the hidden hideout. Much like Alice's original home in Wonderland, this hideout was constructed of vines and logs, intricately interconnected to form several makeshift rooms.

We followed the pattern of hollows and stood in the center of the now-abandoned fort we had hailed as our own Neverland castle. It was haunting without children darting around and playing loudly— like the life had been sucked free of the space. Empty, it felt almost more akin to a tomb.

We took our time, looking around the whole area, but lost in our own thoughts and memories as we pursued, we didn't speak. None of us likely had the words even if we had wanted to talk about it. This place, as different as it felt now, was still sacred to us in ways no one else— save for Wendy— would understand.

Lionel stooped to uncover something that had been buried in years of twigs and debris.He dusted it off and stared at it for a long time. It was Micahel's old teddy bear that he took with him everywhere. He had been the youngest of the Lost Ones, and had been a dearly beloved little brother to all of us. He was still only six when the Darling children ventured into Oz, and neither boy came back. My stomach pitted with grief as I recalled seeing all three Darlings plummet from the sky all those years ago. Their wails of fear permeated my brain, and it took everything I had to not become completely consumed in guilt and grief.

I approached Lionel, and rested a hand sympathetically on his shoulder. He gripped onto the stuffed bear, his fingers digging into the plush surface. Then he slowly rose to his feet and fastened the small, dinged bcar to his belt.

"For Wendy," He sniffed with a sad smile. "I think she'll want to have it."

"Good on you, Mate." I patted his back and turned away. He hadn't been there when the tragic event had happened, but he had been there for the aftermath of my return to camp without the three Lost Ones I had gone to retrieve. All of us being young boys, we hadn't really known how to process their loss to our ranks, and had each come to terms with their presumed deaths as them simply having gone back home like countless others had before. Wendy and John had brought it up before their adventure to Oz, so it wasn't too far of stretch of the imagination, and it helped us all cope.

But, the cruel reality was that they were the only Lost Ones to have ever died and not returned home. It was my biggest failure, and my deepest regret. Part of me wished we had been able to find Wendy to bring her with us, but another part of me was glad she wasn't here. It might be too overwhelming for her.

I approached the part of the fort that had been John's favorite haunt,and dug around through a pile of old discarded items left behind by all the many children who had graced our hideout, until I uncovered what I had been looking for.

John's coveted top hat.

Perhaps bringing back the pieces of her brothers would allow her some room to grieve and gain some closure. Like Dorothy, I had to wonder if a part of her had survivor's guilt too. I knew I did.

I spun the hat between my hands and rejoined the other two. "We didn't find any shadows, but somehow I still think it was good we came here today. I know we need to find somewhere to have a more permanent camp, but I'm not sure the hideout is up to company until we get the others back."

"I think you're right," Tip agreed, reaching out to run his fingers sentimentally over the brim of the old hat. "God, John and Michael. They were both too good for this world, weren't they?" He whispered.

The lump in my throat kept me from responding verbally, so I merely managed to nod my agreement.

Lionel patted the teddy bear at his hip. "That they were."

We stayed in the somber moment a few heartbeats before breaking apart to finish our exploration. Exhausting our searching efforts, we were about to leave when Tip's body went rigid. I zipped over to him.

"What is it? Do you sense something?" I asked, looking around wildly, drawing my dagger. "What do we need to cut up?"

"I don't think the darkness just manifests on Imagineds and contributions, but also can embody phantom memories…" Tip's voice wavered and he swallowed hard, pointing a shaking hand towards one of the hollows. "And I had really hoped this wouldn't be the memory it chose for me today."

I followed his gesture and bristled when I saw in the hollow two bright eyes staring back at me. "Bloody hell! What is that?"

"That would be my phantom," Tip cringed, lifting his dagger. Lionel and I follow suit, retrieving our own knives, eyes peeled for other shadows.

The eyes squinted in a grin, and a shadowy wraith about the size of a young girl hopped to the ground. She twirled and dithered about, then it opened its mouth, becoming the first of the beasts to speak coherently.

"Hi there! I'm so glad I found you."

"What memory is this? Is this from before you came here with me?" I frowned, and looked sharply from the wraith to Tip, knowing that we hadn't ever had any young girls other than Wendy in Neverland. His knuckles were white around the hilt of his dagger.

"Please, I need some help. No, no! There is no time for you to get more help. I need you to come with me now. It's life or death." The shadow raced up to Tip, and to my surprise, he let it, rooted in place while Lionel and I leapt away. *"My name is Mombi and I got lost exploring. There is this creature though, and it's in danger, but I am not strong enough or tall enough to help it. Hurry!"*

"That's not what I meant when I said to embrace it!" Lionel cried in disbelief.

"What does it mean that its name is Mombi?" I demanded of Tip, as the shadow melted off of him and sauntered away before disappearing in thin air, like she had run through space and time, leaving us all braced for her return. "I know she kidnapped you, but I always assumed that she had done that as an adult."

"Who is Mombi again? She sounds like an enemy," Lionel asked briskly, eyes darting from me and Tip to where the phantom had disappeared.

"She is. She's the one that stole Tip away, and held him captive all this time in Oz. She's also who took over Wonderland from Alice with The Wizard," I growled.

"I followed her that night. Then they stole me away." Already, I could see Tip's eyes glazing over, clearly visualizing these moments as they had happened.

"Oh," The lackluster word was all I could manage. "Didn't you say you were kidnapped? Am I remembering that phrasing wrong, because that kind of painted a bit of a different picture. You went to help a creature? And Mombi was a young girl when you met, not an adult? You need to fill in some blanks here. I thought she was your captor."

The shadow reappeared in the center of the fort, and began to twist and morphed into a slightly older form, before racing over to Tip again, this time linking arms with him, and leaning its head against his shoulder.

"Oh, no. She jumped to when I woke up. I didn't think it would be more than one phantom memory…" Tip breathed, turning his head ever so slightly to peer at the shadow, like he could see a clear person in the mess of darkness writhing next to him. Torment swirled in his gaze, and his cheeks started to flush red.

"You need to strike her down, Tip. We can't do it for you." Lionel barked impatiently, while my intrigue piqued. The lost memory was telling a story that Tip, for whatever reason, had chosen not to relay to the rest of us about his time with the Wicked witch. They evidently had been friends.

"It's been so frightening here in this place. I'm so sorry you got caught because of me. But I am also so glad that I met you and we get to be together at least."

"That's… unexpected." I took a tentative step towards the wraith, wondering if we should be stabbing it about now, like Lionel had told us. But, Tip seemed lost in thought so I hesitated, only because the shadow wasn't outwardly attacking. Maybe he needed to relive the memories to process them and the thing would just vanish. However, hadn't Lionel also warned us not to give it time to get into our heads?

"You'd like to kiss me, wouldn't you, Tippetarius? You look like you do. Go on then! You can kiss me. Mmm, someday we will escape and we can spend the rest of our lives together. You'd like that, right?"

"Ummm." My mouth gaped in disbelief. They were *more* than friends? "You didn't. Right?"

Tip gave the smallest of nods to indicate he had, in fact, kissed Mombi, and shocked didn't even begin to cover how that made me feel.

The wraith twirled around and morphed again, now a silhouette of darkness in the likeness of Mombi's adult frame.

"I don't like the look of this," Lionel growled as he leaned deeper into his braced offensive stance. "He's completely entranced, and he's the only one who can take it down. I told him no mercy. Tip has never been the extra emotional type."

The phantom wrapped its wispy arms around Tip's shoulders and gazed up at him. *I'm so sorry they made me hurt you. I wasn't in my right mind. I'll never do it again, I promise. You believe me, don't you, Tippetarius, my love? Let me make it up to you..."*

Her voice was something lost between pouty and alluring. She ran her hands down his chest and nuzzled her head into the crook of his neck. When her hands got to the base of his shirt, she tugged it off in one fluid motion.

"No way," Lionel breathed in utter disbelief, seemingly to finally understand the depth of Tip's hidden connection to the witch, and to the memories this phantom was acting out.

"Whoa, whoa, whoa. Time to snap out of it, Mate! You're letting the thing undress you. Stab it. Stab it now." I cleared the distance and threw my shoulder into the shadow, forcibly shoving it away from my friend. Whether I could take it out or not, I had to at least help get Tip moving again. Seeing him so rattled was very off putting, and seeing that thing run her hands around on him like she owned him made me blood boil.

Tip seemed to snap out of his half daze, his breathing rough and ragged, he looked around wildly, like he'd forgotten where he was. The wraith, meanwhile, had become agitated, and fixed me with a cold stare that slowly turned red.

"Uh oh. I think you made it mad," Lionel groaned, coming to stand beside me, ready to take on the beast as best we could.

In response, it began screeching and bolted for me. Its slender hands changed forms into long claws, and the face yawned open with a glowing jagged smile of malice. It was a terrible nightmare of a creature. This was the horrible thing Tip's unresolved issues had created, and it was very oddly specifically terrible.

"Vile snake!" I hissed as I brandished my knife, aiming to impale it in the shoulder, hoping even if I couldn't kill it I could still fight it like I had with Tentis. But to my dismay, just like Tiger Lily's arrows to my beast, my hand sailed right through it. I felt a sharp pang in my chest as the claws dug into my chest, forcing me, with surprising strength to the ground.

"Damn it!" Lionel swore, trying to get a grip on the beast to pull it off of me. "Tip!"

"*I'm sorry I hurt you. They made me. I won't ever do it again.*" The voice coming from the creature was no longer alluring, but had a deep echo around it, layering over something harsh and hissing, like the demon it was. It felt like grit and thunder in my ears.

"I'm also sorry you're hurting me, actually. Feel free to stop," I groaned, as the breath was knocked from my lungs. I saw blood pooling around the claws, and knew I needed to do something fast. Tip had been knocked out of one stupor, only to be held in some paralyzed state of horror.

"Tip!" Lionel shouted again, growing desperate. Tip had been knocked out of one stupor, only to be held in some paralyzed state of horror. I'd have to get a little added help if I wanted to make it to see another day at this rate.

I called to Shadow, but when he materialized, the wraith dug her other set of claws into one of his arms, holding him captive from tethering her. That was new, and seriously unfair.

"*I'm so sorry. I'll never hurt you again. They made me. You know I love you. I'll make it up to you.*"

"I know no such thing, and I don't think you're very sorry either!" I bellowed at the creature, thrashing wildly. "Tip! You're being entirely useless over there while your shadow-girlfriend is trying to *kill* me. Some assistance would be appreciated."

"I don't know how to make it stop," He replied weakly, though he did manage to take a single step towards me. "She…"

"Bloody hell, what did she do to you to rattle your brain so? *Stab it!*"

"I didn't want to hurt her…"

"Might I remind you that she seems to think she is *Mombi*. you know that Wicked witch you spit nails about all the time? The one you hate? So, stab it, before I am run clean through. Damn it, that hurts!" I ground my teeth together as the claws penetrated further into my flesh. The terrifying creature was laughing. *Laughing.* It was enjoying my pain.

Lionel marched over and decked Tip in the face before grabbing him roughly by the shoulders. "Get it together or you're going to watch it tear Peter apart, and likely me next. That blood will be on your hands!"

"Gah!" I cried out in pain and frustration. I hated seeing Tip in such a frazzled state. It was like he was entirely some other person that I didn't know, and that was the most unnerving part.

"If you hate this Mombi like you've said, then strike her down." Lionel shook Tip again and shoved him towards me.

"Mombi... Right. She's a terrible, evil Wicked witch. She's not that girl." Tip nodded and took a swing at the wraith, only to stop when it whipped around to look at him, no longer in the demonic form it had shown me.

"*Tippetarius, my love? You won't hurt me will you?*" Her voice was meek and shocked once more.

"Blast it all," I swore. I needed to think quickly.

"This thing is clever and manipulative, Tip. You said yourself, she isn't whatever girl you think you're protecting. This is a monster," Lionel reiterated firmly. I was extremely fortunate we had him with us, or I think I would have been run clean through already. Thank goodness we hadn't let him come here on his own.

Clearly, Tip was not menally prepared for this kind of encounter. If I had known more specifically what his struggle was prior, I might have come in with a better plan. I had expected it to be some internal struggle that the Tip I knew would be able to reason his way out of, not this strange tangled tainted love affair. If Shadow couldn't do anything, perhaps I needed someone a little more powerful… An idea formed in my brain, but

I didn't know if it would work like it did with summoning Shadow. I had to try.

"Ida! I need you," I called out, allowing my body to emanate a glow like I had back in Oz when she had come to me before. "Can you take this thing back to the Shadow World, before it kills me? Since Tip is being bloody useless!"

I loosed a breath of relief, as Shadow's form vanished and was replaced by a much more solid shadow form, that I knew was the witch I had called for. She lifted off the ground, a tangible silhouette in the air, just like the wraith.

"I can take her back with me, but she will return until she is defeated for good," Ida's echoing voice was like a sweet melody of relief to my ears.

"Ida," Lionel breathed with recognition, and I realized he must be familiar with the odd shadow witch from his time in that world. "Good thinking."

Opening her arms wide, the depths of her shadows expanded like a cloak, and in one fluid movement, Ida enveloped the wraith, like a tidal wave. Then, quick as she had appeared, and without a single word more, she receded back into the ground, and Shadow flickered back into place.

I bolted to my feet and panted. Then, I walked over to Tip and opted to land a punch of my own to his gut, lest he still was under whatever spell had possessed him. He jolted and doubled over with a grunt before recognition and clarity began to appear back in his eyes.

"Damn it. What a useless piece of garbage I am! Weak! Damn it!" He raged at himself, grabbing at his head.

"What the hell was *that?*" I demanded crossly. "We will have to deal with that thing again later, but for now, start talking. You had some sort of *relationship* with Mombi before all this? Which seemed *pretty intimate* for all your bellyaching about that stuff with me and Alice—and she doesn't take my shirt off. Never mind that, but why was she able to control you like that? I've never seen you act like that. You'd let her skewer me rather than strike her down?"

"Hey! Back off," Tip growled, anger still fresh and raw in his eyes. He rose to his full height— which was annoyingly a little taller than me— and forced me to take a step back with a shove to my chest. "I don't see you trying to stab your own little Wicked witch when she goes off the rails."

"Alice isn't Mombi! She's not evil!" I barked back, a wave of indignation and frustration welling up in me too. I returned the shove, balling my hands into fists, and Tip glared back at me "And this was a shadow, not a person. I can tell the difference which is more than you can say!"

"Shut up, Pan. You have no idea what you're talking about. That little witch of yours has you completely under her spell and it's just as pathetic so don't get off lecturing me."

"At least I can keep my clothes on! That's more self control than you've got. A little hug and kiss and you're down for the count? Who's the pathetic one here?" I taunted, uncharacteristic rage bursting at the seams with a primal heat pulseing from the inside out. I was never goaded so easily by anyone other than The Wizard. I heard a dull cackle of my inner demon laughing in the back of my mind, reveling in my anger.

Tip's lip curled in an equally uncharacteristic wrathful display, and before I knew what had hit me, his fist connected with my jaw, sending me stumbling backwards. Something in me snapped and I shot forward ready to engage in the fight despite my bleeding wounds.

"Hey! Knock it off you two," Lionel shouted, shouldering his way in between us to keep us from getting into an all out fist fight. "Peter got injured, and I can tell it got into both your heads so straighten up and calm down. You aren't each other's enemies. Peter, keep your unhelpful comments to yourself. Tip, you were supposed to kill the thing, and didn't, so, it's fair for us to want some answers."

"I know! I know," Tip shouted, then quieted down. "I loved her, alright? She tricked me into believing she was Good and kind. And I kept ignoring all the little lies she left behind because I *wanted* her to be Good. She'd always claim to be under someone's control and that they made her do the terrible things, or she stood by and watched, claiming they made her. I believed it was worth the pain just to get the woman I'd fallen in love with back. I believed we had both been taken and were in that hell together. I *thought* she was being controlled, but I found out that it was an act and I was just a plaything. None of it was real. Not one damn moment. That woman whom I loved never existed."

"Well… blast. That sounds terrible, Mate. I'm sorry. Why didn't you tell me? We could have planned something better. Or, gotten you to a better place to face it at least." I sagged, the churning anger in my chest melting away to sympathy.

"I didn't want to drudge it all up into words. I'm ashamed of it. I've never been more ashamed of anything in my life, than how foolish I was with her. That's why I didn't want you two to come with me, and I left before we could find Wendy." Tip stared at the ground with deep remorse etched into his face. "I thought I was stronger. That my anger and hatred had made me stronger. I thought things had changed and I wouldn't be weak. I thought I was healing and that maybe I was moving on… But, I am weak, just as weak as I was then when I couldn't do anything other than get out." He clenched his fists, and I sighed, patting him on the back.

"Afraid that's all we can do sometimes. Getting out seems to be the first step, and from experience, that takes strength and courage too," I consoled my friend.

"All three of us have been locked in a prison we had to escape," Lionel added, placing a hand on Tip's shoulder. "Some of us even had to be rescued because we couldn't get out ourselves. It's nothing to be ashamed of."

I rolled my shoulders back and extended a hand to Tip. "Sorry, Mate. I never thought we'd come to blows over something so stupid. I don't think for one second you are pathetic. You are right. I have no idea what it was like to have gone through what you did. I got pretty lucky with Alice, all things considered, so I'm in no position to judge."

"I know you don't." Tip accepted my hand and gave it a solid shake. "And I know the witch— er, Alice— isn't the same as Mombi. It's just hard to trust another Wicked."

"Dorothy has that title too, you know." Lionel flashed a leading smile at Tip. "Do you trust her?"

"I think I do." Tip frowned. "She's different from the other Wickeds. She doesn't have a truly hurtful bone in her body. She's standoffish, but I can tell she cares more deeply than meets the eye. You can see it with how she talks about her family, or how she handled the Mouse Queen, and plays with her dog. She doesn't have that notorious violent streak of a Wicked."

"Hmm. Maybe consider why the two of you click so well then—And don't bother denying that you do. She sounds like a better and more forward focal point than whatever terror you ran away from." I shrugged, and inspected my chest. "Come on, Lads. I'm afraid I am in need of some bandages. We will face this battle another time with a better plan."

"I hope Wendy is there when we get back." Tip nodded, though he didn't acknowledge my suggestion about his obvious taking a liking to the freckled farm girl. He did, however, look to be seriously contemplating my advice behind his stoic expression, and I fully understood why the Wonderlandians liked to tease me and Alice at that moment. It was great fun so long as you weren't on the receiving end!

"Yeah, she is pretty good at wrappings. I guess it's her shadow we will have to tackle next. I wonder what that will look like," Lionel mused, as the three of us stumbled to the exit of the fort. "I just hope that isn't where she ran off to all alone this morning to prove something. She never was very good about asking for help, though she freely gives it. I'd hate to see it get her in a bind."

"No, Tiger Lily said she saw her walking in the woods earlier, so she's about somewhere near the others. She contributed the Mermaid Lagoon, meaning I think whatever it is, it will involve swimming and near drownings, so best leave Dorothy out of that one," I said, stooping to retrieve John's hat that had been hastily discarded in the fight. "But whatever it is, we just need to be there to back her up and be her support in place of her brothers. She's always so kind, we really have no idea what sort of hurt she's hiding behind that smile. Obviously, I can relate!" I gestured to indicate Neverland as a whole and my habit of hiding behind a good round of fun and laughs.

"We will protect her," Tip said adamentally. "I won't stand for anyone hurting her."

"Same. She took care of us when we needed her most as children, and never complained about one moment of it. It's the least we can do to repay her," Lionel agreed, and reached to pat the teddy bear. "And we owe it to them too."

"For the Darlings." I raised John's hat in the air in a call to arms.

"For the Darlings," Tip and Lionel echoed before we took our leave back into the hollow tree, once more a united front.

Eighteen

Dorothy

With the boys off on their quest, and Alice looking for where Wendy disappeared to, I found myself sitting with a group of mumbling and grumbling pirates. I tucked my knees close to me, and held Toto on my lap, lest any of the brutish looking men get any wild ideas about harassing my dog.

It felt almost too quiet with all the other hoodlums gone. I smiled to myself at the notion that I had grown used to their constant company and commotion. Dare I say, I think I even missed their presence a little. Was this what it was like to have friends? I supposed it wasn't as terrible as I had once thought. A lot had changed for me in a few brief days, so it almost felt like I had lived a short lifetime in this place with these people. I supposed constantly being on the run and getting traumatized did wonders for bringing you closer to others. I rubbed my arms, feeling a little cold.

It was likely around mid morning, Alice and Wendy should be on their way back by now, if Alice had managed to locate her yet. I wasn't sure when Peter and Tip would return, or how long they intended to hunt shadows. A small shiver of fear pinged through my body, and I hoped all four were faring well in their endeavors. While I appreciated the safety of staying behind, it was a little unnerving not knowing how everyone else was doing, and I wasn't a big fan of the feeling. They were my allies, after all.

"The downside of connection is worry," I looked up to see that

Tiger Lily had approached me, along with Hook.

"Oh, I'm not worried," I blustered awkwardly. "Well, maybe just a little. For some absolutely absurd reason, I kind of wish I had gone with them."

"Which group would you have tagged along with?" She asked, and smiled pleasantly. I was relieved to see that her rigid personality seemed to be melting away into something more friendly and personable since I'd first met her. Whatever Peter had said to her yesterday had obviously quelled her animosity towards us, and it seemed she was at least trying to be sociable.

I pursed my lips in thought, drumming my fingers in my lap. "I guess I would have gone with the boys."

"Interesting," Tiger Lily acknowledged my answer with a small smirk. "Very telling."

"Of?"

"Priorities," She replied coyly. I wasn't sure she was implying something pleasant with that tone.

My mouth formed a terse line. "I just don't think looking for where Wendy wandered off to takes an army. But, after everything I've seen the past couple of days, I'd be lying if I said I wasn't nervous for Tip to be facing whatever it is he has to face." I thought of the Mombi wraith that had chased us in the maze, and my skin prickled. I was almost certain that it had been Tip's shadow seeking him out.

"But you'd choose to go fight head on with the boys. From what I've heard of you, that sounds like a bit of a change from when you first arrived here, Lass," Hook threw in, his expression discerning yet unreadable.

He seemed to me like one of the high school boys that would hang around the market with slick hair and a cigarette, oozing too-cool-for-school. Only he was rougher somehow, and his nonchalant demeanor, I could tell, was one hundred percent authentic.

"Haven't you been an ally of ours for like five minutes? How could you possibly know a thing about my history here?" I quibbled, choosing to look intently at the fur along Toto's back rather than make eye contact.

I was taken aback by his assessment of me. He was right. When I arrived, and prior to my arrival, I wouldn't have given two figs over anyone one of these people. I also wouldn't have found myself in the epicenter of a brewing magical war in a foreign dimension where I palled around with a witch, a couple warrior teens, pirates, and flying young men with pet fairies. Nor would I have thought to throw fireballs around for sport.

"I have my ways. Watching, and listening. We will just call it instinct for now." Hook joked with a wink that made me smile.

"A lot has changed in a short amount of time. It's been a type of experience that feels like its cramped years into a week," I replied as I stroked Toto's ears. Even now I was surprised by how easily this conversation was flowing overall. "But, I like to think I'm somehow becoming better for it all."

"Maybe it has been years. Time moves strangely here. When they get back, you ought to have Tip or Wendy show you some general fighting moves. From how Alice explained it, you can't hit the other witch with your magical attacks," Tiger Lily suggested, examining the tips of her long sleek hair. "I enjoy her. She has a real fighting spirit and would have made an excellent Lost Girl. Peter really messed up not bringing her to begin with. I'll bet things would have gotten less bleak had he thought it through."

"I suppose I can ask Tip," I nodded, a little bubble of anticipation forming in my stomach at the thought. I knew Wendy was skilled, but after our interactions by the lake, I knew I felt more comfortable with the odd Lost Boy. For some reason, it felt easier to just be me without apology around him.

It surprised me how even though we bickered a lot, we seemed to have formed this bond and friendship since our first encounter. I felt like each time I was around him, a little bit of his hardened exterior fell away to reveal who he had been before he'd endured whatever it was while in captivity. Alice and Peter both seemed to wear their hearts on their sleeves, and Wendy was pretty easy to read too— She clearly liked to care for and mother people, and was sort of like the group's unspoken nurturer. But something about Tip, I found intriguing. I was drawn to get to know him better. In a world of such extreme and impossible things, he felt very sturdy and real, like a grounding point. Perhaps at the end of this he'd be my best friend of the lot. I'd never had one of those before.

The idea made me smile to myself, then, I faltered as I realized at the end of this whole conflict, we'd all be separating. Assuming Alice and I made our way home, where would Wendy go with no family likely left alive? And Alice herself would probably need to go back to England.

Given that everyone except for Mombi, Tip, Lionel, and I seemed to be from there, I suddenly became concerned that that's where I'd be dropped off when we returned and *I'd* be the one having to find a way to Kansas. How was I going to manage that without a passport or money? And what would Tip do? Would he stay here with Peter, or return to where he had come from? What was the point of making friends just to lose them again?

With a sickening feeling, I realized I wandered into dangerous territory and gotten attached to the others. How had that happened so quickly? I was instantly engulfed in the weight of what I stood to lose at the end of the road here.

"Well, that's not a very pretty face," A cold cruel voice whispered in my ear. A thousand needles pricked my spine and I leapt away, Tiger Lily and Hook doing the same and drawing their weapons.

My eyes widened and my stomach pitted when I whipped around to face who I assumed would be the shadow wraith of Mombi, but what I saw was far worse. Standing in front of me, clad in deep crimson and black, was the real flesh and blood witch.

Fire erupted instinctively from my hand, and more than ever I was glad that Alice had pushed me to work more on connecting with my power. I didn't have any clue of how to have a sword around, but nobody liked fire in their face— Even if I couldn't touch her.

"Looks like I found one of the little Lost Girls sitting down on the job. Isn't it your turn to be doing something exciting?" Mombi purred, tapping her chin slowly.

"Ice and water," I managed to croak out to the braced pirates beside me. "That's what she uses."

"Oh, that's not all I can do." Her ice cold eyes glinted, and her tongue roved over her teeth like some appetite for torment had been wetted, and she couldn't wait to sink her teeth into us.

"What business do you have here, Witch?" Hook growled, his stance firm and unafraid.

"I came to see how the game was going, of course." Her gaze flitted over the rugged pirate and she bit her lip. " Well, aren't you a tall drink of water, Captain Hook."

I grimaced at her seductive tone, but relished in the fact that Hook wasn't the slightest bit thrown by her flirtation.

"Sorry, Lass. I like my women hot blooded with a bit of fire in their soul. You're a little too reptilian for my taste." His mouth spread into a grin beneath his glaring eyes. I couldn't help but snort with amusement at the pirate's brazen dig at the ice witch.

Mombi pouted for a moment, before disappearing and reappearing beside him. She grabbed his throat with onc hand, a surprising amount of strength in her grip, and trailed her fingers down his stubbled cheek and across the length of his broad chest.

"Pity. I guess I'm done with you then. I came to play with *her* anyway." Her eyes flicked from me to the captain and her lips curled into a feral grin. In one fluid motion she heaved Hook across the clearing by his throat, and used her free hand to telekinetically slam Tiger Lily into the nearest tree, stunning her. The rest of the pirates stumbled away, splitting in two to check on their fallen friends.

Mombi turned slowly around to face me and Toto, her face looking positively delighted. "Time to play, Dorothy."

My breathing escalated to pure panic, and there was zero chance I was going to be able to stop and count to ten. Mombi had clearly been holding back when I had faced her in the Ozian Woods before, and without Alice or Peter here, I felt completely powerless. So, I did what I had done since arriving here.

Clutching Toto tight to my chest, I turned and ran. Maybe I could find Alice in the woods where she had gone looking for Wendy. Or maybe I'd run into the boys on their way back from their fight. I couldn't face Mombi on my own. I needed the others, and I felt very alone and exposed without them.

I heard a euphoric laugh behind me, and knew that the witch was following after me. "I only want to play a little game. It's too late for you to try and run away, little Lost Girl. I'll find you."

I raced as fast as my legs would carry me through the peaty forest, swatting away small branches and lichen as best as I could as they whipped past me in a blur. I threw a terrified look over my shoulder and couldn't see any sign of Mombi behind me, so I ducked behind a tree and tried to catch my breath and get my bearings. I didn't even know for sure if I had gone the right way to find Alice or the others. Then the laughter sounded again— close.

"Where do you think you've gone to? Trust me, you can't hide from me," She sang out. "I can hear those sharp little breaths of yours." She appeared next to me and pinned me against the tree, causing me to drop Toto. "You're not very good at hiding, Dear."

"The rebound," I spluttered frantically, just as I had with The Wizard. "You won't use magic on me or it'll hurt you too."

"Oh, do you think you've won the game with that line?" She cooed patronizingly, and stroked my cheek with the back of her hand before striking me with it as full force. Her rings cut into my flesh, and split my lip from the impact. "First of all, I don't need to use magic to play with you, Lost Girl. Second of all, I have never been good at following the rules so much as finding ways to break them."

I spat the pooling blood out of my mouth, adrenaline being the only thing to keep me from crying at this point. "What is that supposed to mean?" I challenged, and I noticed that Toto had slipped away with his nose to the ground, obviously on the trail of something important—hopefully help.

"It means so long as I have this ring," She wriggled her finger in my face, and my dazed eyes took in the fuzzy image of a shimmering silver gem, that reminded me vaguely of my magic slippers, only more transparent and glasslike, set in an oval ring. Something was moving inside it. "And you have those shoes, you and I can use magic all we want."

"So that's what happened back in Oz," I muttered mutinously, thinking back to why nothing had happened to either of us when our magic had collided in Gugu's Forest.

"You're no fun to play tag with. How about we rough things up a little bit?" Her eyes were crazed as her wild grin sobered and she returned to petting my injured face. "I can feel your horror. Your face is so much prettier when it's afraid. Like a doll that's been good and broken."

"What the hell is wrong with you, you crazy, psycho sadist!" I shouted at her, wriggling with all my might against her overwhelming hidden physical strength. I set my hands ablaze, and felt sick satisfaction curl in my toes when the witch jumped back, her eyes blazing.

"Crazy, am I? Didn't your mother teach you not to play with fire?" She was choosing her words very carefully. "Or was it not to play with *water?*" She summoned a dripping orb into her hand and raked me over with cruel, predator eyes.

"What?" I gasped, rubbing the blood from my face now that my body was free. I didn't know why this insane woman had it out for me specifically.

"I heard that water really makes you freeze up." She raised her eyebrows knowingly at me. Her face was animated and eager. "I'd love to see you make more pretty faces, so let's play a new game of 'how long can Dorothy hold her breath before she loses her head.'"

Her hands shot forward and the water sliced through the air, bonding to my ankles and crawling up my legs. It stretched and contorted, expanding on either side of me in the makings of an orb forming from the bottom up.

After two close encounters with the lake and then the ocean, I had no tolerance left in me for any more water debacles. My body tensed beyond mobility as my eyes locked on a drop of scarlet slipping from the cut on my cheek and hitting the water, spirals of vibrant red curling in those familiar whisps. Flashes of the sinking car, and the floating bodies appeared between each blink. Pressure mounted in my skull with each agitated thought. I was shaking like a leaf. It was like my body wanted to tip into madness, but there wasn't enough left to relieve the pressure. I was an empty tea kettle left on the stove.

"Ah!" I yelped helplessly. I needed Tip. He knew how to calm me down.

"I can practically see the steam coming out of your ears. Are those beautifully violent memories making your brain melt? Let's add a little tea to that burning kettle shall we? It really makes you so much more fun to play with. Who knows? Maybe you'll be the wildcard player after all who kills everyone off for us!"

She flashed up a large teapot, and I knew immediately she had somehow brought it from Wonderland. With a silky saunter she approached the orb and poured the tea into the water, the brown twirling with the remaining crimson as it seeped into the rest of the clear liquid.

"This should teach you not to play with someone else's toys, you ghastly little wretch."

"I have no idea what you're talking about!" My voice rose into a screech of pure terror as the water curled around me, almost completing the bubble and trapping me suspended in the cold unforgiving liquid tomb of insanity.

"I don't like to share my playthings, so remember to keep your hands off. If you live for another round." Her words muffled as the water covered my ears and swallowed up my head. I sucked in a final breath, and tried to center my thoughts, but I could see the tea swirling in front of my eyes and everything in me felt the insatiable urge to open my mouth and drink it.

My heart hammered and my vision began to stretch and contract in the usual way before I succumbed to the insani-tea. Was I absorbing it through my skin? I thought my body didn't want to tip into the madness a moment earlier.

My tongue tingled and a moment too late, I realized I had opened my mouth, allowing the intoxicating liquid entrance to replenish the crazy as the orb of water expanded around me.

My fear was spiraling and I could feel my fingers twitching with violent intent. I was a cornered animal, ready to rip and tear my way to safety. I blinked and saw dark forms of lifely bodies appear in front of me, faceless and wispy.

I screamed, rattling the water and I jumped back, but the bodies shuttered and gripped me from behind.

Why did you leave us behind, Dorothy? Who was that voice in my head? I didn't recognize it, and yet it felt familiar.

You left us behind and now your punishment is to never have a moment's fun or another living connection again. I jolted with physical pain tearing through my body as I realized I was hearing my mother's voice.

I was fading in and out of delirium, trapped jumping between clarity and insanity trying to sink its claws in. In one of the split seconds of reprieve, I heard muffled voices shouting outside the bubble, followed by frantic barking.

Toto found help.

"What did you do to her?" I could make out Tip's voice, low and full of malice, as he spoke to the witch, before it twisted itself up into sounds of nonsense.

"Hello, my lovely Tippetarius. Oh, I've missed you," Mombi chuckled, the sound splintering into broken glass hitting the ground. "My, you've got such a dark look on your face. Mmmm, how tempting you are. Maybe I'll try to sway you yet, just like old times. If you'd just *tip* far enough…"

"Not a chance, *Witch.*" The sounds of the words thundered and boomed against my skull.

"We'll have to see about that later, won't we?" She purred. "I've been sitting at the board just *waiting* for you to take your turn, and here you all have been hiding away. How very unsportsmanlike." Her playful tone hardened in an instant. "You need to make your move before the clock runs out, or you forfeit the game The Wizard so graciously agreed to play with you all."

"Gracious, my ass," Tip scoffed and lifted his knife, pointing it at Mombi.

She clicked her tongue, and brought her finger to her lip coyly, then widened her eyes. "You don't want to hurt me, do you, Tippetarious?"

"Bloody hell, not that again," Peter spat. "Yes, he does. So do I, in fact."

"Your new little favorite witch seems to be struggling. I do hope you let her know you're mine, and have been mine, so I will have you again," She smiled at Tip and pointed past him to where I was watching their flickering images through the rippling water. I hadn't even realized I was banging on the inside with my fists. "Should I end her suffering?"

"You won't go near her," Tip shouted, his face twisted in anger. I blinked and all his features melted from his face, and he was reduced to a puddle. My sanity was at its breaking point and I slipped fully into the madness.

"Too late," She laughed in such a sensual way. "She's making all those pretty faces I asked for over our tea party."

"You gave her more tea?" Peter gasped. "Uh oh."

Everything faded away into hues of black and red, and I was freefalling through it. I opened my mouth and screamed at the top of my lungs, something sloshed and shattered around me, and a thousand tiny scorching bubbles raced past me before I sank into the shadows, dark wisps curling against me. Everything was freezing as a current of wind coiled around.

This is where you left us. I heard my father's scathing words, and saw the floating body reappear in front of me. *How dare you think you could make friends after what you did. You aren't allowed to care or be cared for ever again. You aren't deserving of fun or magic. You must stay contained and collected. All alone forever.*

"No!" I screeched, and flames erupted from my entire body, blasting the shadows away for a few heartbeats before they hissed and doubled down, pinning me to the ground with long claws. They rippled like they were each made of up large black raindrops. All around me the red and black atmosphere morphed to form a cone with me at the narrow base, all the drops of darkness beading towards me. Each one struck me, and I felt some painful emotion rip into my chest.

Splash, guilt. Splosh, grief. Splish, loneliness. Splash, longing. Splosh, fear. Splish, fury. One pelted me right after another. I felt sodden and heavy under the weight of it all, dripping darkness. I didn't deserve to be alive. I didn't deserve happiness. I didn't deserve friendship and love. I shouldn't have allowed myself to feel close to the others earlier.

I screamed and screamed, till my throat was raw, throwing my hands over my face. Flames burst from my feet and crawled up my body, and I could feel them burning at my clothing but not my skin.

"Stop taking things from me!" I bellowed at the flames, and aimed them haphazardly away from me. "I don't want your fire and dewdrops!"

"Oh, Miss Dorothy, why did you light our village on fire and leave us to die?" Boq's voice wailed at me from thc top of the barrage of liquid emotion.

"I was trying to protect you! I ran away so the flames would swallow me instead of you but the lily pads crumbled under the bullfrogs and I fell into the cactus pond," I babbled, still spewing fire. A biting wind started blustering around me, tugging at my hair and body.

The cone collapsed in a gust around me into a flat plane, and lit the ground red from beneath, a current of blood sloshing at my silver feet.

"Run run, river of dread, swallow me up till I'm cold and dead." The song tumbled out my mouth and I clasped my flaming hands around my face. Whose blood was running around me? I didn't want to hurt anyone else. "No! I don't want the nonsense. I want the sense back. I need light. Light bright, light bright."

Trees of obsidian sprung up all around me, and shadowy wraiths started snaking around in all directions. Some vanished mysteriously as they prowled forward, and in their place were tiny specs of light.

"Light bright," I whimpered, and stumbled over to one of the specs to snatch it into my hand.

You feel guilty about that?"

"A bit,"

"Don't."

Tip? His words emanated from the glow in my hand. I whirled around, and chased after another glimmer in the dark, tearing one of the wraiths in two with my bare hands on the way

"I think we qualify as friends, at least on my end.....tell me your tale of woe then, friend."

Could I really connect with someone again? Was I allowed after everything I had done? I caught another light in search of an answer.

"You just need more faith and trust."

"Not that again..."

"In yourself. You're the only one in control of yourself. So, have a little faith, and trust yourself to stay in control. How else can a self proclaimed realist adjust to an unrealistic world? Take control of yourself because it's all you can control when things are uncontrollable. The splendor comes afterwards.

A shadow tried to latch onto me, but I grabbed it by the face and set my hands ablaze. It shrieked and withered beneath my grasp. I clutched the balls of light to my chest and released spears of fire, wrapped in tiny tornadoes to strike every remaining wraith in the dark forest.

My world was spinning, and it had started raining black tears and scarlet raindrops. I breathed heavily, and felt like I was holding something tangible in my hands where the light was still aglow.

Have faith in myself. I don't need to run, I can weather this fight. I can take control of myself. I can turn this evil madness into something fantastic. I can't save who I left, but I can set them free out of the shadows and into the splendor. I looked to the sky, letting the storm of emotions wash over me and bathe me in the blood of my memories.

"One," I wheezed, taking it all in. "Two. Three...."

"Four, five, six." I heard Peter and Tip's voices clearly, and dared to open my eyes. The bleak thundering sky flickered, the red and black rain being replaced with drops of silver and white, coating the darkness in light. I slowly craned my neck from staring above to looking in front of me.

Tip and Peter were both holding onto my hands, while Toto pressed his body against my leg. "We've got you Dorothy. You're okay."

The two floating bodies appeared behind the boys, causing me to tense for a moment. But then the shadows evaporated, leaving the clear—albeit intangible— images of my parents smiling at me. I could see their faces. I remembered them, and they weren't angry with me. They were looking at me with love and hope for my future. I wanted something marvelous for them, to send them off, so I willed it with all my might, daring to imagine the most spectacular farewell. Sparkles of starlight swirled around them and they lifted into the clear blue sky, no longer bound to the bottom of the lake.

I squeezed Peter and Tip's hands, reveling in the connection I felt in their touch, and the genuine concern on their faces. They cared about me. I cared about them. I was allowed to care. I was allowed to dream and not fear the unfotrobable waves lifc threw at me for risk of losing anything else precious to me. It would be an uphill battle to undo all the destructive habits that had formed, but with a sigh of relief, I gave myself permission to start that battle. I could be happy. I was allowed to *feel.*

"Seven, eight, nine, ten," We finished together. My eyes filled with tears and I threw my arms around both boys and hugged them tightly, rubbing Toto's head with a free hand.

"You defeated your shadow, Dorothy," Lionel spoke quietly from the side of our hug, smiling reassuringly. "It was a nasty one too. Plus a whole slew of other smaller ones. We cut down some of them but you did this crazy fire move and took them all out."

"Good job, Dorothy." Peter nodded approvingly. "You even seem to have discovered some essence of wind or air magic. That will be fun to figure out later.

"How'd you do it?" Tip asked, his eyes searching as they stared into mine. "How'd you defeat your beast?"

I felt very sleepy, and everything was growing fuzzy. "I heard you," I mumbled sleepily, sagging to the ground in desperate need of a nap. "I heard you calling me your friend. You were the tiny spec of light telling me to have faith in myself."

Nineteen

Wendy

I wandered and weaved through the Neverland trees, touching each one I passed, to remind me that they were real. I had so often dreamed of returning here during my time in The Wizard's captivity, it was always a crushing blow to wake up and realize it was all a dream.

The boys were likely well on their way to the hideout in the Hollow Woods by now, and though part of me wanted to be with them, and to see my old home again, the other part of me feared seeing the ghost of what it had once been.

I wondered if any of them had noticed I was gone. Perhaps I ought to head to the Mermaid Lagoon and look for my own Shadow Beast. If I somehow bested it all on my own, it would help in the grand scheme and maybe remind them I belonged here with the rest of them.

"There you are," Alice's voice called to me, snapping me from my rolling inner thoughts.

"Yes? Did you need help with something?" I asked hopefully.

"Nope. Just came to tell you you'd better come back to our little base. The last thing we need right now is for you to wander off and get lost." She shook her head, and I felt a jolt course through me.

"I'm the one who's lived here. You should be the one worried about getting lost, not me." The biting words slipped out my lips before I could stop them, and my stomach dropped.

Alice raised an eyebrow, her cool blue eyes looking me over

slowly. "Why are you out here? Don't you see how unhelpful your sulking is?" Her compass was spinning, and I could see her fingers turning white where she was gripping her arms folded over her chest.

Her words might as well have been a steel blade for how deep it cut me. *Unhelpful*? *Sulking*?

"I'm sorry. I didn't realize there was a monopoly on taking a moment to one's self. I'll be sure and think about my missing brothers and estranged friends at a more convenient time next time." I smiled, and blinked slowly, oozing sweetness and guilt.

"Your friends are hardly estranged," Alice snorted, rolling her eyes.

"How would you know? You weren't here to know how close and happy we all were back then. That was before your time." I couldn't stop the passive aggressive words from spewing out like venom, and my body trembled against every syllable. Everything had been fine before she got here and would still be fine now if she hadn't come. My bitterness stung my tongue like bile.

"Funny. I wish I could say the same to you, you know. But, actually, I think having you back really reminded Peter of what he had been missing and showed him what he really wanted." She dipped her chin and smiled at me viciously. "That's how he was able to realize he loves me. Not some child's crush, but real, true, grown up, *love*. I think I should really be thanking you for helping him connect those dots."

Each word was a twisting dagger in my stomach and it took everything in me to remain composed, though I could feel heat rising in my cheeks, and was certain my face was turning scarlet with frustration, betraying my true feelings. That wasn't the kind of help I was offering.

"I don't think he realized what he was missing," I said quietly, looking down at my feet, unable to both look the witch in the eye and get the words out.

"Oh?"

"I haven't been back long enough to really show him what he's missed." Why should Alice get to lay claim over Peter's heart? If I reminded him just how helpful and adventurous I was, dealing with the temperamental hot head wouldn't be nearly as appealing, I was certain.

But, the feeling of possessive power faltered, and was swallowed up by regret at my meanspirited jabs. I needed to resist the urge to try to stoop to the Wicked traits that separated me from Alice.

"Sorry, I'm just feeling a bit overwhelmed by how much everything has changed." I dared sneak a peek at Alice, and saw her jaw set under pursed lips while she clutched at her compass.

She was going to smite me, I was sure of it. And nobody would notice or care.

"If you had this necklace, I'm sure you'd just make sunshine and rainbows at every turn. Your typical obnoxious kindness both nauseates and impresses me," Alice commented, though not unkindly, after a lengthy pause then shivered. "Does it feel colder here to you?"

I nodded slowly, realizing that she was actually giving me a pass for my harsh words. Perhaps she understood more of how I was feeling than I knew. Or, at the very least, could understand and empathize with my loss. I didn't actually know too terribly much about her on a personal level. I burned with shame and regret, and knew I needed to be kinder.

"It is a bit chilly," I agreed, and rubbed my hands up and down my arms for a little warmth.

Alice's eyes darkened. "I'm not sure I like the feel of this. Something's not right."

I felt the hairs on the back of my neck rise on end, and I scanned around our immediate surroundings. I felt it too. There was something not right at all. Was it a Shadow Beast?

"My, how far you've flown from your cage, Lost Girl." I heard Mombi's voice hiss in my ear and stiffened. I'd have thought I'd imagined it, but then I felt an ice cold finger run the length of my arm up to my shoulder. "I came here to take a look around and play with Dorothy, but I was lucky enough to bump into you. Very lucky indeed."

"You!" Alice shouted, her face twisting in anger. Quick as lightning she formed a blade between her hands and aimed it next to me.

Mombi laughed and grabbed my cheeks to forcibly turn my head to look into her frigid blue eyes. She stared cruelly at me, and her mouth curled into a twisted, insane smile. "Run, run little Lost Girls. Run on home," She cooed then turned to Alice, flashing away from my side to appear behind her, just as Alice charged forward with her blade forward.

"Ugh! I will rip you apart limb from limb for all that you've done!" She screeched, her voice pitched in absolute irate rage at the ice witch.

"Tsk, tsk. Better mind those Wicked thoughts, Little Lost Witch." Mombi's words were saturated in a pouty patronizing tone, like she was chiding a small child. "Looks like you haven't taken very good care of one of my favorite little toys. It's liable to break at any moment. Reckless girl. I could repair it, you know. And you could come to your senses, and leave the boy behind without a second thought. Mmm, that idea is so tempting, it's positively *Wicked*."

"I'd rather die!" Alice bellowed, swinging her arm around to arc the sword behind her. She had the basic idea, but she needed to refine her movements if she ever expected to strike a moving target.

"Well, that works too. Either way, we win," Mombi laughed, disappearing and reappearing next to me. "And you will always be lost won't you? That dark little dungeon was the only thing shielding you from the reality where you are obsolete and unwanted. It was the last wall of hope you had. Now, that illusion is shattered, and you'll always be lost and unwanted. A waste of space within this group you've burdened with your very existence."

I felt myself shrink under her words. How had she so poignantly struck the nerve of my deepest, most despairing thoughts. My chest instantly felt hollow and hopeless, knowing there was some twisted truth in what she was saying. If I had lived the rest of my days in that dungeon, I would have died holding on to my dream of my happily ever after. Now that I was out and knew the truth, that dream was truly shattered beyond repair in my hands.

"How dare you?" Alice's voice was cold and low. Her eyes were blazing with fury, and I saw her compass spinning with more and more velocity. "You vile, loathsome creature. How dare you say that to her. To try to twist her feelings into believing her captivity was for her own good. To tell someone their existence is inconsequential and a waste like it's nothing. Making her think that being alone is better than being with those who cherish her."

"Ha. You don't cherish her!" Mombi cackled. "You'd be more than happy to see her locked away and not be your problem anymore. You're the Wickedest Wicked Witch, Alice! You don't get a name like that making friends. You get it by killing and destroying. One of these days very soon, I'm sure you'll realize that that moral compass has just shown you who you truly are. Walking chaos, calamity, and destruction begging to unleash. And when you do, that little spec will be your first target for daring to love what's yours. Even if the boy becomes just a toy in the end before we bring him to his knees and erase his existence."

I balked at this witch. She not only seemed to have some insight into my insecurities, but also was able to hit Alice's struggle with her compass on the head too. Either we were terribly readable foes, or she was unnaturally insightful to pain and suffering. She was striking our weak spots, looking for vital points to run through.

Clearly she had said the wrong thing to Alice, because she summoned lightning to her hands and aimed it for Mombi. She dodged Alice's attack with another cruel laugh echoing between the fibers of time and space, before reappearing a little ways away from us. Alice's eyes glittered with hatred, and she looked fiercely at me, lifting her chin high, the very picture of pride and defiance.

"The next time she dares speak to you like that, Wendy, you draw your weapon and fight. Fight to prove her wrong—to prove it to yourself. Fight to protect the existence of not only those around you, but to protect yourself. Don't let anyone tell you are a waste."

I stared wide-eyed at Alice. The Wickedest Wicked Witch was standing here, despite our quarrel, infuriated on my behalf, on Peter's, and on her own. She was angry that her home and Wonderland was taken, angry that she had been used, angry that she and her friends were in this very position at all. She was fighting to protect us all, as well as herself. Her convictions were so strong, and innately connected to who she was. Her loyalty was an unbreakable pillar in the raging storm of doubt we all were floundering in. I was awed by her strength. It often came off surly, impatient, and impulsive, but she was driven by fear— both the abundance and absence of it. All of it centered on the fear of what she had to lose, and what she valiantly protected.

She stood there, unwavering, her eyes two roaring blue flames, jaws set, fists clenched. She was a force of nature, and I could see now why Peter had grown to admire her so much. I wondered who she had been before the Wickedness had plagued her, and could only imagine how she would wield her powers for Good. I knew then that whatever obstacle was put in front of her, she'd burn, claw, punch, shred, and obliterate it.

Despite the faint shudder of envy at this power of hers in the face of my weakness, I felt her presence anchor me, in my driftless sea of dark loneliness. I'd wondered how Peter could have stayed beside her when she's done so many terrible things, some of which he'd witnessed with his own eyes. But, I finally understood. She wasn't really Wicked. She was Alice. And Alice was Good. No broken compass could change that roaring light within her and that's how she'd survived this long here.

"Right," I said, exhaling deeply. I drew my sword and stepped up beside my ally, pointing it alongside hers at Mombi. "We are never truly lost. Neverland will always be where the Lost Ones go home. It is a sanctuary you will never be able to destroy. You can't even touch it." My words were clipped, as both pride and anger twirled in that hollow space in my chest. Alice must have lent me her strength because I didn't even tremble this time.

"Oh, is that so? Your other lost friends might have something else to say from where I left them. Unless Dorothy has managed to kill them all already. I always loved a good game of tag. The speed, the chase, the fear in the hunted." Mombi quirked an eyebrow, and frowned, her eyes latching onto a cast shadow of a tree.

Alice and I exchanged a concerned glance, but said nothing. I could feel adrenaline building in my muscles, ready to unleash.

A shadow creature slowly morphed and gloved out of the darkness, red eyes glimmering as it licked its lips at the ice witch. It stalked past Alice and I, clearly drawn towards a specific prey.

Mombi swore under her breath, and blasted the thing with water, destroying it in one hit. But, more had climbed out of the shadows of the forest and were clambering towards her.

I realized they must be drawn to large amounts of negative thoughts and energy, making the Wicked witch with no semblance of light in her body, a beacon to consume.

"And," Mombi hissed, disappearing and reappearing behind us. "Tag you're it." She placed her hands on our backs and shoved towards the wraiths.

"Ah!" Alice's squeal of surprise turned into a cry of anger as she tumbled against the outstretched claws of a beast.

Quick as my racing heartbeat, I counted the remaining six dark entities and made swift work of dispelling them against my sword.

"Are you alright?" I asked, puffing from the exertion as I kneeled to inspect the new wounds on Alice's thigh. Crimson was showing through where the claws had torn at her trousers.

"I'm fine," she huffed, her compass slowing as she took a deep breath. "We need to see what she meant about Dorothy."

"You don't really think she'd *kill* our friends do you?"

"If she lost her head, I have no idea what she's capable of. We just have to hope that Mombi was bluffing." Alice grimaced and staggered to her feet.

"Here," I offered my shoulder, and after a moment of static hesitation, Alice nodded and leaned against me, limping along as fast as she could manage.

"Thanks," She gritted her teeth and I knew her injury was more painful than she was wanting to let on. "I want to say something to you."

"Yes?" I bleated, awaiting the impending lashing I'd likely receive for something I'd done.

"I see you drowning, you know. I know that's why you wandered off and isolated yourself. It's a terrible feeling, and I don't wish it on anyone. What that witch said, you pay no mind to it. You determine your own worth, no one else."

"Oh," I squeaked, completely taken aback. I opened my mouth to reply but found myself at a loss for words. She was fierce, beautiful, valiant, *and* she was compassionate? I never stood a chance against her.

"Alice! What's wrong?" Peter waved to us from a distance and I felt the color drain from my face when I saw the fresh blood running down his chest. Beyond him, a shirtless Tip was carrying an unconscious Dorothy, and I could see her face was beaten too, bits of her clothing charred. Had she fought Peter? Lionel brought up the rear and my heart jumped when I saw what he had in his hands. My brother's hat.

I was torn on who to run to first; Lionel with John's hat, or Peter with his wounds to tend. Peter made the choice for me by lifting in the air and zipping over to take a look at Alice's leg.

"I know Wendy didn't do that, so what happened?"

"We were graced with the presence of that vile witch. She came here to taunt us. Shadows tried to glom onto her though, and she shoved me into one. Bloody coward."

"You too? She was terrorizing Dorothy and had her stuck in a bubble of tea water."

"She had *more* tea? Oh, good grief. Did you have to knock her out again?"

"No, actually. She had a real breakthrough and defeated her Shadow Beast that must have manifested back in the corn maze or something."

"Peter," I physically stepped between him and Alice, before I knew what my body was doing, my eyes having not left his chest for the entire exchange. "Can you please remove your shirt?"

"Uh, what?" Peter looked startled and flitted back a step.

I gestured to his bloodied torso. "You're injured. I need to see the damage to get it cleaned up."

"Oh," he seemed to sag with relief. "Right. Love, would you care to make me some bandages?" He looked around me at Alice, who nodded and flashed up some material, plunking it into my hands. "You can take care of Alice first."

"Don't mind me." Alice waved me toward Peter. "Hey, why is Tip shirtless? He doesn't look injured." She jerked her head where he and Lionel were getting Dorothy situated as best they could on the ground.

"That's… a long story." Peter shrugged and peeled the shirt off his back, every muscle rippling in the process.

"How'd the hunt go?" I piped up again, a bit sharply.

"Eh, another long story. But, long story short— not great. Tip wasn't properly equipped to take on his beast so I got a little impaled and here we are. We will try another time."

"Oh, poor Tip. I hope he doesn't beat himself up over it." I clicked my tongue sympathetically as I worked on wrapping Peter's chest. "There you go. Good as new."

"Thank you, Wendy. You're a lifesaver! Oh, you ought to go see Lionel though. He has some things we thought you might want. I'll get Alice's leg wrapped up."

"Sure," I reluctantly shuffled away, unsure of how to feel about John's hat resurfacing.

"Hey, Wendy," Lionel greeted me with a small dip of his head. Seeing my eyes already locked on the hat, he handed it to me without pause, then reached for his belt to retrieve dear Michael's teddy bear. The fabric was dingy and the thread of one of the button eyes was coming loose. "We found these in the hideout and thought you might find a little closure in having them."

I accepted the items and stared at them, somehow overflowing with emotion, while also feeling starkly numb. "Closure?"

"Yeah, you know. So you can make peace with what happened—"

"What happened, Lionel? Were you there? Did you see?" My words were razor sharp. My eyes darted to Peter wrapping Alice's leg, to the bandage the wounds of the Shadow Beasts, and back to the items in my hands. First Peter had been my hope. Then Neverland. Both had fallen short. A burning ferocious force within me refused to let the hope of my brothers be taken from me. I needed that hope to keep going. I was fuming and the insinuation that that was to be taken from me too, made my lip start to curl in the beginnings of some sort of primal snarl.

Lionel looked alarmed and waved his hands in dismay. "No, no. Of course not. I just thought that the likelihood—"

I cut him off again, sobering. "Thank you. I'm sure both John and Michael will be thrilled to have these back when we find them." I nodded curtly and spun on my heel to stalk off to an isolated portion of our makeshift camp, my fingers gripping the teddy bear and hat brim so hard, they yielded beneath my touch.

It was an odd turn of events that had been entirely unexpected. I was relieved that everything had ended well enough following our startling encounters, but, despite Alice's good advice and strong conviction, Mombi's earlier words yawned open in my chest once more as I clutched the hand of Michael's bear to my chest.

If Mombi wasn't here, who did I point my weapon at for how I felt? Alice? Peter? Lionel, Tip, or Dorothy? No one was taking anything else from me. I couldn't survive it.

And I feared more than ever I had nothing left to give.

Twenty

Dorothy

"Alright, I'm ready. Teach me your most barbaric ways," I faced Tip, feeling particularly cranky about the whole tea debacle, and slowly curled my hands in fists. "What do you got?"

Tip raised an eyebrow at my surly eagerness, and folded his arms. "Barbaric?"

"Yeah! I want to kick some serious butt, here. I'm a complete novice so you have your work cut out for you." I nodded intently. "Go ahead, I'm ready."

After my nap, we had reconvened to go over any pertinent information that everyone had found out. Alice had reported also running into Mombi and that the extra, less powerful, shadows seemed drawn to strong negativity and Wicked thoughts. Tip, Lionel and Peter, had returned less than victorious about their endeavor to defeat Tip's shadow, and all three boys seemed rather tight-lipped about the ordeal, other than letting us know the wraiths could manifest memories as well— which made sense given my own experience with my parents— and Peter had some shadow-witch on the inside that could help restrain a beast in dire situations.

Wendy had remained mostly silent during our little meeting, and the pirates were still licking their collateral injuries, while the Wonderlandians and Ozians puttered about with relative ambivalence. Only Jack and Saw-Horse expressed more direct interest in our immediate human grouping, and most of that was on Tip's behalf, I was sure. Still, they had been there with him when I woke up from my impromptu slumber and made sure I had anything I needed, making me feel more endeared to them all.

By the time everything was said and done, the sun was setting on another day. Lionel had opted for a little fun and games with the Imagineds, and Toto had wandered along, tail wagging, to bark along at the brewing shenanigans. Wendy had wandered off, though still a stone's throw away this time, saying she was going to ponder what she might face with her Shadow Beast, and Peter and Alice had slipped away for Alice to show Peter some lessons in magic away from where others may inadvertently pay the consequences of being unwitting bystanders. That left me and Tip free to do as we chose. Feeling fired up, I had impulsively asked him to give me a sparring lesson, lest Mombi get a physical advantage on me again, I'd be better prepared and not get the snot beat out of me. Plus, I didn't want to be stuck taking her at her word about how the rebound didn't affect us like it should. For all I knew, she was luring me into a trap.

A combination of indignation and embarrassment for my behavior, along with my new burgeoning friendships, and relationship with splendor over logic, made me eager to fight to protect it all. I'd marched over to Tip and prompted him to start our lesson, setting up several torches around a new area, out of view from prying eyes. Odds were, this lesson was going to not be a pretty one, and I'd rather not have the others mocking me. Tip's inevitable mocking would be plenty as is.

"Alright there, Feisty Pants," Tip laughed, pulling me back to the moment. "Let's see what you're working with first. I saw you being plenty 'barbaric ripping wraiths apart with your bare hands, but we can't count on another spirited reaction like that. Why don't we start with basic fist fighting? Take a swing at me."

"What?" I squawked. "I don't want to hit you!"

"Isn't that the whole point of this?" Tip brows jumped up and down. "Come on, then. We both know you've wanted to land a good hit on me since we met," He goaded.

"I don't want to actually hurt you."

"You won't. Trust me," He scoffed, spreading his arms out wide.

"I could too!"

"You'd have to actually hit me, first. And that's not gonna happen." The fire made shadows dance across his face, but there was a competitive and almost playful gleam in his eyes. He really did seem to be coming back into his own skin while back here in Neverland, regardless of whatever demon he hadn't been able to face earlier in the day. He was right, too. When we'd first met and he'd been so uptight and surly, I had most definitely wanted to punch his stupid smug face.

"Are you challenging me, Tippetarius?" I narrowed my eyes and raised my fists.

"Not much of a challenge since you won't be able to do a thing about it, but sure. A challenge." His nose crinkled patronizingly, instantly making my blood boil with the desire to prove him wrong.

"Gah!" I lunged forward, swinging a fist, but Tip easily leaned out the way. His foot slipped around mine, pulling me off balance and then he gave me a light push, sending me toppling to the ground.

"Sloppy work, Miss Gale," He chided. "You have to not leave yourself open— I could have easily struck you instead of pushing you. Also, you need to learn to shift your balance in your legs. You're too rigid."

"Couldn't you have told me that instead of bruising my tailbone?" I grumbled, pushing back up to my feet, and dusting myself off.

"Experience is the best road to muscle memory, so your body instinctively knows what to do."

"I made a big mistake trusting you for this, didn't I?"

"Probably. Why'd you make that terrible decision in the first place, again?"

"You said we were friends and said I could always trust you to have my back when I woke up and thanked you for your help with the insani-tea!" I snapped, though my words had an air of laughter behind their indignance. "You said we'd all bonded or something."

"Did I say that?" He feigned memory loss and tapped his temple. "Bonds usually make it easier to push buttons too. Did I not include that part?"

"If you don't mock me a little less, I'm replacing you with Wendy," I threatened halfheartedly, and to my surprise Tip raised his hands in defeat.

"Okay, okay. I'll be good. You just make it so easy to tick you off."

"So?"

"So, it's funny," He chuckled, narrowing his eyes at me as I scowled at him. "You're funny when you're mad, and I can often use a laugh. It's a better thing to focus on."

"Rude!" I gasped.

"So you've said, before. What are you gonna do about it?" Tip taunted, grinning from ear to ear, clearly enjoying himself, and I guess he really could use the reprieve of letting loose a little. "It's just you and me here, so get comfortable, think it out, and remember your fancy little shoes won't help you now, since we aren't doing the fire thing."

"You are really annoying," I growled and tried to imagine myself as less rigid in my stance.

"Good!"

I lunged forward again, taking a swing with my other arm in an attempt to throw him off, but he dodged, and grabbed me by wrist, spinning me around so I thumped against his chest, with my arm pinned to my back. His free arm mimed holding a knife to my throat. I was immobilized in an instant.

He lowered his head to my ear. "Oh, come on. I saw you frolicking with Toto earlier. You've got fancier footwork than that." He released me emphatically and stepped backwards, causing me to stumble forwards.

I whipped around. "Ugh! You're infuriating."

"I can't take you seriously," He sniffed, folding his arms with a shrug.

"Why not?" I demanded.

"You are too cutesy when you're angry. It's like picking a fight with a bunny or something, and is hardly intimidating," He smirked, only causing my indignation to grow.

"What the hell does that mean? I'm note cute when I'm mad! I'm just mad," I cried in disbelief.

"Mmm. If you say so, but I beg to differ."

"I want to punch that stupid smug look off your face!" I shouted, tying my loose hair back into a knotted bun to aid visibility.

"There it is!" Tip cheered, clapping slowly. "I'm right here, Twinkle Toes. Come get me." He brought his hands to his chest and beckoned me closer with his fingers.

"Grrr." I looked crossly down at my feet and tried to think of something— anything to get the upper hand. Perhaps there was some clever way to fight with the magical advantage without striking him. Despite how irate he was making me, I *was* having fun, and it would be a terrible shame to burn him to a crisp on accident.

"I'm waiting!" Tip taunted, spreading his arms wide. "Get your game face on!"

I briefly recalled, the night before, Peter regaling me with an unsolicited account of Alice taking down the Red Queen, and remembered that both of those witches had used their magic on surrounding objects as a loophole to strike or restrain the other. I didn't have a super clear idea of how to go about doing that, and I didnt know any fancy telekinesis, but an idea did come to mind as an alternative. I even thought up a spiffy thing to say along with it.

"You know, Tip?" I drawled, summoning fire into my hands, and tossing the flames up and back and forth with a nimbleness that made me squeal victoriously internally. My small moments of practice were paying off and making me look good. "You seem to want to play with fire here."

Tip raised his brows, and I saw an intrigued spark in his eyes as he stared me down. "Breaking the rules, *Wicked* witch? No magic hits, cheater," He chided.

"Well, when someone such as yourself plays with fire…" I kept on my planned speech for maximum effect, then faked to throw one of the orbs of fire at him, catching him off balance as he went to dodge.

Next, I slammed my other hand into the ground, imagining it cracking and quaking. Neverland heeded my call to imagination,—

something I never would have thought to rely on even this morning had it not been for my last craze— and the land obeyed, succeeding in knocking Tip to the ground. Quick as a flash I rushed and stood over him, stepping lightly on his arms with the tips of my shoes to pin them down.

"You might get burned!" I finished smugly. "How's this for a game face?"

"What a clever little speech. I bet you're feeling pretty pleased with yourself for that trickery." Tip clicked his tongue and his jaw set beneath a bemused smile. "And here I thought you were above such mental tactics. Silly me."

"I am pretty pleased, actually," I laughed.

"But…" He started, the competitive glint returning to his expression.

"But?" I repeated warily, stiffening. This wasn't going to bode well for my tailbone.

Next thing I knew, Tip used his superior strength in his arms to yank them from under my feet, repositioning them to push hard on the front of my ankles. With a squawk of surprise, I lost my balance and body slammed into him on the ground.

"Oof!" I puffed, the air fleeing my lungs from the impact. But, Tip was ready and had braced himself, wrapping his arms around and flipping us like a crocodile in a death roll. Our positions now reversed, he pinned my legs by straddling over top of me, and restrained my arms to either side of my head with his hands.

We were both panting for the moment of exertion and surprise, eyes boring into each other with adrenaline pulsing. Then, he snickered and a full roaring laugh erupted from his lips as he stared down at my glowering expression. Watching him laugh like that felt contagious and before I knew it, I was laughing too, thrashing about wildly.

"What the hell was that?" I demanded, my eyes watering. Tip released his hold on my arms and I shoved against his chest with one arm as I propped myself up on my other elbow. My hair dislodged my makeshift bun and fell free over my shoulders, wild curls spindling around my face. "Get off me, you big oaf. You're *heavy!*"

Tip slipped off of me and crouched, holding out a hand to help me to a seated position, still chuckling lightly. "Oh, man. That was fun. Thanks for that."

"High praise from the sourpuss!" I cheered sarcastically, still smiling. Then I added, playful and begrudgingly, "I had fun too. I've never wrestled anyone before. Well, except this goat once, and I lost then too."

"More of a lover than a fighter, I take it?"

"I guess so. He was being a pill, but I couldn't bring myself to be too stern with the guy when he looked at me with his big sad eyes. He just wanted to go do goat things."

"Go do goat things? What an amusing sentiment. Perhaps I should aspire to do goat things," He mused, his words broken up by short chuckles at what he was saying. He tilted his head and squinted at me. "I'm surprised you let that girl in Kansas push you into a bush with those raw talent moves you had up your sleeve. Getting me on my back is not an easy feat. I'm a pretty decent brawler."

"Well, next time I guess I can wave a torch around like a madwoman and get a similar effect to throw her off guard," I mused with an amused frown, picturing throwing a fireball at Felicity Arroyo's pinched face. "Then I'll tackle her and use that pink taffeta to tie her up by her toes!"

"Very creative. And when they haul you away to the asylum for doing all that?" Tip queried, gesturing for me to continue.

"Well, then that's when you come in and use the big guns on them!" I declared, miming some rapid punches and rolled my eyes. "Obviously." I fidgeted with the hem of my top a little, trying to seem nonchalant. "Have you, um, decided what you're doing when this is all over?" I broached the question that had been lingering in my mind since this morning about what everyone was planning to do after the big fight.

He tilted his head, eyes still bright from the joking. "What do you mean?"

"Um, when this whole war-of-the-directions business is straightened out," I gestured vaguely around us. "I was thinking about it earlier today. Do you think you're going to stay here in this world or go back to where you're from?"

"Oh," Tip's expression sobered, "I hadn't really thought about that. There isn't really anything there for me anymore. I was an orphan, and it's been nearly a century, I think, since I was there, based on when you are from— as you were so fond of pointing out before."

"Oh, right. That would make sense." I tried to ignore the trickle of disappointment pooling in my chest. Had we been in the real world, our timelines wouldn't have ever crossed and we would have never met. That notion felt very strange to me now.

"But, I don't know," He answered, catching my eye with a searching glint, like I was holding some hidden answer he was trying to see.

"You don't?" I perked up, then kicked myself for sounding hopeful. What was wrong with me? Leave me alone for a morning and fire me up with an emotional epiphany, and my sentimentality went haywire apparently. Though admittedly, it had been Tip's words that had led me out of the darkness, and his and Peter's solidarity that broke its hold over me. That shouldn't be something I scoffed at.

"Uh, yeah. I'm not sure yet. I'll have to think about it and see how things stand when we get to that point."

"Very pragmatic of you." I smiled and nodded, feeling very small and shy all of the sudden.

Why was I feeling so strange? I knew I wasn't really familiar with interacting with friends, but friendship with the others didn't feel like this. I thought of Peter and Alice and gulped. I wasn't catching the love-twins' infatuation bug, was I? I had barely decided it was okay to have friends. I wasn't ready for more than that! Not for this sourpuss. Maybe I needed another nap. I squinted at him and he smiled self-consciously. Well, maybe he wasn't *so* sour anymore…

"You okay?" Tip poked me in the arm and I about jumped out of my skin. "Sorry."

"No! I mean, I'm fine. Just got lost on a train of thought trying to figure something out."

"Anything I can help with?" He offered casually, throwing his arm over his knee as he resigned to sitting on the ground across from me, torches still dancing ablaze around us.

I smiled. "Not right now. Probably never, really. But maybe someday. I guess we'll see. No matter! Forget it." I grimaced at my own awkwardness. I didn't need this in my life.

"Uh uh… Well, that was terribly cryptic." Tip looked skeptical but also bemused by my vague answer. "I haven't made up my mind yet, but, after today, I did think of something I'd like to ask of you." He looked at the ground, and pulled out the dagger I had made back at the apple trees in the corn maze.

I tucked my hair behind my ear self-consciously and tugged the rest of my unruly mane to start taming it. Tip reached up and caught my hand, then gingerly untucked the curl and shook his head, speaking softly. "It looks better that way. Wild and free and unafraid." Then he flinched away, like he'd just realized what he'd done, and cleared his throat.

A heat crept into my cheeks and I looked down at my hands awkwardly. My heart was suddenly hammering in my chest, and I once more questioned the infatuation bug. "Um, what is it you want?" I gestured to the dagger. "Is this where you finally have lulled me into complacency and strike me down?" I joked.

"Ha. No, but that would have been smart on my part," Tip snorted, flipping the knife to hold it by the blade, showing the hilt. "It's a two-part request. First, would you be so kind as to explain how you came up with this handle?"

I looked at the knife and pointed at each area, feeling rather proud of that creation. "Oh, well when I was concentrating on making it materialize, the design just sort of popped into my head. I thought of things that were closest to you. So, here is a reference to Saw-Horse, and this part is obviously a nod to Jack. And these two little stary bits at the top are a thinly veiled allusion to your favorite fairy-boy, Peter. The second one is just supposed to be a nod to Wendy too. But, the pointier one is for Wendy because she's clearly the sharper of the two mentally, plus she's into the weapons thing," I concluded and smiled fondly at the knife. "If I'd known about Lionel, I bet I would have found a way to add him too."

"Wow, that's quite a bit of creative thought you put into an apple knife," Tip laughed, and nodded slowly. "I like that about you. You've always got a lot of things happening upstairs." He tapped his head. "Not all of it entirely sane or rational, but it's always happening regardless."

I swatted him in the arm and grinned with feigned terseness. "And you said I wouldn't land a hit."

"Ah, you've bested me and my ego in one fell and pitiful swoop." He hung his head in mock defeat.

"Alright, well what's the second part of the request?" I crinkled my nose and prompted Tip to continue. "I'll warn you, if it's magical, you might just get corn."

"I kind of figured that was your reasoning behind the design. So, while I appreciate the dagger, and I will use it… I don't have my own sword anymore. I was hoping you could make me one like this?"

"Oh, sure—" I started to agree, but Tip kept going.

"Only this time, I was wondering if you'd add something to make a little piece of you in the design this time." His eyes twinkled in the firelight as he brought his gaze away from the knife to look at my face. I blinked back at him, taken aback.

"Me? But, these were supposed to be your closest companions," I blustered, feeling I hadn't earned a place amongst that category.

Tip smiled softly and nodded again. "I know. And, whether I stay behind or find my way in the other world, I realized, thanks to something Peter and Lionel said to me about focusing on better things, that I'd like to make sure I have something to remember you by, Dorothy Gale. I think that means you've made the cut."

"Oh," I breathed, my palpitations growing. "That's…" I felt lost for words.

"Yes?" He continued to stare pointedly at me, I felt squirmy beneath his unrelenting gaze, that seemed like it posed some sort of additional question, I didn't quite understand yet.

I shook my head, likely over thinking it again. "Yeah, I can do that. I think. Again, it might be corn or fire that comes out. I have no idea what to include to represent me, though. Oh, God. Please don't immortalize me as a cornstock," I pleaded, lost in a ramble again.

"I've got an idea," Tip started and pointed to my hands. "I think it should be a flame. That way I will never forget that wacky Wicked witch I met with crazy firehands. The one who couldn't turn away from the pleas of a little mouse, and chose to use her one wish of salvation to do Good for someone else. And the pretty bad ass farm girl who took down a pack of monsters single handedly, despite being more less poisoned by questionable tea. You might have had a rough start with that fire power, but it definitely left an impression in this world."

"As long as we keep that lovely painting of my time here, and agree to forget the whole setting the Munchkin Village on fire and ripping apart those monkeys... Or crying everytime I get splashed, I think I can manage that. I think I can be fiery," I mused, taking the knife and inspecting the handle more closely to decide where I wanted the fire part.

"Your flame isn't normal either. It's odd, like you."

"Gee thanks." I rolled my eyes.

"It's brighter." He elaborated cheerfully. "Unusual and unique. Hard to figure out. It's more like ultraviolet light, but a flame will do just fine."

"Ultraviolet makes me sound awfully spiffy, but I'll take it. Now I just gotta find a place for it on here that looks good..."

"You're right. I already have the knife with the others on it. Just make the sword with the flame. When I use it in some ferocious battle, I'll imagine it's got that ultraviolet power."

"What power is that?" I snorted, finding it a little refreshing to see that even the most mature and stoic of the group was still that playful Lost Boy at heart.

"It's... I don't know. It burns, but it's also too cold without it around. It's the good and the bad, and the undecided."

"Sounds like a hot mess," I joked, and Tip shrugged.

"I like it. I can't really explain why, but I do, so that's that."

"You sure you want just a big flashy sword hilt covered in my fire as a reminder of what a thorn I've been in your side?"

"Exactly so. Lest I ever brave another Wicked witch again, I'll remember that they aren't *all* bad." He tapped to the toe of my shoe that was sprawled next to him. "You're intriguing, as Peter would have me tell you."

I smiled inwardly to myself. Intriguing wasn't something I ever expected anyone to find me as, and normally, I'd worry it was another word for weird, but I liked the way Tip said it, and I knew it was a compliment coming from him. It sounded less like *weird* and more like *special.* I'd never been special before. I closed my eyes and clasped my hands together, the image of the sword coming to my mind's eyes.

I pulled apart my hands and watched as the sword formed between them, the tip and the hilt appearing last. I looked at my handy work, admiring the way a silver flame coiled down from the top of the hilt, spreading into ornate winding wisps around the cross. I could scarcely believe it had worked on the first try, and I snuck a quick peek around me to see if anything had been set on fire or any rogue corn stocks or apple trees had popped up.

"Wow, that's really beautiful." Tip looked over at the weapon and widened his eyes in his approval. "You're a quick learner."

I offered it to him, careful of the blade as I held it sidewise. "There you go. One Dorothy-sword, as requested."

"It's perfect."

"You know, your sentimentality must be contagious."

"What makes you say that?" Tip tilted his head to the side, his brows knitting together in contemplation.

"When I go back, I might need something solid to remind me this wasn't all a dream. So, I kind of want a cool knife, or something, to remember you by too. "

"You do?" Tip looked honestly surprised to have the gesture

reciprocated.

"I mean, yeah. You've actually been a really good friend to me here. I'm not very experienced with it, but you're very sturdy and reliable. You're considerate too, despite yourself. When you're not being rude, that is. Even if you drive me madder than the tea does sometimes, you're good company overall. I think I'm really going to miss you all when we part ways. Tell anyone else I said that though, and I'll be forced to deny it."

"Even Peter?"

"Even Peter. But, seriously, before I change my mind, help me make something that represents you."

"I'm not sure I trust you with a knife."

"Oh, hush. I'm more likely to hurt myself than someone else, anyway."

"That is part of the concern," Tip laughed.

I waved him off. "I'll make it small and cute, just to prove that cute things can pack a punch too. I'm tempted to make it a bunny out of spite, but I think I'll make it an anchor."

"An anchor?" Tip repeated, mystified. "I'm not sure that's a good thing to be visualized as… Like I drag everything down?"

"Well, when I was in the ocean, it was you that found me. And when I was panicking after the lake, it was you who centered me. Same with today. You and Peter brought me back down to earth— or um, grounded me. You are good for anchoring when one is adrift in their own inner torment, I think." I nodded, feeling resolute in my decision. I clasped my hands together once more and pulled them apart a short distance to make a fairly small and unassuming knife.

"Perfect for slicing apples!" Tip cheered.

"I like it. Now, if I get the chance, I can stick it in Mombi's stupid face. Teach her to terrorize me with tea!" I puffed indignantly.

"There's that *bad* side I was referencing earlier," Tip shook his head. "Can't say I don't share the sentiment though. I'm sorry she went after you today like that."

"Seriously, though. She was more insane than me!" I puffed in exasperation. "She kept going on about me playing with her toy and how she didn't like to share her playthings, bla bla bla. I have not played with or taken any plaything of hers. The whole thing made no sense, just bad luck I guess."

Tip's face paled, then flushed with color as some unspoken realization flickered over him. He coughed, then rubbed his face and shook his head. "Yeah, er, she definitely gets pretty possessive."

I pursed my lips pensively, oscillating on whether or not to broach the topic of my theory that she was his shadow. Finally, when the silence seemed to stretch on, I blurted it out. "Um, well, about what happened earlier, it's just us, if you feel like a little chat. My poor tailbone needs a few more minutes anyways."

The firelight, which had now burned down my torches significantly, cast dark shadows dancing across Tip's face, where the smile was melting rapidly from his expression. I saw his jaw tighten, and felt a wall of defense immediately spring up between us.

"It's… hard to talk about."

"Oh, I don't mean to pry or anything. Just a sympathetic ear to your tale of woe. You heard mine, after all." I threw my hands up in front of me, gesturing back and forth awkwardly. "If you don't feel comfortable…"

"No, it's not that. I think it's just that I am more ashamed of it than anything. But, in light of what happened, I'd probably do good to talk about it with someone new. Just, I hope it won't make you look at me any differently." His eyes could have drilled holes into the ground with how hard he was staring at it, clearly avoiding catching my eye.

"I'll always view you as the same sourpuss you always are, worry not," I promised, succeeding in getting a smile out of him. "I think we've *bonded* enough to weather some baggage," I echoed his earlier bonding sentiment and leaned back on my hands. "You heard my darkest moments and survived me literally losing my mind, and yet, for some reason, are still hanging out with me— which honestly makes me question *your* sanity a little— and, well, what you told me after all that with the water stuff, really helped save me today. So, I'd like to return the favor. Unload."

The truth was, while I meant what I said, I was also insanely curious about what was troubling him since he seemed to always have all the answers. He fidgeted for a few moments, clearly weighing my words, but struggling to form his own. What puzzle within himself could he not solve?

"The thing is… Mombi and I have a questionable past," He fished to find his wording. I already knew she had kidnapped him when he was a child, so I wondered why he was finding it hard to start his story.

"Right…"

"It was, um, intimate in nature." His voice was barely more than a whisper, and the words were strung together in a mumble that was rushed and apologetic.

"Oh!" I couldn't keep the surprise out of my voice. "As in…?"

"Yeah, as in." Tip hung his head in shame, still avoiding eye contact. I felt a heat run through my body at the thought of intimacy between Tip and the horrid Wicked witch, and couldn't help but feel completely lost. "She pretended to be someone else. Someone that reminds me a lot of you, actually. It's why I think we get along pretty well, and why I got so defensive when I found out you were a Wicked."

"Er, I'm not sure what that's supposed to mean. And, furthermore, I don't think I like being lumped in with her, thank you very much," I huffed indignantly, folding my arms.

"She acted kind. She pretended to be Good and honest, and fun. She played pretend with me to make me view her as a beacon of light in my small captive world, but having no prior experience in the area, I got infatuated by that fake side of her, ignoring that things were too convenient or too perfect and staged, and it was game over for me."

"Oh. So, you didn't know she was behind it then?" That made more sense, and my offensive lessened.

"Not for a long while. She was still young when we first met. Maybe a year or two older than me by the looks of it. She found me in the Never Woods, and told me there was an animal in need of help," Tip explained, rolling his fingers over the sword handle in agitation.

"Oh dear, that does sound eerily familiar, doesn't it? No wonder you reacted so harshly when I went to help the Mouse Queen." I cringed at the similar nature of our initial interactions.

"Only, unlike you, she never had any creature, and I was knocked out before we reached it. No doubt, she laid the mouse trap as a cruel reminder when she found where I went in that purple forest." His grip tightened angrily on the sword, and I half expected him to brandish it at the memories.

"Oh, God. And I walked right into it. Tip, I'm so sorry."

Tip shook his head. "It wasn't your fault. How would you know? The core difference was that you actually intended on saving whoever was in distress, regardless of my pushback. Nothing staged or fake about it. You're definitely not perfect— and I mean that in the best possible way. However, needless to say, I then reacted poorly when I heard you were a Wicked witch too. I could tell— no *feel*— that you two were different, but I just sort of reacted. So, for that bit, I must apologize. There were plenty of red flags that I ignored before that you don't share with her and I know better now. I'd only just gotten away so it was pretty fresh. The whole Wicked title is heavy and hard to ignore after everything."

"Don't worry about it. It was a doomed first impression from the start, I think. I have a habit of that, apparently." I shrugged, and hugged my knees to my chest. "Plus, me and my imperfect self can get a little blunt and hot headed sometimes and not say the most polite things back."

Tip nodded emphatically to my sentiment causing me to scowl at him insincerely before waving him on to continue his story.

"I was put to sleep for a while, and then woke up, growing up some. Mombi grew too. The whole time she acted like she was a captive too. I thought we were in this whole ordeal together, and she pretended to be my closest friend, while we were 'forced' to tend the little farm we lived at and help with research development for magical trinkets. Things sort of ramped up from there and we… Well— this is the hard part to get out— I developed feelings for this version of her that didn't really exist. Then one day she started changing. She started hurting me— physically, mentally, and emotionally. We'd always made the best of things, but once we had gotten really attached, little things started slipping up where her true nature showed through. Afterwards, she would act like she'd been put under some sort of spell and talk me around, because she knew deep down I wanted to believe her."

"Wow. That's truly insane and horrible and awful and..." I floundered for words. The whole thing made me feel ill. Tip was such a serious person, but I believed he was pretty genuine under his defensive sarcasm. It had a way of showing through in imperative moments. To think that someone had twisted that part of him and used it to hurt him on such a deep level, made me positively sick.

Tip nodded, and dared to look up, a whole storm of emotions in his gaze, glinting in contrast to the reflected orange flames, like a fire was raging through a meadow. It was devastation buried beneath shame and repression, and I knew it well.

"Yeah, so I was stupid. So incredibly naive. I kept thinking there was hope, and that this woman who had loved me, who had planned a future life with me when we finally got away— she would never hurt me on purpose. And as the tortured times increased, I kept holding on to the rarer moments when she would be back. Gah, even just hearing it come out of my mouth sounds so contrived and stupid. How stupid could I have possibly been to believe that stuff?"

"That's heartbreaking, Tip. I'm so sorry." I felt my eyes sting as I saw pain glittering in his.

"She'd always said that she didn't mean to hurt me, and promised she'd fight it the next time. She'd swear she wouldn't do it again. But she was all I had—or well, I *thought* she was all I had. So, I believed her and endured it. Then, one day, I found out the truth. She slipped up majorly, and I found out that the 'they' she'd always blamed for her Wicked actions was none other than her true self and The Wizard. The whole thing had been a plot to break me and turn me into a submissive servant. I guess as Peter's closest and oldest friend, they assumed the best ploy was a long game like that. From then on, she treated me like possession. A toy to play with and abuse."

Did he say toy?

"Any time I would get the gumption to try to fight back, she'd flip that switch to that Good woman… and I just couldn't bring myself to hurt her. Some part of me still worried that I would be hurting who I thought she was. So, I planned my escape, got Saw-horse and Jack and left. I took her powder of life potion too, out of spite, because that was her most recent experiment I had been forced to help with. But, when she found us in the woods and she said I had taken something of hers, it was more than the powder. It was me."

"So today…" I prompted, squirming inwardly at the connection that Tip might be the aforementioned plaything Mombi didn't want to share with me. But, how could she have known we were becoming good friends? Had she been spying on us? I glanced around the clearing self-consciously.

"The shadow that chased us in the maze was mine, but I'm sure you already figured that out. She was the young version there, but today, in the Hollow Woods, it was all the phantom memories of her through the years. And I was still powerless to do a damn thing about it. I couldn't even bring myself to strike the beast down when it was going after Peter. He and I even got into a bit of a fight over it. And I—" He looked away sharply, his voice catching in his throat. When he continued, he tried to hold his words steady beneath a small tremble. "I'm even more ashamed of that than all the rest. I was so, so painfully stupid and weak."

"I don't think love is weak," I surprised us both by reaching out and squeezing his hand for reassurance. "This is new to me, so it may sound trite but, I think it's a strength. I also think it's terrifying. Like one of these fancy weapons you wave around. Dangerous. But, if you know what you're doing… It's strength."

Tip glanced down at our hands, with a small almost inaudible sharp intake of breath, and I quickly retracted it. "And I sincerely hope that that woman you fell for is a real person out there for you somewhere."

Tip looked up at me, mystified, then he smiled and averted his eyes once more. "I'm actually starting to think so too, despite my better judgment."

"Good. That's good. There, see that right there is huge, and you… I'm in awe of you, Tippetarius. When I face that horrible piece of trash, I think I am going to unhinge just a bit, unapologetically."

Tip smirked and sighed. "Nah. I don't want you to accrue more Wicked deeds on my behalf."

"I think it'll be really satisfying though!" I argued, taking my little knife and jabbing it into the air a few times to emphasize my point. Then I sobered. "So, today was pretty rough then. You faced the shadow and then real Mombi showed up here. You stood up to the real thing just fine."

"Nope, I still hesitated. I'm still weak."

"Again with the self flagellation. Knock it off. You're not weak, okay? I'd tell you if you were, and we both know I would. I'm no sultry ice witch by a long shot, for many reasons," I rolled my eyes. "But you did save me today from her—Yeah, I saw you guys come rushing in with Toto to help, and I didn't see any hesitation. *You* did that, my friend. You were there when it counted. you've been there, and I'm not a shadow-thing or whatever happens when they win. Plus, she was gone when I came out of it, so obviously something happened. Can we count that as a victory?"

"I guess you have a point. I couldn't just let you get hurt." Tip shrugged, a slight air of bashfulness in the movement. "However, she left because you started getting batty and the smaller shadows were fixed on her. I didn't do a thing to make her leave because she pulled the line she always does and I froze." He shook his head mutinously.

"You just gotta find something to love more than the memory of what could have been. You know, look forward at something new to love. Even if you don't love it yet, and it takes a while to get there, you can still look forward to watching it grow at whatever pace it takes. Just give yourself permission to feel again. Trust me. It'll grow."

"Well, thanks to an unsolicited chat from a one nosy Peter Pan, who suddenly thinks he is wise and knowing, and Lionel, I've finally started exploring those 'moving forward' options with a more open mind and I'm trying to trust my heart even if it's taking me in a peculiar direction. You were busy snoozing during this big self reflection."

"Hey, I've had a long day too! Anyways, that's the first step, so don't belittle it. You got this." I grinned encouragingly and felt a tingle down my spine as Tip smiled back, a fondness in his gaze.

"For the first time, in a really long time, I have hope. Thanks Dorothy."

"For what?" I asked, but Tip just shook his head again and pushed up to his feet.

"Come on, enough chit chatting. Let's get some training in for real."

"Wasn't that what we were doing earlier?"

"Nope. I was just messing with you. How can you fight better without instructions?" Tip beamed, a light of mischief that could rival Peter's, emanating from him. "You really do make it so easy to mess with you, and give the best reactions."

I gaped at him and begrudgingly accepted his hand to get back to my feet. "Are you kidding me? You are the worst!"

"Well, if you're going to do anything, do it well I suppose. And if messing with you makes me the worst, then I suppose I'd better be the best at being the worst." He shrugged cheerfully. Alright, get in your stance and I'll tell you what to do this time. For real."

"How can I trust you?" I complained, though my tone remained light and teasing. Tip stood next to me and stretched, clearly getting ready to actually mean business this time. Apparently picking on me was just a warm up.

"You can trust me. Always." He spoke with an edge that told this time, he wasn't joking, so I nodded.

"Alright, against my better judgment, I guess I do. You'll lead this time, and I'll follow? Is that a trust metaphor now?" I laughed.

Tip smirked. "You got it."

My heart felt light as I went to my beginning stance, and this time, Tip kept his word and began teaching me for real. It was a strenuous workout, and my feet dragged the whole way back to the camp. But, when

I crawled into my little makeshift bed that I had managed to magic up on my own, I pulled out my new little knife and ran my fingers over the anchor, smiling until sleep claimed me.

Twenty-One

Peter

"Gah! Don't break the damn place, you idiot," Dorothy swore, arms outstretched in alarm. "You'll take down the whole forest at this rate!"

"Uh, I'll try and fix it…" I zipped over to the fallen woods, I'd just knocked down with my magical practice. and inspected them thoughtfully. The nearby onlooking munchkins bowed awkwardly and raced away, no doubt afraid to become collateral damage. What was that saying about curiosity killing something?

I touched the nearest trunk and faltered.

"Actually, I have no idea how to do that." I turned sheepishly and whistled back over to my friends. "That's likely enough of that for now."

"I don't suppose you know how to dry us off?" Wendy asked, giving me her best no-nonsense staredown as water dripped from her soaked ginger hair— more collateral effects from my attempt at wielding more precise water magic. I'd doused the lot of my friends, but it had been amusing to watch them squawk and flitter about. Tink was in the sky with me, and pointed and laughed at their misfortune. Sometimes, I wondered if she was my original bad influence.

"Sorry, Love. Don't know that one either. I could try some of that powerful wind stuff again?" I offered sincerely, but Wendy waved her hands in front of her, shaking her head adamantly.

"I think I'd like to remain blissfully unaware of what it is like to be swept up in a cyclone, thank you."

"It's not fun," Dorothy commented with a frown.

"Especially when they chase you," Alice grunted her agreement.

"I think with Peter and his magic, Mombi won't know what hit her," Tip asserted, with a small smile of approval. "I doubt they will even be expecting him to use it. Their goal was to break him in that old room in Oz, not empower him to accept the magic. We can likely use that against her."

"How do we know that The Wizard won't be with her?" Wendy asked, grimacing with concern. "Or, how long will they leave us alone before striking more directly first?"

"We don't," Alice replied solemnly. "But, if we can all be at our best, I believe we have a chance of at least getting Wonderland back in the near future. Though, it does seem in a way, the shadows are our enemy but they also go after the truly Wicked. Therefore, we have the old saying, 'the enemy of my enemy is my friend' on our side, for the time being."

"If The Wizard is with Mombi, it likely will just be for the night anyway," Tip threw in with a sneer. "She had been in Oz all those years but was always at that cursed little farm and he didn't make frequent appearances there."

"That's because you go to see The Wizard, not the other way around," I muttered, an instinctive feeling of revolt settling in my stomach as I thought of Mombi's obvious infatuation with my father— especially since we shared an unfortunately uncanny resemblance. I didn't know exactly what it meant, but something told me late night visits between those two weren't made up of pillow fights and stolen kisses. I shuddered, trying to physically shake the notion away.

"Goodness," Alice hissed, a small heat rising in her cheeks. "Let's not go on about all that." She looked sharply at Tip who rolled his eyes but let it go.

"So, do we risk seeing what else Peter can do with his odd god-like powers— which, by the way, I find it extra obnoxious that you seem just naturally gifted at being able to control them— or what are we doing next?" Dorothy interjected, pointedly shifting the conversation as she scuffed her shoe uncomfortably, not meeting anyone's gaze.

"He could do with a bit more control actually. Everything is coming out very powerfully, but there is a lot of collateral damage. We don't want you turning Wonderland to sodden ash and dust," Alice countered. "So, why don't we make this a little more interesting?"

"What do you have in mind, Love?" I asked, perking up. I felt a game coming on, and games always made things more enjoyable. This might be serious business, but no one ever said serious business couldn't have its elements of entertainment too.

"Dorothy, let's spar him. You're really getting the hang of your fire and it's good practice both ways."

"I'm sorry, but do you have a crazy death wish?" Dorothy scoffed, folding her arms over her chest defiantly. "I thought you were trying to play it safe with the magic stuff until you figured out why you are cracking?"

In response, Alice merely tossed a ball of lightning lightly from hand to hand as she looked at me. Her eyebrows raised to beckon me to the challenge.

"Come on, don't be chicken, Dorothy!" Tip teased lightly. "We can go tutor the Imagineds in the ways of war, Wendy. Let's leave them to it... If Dorothy isn't too chicken to fight back, that is."

"I'm not! Stop trying to antagonize me, you rude boy," Dorothy objected, clearly flustered.

Tip merely smirked and walked away, whistling nonchalantly, with Wendy close at his heels. "Give him hell!" He called without turning around, raising his hand in farewell.

Dorothy sighed and summoned fire to her hands and stood next to Alice opposite me. "Trial by fire it is then, I guess. Don't blame me if your boyfriend accidentally kills us."

"Maybe you should give me some dust to even the playing field, since you see us as equals and all. A queen of Neverland needs to fight in the air." Alice narrowed her eyes playfully, lifted her chin to play the role of regal queen, and held out her hand expectantly.

I'm not giving her any of my dust. The audacity of that girl is beyond me. Honestly, Peter, you can't be trusted with girls. You choose the worst ones. Tinkerbell jingled in my ear. Fairies of Neverland had the ability to choose who could understand them speaking, while others could only hear the sound of twinkling bells in place of words.

"I'm not the one withholding this time, Love." I grinned, and nodded to the agitated fairy beside me.

Tinkerbell had been my first Imagined and had led me to Neverland originally. She was once always by my side, and my fiercest protector… Until Wendy came into the picture. Tink had no warm and fuzzy feelings about Wendy's more obvious infatuation with me, nor my budding returning crush on her. So, to protect me from the perceived evil that was matters of the heart with young girls. Tinkerbell had made it her sole mission to terrorize Wendy and try to drive her away. When that didn't work, she had started returning more and more to the Pixie Village, and going on less and less adventures with me— though, like the instance with Tentis, she almost always came if I was ever in truly dire straits.

"Are we doing this or what? I have other things I'd rather be doing."

"With Tip?" I asked, my tone leading. I landed beside her and rested my arm on her shoulder. "More wrestling and such?"

"Shut up, Fairy-Boy." Dorothy pushed my arm away and glowered at me. "It's practice too. Some of us like to be prepared for things."

I grinned and squared off my stance, raising my hands in front of me offensively. Wiggling my eyebrows up and down, I dipped my head in acceptance. "Let's dance, ladies."

~*~

After that initial successful sparring match, we made a tentative plan of attack for taking back Wonderland, opting to put off fighting the personal Shadows until Tip and Wendy were both a little stronger. Instead, we made a conscious effort to do sweeps of removing the lesser shadows in patrols. Though I knew I needed to help Neverland, I also was getting anxious about the remaining Lost Ones stuck in captivity and wanted to see them set free.

Wendy and Tip had doubled down on training and drilling our attack plans into the Imagineds, each one taking windows of time to help instruct Alice and Dorothy on physical combat. Lionel was unceremoniously elected to lead the main attacks on the lesser shadows, and made sure we were all rotating to do our part to help the remaining Imagineds as best we could. Even Tink was conducting flying lessons, with some of the Imagineds she deemed worthy, with her stores of pixie dust, making use of her tiny militant personality should we opt for an aerial advantage in our ambush. Dorothy, Alice and I all were dragging, having to spend all of our energy on both magical and physical sparring sessions.

And when we weren't doing that, Alice was testing out some compass theory she had come up with on her own and was being annoyingly private about. I would have liked to have taken some time to cloud watch with her and enjoy our newly proclaimed romance, but that apparently wasn't on her mind at the moment.

Dorothy had to tough out a few more bouts of insanity from the tea Mombi had fed her, and thankfully, she had seemingly found a way to turn it positive, and even utilized it for imaginative power. She inadvertently added several new additions to Neverland's terrain. Tip was usually somewhere around her these days, lending a hand or observing her antics and laughing at it. Seeing as it seemed to be healing both of their wounded spirits, I didn't feel inclined to interrupt. If Dorothy was a future for Tip to focus on, and it helped him move past his pain, then maybe his Shadow would hold less power over him the next time they met.

Wendy had become consumed in helping Lionel search for shadows and trying to take care of any little need that arose in our camp, ultimately running herself ragged. Several days in this routine had transpired, and it was looking like the tide was turning in our favor in our plight with the blight on Neverland. Not many scouting patrols were needed anymore, which left my free time unaccounted for. Since the others all seemed busy, and the Wonderlandians were… well, they were just there doing Wonderlandian things, I found myself unwinding with nonother than my friendly childhood nemesis, Captain Hook.

I squinted my eyes, aiming for a crudely drawn target on a tree a good twenty paces away. I held in my hand one of Hook's pistols— something I hadn't gotten to use in ages— and was partaking in a friendly shooting competition with the pirates.

"You're sure taking your time," Tiger Lily complained behind me.

"This is supposed to be a *leisurely* activity, Love," I reminded her, but finally pulled the trigger. The bullet went whizzing through air and struck to the left side of the center circle.

I passed the pistol off to the crew, and felt my little moment of self inflation evaporate as each one managed to hit an exact bullseye. I was definitely out of practice. Perhaps a knife-throwing contest would wind up more in my favor.

"Isn't there something more useful you ought to be doing?" Hook drawled, setting to work cleaning his weapon. His dark brows knit together in concentration, creaking little creases in his forehead as he looked up at me.

I shrugged and flopped onto my back, floating ambiently in the air with my hands tucked behind my head. I was feeling a bit listless and agitated being the only one without something imperative to be working on. Perhaps everything in the past few weeks had been altogether too serious and my body was in desperate need of relaxation and fun. Too jolly bad I was surrounded by resident workaholics and canoodlers.

"Have you paid any thought to when this is all over? If we don't die." Tiger Lily held out her hand for some dust to join me in lounging, and I obliged by retrieving a handful from my pouch.

"I honestly can't even see that far ahead," I lied, closing my eyes to drink in the fresh air and near-sunlight dappling the forest.

"Classic Pan for you, right there," Hook snorted. " Why worry about tomorrow when today is infinite, is that right?"

"Don't be silly. Tomorrow will come, and it will be another glorious day like today."

"Until it isn't," Tiger Lily pressed, folding her arms. "What then?"

"Why are you trying to invite trouble, Lily?" I tried to keep my tone neutral, but I felt frustration beginning to brew in my chest.

She whipped her head over to look at me, her gaze piercing and unrelenting. "Because you need to think about it!"

"Well, I don't want to think about it right now. I want to relax," I argued back, my fuse shortening. It had been shortening more and more as the pressure amped the closer we got to big impending conflict with our foes. And beyond that, I had to find and free my friends, only for them to likely go off on their own merry ways.

"Not thinking about things created all the shadows that killed half of Neverland's Imagineds. We don't need more."

"I don't need reminding of that either. Ever consider the fact that thinking too far ahead might create shadows too?"

"But—" She started to counter, but it was the last straw.

"Everyone leaves *again*! That's what happens, Lily. Happy?" I dropped to my feet and stalked away, waving my hand in a single jerked motion as I shoved the other one in my pocket. "Thanks for the fun, it was a real blast."

I knew it wasn't like me to lose my temper, and I didn't like it. But, while Neverland had always served as a safe haven and home, and I had more appreciation for the Imagineds who dwelled there, something in my gut still didn't know if it would be enough when everyone went back to their world. I had grown so much since I'd reigned over this direction as a young child. I'd felt brotherhood, true friendship, loyalty, and love. Even Dorothy had come to feel like a sister, despite her prickly self. I had my family here, and the remaining members were out there lost somewhere. But once I found them, it was only the beginning of the end before they left again.

I shook my head, trying to physically knock the turmoil from my brain. Perhaps I had been drawing in so much pain with my shadows, that I was stewing in it. I was angry, and bitter, and already feeling phantom loneliness stirring within me. These were all things that drew out my big demon shadow, though he hadn't fully appeared for me to try and fight since the attack with Alice and Tiger Lily. Rather, he liked to appear in my mind and behind my ears to remind me he was there, out of reach, waiting to consume me the moment everything fell apart.

Yet, today, I was having a particularly rough time finding a bright side, and frankly didn't feel like dealing with banishing the darkness or absorbing anything else. I'd been content with life in Wonderland with Alice, but that had been disrupted. I'd been reunited with my old best friends, and made a new one, but that was all hanging in the balance. I'd fallen in love and been loved back at last, but she had to go and I knew now I couldn't keep her here with her compass damaged the way it was or she would die— whether she admitted it to me or not. I'd found my old caretaker, but she was lost to the Shadow World. I'd felt connected to my mother at long last and healed so many wounds, but it was fleeting. I would never truly know her because she'd been taken from me.

And for what? A power boost. That's what she had been in the end. A bloody power boost for The Wizard. My family was dead, insane, evil, or in some instances all three. And the family I had chosen and made was destined to leave me behind.It was all so unfair!

On cue the inner demon cackled, booming and bouncing around my skull. I threw my head back with a mutinous groan, wanting to wail and to rage at the heavens. I could feel my storm magic being called upon, swirling around me. Alice had always tried to let steam out of the pot with her magic, so maybe I ought to give that a whirl. I didn't like that these intrusive thoughts were pointing out all the negatives. But, I didn't know how to make them stop.

As if in answer to my mental check, I heard a pair of voices in the near distance. *Tip and Dorothy.* A devious smile curled my lips. I was *Peter Pan*, the eternal optimist. Brooding wasn't something I did. Mischief and games were what I did. And I didn't need to attack everything in sight to release some pent up pressure, like the beast would lead me to believe. I needed some fun and games.

I zipped over to where I finally spotted the pair walking towards the new growth of apple trees that Dorothy had materialized at some point, with empty buckets in their arms. They were engaged in one of their usual bantering sessions, completely unaware of my presence. True, I had been urging Tip towards Dorothy, as it was obvious to me that they had some spark of connection between them. Tip and I had talked at length about healing his wounds, and opening himself back up to the world a few days back. He had promised to start keeping an open mind about such things.

I liked to be more aware of these feelings I was constantly learning about these days, and I wanted Tip to move past his harrowing trials with Mombi. But, in this moment, I needed to blow off some steam and I wanted my friends back to myself for just a little while.

I conjured up a ball of water and hovered it stealthily above their heads. "Three, two, one." Then I released and delighted as it barreled down on top of them.

Dorothy let out a startled shriek, while Tip looked glumly forward, the very picture of a wet blanket. She whipped around wildly, fire forming instantly in her hands.

"Peter!" She shouted, angrily, water beading down her face and dripping from her hair. "I'm going to ring your neck, you pest!"

"Don't go burning down the forest. Let's just get you dried off and—" Tip tried to rationalize while he wrung out the bottom of his shirt, but stopped short and sighed, as Dorothy spotted me and took off. "Good thing I have a bucket I guess…" He meandered towards the shore to get water.

Dorothy, meanwhile, having gotten significantly more adept at handling her fire magic in the past few days, had formed her flames into a point like a knife and was aiming to throw it at me.

"Oops. I forgot she's a lot more precise in her aim now," I mumbled to myself and grinned at her. "Good, I got your attention!"

"A simple 'hello' would do just fine next time. Now hold still so I can hit you!" She hissed. "I hate being splashed, and you know it, Fairy-Boy. So, come here and face the consequences!"

"Face the consequences? Doesn't sound like me," I taunted,

perching in a tree.

"Dorothy, don't hit him up there. I can't get the bucket of water there very easily—" Tip had rejoined us and was once more stopped short as Dorothy hurled her flame-knife at me with all her might.

"Missed me!" I cheered as I flew out of the way with ease. "You were right, Tip. She does have terrible aim." I pointed to where the fire had caught on the trunk next to where I'd previously been standing.

"Do not! Tip, why do you keep saying stuff like that? It's rude!" She snapped, turning on a bewildered Tip to glare at him, before growling and chasing after me again, flinging more fire as she went.

Tip looked woefully down at his bucket of water and up at the high elevation of the fire burning in the tree, and sighed heavily. "I guess I need to go find that lizard and borrow his ladder."

"Best not involve Bill," I cautioned as I circled overhead like a hawk. "He will steal your best girl for late night adventures. Ask Alice."

"She's not my best girl!" Tip blustered, blushing.

"Who, Alice? I should hope not. She's mine." I reveled in the nonsense I was spinning and the buttons I was pushing. I could physically feel the enjoyment pushed the demon back into his corner.

"You know what, Dorothy? Have at him!" Tip smiled wickedly at me and rubbed his fingers together. "Make it more interesting, Pan, and give us some dust."

I whistled and dutifully sprinkled pixie dust on Tip and Dorothy, now that I'd finally got Tink to relinquish a small amount for emergencies—and if tea was a direction, fun was definitely an emergency. Tip dropped his bucket and immediately leapt into the air while Dorothy flailed as usual.

"Ugh, I like my feet on the ground! Flying gives me tornado and tea flashbacks."

"Don't let the fear cage you, Dorothy!" Tip called to her from where he and I were darting nimbly around the various trees and branches.

"Spread your wings, Little Phoenix!" I crowed at her, and mimed flapping.

"Phoenix?" Tip echoed.

"Well, yeah. The fire, obviously," I laughed.

"Oh. Right."

"I'm not a bird! I'm a ground-dweller. Like a hedgehog," She wailed as she ascended even higher.

"Ever seen a flying hedgehog, Pan?" Tip gave up on chasing me and hovered with his hand pressed thoughtfully to his face. Ha, he'd joined my team.

"Why, I believe there is one just over there!" I joined him and pointed in mock awe at Dorothy.

"Oh, shut up!" She shouted, but we could see her smiling at our fun. "Now you're both going to harass me?"

"I told you before, you make it too fun," Tip teased, his face bright and animated. Just like old times, same Tip, older face.

"Don't lie, Dorothy. If your thoughts weren't happy, you wouldn't be able to fly." I wagged my finger at her and laughed.

"That's a fallacious argument," She sniffed.

"What? You and your big words. Your insults have little effect if I don't know what they mean."

"'Ignorance is bliss' was an expression made for you, Buddy," Tip snorted and shook his head.

"Well, in any case, I can't steer," Dorothy whined as she bobbled about in the air awkwardly.

"Here, let me help you. You have to tilt your body into it," Tip offered, taking her hand using it to tilt her at an angle.

"I'll just end up upside down."

"Not if you use control… Oh, look at that. You did turn upside down. Whoops."

"Ugh," Dorothy groaned, hanging in the air with her sparkling shoes pointed to the sky.

"Now you're a possum!" Tip snickered.

"Come on, Dorothy, you can do it! Use your imagination and work up some of that blissful madness when you're more fun and hop on clouds and stuff," I prompted her, and Tip nodded his agreement, making a sarcastically pulled face at her.

"You want the madness? Alright, I'll give you both the madness!" Her face was bright, and she closed her eyes as she embraced something that had terrified her a few days prior. She'd really grown, and both she and Lionel were prime examples of how freeing defeating one's Shadow Beast was.

Next thing we knew, Tip and I were being propelled towards the ground by something at our backs, and Dorothy was once more vertical. She'd managed to assault us with some of her favored bouncy clouds she had compared to something called *cotton candy*.

As we both pulled up to avoid smashing into the ground, two large corn stalks erupted from the ground, and sucked us into the leaves where the cob should have normally been.

"Why is it always corn?" Tip gasped between laughs as he struggled to free himself from the leaves.

I broke free at the same time and we both landed on the ground to catch our breath. "Well, that was definitely random."

"Slippery little things, aren't you?" Dorothy mused, using her cloud puffs to hop down to the ground, no longer floating aimlessly. But no sooner had she spoken than Tip and I were doused in some form of slippery, fruity liquid. Our feet no longer able to find traction, we both tumbled to the ground in a heap.

"Ah!" We squawked in unison.

"Oops, sorry. This mad imagination thing is still a little hard to control," Dorothy apologized but her beaming face made it clear she wasn't really sorry.

"Is this jelly?" Tip asked, touching his hair clumped by stickiness.

"I think it's jam," I replied, daring to lick a little off my finger.

"What's the difference?"

"No idea."

"Jelly is strained, jam is mashed," Dorothy explained. "This is jelly. I wish I had some toast right about now to go with it."

In response to her statement, it began raining down pieces of toast on top of Tip and I. A mere moment later and were already buried up to our eyes in bread, with a few stray pieces atop our heads like hats.

"Well, this just seems excessive," Tip mumbled from beneath his mound.

"You shouldn't trust sugar pops with a toadstool if you don't want sassafras to dance with paprika!" Dorothy blurted out, her eyes glazed for a moment, before she gasped and covered her mouth.

"This is probably why Wonderland's magic is best served *in* Wonderland where imagination magic isn't quite as readily available," I chuckled, then pointed to the sky where it was still raining bread. "Dorothy?"

"Sorry, I'm trying to turn it off but it's a bit tricky to stop the weird thoughts once they start." She hiccuped and suddenly disappeared.

"Dorothy?" Tip called, trying to scramble out from under the toast, slices clinging to the jelly on his body. "Did Alice teach her how to do that?"

"Ummm. No?" I frowned.

"Butterscotch or cinnamon?" Dorothy's nonsense rambling sounded behind us, and she rocked back and forth like a child with her hands clasped behind her back. "Ha, I think I've lost my head a moment. Have either of you seen it?"

"That's—" I started but stopped as Dorothy shot a ball of fire in Tip's direction. He dodged and stomped out where it had ignited some of the bread.

"Oops. I think she went a little too far into it," Tip observed wryly. "Hey!" He shouted when one of his boots vanished from his foot and appeared in my hand.

"Well, that's a new trick…" I observed, plucking the shoe from my hand and handing it back to Tip.

"Maybe you should tackle her again," He grumbled as he slipped it back on. He was referring to Dorothy's first dip into insanity following her harrowing shadow battle. It had caused her to start lighting fire, and I'd tackled her to smother the flames while she managed to turn the flames to something else less destructive.

"I only did that because she was burning things at alarming amounts that time. Why don't *you* tackle her?"

"I don't want her to get the wrong idea."

"That you're *restraining* her?"

"It's different if I do it!"

"Why? Don't you do that stuff while practicing fighting?"

"Good grief, Pan. Take my word for it. I'm not tackling her for the sake of it."

"Oops. We lost her again." I looked around the immediate area to see a distinct lack of Dorothy. "But at least it stopped raining bread. She seems rather adept at imagining food. Maybe we haven't been feeding her enough," I mused, lifting into the air.

"Oof." Tip's grunt sounded as Dorothy reappeared directly over top of him and crashed onto his back, knocking him down with the dazed farm girl sitting ontop of him. "Found her."

"Hello, Dorothy. You back with us? Let's step out of the madness now. Yes, see let's visualize a set of doors, and as you walk through those doors you leave the madness behind you." I crouched beside the befuddled girl and spoke encouragingly next to her ear. "How's that, Love? Are you back with us?"

"Don't call me that!"

"She's back!" I cheered, and lifted back into the air. "You know, if you ever used that type of magic in a fight, your enemy wouldn't know what hit them because it makes no sense."

"Where did Tip go?" Dorothy asked, rubbing her head and closing her eyes. "I didn't make him explode, did I?"

"Um, he's right there," I laughed and pointed to beneath her.

"You must have mistaken me for a cloud to land on," Tip joked from where he was squished into the ground.

"Oh, God!" Dorothy leapt to her feet, embarrassment tinting her cheeks red. "Sorry… I didn't know what I was— Um, I need to go."

"Go where?" Tip laughed at her blustering.

"Anywhere but here."

"Oh, don't be so uptight, Dorothy. We were having great fun!" I twirled around her to intervene in her exit.

"I'm not being uptight!" She snapped, folding her arms.

"You know, I think we left that part of the forest burning," Tip commented, getting to his feet and dusting himself off. "We should probably fix that, don't you think?"

"Oh, yeah," She repeated, staring at the ground mutinously.

"What's got you so cranky?" I asked, poking her in the arm.

"I guess *I* will be the responsible one and go put the fire out… Again," Tip sighed and retrieved his bucket of water before striding off in the direction of the small fire still burning.

"First of all, I am mad because I thought I was controlling that stuff better. Secondly, it's embarrassing to still be the weakest link," Dorothy sniffed. "I'm tired of being the one who doesn't know what she's doing. I'm not an unintelligent person, but all this foolishness always leaves me feeling so painfully stupid and inept."

"I think you've shown a lot of progress since you set the woods on fire mostly intentionally this time!" I tried to joke, but Dorothy didn't laugh. "Er, I mean… Insanity is probably a tricky weapon to wield, right? I imagine you have to have really strong convictions to use it effectively."

"Strong convictions?"

"Yeah, like something worth fighting for. The Red Queen was off her rocker and entirely bonkers. But, she did have this sort of clear vision that it was all linked to the love and grief of her sister. That's likely how she controlled it."

"I guess. I *do* feel convicted though. I don't want any of you to be hurt," Dorothy muttered miserably. "I went from not caring enough to caring too much."

"It will click eventually." I patted her shoulder briskly.

"Says the prodigy."

"Hey now. It took a lot of growth on my part to even use magic at all. Alice was actually probably the most automatically inclined with it. I can't make a weapon worth two specs of pixie dust, like you can. Tip showed me those fancy weapons you made him. Everyone is different, so best not to compare your progress."

"This is weird." She finally cracked a smile.

"What is?"

"Us acting like friends."

"We are friends whether you like it or not. What, only Tip gets to be in your good graces?"

"He doesn't drop water on my head for attention," She replied pointedly, but behind her alleged annoyance was a soft smile.

"Oh, that. I just needed to blow off some steam. I got a little testy myself today, and bickered with Tiger Lily. I'm not really used to staying put under all these stressful things."

"Why didn't you just say so?" She rolled her eyes, and I scuffed my foot on the ground as I landed. "We would have listened. Everyone needs a break at some point anyways or we will all get burned out."

"It didn't seem important. You all are doing good and useful things and I'm just… here. And I'll always be here. Long after everyone is old and gone, I'll still be here, biding my time," I trailed off, the forlorn feeling blossoming in my chest once more.

"I've been thinking about it a lot too," Dorothy spoke softly, her brown eyes glittering.

"About what?"

"About what happens when all of this is over. It will be really weird to all go our separate ways after everything we've been through together." She waved her hand to generalize what she meant.

"True. I know I won't be alone but… I'm not going to say I'm looking forward to watching you all vanish," I admitted, and looked away. I hadn't really been looking for a heart to heart, but there I was.

"Lionel seems pretty well adjusted to this place." Dorothy pointed out.

"I suppose that's possible." I shrugged, not daring to hope it might have some real merit.

"Tip will stay behind, I'm sure."

"I'm not so sure about that."

"Why wouldn't he?" Dorothy asked, confusion lacing her words, like staying was the only obvious choice for our friend. I, however, wasn't convinced of that anymore.

"He's got to follow his heart," I replied matter-of-factly.

"That's awfully philosophical coming from you. He loves it here, and it's his home. I'm sure his heart is going to stay in Neverland," Dorothy insisted, and I almost wondered if she was trying to prepare herself for the separation by telling herself it was a done deal.

"I think his heart is going back to Kansas, just the same as mine is going to England." I looked her in the eye and shrugged.

Dorothy's eyes widened in surprise then narrowed. "Don't be ridiculous."

"Is that what I'm being? Funny, for once, I thought I was being realistic," I responded with a sad laugh and a pained smile.

Whatever Dorothy had been about to say was interrupted as Tip hailed his return. "Well, I got the rest of the flames put out. Dorothy, if you could please try to control your temper, it would be much appreciated. Thankfully, your weird bread storm actually smothered most of it, though the whole area smells like soggy burnt toast…" He trailed off as he took in Dorothy's and my demeanor.

"You should just go with her," Dorothy looked at me meaningfully. "I'm sure we could figure something out."

"And what would become of Neverland and the rest of this world? Just hanging out in another direction led to total chaos here. For all I know, the magic I inherited from Ozma is the only thing keeping this place running."

"Well, that's the part we'd need to figure out, then."

"Er, I feel like I missed something…" Tip commented, his brows furrowing as he looked back and forth between us.

"The stress is getting to Peter," Dorothy answered, not taking her eyes off me, wheels spinning behind her gaze.

"Well, that's nothing new," Top scoffed, patting me on the back before slinging a friendly arm over my shoulder. "Guess we'd better do something about it then."

"You sound like you have an idea," I laughed, appreciating the friendship and consideration they were both showing me.

"We should have a race, take a swim,— well maybe not Dorothy. Climb a tree. Something of that nature. That sounds like a very Peterish thing to do," Tip suggested, looking once more from Dorothy to me.

Dorothy shook her head, and smiled. "Count me out. I need to get back to Toto anyway. I left him with Wendy after his grand attempts at keeping pace with the Imagined's training tuckered him out."

"Spoilsport," I complained. "Oh, right. Before I forget, when did you learn how to teleport?"

"If I knew how to teleport, would I still be in this wacky world?" She replied tersely.

"He's right. You were popping all about like the Cheshire Cat." Tip nodded and pointed to the silver slippers. "You might just be close to figuring out how to use those things without that supposed charm The Wizard mentioned."

"Oh," Dorothy's eyes widened. "Well, then I guess I probably should go talk to Alice then. Maybe we can figure something out together."

"First we should—"

A loud bang sounded in the distance, and a surge of energy coursed through the air. All three of our hair began to rise with static, and I could feel ambient electricity pulsing.

"That's coming from the camp!" Dorothy cried in dismay.

"Alice," I breathed and was barreling through the woods in her direction in an instant. Tip and Dorothy followed hot on my heels, racing on foot. We burst into the open to discover the camp in disarray, smoking and smoldering. I began searching the wreckage for signs of life, dread rolling down my spine. It looked completely deserted.

"Toto?" Dorothy called frantically.

"Here, I'll help you look for him," Tip offered, kindly.

"Toto!" Dorothy called again, desperation choking her voice. "Every damn time we are separated."

"We'll find him, don't worry."

"I shouldn't have left him behind. He's all I have, and I can't… I can't…" Her breath began sucking in big gulps, her eyes wild.

"Calm down, Dorothy. It's going to be alright. He isn't all you have, remember that. You have all of us now too, and we will help find him." Tip paused his searching to aid Dorothy. "You need to slow your breathing. The last thing that will help find him is you losing your head, in the bad way, or making new shadows come pouring in."

"That blast was from Alice, I'm sure of it. And, she wouldn't intentionally hurt an animal, no matter where her morality is spinning." I tried to remain calm, but I was becoming increasingly agitated at not yet being able to find either Alice or Wendy.

"Peter!" I breathed a sigh of relief as I heard Wendy calling from a stack of fallen branches, likely snapped off from the velocity of Alice's outburst.

I shot over to her and helped untangle the debris, until she was able to pull herself free. There were several thin and shallow scratches covering her face and hands, but nothing looked like a serious injury.

Toto hopped out after her and bounded to Dorothy who crouched and accepted him into her arms, burrying her face into his fur as he wiggled and licked at her forehead with a wagging tail. Tip squatted beside them and scratched Toto behind the ear, receiving his own friendly lick from the dog.

I looked past Wendy, expecting to see Alice but faltered when I didn't see anyone else in the heap of branches.

"Where is she?" I asked sharply. I couldn't put my finger on it, but something in the energy she'd dispelled felt dangerous, and I couldn't shake the nagging feeling in my gut that Alice wasn't alright.

"I'm not sure. She was trying to do something while everyone else was busy doing things outside the little camp and her compass went out of control. She tried to shield us with branches…"

"Uh oh." Tip's tone was grave. "It didn't break, did it?"

Fear pierced my heart and I felt cold sweat gathering in my brow. Blast! I had been so caught up on the future and cheering myself up that I hadn't been here to help Alice stay grounded. If I had been playing tag in the woods and she'd succumbed to the compass all alone, I would never forgive myself.

"Why didn't you do anything to stop or help her?" I demanded, my rising terror making the words come out sharper than I intended.

"I don't know." Wendy's eyes were wide as the moon. "I don't know," She repeated weakly looking around wildly, her eyes welling. "I don't know where she went. I don't know. I'm sorry I didn't help. I should have helped."

"She's in shock," Tip hopped to his feet and approached Wendy. "Come on Wendy, it's alright. Let's get you some water. Dorothy?"

"On it." She gave Toto a final squeeze and flashed up a glass cup— Alice had gotten her more confident making small objects now as well— which she filled with water from a canteen and passed it to Tip.

Wendy was trembling and looking up at me with such anxiety, I couldn't stand to look any longer. Whatever had happened really must have rattled her, and that certainly didn't bode well for Alice.

"I'm going looking for her," I declared and tried to discern which direction looked to be the focal point of her discharge.

"Mr. Peter Pan, sir?" A timid voice called out and I whirled around to see Bill standing with a grim expression and his hat in his hand. I noticed his tail was missing, and in its place was a bloodied stump. Accompanying him was one of the defector Card-guards, holding a broken spear, and the March Hare, patches of fur burnt and steaming.

"Oh, no." I felt like my heart was ready to burst out of my chest, and all the strength was draining from my body. "What happened, Bill?"

"The Queen became unstable and was trying to get away from everyone…" The lizard replied shakily. "We tried our best to help her. She is our friend, after all, and that awful compass won't ever change that. We wouldn't abandon her. But, she couldn't contain it… Well, you'd better come, sir. She's in pretty bad shape."

"Dorothy, give me some bandages. You stay here with Wendy and try to keep her calm. Pan, let's go," Tip asserted, taking the bandages Dorothy hastily created, and walked confidently toward me. As he passed to take the lead, he gripped my shoulder and gave it a squeeze. "We'll get her taken care of. Chin up."

I nodded, a lump lodged in my throat making it impossible to speak and followed behind Tip and the Wonderlandians. The path they took didn't lead too far out, but I could see scorch marks on the ground as we approached a cluster of smoking jagged rocks.

My stomach leapt to my mouth and my heart dropped to my feet as I spotted Alice's motionless body, laying in the center of the of large broken stones, her body covered in blood, tinging her lovely long blonde hair crimson.

Cheshire was sitting on her chest, tail flicking in uncharacteristic concern. His immaculate white and ginger fur was scarlet where he was making contact with Alice. He flicked his ears and, without an air of nonsense, said, "She's still breathing."

Tip and I rushed forward. As we reached her, I realized the blood was leaking from a pattern of cracks all over her body— deeper than the last time. I dared to look at the compass and saw the cracks had grown and the metal was dented, but it was still intact. She'd managed not to break it completely.

I crouched at her head and gingerly cradled it into my lap, a shaking hand stroking her head. Tip, meanwhile, sprung into action to perform triage to her many wounds. My stomach was doing flips, and all I could do was mumble reassuring phrases to her as I tried to ignore the fact that she hadn't opened her eyes yet.

"It's going to be alright," I repeated over and over again, though I was trying to convince myself just as much as her. Any possible indulgent glimmer of hope that Alice might be able to stay here with me and rule over Neverland afterall — small as it might have been— had snuffed out. I was certain if she stayed now the compass would definitely kill her.

"Peter?" I looked down as Alice managed to croak out my name then had to quickly look away. Seeing her in such a state was making my head spin, swimming in shades of blood.

I swallowed and gritted my teeth, looking back and working up a smile. "I'm right here, Love."

"I'm sorry." She whimpered pitifully. "I messed up."

"Don't worry about it. It's going to be alright." I went back to gently stroking her forehead. "But no more Wicked magic for you."

"Are they okay?"

"Who?"

"Bill, and the others?"

"Funny that Bill is the first to come to mind."

"You can never tease him again. He saved me. They all did."

"They are a little banged up but everyone is fine. You, on the other hand, are full of cracks again. You look like a teacup after the Hatter's had his hands on it."

"I know. I was just trying to control the pull of the compass and…"Alice's big blue eyes blinked slowly and her voice trailed off, her breathing labored.

"Alice?" I asked, trying to shove my rising panic down.

"She's lost a fair bit of blood here," Tip commented from where he had finished wrapping Alice's arms, and was tearing at her pants to have access to her legs. "She's going to be worn out. She was pretty affected when it was just her arm, and that was without the blood loss and a much smaller portion of her body.We just need to keep an eye on her pulse and breathing."

"You don't mean…?" I couldn't finish the question.

Despair. Unleash your anger and force that ice witch to fix the compass and save her. The Shadow-Peter growled in my mind, slipping through the layers of anxiety.

"She's not out of the woods yet, but we will get her there," Tip sighed, but his face was set with determination.

"I never knew you were this skilled in a crisis," I replied weakly, blinking rapidly.

"There was a whole life I lived before coming here, you might have forgotten," Tip paused and glanced up at me. "Twelve years of rough living, seven of them orphaned. I had to be alright. There wasn't another option, which was why coming here was such a sanctuary."

"Yeah, that's why I brought you back with me. That was such a long time ago, I'd forgotten." I fixed my eyes on the ground.

So much for a sanctuary. Tip and the others had been stolen away one by one. John and Michael likely had been killed, Wendy imprisoned, Alice collared and tormented, Dorothy pushed into a game she didn't sign up for as a pawn. Even the Imagineds had suffered and been caught in indirect crossfire. Coming here, and staying with me wasn't a paradise. It was a living Hell. The Wizard and his vendetta made damn sure of that.

"Don't look so glum, Buddy. She's going to be alright. Remember that the cracks healed up in less than a day last time. These are a bit deeper but they will fade too. She won't be broken forever. Now, we need to get her back to what's left of camp." Tip finished using up the bandages Dorothy had provided him and beckoned the Wonderlandians over to help support Alice's body.

I was filled with such anguished rage— at The Wizard, at Mombi, and at my own existence for all the damage it caused other innocents. I could hardly see straight, knowing he'd succeeded in hitting me where it hurt, whether Alice stayed here or went back home— either way, I'd eventually never see her again.

I reached for my pouch to sprinkle her with pixie dust but faltered. "Let's carry her. I don't want her first time using the pixie dust to be like that." The others nodded with understanding.

We lifted Alice carefully, Cheshire staying loyally rooted to her chest, and carried her back to the camp. Wendy looked to have recovered from the worst of her shock and she and Dorothy were trying to straighten up what they could salvage. The pure destructive blast that had burst from Alice, to have done so much damage even with her at a distance, it was a wonder she had managed to survive at all.

After getting her situated, I thanked Bill, the March Hare and Card-guard from the bottom of my heart for however they managed to save her, and then rejoined Tip, Dorothy and Wendy.

"We can't put this off any longer or it's going to kill her," I declared darkly, plopping down next to Tip. For the first time, I was actually entertaining what the demon had suggested. I certainly had a lot of pent up anger I could unleash on Mombi to make her fix the compass and get Alice out of danger. "She can't use any more large stores of magic or she is going to shatter the compass completely with the next uncontrollable outburst."

The rest of the group nodded along solemnly. There was no running away this time. I took a deep breath, knowing I couldn't play my days away from this point onward. Then, I exhaled with newfound conviction settling in my bones.

"As soon as those cracks close back up— because we all know she won't abide by being left out of the fight— we make our move."

Twenty-Two

Alice

It had taken me the better part of three days to recover from the unfortunate outburst of power that had almost destroyed my compass and killed me in the process. My cuts were finally fading, and I had to make the conscious effort not to dwell on the lingering anxiety I felt regarding my tumultuous fate in this world. I didn't even really want to talk about it, for fear of finishing what I had unwittingly started.

"You wanted to talk to me, Witch?" Tip's gruff voice announced his arrival, and I looked up to see him staring down at me skeptically. Though, I did notice he was not throwing hateful daggers at me with his eyes since he'd encountered his Shadow Beast a few days earlier.

"Yes," I took a deep breath and gestured for him to please take a seat across from me.

"Peter is rather put out that you shooed him away for this ominous *private* conversation," He commented, with a jerk of his head to show Peter flitting back and forth, half listening to something Wendy was trying to tell him, his eyes fixed on me.

"He has hardly left my side in three days," I sighed.

"You gave him quite a scare."

"I know that. And that is precisely why I wanted to talk to you alone. I have some questions about my compass." I reached up and gingerly lifted the trinket to dangle it in front of my face.

"I see. Does this have to do with the other day?"

"When I went into the Shadow World, the compass had been spinning but came to a dead halt once I was inside. I had this feeling of freedom, like I couldn't find a single negative bone in my body. Then, when I summoned my fire to help Lionel, the flames were silver and white. They went back to normal when I was in Neverland again."

"Interesting," Tip mused, rubbing his chin thoughtfully. "So the compass stopped working once you left the world. You must have gone back to your natural self."

"I thought that might be the case, but I didn't understand why that would be. I was told by Avrilia that if I went home to my world the compass and magical effect would all go away, but it was always just a theory that I was chasing. However, I thought the Shadow World was still part of Neverland?"

"No, I think, from what Lionel has told me of it, it exists in its own plane or dimension that has an access point through the thorns—Not unlike the Northern Star, once upon a time had been, to our original world." He tilted his head. "But, it sounds like you already have that part worked out, so what are you needing to ask me?"

"The other day, when I sort of…"

"Spontaneously combusted?" Tip finished for me with a smirk as he referenced our time back in the caves.

I smiled, appreciating that despite our bristles and bickering, we at least had an inside joke between the two of us that indicated some semblance of friendship lurking. "Yes, that. I was trying to get the white flames back."

Tip narrowed his eyes. "I see."

"I think it was Good magic."

"It probably was."

"You don't sound surprised." I raised my eyebrows suspiciously.

"That's because I'm not."

"Care to elaborate then? Because it sounds like for all the grief you've given me about being Wicked, you seem to be saying I have Good in me too."

"Two reasons. First, didn't you say you first absorbed Glinda's magic from her puppet?"

"After removing her heart-thing, yes," I grunted. "Which would typically be considered Wicked."

"But *her* magic was Good. If it was her magic imbued in her. Transfer of magic isn't quite as black and white as everyone seems to think. At least not in the same way they think, anyways," Tip explained, leaning forward, gestures and miming punctuating his words.

I thought of Avrilia and her telling me the same thing about my view of morality. "How would you know about the moral scales of magic?"

"Mombi," He answered simply, then added for my benefit when I gave him a dubious look, "She is an inventor and scientist of sorts, as I've said before. Her whole thing is studying and experimenting with the confines of the magic in this world. I was around for a lot of that, and was made to help and partake in experiments with a lot of her trinkets— though thankfully none of them had any lasting effects."

"Like the compass?" I squeezed it in frustration that I had to push down for the risk of setting the compass ablaze and killing me and everyone here in the process.

Tip nodded. "Which brings me to my second point. That is a moral compass, yes?"

"We've established that, yes."

"And it's broken?"

"Again, yes."

"Well, doesn't morality go both ways?"

"I don't follow," I crinkled my nose in confusion.

"You've allowed your negative emotions to control the pull of the compass. No one is in control of it other than you. Sure, it might wander off course on its own from being broken, but you can lead it back to North. I'm sure it probably takes a fair bit of effort on your part, but—"

"What?" I demanded, interrupting Tip, dumbfounded. "I have never had control over this blasted thing!"

"Well, control might not be the best word."

"One moment you're calling me evil, the next you say I'm capable of Good, and now I'm back to willfully Wicked? It can't be both!" I tried to keep my voice level, reminding myself I had been the one to initiate this encounter.

"It's *because* you have both that I give you grief, Witch," Tip scoffed. "Actions are a driving force of morality. You succumbed to your negative actions the first time the compass swung out of control and let Wickedness claim you. *You* did that."

"I've fought this bloody compass nearly every step of the way! How dare you accuse me of doing otherwise!" My voice rose as anger began crashing freely through my body, setting all of my nerves on end. When pain shortly followed, it reminded me to settle down.

"Oh, don't be so high and mighty. It's how the compass works. Traditionally, it was meant to allow someone else to control the pull from Wicked to Good and everything in between. Just because the control was broken doesn't mean North was erased."

"I refuse to believe—"

"What? That you could possibly be at fault for your own actions? Take some responsibility, Witch," Tip snorted. "You were scared, and fear is a powerful agent to Wicked actions."

"I never—" I spluttered but Tip cut me off again.

"Fear is also a double-edged sword. Fear of doing bad things made you do bad things, and you became one big Wicked self-fulfilling prophecy. Staying rooted in fear, anger, and resentment leaves you just that; rooted. You will never move forward towards something better."

"Gah!" I exploded and threw a ball of fire at Tip's face, which he narrowly dodged, sending the flaming sphere spiraling into the ocean beyond him.

"Your temper seems to be another agent for you," He commented wryly, waving to Peter, who perked up at the altercation, that everything was alright. "It, mixed with your fear, makes you like a cornered animal, and lets the Wicked right in. Admitting your own faults might be a good way to gain better control of the compass' pull. Though, I don't suppose

I need to tell you that pride is another of those seven deadly sins. Right?"

I opened my mouth to yell at him, but images of the Munchkin Village broke into the front of my mind, causing me to take pause a moment. That had been an instance where I had fought the compass fully and won. I had recognized that what I was feeling was wrong, and had faced the fear of the fire to do something Good. Afterwards, I had felt lighter, and more like my pre-compass self than I had in ages. It was the closest I had come to how I had felt in the Shadow World too.

"I see those wheels turning. Are you starting to see what I am getting at? When you went into that place, your compass stopped working, and you felt disconnected from your fear and anger long enough to let your hackles down and remember who you are at heart." Tip's face was serious but not unfriendly, and I knew he wasn't trying to hassle me, but also wasn't pulling any punches.

"So, it wasn't misguided to try and find that magic out here?" I asked hopefully, only to scowl a moment later when he shrugged.

"Without talking to me first to rationalize out the situation and going in blind, it probably wasn't the best idea. Especially since you already knew that your Wicked magic was doing something to aggravate the compass."

"And now? Now that you've explained it to me, is there some other way I can connect to it?" I bit my lip and willed him to have some grand and easy solution.

"I think you just need to keep doing what you're doing," He said after a moment of thinking.

I drooped. "Well, that was anticlimactic. What I've been doing has made it all worse."

Tip shook his head. "No, not so much with the magic. I think you need to stop obsessing so much on it, because it only makes you more fearful and aggressive. You need to focus on the little things that make up the best part of every day you've spent here. Relax a little and enjoy yourself. If you can let go of some of the fear, you might actually have a little more control of what affects you and what you in turn have affect on."

"I can see why Dorothy finds you so insightful," I admitted begrudgingly.

"She does?" He perked up a little.

"Yes, and your ability to read everyone like a book is very unsettling," I snipped back, then smiled. "But it is useful. Thank you for indulging me. I will try to let go of obsessing on my fear and aggression, though with the big altercation coming up, I'm sure that will be easier said than done. Maybe I ought to try enjoying the fighting…" I half mused, half joked.

"Just don't use big stores of magic in the fighting, and I think you can manage it. Besides we have you going to a part we don't anticipate being highly populated, based on Tiger Lily's scouting mission yesterday." Tip nodded encouragingly and pushed back up to his feet, turning to walk away.

"You sound like Peter."

"Must be a method to his madness. There is a healthy place between drowning in fear and avoiding anything negative though. Meet in the middle somewhere."

"Hey, Tip?" I called after him.

He turned back. "Yes, Witch?"

"Thank you. For the other day. And the time before that. And the one before that. You've saved me several times over, and despite everything, I am really grateful you're around." I nodded in turn to Peter and Dorothy. "You've played a hand in saving them too. So… Thank you."

Tip looked taken aback by my sincerity but smiled and turned back around with a wave of his hand in farewell. "You're welcome, *Alice*."

I felt a small burst of victory at Tip's choice to use my actual name instead of his unsolicited nickname for me. Getting to my feet, I crossed the camp to meet Peter halfway as he headed over to me.

"What's got you smiling like the Cheshire Cat?" He asked with a puzzled look at Tip, who was now sitting with Jack, Saw-horse, and Dorothy, being lectured by Caterpillar about some naming nonsense. It was honestly a nice sight to see the various Imagineds from West, East, and South all interacting pleasantly with one another, making Neverland a communal home and refuge. It felt akin to Peter's intent for the place to begin with— a sanctuary and paradise.

"He called me Alice," I replied smugly.

"Well, look at that. Tip, you big softy. You finally wore him down," Peter cheered, then looked at me with a devious expression. "Now what were you two talking about?"

"Nothing to worry about."

"Oh, come on! I'm dying to know."

"And they call me the curious one. If you must know, I was just asking some questions about the compass. And how to keep it… less active than it has been."

The smile fell from Peter's face and he grabbed my hand to inspect it. "How are you feeling, Love? I saw that fireball. Did you break again anywhere? I'm willing to do a full body search."

"Peter!" I scolded and swatted him.

"What? Answer the question and you have nothing to worry about."

"I'm *fine*." I leaned on the word for emphasis. "You're more fussy than Wendy these days, good grief."

"Can't help that I care. Sorry, Love." He tapped my nose affectionately. "Well, did you at least get the answers you were wanting?"

"I sure did. And apparently I need to relax a little— as much as I can manage anyways— before our little fight tomorrow." I tried to swallow down my intense desire to connect with the Good magic. Trading one fixation for another didn't seem helpful. But, it was also worth it to me to try to find a way to overcome the compass in this world because, with everything that had happened in the past week, it was finally becoming clear to me that my desire to go back to my home world was waning, while my wish to stay here with Peter was growing. But, I could only do that, if I could find a way to beat the compass. "Want to go watch some clouds?"

I could have sworn I saw stars shimmering in Peter's eyes as he beamed at me. "I've only been asking for ages! But," I raised a finger.

"I actually have something that I think will be even better than cloud watching, I've been waiting for you to be up for it."

"What's that?"

"We are going to the Pixie Village."

The next thing I knew, Peter had scooped me into his arms and we were zipping through the Never Woods like a bolt of lightning towards a lightning rod. This was the first time he and I had flown together since before all this nonsense had started. And before we had told each other we loved one another. In fact, I realized the last time Peter had held me like this, I had been terribly self-conscious about wanting to cuddle in against him.

But now… I looked up at him before nuzzling into the crook of his neck just below his chin. Keeping one arm around his shoulder for support, I rested the other on his chest, trailing it back and forth lightly. I had wondered countless times what it would be like to do such a thing.

"Whoops," Peter gasped, suddenly veering sharply to the right to avoid flying straight into a tree. "Sorry," He mumbled, heat flooding his cheeks.

I tilted my head back and laughed, moving my hand from his chest to cup his face instead. I pouted my lower lip and widened my eyes innocently. "Awe, did I distract you?"

"Just a little bit, Love. Not that I didn't like it, it just was, um, distracting. Just as well, because we are nearly there, but we can make a little stop first," He puffed, angeling our trajectory to land. When he placed me down, his arm lingered at my back, and instead of releasing me, he pulled me close to him and kissed me. "I've been wondering what that was like for a long time."

I kept my eyes closed and drank in the bliss engulfing me. This was the future I was trying to aim for. I needed to let go of the tormented emotions regarding my family and the guilt I felt about getting back to them. My time in that world had passed. I'd be an old woman now if I had never gone into the rabbit hole, and I could only guess how much lonelier my life would have been. I wouldn't have made it to right here, at this moment.

This tiny little moment in an infinite timeline, happy and at ease.

"I've had thoughts like that too," I admitted, then pointed a finger in his face. "Care to make it a game then?"

"A game?" He smirked and quirked an eyebrow at me before deliberately pushing my finger to the side. "Watch where you point that thing. I know how much damage you can do with one finger."

"Not right now," I waved him off.

He squinted his green eyes at me intently, clearly back to worrying about my compass again.

"Peter, the game?"

"Alright, tell me the rules of the game," He conceded, leaning against a tree where we were tucked into a small grove of ash trees. "After the last couple days, I could do with a fleeting moment of fun and games, just us two, before we rejoin the others."

"Okay, then for five minutes we are going to say everything we've been thinking about each other that we haven't really ever said directly to each other. It'll be like a challenge, one statement for the other and the first one to chicken out loses. We both get one freebie to pass on though. Then we go back with our new understanding of each other, and face this whole Wizard trying to kill us business. Peter Pan," I extended a hand and feigned seriousness. "King of Neverland, do you accept my challenge?"

He took his time pretending to mull over his decision, rubbing his chin and making a lot of hmm noises before accepting my hand and giving it a firm shake. "You're on, Alice Liddel"

I narrowed my eyes playfully. I could tell by his posture that he was ready to give me a run for my money, but I bet I could get him to call chicken first. He was shameless, but I'd also seen him get squirmy more than once, so I knew I had a decent chance at victory. "I've imagined a romantic future for us if we both grew up all the way, more than once. Go."

"Since we first met, I've always found you insatiably attractive. Go." Peter stared at me with a big crooked grin on full display, though his gaze never wavered. I could see him blushing, but he wasn't caving.

I felt my cheeks flush too, but I held his gaze and relished the competition. "I've always really fancied your muscles. Even when we were younger."

"Ah, tell that to Dorothy, will you?" Peter sighed dramatically, gesturing to the beach. "She seems to think Tip is the only one with muscle."

"That's alright. I don't want her thinking of your muscles, thank you very much."

"Jealous little bat." Peter clicked his tongue. "If Tip or Lionel made a romantic advance on you, I'd definitely punch them in the teeth. Friend or no. Go."

"I wanted to kiss you long before the whole deal with your lovely aunt Jabberwock. Go."

"I wanted to play tag and wrestle and tickle you as an excuse to touch you. It became a rather persistent itch to know what it was like. You have rather soft skin, you know. Go."

"You're my favorite person I have ever met and…" I almost blurted out my desire to stay in Neverland with him now, but I trailed off, wondering if it would be fair to get his hopes up, especially since it was a relatively new revelation and I needed to be certain I didn't change my mind again, and could find a way to fix the compass.

"And?" Peter leaned on the word.

"Pass," I squeaked, taking a deep breath.

"Ah ha! There goes your free chicken." Peter crowed victoriously, though my pass hadn't been from embarrassment. "I did not expect to be better at this."

"Hush, it's your turn." I rolled my eyes. "Time is almost up."

"I got a good one to shock you. I don't knock on purpose," He returned to slouching against the tree, face beaming, eyebrows waving.

My jaw gaped and I laughed hoarsely, before punching him in the arm.

"It became a morbid curiosity to know why you were so private." He threw his arms up defensively.

"I don't ask you to drop your trousers!" I chided, wrapping my arms around myself self-consciously. "Some things are just private, because they are."

"I can, if that would make you feel better," Peter shrugged, causing me to smack my face with my hand, scarlet red.

"No! Now is not… I don't need to. Ugh. Good grief, I forget you weren't raised with an ounce of decorum."

"Sounds boring," Peter sniffed, but plucked my hand from my face to smile deviously at me. "What's the problem, Love? Too embarrassed to continue? You look pretty red, so I'll accept your defeat now."

"Ah, so that's your angle!" I hissed.

"Tick, tock." He tapped his wrist rhythmically.

"Fine, try this one on for size!" I raised my eyes to bore into his, going for shock value as well. "You're a better kisser than your father."

"Oof! Brutal, but I can't say I'm not a bit relieved to hear that. Actually no, it's still not something I wanted to hear. Let's never speak of it again." He wrinkled his nose in disgust. "And maybe we can agree that from now on, you won't kiss anyone? Other than me, of course."

"I didn't exactly ask for it. He just sort of ambushed me," I grumbled, shuddering at the memory.

"Well, how about my request? I've recently adopted a more mature nature, and I think it to be a reasonable thing to ask for those such as us— coupled and whatnot." He put one arm behind his face and waved his other hand in front of him dramatically, with no small amount of pomp and stuffiness.

"Who else would I kiss?" I sighed, shaking my head.

"Bill, obviously." Peter rolled his eyes and cupped the side of my face, making me feel so small and delicate in his palm.

"Oh, that's a tough one. Alright, I agree not to kiss anyone else. Happy?" I quirked an eyebrow and batted my big blue eyes at her, all innocence.

He cleared the space between us once more, pressing his lips to mine, softly at first, then a bit more aggressively. A sudden hunger overtaking me, I realized there were definitely perks to be found in growing up beyond my getting prettier, and his getting more handsome like we had once talked about. Apparently, when you were older, you could actually do something with that attraction. *I should have done this ages ago. I didn't know what I was missing.* And something told me, he was thinking the same thing.

We separated, and leaned our foreheads together. The moment was both heated and so incredibly fragile. Tears started to well in my eyes as the reality of having to leave him behind crashed over me. When I went back, there would be no more moments like this, and I couldn't believe just how blinded I had been by the manipulations pointing me back to my old unhappy life. How cruel I had been to Peter to treat him as so easily discardable. I didn't deserve him or his love.

What if I went back and Wendy stayed behind and they got married? I'd likely have to get married someday too, but could I ever readjust to society after living wild and free so long? How had I never thought any of this through? I had been fighting to leave what I loved most, on the off chance my old world might appreciate me more. And just like that, my heart started breaking, and a new wave of fear bled through the seams.

"What's wrong, Love?" Peter asked, staring down at me with wild-eyed concern brewing in his gaze. "Did I do something?"

"No. You're perfect." I bit my lip and laughed softly to myself, wrapping my arms around his neck, and twisting my hands through his hair.

His grip tightened around my waist, and he trailed one hand lightly up and down my spine. "Intoxicating, positively intoxicating," He mumbled mostly to himself, and I wondered if he even realized he had said the thought out loud.

"I can't do it, Peter," I whispered, my voice edged with emotion. "I can't lose you. I can't leave you. You were right. This is my home now."

"But you have to go back for…" He responded lazily, still a bit entranced with all of the new physical touching and closeness. "Your family and the Wickedness stuff or whatever. The compass. I've accepted your choice. I'm not trying to get in the way anymore."

I nuzzled my head against his affectionately. "I can't do it. You mean more to me than going home does. I just was too blinded to see it." I pulled away and rolled up sleeves to show the remaining fissures across my skin. "I was breaking apart from the inside out while I tried to internalize all of my Wicked emotions about everything I'd found out like you lot have been doing with your shadows. I had realized that I had been a pawn in The Wizard's game from the moment I got here. The White Rabbit could have also been a trick for all I know, and that's why I can never catch him. The compass was made by Mombi. I was just a tool to be a last ditch way to destroy you, and I couldn't take it. I got so worked up, I had to try to calm myself down and I tried thinking about going home. But I couldn't picture it… until I started thinking about you. And that's when I realized that home is with you."

"Alice, I think—" He tried to spit the words out, but I kept going, not wanting him to have a chance to counter me.

"And, when I was starting to drown, all I could hope was that my death wouldn't hurt you too badly, and that I wished I had come right out and told you just how deeply I care." I stared at the compass. "And that I'm sorry for all this time I didn't see what was happening. That I couldn't see how I was hurting you." I kept my eyes lowered because tears of guilt had started to brim in them. Emotions over the past, present and future were all stirring together.

"I see now, that if I leave you behind then I am playing right into The Wizard's hand and I refuse to do that." I looked up at Peter and my gaze burned with a heated intensity— resentment, bitterness and orneriness all churning in their blue depths. But, that spark of willful defiance was part of what made me who I was.

"I think you should go back." Peter's words came out blunter than I had expected and I blinked at him, taken aback.

"What?" I was incredulous. "*Now* you want me to leave? Is this all just another stupid game for you or something? I—" And now my tone had shifted into a rising fury of indignation, but he took my hand and shook his head.

"It's not a game, of that I can assure you. But, you just told me that you literally almost ripped yourself apart because of a cursed compass my father arranged for you to get tangled up with, just in an attempt to get at me. I can't let you take that kind of risk."

"But—" I started, and he shook his head again.

"And just so you know, something I never got tell you, because I had lost track of the memory in the cobwebs of my mind or something, was the reason I was at the crossroads when you arrived. I was led by a little white rabbit I had never seen before with a pocket watch. I'm not sure what he is or why he can never be caught, but I do know he is Good and he wasn't a trap or a trick. I think he took the memory from me somehow— and I don't know why he would— until the other day when you told me you loved me, and I saw you playing with your hair like when we first met, and it all started to come back into focus. But, all those years ago, I made a wish years ago, and he granted it." His brows knitted like he was struggling to form a clear mental image of moments passed.

"What was the wish?" I asked, my irritation melting into my insatiable curiosity, and the romantic and shocking element of Peter's story.

"For someone who wouldn't leave me, and would choose to stay with me. Then he led me to you."

"And I do choose to stay with you!" I implored, squeezing his hand before folding my arms defiantly. "You can't change my mind."

"But the compass, Love. What happens the next time you go off the rails? You want to give me prime viewing of you shattering to pieces on a sunny afternoon in the garden?" He countered. How was *he* the mature and selfless one here? "Besides, wish granted. You chose to stay, but now you need to go."

"No."

"Well, now you're just being obstinate."

"I won't go off the rails," I insisted, flashing my best innocent smile.

Peter smirked. "Ah, so all the other times were by choice then?" The light stagnated in a sort of permanent dawn gleam, even though the sun would be high in the sky above the trees surrounding us. We were suspended in a globe of peace here, and I closed my eyes a moment to drink it all in. My new closest friends, here safe in Neverland. This quiet secluded space where Peter and I discussed our future beyond childhood games. Woodland scents tickled my nose. It reminded me of pure serenity.

"Um, no. But I have new information now," I replied, my face lighting up. "Tip was familiar with the compass because of his time with Mombi, and he pointed out the simplest of facts that will probably make you feel just as foolish as me when you hear it."

"Well, with a lead like that, I am ready to be baffled by this obvious discovery." Peter lifted his eyebrows up and down and exaggerated his enthusiasm, causing me to scowl at me.

"The moral compass is still a compass," I replied flatly to his sarcasm.

"So, we don't have to get lost…?" He fished for the astounding new piece of information that would turn the tables of our debate.

I squinted at him and waved away his comment. "No. We've been focusing on the compass as a *Wicked* compass only. But, it still has a North. Remember what Avrilia told me about fear being an agent of Wickedness? Well, I had become so afraid of my own fear causing me to do bad things that I… er, did bad things. However, there is still a Good side to tap into with *Good* magic. I mean to try to figure out how to use it."

He frowned in interest and rubbed his chin thoughtfully. "Alright," he conceded at last. "You were right, we both probably should have put that together ourselves and it does sort of help, but I'm not ready to gamble your life, Love."

"We can go back to the others and carry out our game plan." I lifted my chin with the same confidence I had made myself wear so many times before as I faced some new challenge or adventure. "We are going to win this game with The Wizard, take back Wonderland, and we are most definitely overthrowing The Wizard too. We will do it for us, for our friends, and for all the Imagineds." I spoke fiercely and my eyes were blazing. I was ready to fight, and I hoped my intensity was infectious. We would fix this one fight at a time.

Peter grinned and offered his hand out to me. "Come on, let's go look at the Pixie Village. It's just a little ways though here," I puffed a sigh at his obvious dodging the concreteness of our conversation, and followed him through the woods, my future here still uncertain.

Upon clearing away the fronds and branches that opened up to a small moss speckled clearing, we slipped through to an unexpected scene of chaos. My eyes stretched wide in horror and Peter bristled. All of our previous happiness had snuffed out entirely.

In front of us was the Pixie Village, broken and in ruins. A giant purple Spider standing in the center of the mess. Tiny half-shadowed bodies littered the ground around it. The little structures of the village were smashed and coated in webs.

"Gah!" Peter roared and blasted the arachnid with a powerful strike of magic, disintegrating it. I braced myself for the appearance of Mombi, or the chill that tended to precede her presence, but felt none.

"Are they…?" I asked quietly, kneeling to the ground to inspect one of the fallen fairies.

"Dead." Peter spoke through gritted teeth. "Tink? Is she here? Is she…?" He couldn't form the words, they were choked with such emotion.

I quickly scanned the surrounding bodies, looking for the feisty pixie, but shook my head when I saw no sign of her in the body count. "She's not here."

"Good. Good," He breathed rapidly. "Tink? Are you here somewhere? I swear that witch has gone too far. I'm going to—" He voice was dark and husky, reminding me of how his demon sounded, and a chill ran up my spine. He stopped himself from finishing the statement and composed himself, clutching at his head. "Tinkerbell? I need you," He whispered.

My heart ached to see him hurt so, and sound so utterly defeated. Clearly, Tinkerbell meant a lot to him. A soft jingle sounded, and a handful of tiny faces poked out from behind nearby trees. The surviving fairies.

Among them, I spotted Tinkerbell, and saw Peter sag with relief. He shook his head slowly. I knew seeing his beloved fairy alive softened the blow a little, but not really. I knew he was taking on the guilt of the fairies and was filled with grief and despair. I couldn't stand it, and had to do something.

"This was not how I imagined you getting to see the Pixie Village. And it was supposed to be an adventure too," He groaned, kicking away some of the spider webs.

"No, this wasn't how I imagined it." I screwed my eyes tightly closed. Fairies and flying had been something I had idolized for years. I had spent so long dreaming up what their home in Neverland looked like, and what it would be like to fly with them and Peter if he ever brought me here someday. My lip trembled and I clung fiercely to that image in my mind, refusing to accept anything else.

Mombi couldn't break Neverland and scar it like this. I absolutely refused it with every fiber of my being. She and The Wizard wouldn't hurt Peter in this way, or Neverland, or my own dreams of what the fairy village would be. It was the start of Neverland, and there was no doubt why she had slipped in to attack it while we were elsewhere, and the shadowed fairies were like collateral results of the wraiths being drawn towards her Wickedness again— Sacrifices. She had desecrated sacred ground and ran away.

"I imagined it with little houses made out of rocks and mushrooms and other small things." I started describing my own version of the village, keeping my eyes closed and gesturing broadly, like my words alone could somehow rewrite history. "I imagined things being made out of lost things that they would find and salvage so everything could be found, and nothing stayed lost. And there were leaves for curtains in the houses. They cover this whole area. There was a river of pixie dust running through here, and the fairies would use tiny acorn buckets to harvest it. And light. I imagined there would be all sorts of little magical flowers that dappled the entire area with glowing centers that represented the wonder of every child who has ever believed in fairies and wished to see one. The fairies would be dancing and singing to the most beautiful and ethereal music played by some fairy instrument unknown to mankind and—"

I stopped at the sound of a small jingling that made my ears twitch. It was quickly followed by the most elated, jovial laugh I had ever heard from Peter in all my time knowing him. I opened my eyes slowly, startled by the sudden change in his attitude, and stared in awe at what was happening before me.

Golden specs had started permeating the ruined village, dancing and swirling through the wreckage. Pieces of debris and plants were lifting and morphing in a brilliant light. The particles covered the fallen bodies and absorbed their darkness, turning them into more radiant dust to swirl in with the rest.

And the sound.

The sound leapt from twinkling to something somehow both mournful but also filled with joy and hope. It reminded me of old gaelic folk music steeped in wist and wonder as it rung through the village.

Neverland was restoring the village to fit my imagination. I laughed breathlessly and twirled around, dipping my hands in and out of the ambient sparkles, filled to the brim with absolute splendor.

I was fixing it. My conviction and longing had worked and I could scarcely believe it. So this was the true magic of Neverland.

"And," I went on eagerly. "It is protected. Only Lost Ones with the blessing of the fairies can ever see, hear, or know of the village. Nothing will ever harm it again."

One by one, little flowers appeared as closed buds, but like lighting a cathedral of candles, their petals spread out, centers illuminated. From within each flower's dazzling glow, a tiny fairy stepped out, straightening their wings and dusting off the floral clothing. The fairies had been born from the dreams of countless children out there somewhere in a big expansive universe, dimension upon dimension aiding in their magic.

Tink and her remaining kin were slowly filtering into their new home, eyes wide with amazement and gratitude. They greeted the flower fairies hesitant at first, and then with more fervor, the embraced with recognition that told me not only had their village been restored, the lost fairies had been revived. They were singing and dancing, flitting through the air with unbridled rejoicing.

Peter was glowing—Actually physically emanating a soft golden glow from his entire body and he looked at me like I was the most spectacular thing he had ever laid eyes on. I could see the faintest glaze of tears reflecting the shimmering light shifting and creating around us and they were filled with such pride and love.

"You have contributed to Neverland, Alice. Now there will always be a piece of you here. Not only that, but you *fixed* Neverland, and undid this travesty with your pure force of will and brilliant imagination, just as I should have always known you would have. I just don't—" His voice caught in his throat, and I felt my own tears start spilling down my cheeks with the overwhelming blissful emotions. "I don't have words to begin to tell you what this means to me. To see someone imagining in Neverland again, turning something broken into something beautiful. To see *you* so happy here… I don't have words."

I smiled and took his hand. "Come on, let's go back to camp. We have to prepare to pay back this devastation ten times fold. I want Mombi to pay for everything. I want to avenge this village. I want my castle back! You can't just replace those," I lamented and made to hop into Peter's arms like we usually flew together.

But, instead he pulled his pixie dust pouch out, dipping into the new river of golden particles running through the center of the village, and sprinkled over himself for a fresh coat. He whistled to the fairy and pointed to me with an unspoken request directed at Tinkerbell. Tiny glittering tears rolled down her face and she nodded, her face crumpling with emotion.

She jingled, calling something out to the other fairies and one by one, every single one flew around me, in a single unified, beautiful dance, cascading golden pixie dust all over me. It glimmered, a gold ethereal glow around my blonde hair as my eyes widened with delight.

A small gasp of childlike wonder escaped from my mouth as I

immediately floated from the ground while Peter squeezed my hand in his. "You're letting me fly! You've never let me use the pixie dust before!"

I felt just as animated as when I had first flown with Peter over Wonderland and he'd asked to trust him as he tossed and caught me. Fairy wings were tickling my skin, as they continued to orbit around me while I rose higher into the air, carried by the pure happiness of the moment.

"That was when you were Wicked," Peter replied dramatically, and joined me in the air, still tethered by our hands.

I scowled and pursed my lips. "I didn't have magic to be Wicked or Good at all for six years! And I still am Wicked, technically."

"Details." He waved away my reasoning and let go of my hand, allowing me full freedom of flight. "Don't get me wrong, I definitely don't mind carrying you, but, if you are to be my Neverland Queen, even just till the end of this war we are in, I think you should be flying at my side. As equal, mad heads, soaring through the sky. From here on, just like we agreed outside your fort on your second night, let's keep growing—together."

"Together," I echoed, beaming and immediately started whirling about with the reckless abandon of a madwoman, laughing as I did loops and twirls through the air with the fairies.

Peter hovered in the air and watched my joyful flight, laughing happily along with me, and I knew we were once more reminded of Neverland's earnest origins built on bliss and splendor.

Thank you. The fairies whispered to me, and Tinkerbell floated directly in front of my face. *You will never know the depth of my gratitude, Alice Liddel— I don't care what they call you as a witch. From now on, you will be hailed in Neverland as Alice the Good Fairy of the South. The fairies will follow you to the ends of this world and the next should you need it. Our debt will never be repaid.* She gave a tiny bow and flitted back into the throng of dancing fairies filling the air.

I swallowed down the lump in my throat, touched beyond words at the temperamental pixie's acknowledgement.

We couldn't change the past. We could only take our given roles in this world sincerely and endeavor to forge a brighter future from this day forward for ourselves and everyone who was depending on us. Even if there was a war brewing, pain still needed to be conquered, and darkness was on the horizon, as I watched Peter flit through the air to join me with such a bright and sparkling look of glee, I knew. This was going to be our biggest adventure together yet, and just maybe, this was the glimpse into our possible bright future that he needed to see in order to trust me to stay with him.

A quick glance at my compass while filled with such euphoria, I was startled to see the arrow spinning and pausing intermittently, but each time it hesitated on the same direction.

North.

Twenty-Three

Alice

It was our last night in the little camp we dubbed as our safe haven. In the wee hours, before light could fully crest the horizon, we were finally launching our attack to reclaim Wonderland from Mombi.

That truly Wicked witch was flouncing about in *my* castle. Her creepy scarecrows and tinmen soldiers were marching about in *my* Wonderland, and she was ordering around *my* Card-guards— the ones who hadn't been free thinking enough to defect and join us in Neverland. Though nearly all of the main Wonderland inhabitants had managed to escape her temporary reign, there were still those left behind. The Hatter was an actively held prisoner. The chess pieces in the World of Reflect likely didn't know much of a difference, but the rest of the card-guards were still there, and the walrus, carpenter, and other miscellaneous Wonderlandians were unaccounted for. Even those blasted talking flowers that I loathed so much were under hostile takeover. I needed to restore order— as chaotic as order could be in a place such as Wonderland.

Moreover, since discovering that Mombi was the whole catalyst to my misery here in this world, I couldn't wait to unleash on her. Then she just increased the desire by attacking Dorothy and the fairies. I wouldn't let her turn it into a ruin like she had with Pixie Village.

Despite my desire to go berserk with my confrontation with the Wicked witch, I knew I had to be sensible, and I found that notion to be terribly bothersome and limiting. But at least I would have help in my little attack squadron.

As soon as I had been able to, I had made sure to attend to Bill and the March Hare's injuries personally, and repaired the card-gaurd's broken spear following my combustion and now it seemed they were once more in decent shape, and ready to fight for their homeland. Bill's tail was still a stump, but since I didn't have any clue of how to heal injuries with my magic, it was something we had to live with till it grew back on its own. Mombi would be paying for that too.

"Working on your fighting face?" Dorothy commented, coming to sit beside me at the fire. "You look like you swallowed something sour."

"Just was thinking about ripping Mombi's head off her shoulders with my bare hands."

"Well, that's a bit much, don't you think?"

"Not really," I muttered darkly.

"Well, if you did feel the need to do that, between you and me, I don't think I'd stop you. And, I might take the opportunity to cut off her tongue. Oh, God. What a terrible and violent influence you've been on me."

"Me? Who's to say that's not your Wicked side showing? Besides, some people make choices that simply don't warrant mercy."

"Are you going to put her head on the signpost like a spike?" Dorothy asked sarcastically.

"There's an idea… We have to survive the first wave though."

"Please don't mention the word 'survive.' If we start talking about survival, it means there is an equal chance of doing the opposite, and I'm nervous enough already. I'm a counter girl at a market. I'm turning seventeen. I'm not meant to be in a battle, let alone a wacky one like this. I'm meant to be suffering through ringing up customers, embarking on basic adulthood, and my Aunt and Uncle trying to force me to make friends."

"It only took you traveling to a different dimension for their ploy to work, I suppose," I laughed, nudging Dorothy gently with my shoulder.

"And somehow the friends I have made have tried to stab me,

sent me flying out of control, hunted me down to steal my shoes, gotten me locked in a dungeon, and once more hunted down by an all-power, egocentric maniac and his main squeeze." Dorothy rolled her eyes, but smiled nonetheless.

"Well, anything sounds bad with an attitude like that." I wagged my finger at her, and gestured to the rest of the gang coming over to join us. "You're hung up on those pesky details."

"I am glad to have met each one of you, despite those pesky details— or near-death experiences, as I call them— that keep cropping up in your company." She looked around at each of us warmly, starting with me and roving to Peter, Wendy, Lionel, and ending on Tip.

"Are we getting sentimental? Oh! Let's make Tip cry," Peter declared, turning to stare intently at his friend.

"What?" Tip cried incredulously.

"You're the only one who hasn't had an emotional and or tearful outburst."

"Neither have you! Or Lionel, for that matter."

"I did so. Just in private, of course."

"Oh, good grief," Tip sighed and shook his head at Peter's antics.

"Quick, Dorothy, tell him something heartfelt. That should get him going." Peter patted Dorothy's arm with the back of his hand.

She pushed it away. "I highly doubt that. Also, no. I'm not qualified to do heartfelt."

The fire crackled, the sound palpitating through the silence, thick and tangible. None of us spoke for a while. None of us even knew what to say. This was it. We were all going to pick a fight with a foe that had once bested us before. No amount of preparation was truly enough to steady our nerves.

"Hey, Peter?" Dorothy broke the silence, her voice shaking behind a trembling smile. "How about one of your games for our final night in this place?"

Peter's soft green eyes reflected the flickering flames, and gleamed. "What type of game are you thinking of? Wait, I know what will be fun!" He leapt into the air and dumped pixie dust on Dorothy's head, beaming when she squawked and latched onto Tip's arm to stay grounded while her lower body began lifting into the air without her consent. "Come on, Dorothy!"

"Oh, oh no. He got you..." Tip reached halfheartedly after her and faked shocked remorse as Peter plucked Dorothy off of Tip, spinning her into the air. Both boys laughed at her continued squawks of protest as she instinctively flapped awkwardly about. The rest of us couldn't help but snicker along good naturedly.

After a few minutes, Dorothy managed to land, arms stretched out to either side for balance. She took in a steadying breath before her wild brown eyes narrowed into slits.

"So, you two want to fight, eh?" Her hands lit into flames, a powerful wind whipping around her immediate body, and she hurled two fireballs at Peter and Tip. "I can do the fancy magic tricks now too!"

Peter lifted into the air to avoid the assault, while Tip calmly leaned to the side, allowing the orb to whiz past him. He was getting used to dealing with us witches, it seemed.

"Clearly you've been spending too much time with this one," Peter floated behind me and placed his hand on my head, patting it slowly. "Since you've started throwing fire about."

"Maybe you shouldn't be so antagonizing then," I quipped to him, then flicked my eyes over to where Dorothy's stray fire had lit a tree ablaze behind Tip. "You are, however, setting fire to the forest again, Dorothy."

"Damn it!" She hissed and rushed over to inspect the damage. "If you hadn't dodged, this would have been you!" She called over her shoulder at Peter and Tip.

Tip chuckled and sighed. "Hold on, I'll come help put it out. You too, buddy. You heard her. We *shouldn't* have dodged the flaming balls of death she threw at us." His tone was sarcastic but he got to his feet and beckoned Peter to follow him.

"Shouldn't we get a bucket or something?" Peter asked as he floated away.

"Don't you have water magic?" Tip reminded him, and Peter snapped his fingers.

"Oh, yeah! I forgot about that. Watch out, Dorothy."

"Wait—" Dorothy's words were cut short as Peter unleashed a barrage of water against the smoldering tree without waiting for Dorothy to get out of the way. "Gah! Come here, you little gnat!"

Dorothy chased Peter, flinging more fireballs, while he flitted away laughing in pure bliss. Tip sighed, walked over to us, dumped out a bucket of apples, and refilled it with water from the little well we had managed to create. He shook his head and set to work following behind Dorothy to put out her flames.

"Apparently, you've joined their impulsive club," He muttered.

It was an amusing sight to behold, and something about the friendships building here lifted my precarious spirits. Dorothy had been an adversary and target, and now she was an ally and friend whom I actually trusted. Peter treated her more like a sister to annoy, which seemed to have become their dynamic. Tip, as ambiently cantankerous as he was, seemed to have developed a soft spot for Dorothy, and already had one for Peter—who also seemed to bear a sort of brotherlike relationship. Lionel fit in with the boys, usually encouraging the antics or reminding the others of old fond memories of the Lost Ones to make them laugh.

In some ways, a lot of bonds had developed in a short amount of time, but aside from Dorothy, the rest of us all had long standing relationships with Peter, making him the glue of the group. He was like a tree trunk and we were all his branches now being made to intermingle. Everyone seemed to be building deeper bonds with one another— well, except for myself and Tip, though we seemingly had settled into a respectful tolerance, which I suppose was progress of its own breed.

Everyone's friendships were morphing and deepening except for…

"Wendy," I ventured, seeming to snap her out of a sort of trance.

"Sorry, yes?" She blinked at me, and tilted her head, clearly surprised by my addressing her. Since our conversation with Mombi, we really hadn't interacted directly or independently. But, my gut told me that something tortured and ominous was growing inside her, and her connections were stunting. I worried that Mombi had been able to get under her skin.

Who cares about her? My compass hissed through my mind.

I do. I should, anyway. It's the right thing to do. I countered. *You know what it feels like to have no connections to anyone, and to feel invisible. I can do something about it.*

She's a threat to your happiness.

No, she isn't. Peter has proven himself to me, and Wendy is not trying to take him from me. We would have had it out already if she was.

But, she could. If you befriend her, you can use it as leverage.

I don't want to think that way anymore! Where is your good half? I'd rather speak with them. You're just trying to get me to drive everyone away, and all I ever wanted was friends.

"Alice, you were saying something?" Wendy exchanged a quizzical look with Tiger Lily, who had just wandered over from the pirates to see what all the commotion was, and I realized my internal dialog with my compass had interrupted my flow of conversation.

I cleared my throat, and waved my hand absently at the three rushing about to the side of us. "They have hijacked the excitement. Is there anything you would like to suggest for a game?"

Wendy blinked slowly then shook her head. She felt almost vacant. "Nothing is coming to mind. I can't really focus, I'm afraid."

"Are you nervous about tomorrow?" I tried another flow of conversation.

"Not really, I don't think. I'm more just anxious to help the other Lost Ones. Sitting around playing games feels a bit unsettling."

I felt my skin prickle with irritation as the imposed slight at trying to lighten the mood. "Everyone handles things in different ways, I suppose," I replied through a forced smile. "So you feel ready then?"

"I do." Another deadend response. I glanced at Tiger Lily who shrugged.

"Peter asked me to go with him tomorrow." She offered a shift in conversation and I was grateful for it.

"I thought he wanted to go on his own for the purpose of being a more sought after target?" I asked Tiger Lily. She removed her hat and combed her fingers through her glossy black hair.

"He just asked me earlier today. He didn't really say much about why, just that he wanted to use my stealth skills." She shrugged.

"Well, I suppose that makes sense," I mumbled begrudgingly. "I wish I were going with him."

"Well, that's what happens when you blow yourself up," Tip sighed, plopping down to join us again.

"Lose interest?" Lionel raised an eyebrow at the Lost Boy.

Tip shook his head. "No, but they should be right behind me. Once Peter realized he could juggle Dorothy's flames she got frustrated and gave up."

"Stupid master-of-all, magical flying, Fairy-Boy. Taking my magic and making it into a joke…" Dorothy grumbled to herself and sat with a huff.

"I said I was sorry," Peter trailed along after her, still juggling the balls of fire. "But, you can't argue with me that this isn't impressive, right here."

Lionel smiled wickedly and stuck a leg out to trip Peter, who subsequently stumbled and dropped all the orbs onto our bonfire. "Whoops."

"Mutiny," Peter complained, dusting himself off. "Alright, what are we doing here for real?"

"Nothing too strenuous," Tip cautioned, fixing Peter with a stern look.

"We need to be well rested." Wendy nodded emphatically, suddenly coming to life once more. She did that more and more lately. Half the time she was spaced out in her own head, giving little to no responses to the rest of the world, and then in another moment she was fully engaged, trying to be as immersed as possible. I viewed it as her being stuck between a mental space of overthinking, and a physical space of over engaging—neither one netting her the connection she seemed to be in need of. It was hard to watch sometimes.

She's slipped into such a dissociated state while Peter had been regaling her with the story of the Pixie Village when we returned, I had actually seen the light drain from her gaze, only to return a bit later when it was her turn to give me my fighting lesson, and she really gave me quite the workout. I had to wonder if it was because Peter was watching and she was trying to prove her ferocity while I couldn't use magic.

"I don't know if I'll sleep a wink tonight, if I'm honest. But, I'll go through the motions like a good girl," I threw in, pushing away my analysis of the Lost Girl, stretching my arms and arching my back.

"How about Peter Says? Or Truth or Command?" Peter ticked off the options on his hand.

"Is that supposed to be *Simon* Says and Truth or *Dare?"* Dorothy raised her eyebrows at Peter. "If the answer is yes, you're going to abuse it, aren't you?"

"You know me so well, Love," Peter batted his lashes emphatically at Dorothy.

"Don't call—" she stopped short and pursed her lips, closing her eyes to inhale deeply. "Alright, Fairy-Boy. You're the king here, so play away."

"I feel so respected," Peter preened and paused to look at me with concern. "You sure you're up for a game?"

I waved him away. "No, but I am up for *winning* a game."

"Don't be so confident, Witch. You've got some healthy competition here." Tip's eyes narrowed as he gestured to himself, Dorothy, Lionel, Tiger Lily, and Wendy. Though he still didn't address me by my name regularly, the word *Witch* didn't hold the same animosity it once had.

Peter's grin stretched from ear to ear. Dorothy had definitely chosen the right thing to take the tension out of the group, and Peter's uncanny pension for fun and games was reminding us for a moment that we were all young, vulnerable, and human. We didn't know what daybreak would hold, or even if all of us embarking would make it out alive. But, for right now, we were merely Lost Children playing in Neverland, where we loved, laughed, cried, and dreamed all the same.

Peter drew in a big breath and squared his shoulders, lifting into the air to moderate. "Peter says to stand on your head," he commanded.

"Does this count?" Jack laughed, setting his pumpkin head on the ground and placing a wooden leg on top of it."

"I'll accept it. Point for Jack." Peter nodded.

"Oh, boo. None of us can do that!" Wendy complained with a laugh.

"Not so fast, Wendy..." Tip said smugly, throwing himself into a handstand. Using impressive control, he held his body stiff and lowered himself so his head touched the ground. "Ha!"

"Wow, show off," Grunted Dorothy, and with a devious smile, she pushed his legs, causing him to lose his balance and topple to the ground.

"Sabotage!" Tip cried indignantly, looking at Peter as he gestured to Dorothy.

"One point for Tip, and negative one point for Dorothy." Peter pointed to each friend in turn.

Toto yipped and placed his ear the ground before tucking into a roll on his back.

"Sorry, and one point for Toto." Peter amended the tally.

"I think we should all get a turn to be Commander," I suggested, receiving approving nods from everyone else besides Peter. He opened his mouth to protest, but I jumped in before he could. "*Alice* says the last one to crack a smile gets a point."

Instantly everyone's faces sobered. Peter was the first to crack a grin, followed by Wendy, then Lionel and Tiger Lily. Tip and Dorothy held their stoic expressions for a while, turning to face each other in an effort to throw the other off.

Dorothy tightened her face to look angry, and Tip immediately started laughing.

"You know that face makes me laugh. It's not intimidating, it's cute! Like an angry bunny."

Dorothy ran her tongue across her teeth and cracked her knuckles with a victorious sigh. "Exactly. Know your adversary's weaknesses and extort them for victory!"

"Brutal," Peter snickered and Tip rolled his eyes.

"That's one for Dorothy," I tallied and gestured to Wendy to take her turn as commander. And the game went on like that for several more rounds before Hook came over to lecture us.

"As the only *real* adult here, I think it's about time we all get some sleep. Big day tomorrow. Clear out and shut up." He folded his arms and grinned at Dorothy. "Unless you feel like more late night chats, Lass."

Dorothy just rolled her eyes at the pirate's flirtation.

"Oh, go jump in the ocean," Tip groused to Hook.

"Don't tempt me with a good time, Tippy," Hook jeered half heartedly, then turned gave a friendly jerk of his head to Tiger Lily in an unspoken order to fall in line for bedtime. "Let's get back to our quarters."

She nodded and bid her farewells and grabbed her discarded hat before following the Captain to the self-designated pirate area of our camp.

"Night, Lily!" Lionel called out with a wave before grinning at the rest of us. "Boy, is she a looker."

"Alright, enough fun and games. It's time for bed," Tip groaned as he stretched. "Don't want to be falling asleep on our swords."

"Right…" Dorothy sighed and gave everyone a pitiful wave. "Goodnight, everyone." As she walked away, I noticed her pull out a tiny knife with a hilt shaped like an anchor. She rubbed her thumb rhythmically over the handle until darkness swallowed her up near her bed. Similarly, Tip had his hand wrapped around the hilt of his new sword, gripping it tightly as he veered over towards his more secluded sleeping space near where Peter's claimed area was.

Wendy dipped her head and followed Dorothy, while Lionel whistled happily to his own bed, like we weren't about to fight a battle in the morning. He caught my eyes and winked.

"Fake it till you make it, right?" He was willing his jovial attitude to chase away the nerves.

"Just so." I smiled and nodded, then made to head to my sleeping area— which was by far the nicest on account of my magic being the best at conjuring objects— but Peter caught my hand and held me back.

"Yes?" I asked, folding my fingers between his.

"Are you sure you're ready for tomorrow, Love? All healed up? Actually, are you sure you won't just sit the whole thing out entirely?"

"Peter, don't be ridiculous. I could be bursting into a million pieces and you couldn't keep me away from this fight. It's something I have to do. Wonderland was mine and I let it fall. I will fight to return it." I thought of how Bill, Cheshire, The March Hare, and the Card-guard had risked their lives for me, and felt a fresh wave of affection for the creatures wash over me, mixed with stinging guilt ove rhow I had treated the Hare back in Wonderland when I had been searching for Dorothy. "I can't abandon my friends when they need me to fight. Not to mention everything that witch has done to me— to all of us. To the fairies."

Peter brought our clasped hands to his chest and smiled softly. "I know. I just don't know if I can take another incident like the other day. So, I need you to promise me, before we go frolicking into battle, that you aren't going to do anything that makes you rely on the compass for large amounts of power."

"Believe it or not, you're not the only one who doesn't want me to die. I think I'd rather fancy staying alive too, in fact. Besides, I still have to prove to you I am fit to stay in this world. So, please, stop fretting over me like a mother hen. We already have one those flittering about ata any given time. I messed up the other day." I looked at the ground, recalling how I had thought to try and mend my relationship to the compass and restore some of sense of delight, starting with the otherworldly experience with the fairies and flying for the first time on my own. "But, I have been working hard. They won't be making a fool of me in my own castle again."

"And if you aren't in your castle when you fight them?" Peter teased, his eyes bright and filled with equal parts affection and concern.

"Oh, well then that's different," I agreed with a chuckle. "Come on, we better get some sleep too." I tried tugging away but Peter once more held me back.

"Well, actually, I kind of thought maybe…" He started, and rubbed the back of his neck with the back of his hand slowly before continuing. "Remember back in Wonderland after the whole ordeal with the Red Knight?"

"Vividly," I commented wryly.

"That night you were a bit unsettled and you asked me to stay nearby. Well, *I'm* a bit unsettled tonight, and I was hoping that you would stay nearby."

"Oh," I voiced in surprise. "You want to cozy up?"

"It sounds silly when you phrase it like that…" Peter groaned awkwardly. "But yeah, I guess that's the sum of it. Like when we were back in the Emerald Castle, only sans Dorothy and all the awkwardness this time. Just us two together, under the stars— I think it's supposed to be romantic or some such, and who knows when or if there will be another calm night."

"Oh, hush. You don't have to convince me with your Peter-logic," I laughed, and flashed up one wide blanket on the sandy ground of the beach, a pillow for each of us, and a second blanket for warmth. I turned to Peter and tapped his nose. "Be clean."

"Again?" Peter sniffed, and just like before, his body was cleaned in an instant and his raggedy clothing was replaced with the same silk pajamas. "Very posh."

I changed into a similar set and we crawled into our little makeshift bed. I curled against Peter's chest, and he wrapped his arms around me, holding me close. He inhaled deeply, and I could feel his heart pounding beneath my head. I knew mine was racing at the same palpitating speed, but somehow I was calm and this gesture felt right and natural in its own way.

"Faith, trust, and pixie dust," I mumbled quietly, looking up at Peter's face, his eyes pensive. "I hope it's enough."

"We will make it enough. No room for doubt now." Peter looked down at me, hugging me closer for a moment as he pressed his lips to my forehead gently. "It'll just be another harrowing Peter and Alice adventure when it's all said and done. But, with backup, for once."

"We do enjoy an adventure." I nodded amicably, one hand resting on Peter's chest in front of my face, the other clasping around my battered compass. I knew tomorrow was really going to be less of a pleasant adventure, and more of another dance with my inner darkness. I was running the risk of being consumed by that dance partner with each step I'd take, each blow I'd make, and each temptation I'd face. In all technical aspects, I didn't need a Shadow Beast to torment me— I had the compass for that.

"Goodnight, my Love," Peter muttered groggily, already beginning to drift into slumber— something I'd always envied was his ability to fall asleep so easily, while my mind took ages to still.

"Goodnight," I echoed, nuzzling in. And just as I predicted, I lay wide awake long after Peter's breathing deepened rhythmically, indicating he was fast asleep, unable to sleep a wink.

~*~

The light had shifted to a deep blue, emanating a soft glow in the depth of the blue that alerted to early morning. The air was crisp and dewy as our group of ragtag fighters rose from our beds and assembled on the beach. Every face was solemn and resolute. Only the lapping of the Neverland Sea permeated the still air.

My dear Wonderlandians were intended to be the first ones in with me on the eastern outskirts, so as to catch the smallest wave to start with, then move in for additional support as needed. Then, the munchkins, along with Jack and Saw-horse, would spread out around the remaining edges of the land and work their way in, doing well to remain hidden. Hook and a handful of his men were to advance at Nonsense Falls nearest the castle as the group with the most fighting experience, including Dorothy, Wendy, and Tip, as this was scouted to be a hot spot for stationed soldiers the night Tiger Lily performed her reconnaissance. Lionel, being the weakest of our group physically after being in the Shadow World so long, was stationed to remain in Neverland to guard it, should our enemy be planning a counter attack, along with a group of Hook's crew. He wasn't happy about his assignment, but listened to Wendy's explanation begrudgingly, and promised if he saw a distress flare from any of us, he'd be there in a heartbeat.

Tinkerbell was to patrol all flanks to offer dust for an aerial advantage when needed, and had expressed to both Peter and I that the other fairies were staying in Neverland to help gaurd it, but she would come to our aid if she heard either of us call for help. Considering she hadn't made the offer to anyone else, I think it perturbed Wendy that the fairy had accepted me, while still harassing her.

That only left Peter to go in with Tiger Lily. They were going to be the last wave to leave, slipping in once everything had gotten good and riled up in the rest of the directions. Then we just had to hope that The Wizard wasn't paying Mombi a nightcall.

Peter had yet to reveal he was on good terms with his magic to our enemy. Even when Mombi had attacked Dorothy, he had refrained from using one drop of his power, hoping to instead save it to use it as a tactical advantage. Tip was in good fighting form, and would likely do well in physical combat, while Dorothy's own increased magical control made her act as a floater to aid whoever needed it most in their group—Toto, of course, would not be separated from her. She was going to rely primarily on her fire magic, having only discovered the second affinity of wind recently, and didn't trust herself to use it yet.

Once we had our footing, the five of us Lost Ones were going to attack the castle directly. I had changed our outfits to black, hoping to give us an element of stealth once in the woods, and as we stood on the eastern shore of Neverland, we blended with the night.

We'd planned everything out and now the moment had arrived to execute it.

One by one, weapons holstered, everyone began to leave our bubble of sanctuary and strode towards battle, none of us knowing for certain that we'd make it out alive. Yet, there was a collective serene calm cloaking every individual's anxieties, as we all knew we believed in what we were fighting for and trusted our convictions to see us through.

I hugged Peter close, offered a friendly joint embrace to Dorothy and Lionel, and even managed an amicable handshake from the ever-surly Tip, then I nodded to Wendy, not knowing where we stood in that regard, and turned to follow the Wonderlandians. As I marched through the fog of early morning rolling from the ocean over the shore, my oldest friends rallying alongside me, each step filled me with increasing adrenaline that pulsed in my veins, ready to unleash. It wasn't the compass driving this time, though. It was a thirst for vengeance and justice pounding in my chest, eager to break free. It was my own fury, and it wanted havoc and no mercy.

"Everyone ready?" I called out to my group, emanating a small fire in my hand to allow for a light source until we had safely cleared the terrain.

"Present, and accounted for, your Highness," One of the Card-guards reported with a salute.

I nodded to acknowledge him. "Alright then, let's proceed."

We picked our way along a stoney path with tapering undulations into the topmost part of the Never Woods, following it to where it would run parallel with the eastern edge of Wonderland, then veered West.

As we prowled out of the woods, the pale, washing light of dawn was beginning to turn the night from inky darkness to an indigo hue that glistened off the morning mist still thick in the air. Everyone should be finding their way to their positions at this point, and even in the murky visibility, I could already make out the lumbering forms of a group of Mombi's henchmen, the tin soldiers and scarecrows, patrolling the border.

"Ready to fight for Wonderland?" I whispered to my friends, hunkering down into a crouch. Each one stared back at me with round eyes, twinkling with vigor and defiance. Even Cheshire was in his tangible form, ears pricked, and green eyes narrowed to fix on his prey.

"I've never been much of one to fight— It's so beastly. But, I have always loved a good hunt," He purred, licking his lips. "Though who would hunt when there's a good fight waiting. Really brings out the beast in me." He contradicted himself as usual, his claws sheathing and unsheathing rhythmically.

For a moment, I could have sworn they were getting bigger with each motion, but I shook my head to clear it, my eyes likely playing tricks on me from nerves. Instead, I drew my weapon, slowly, discreetly, and my companions did the same of the weapons they had been entrusted with as mad beings.

"Let's go!" I called and launched forward from my crouched position, using my bunched muscles for momentum to propel me forward. No hesitation, no turning back. It was time for battle.

The moment of whizzing silence as we advanced was quickly replaced by the vicious sounds of mutual confrontation. The scarecrows looked like something from a nightmare, with hollow voids etched onto the burlap faces for eyes, and leering black smiles. They swayed and moved in unnatural ways that made them terribly unnerving, their bristling hay hissing as they fought. One threw back its head and screeched an alarm, the sound sinister and piercing, gargling in the creature's throat.

"Can't have that awful noise waking up all of Wonderland," I growled, and lunged for it, despite my crawling skin.

I held a small flame to its abdomen, recalling that no amount of slicing did the least bit of damage, as it could repair itself. Fire was this brainless monster's weakness. It flopped about wildly, and only when the flames engulfed it so heavily that it had begun to singe my skin, did I release it. Within mere heartbeats, it was reduced to a pile of fine ash, and I noticed that amongst the cinders were silver flecks glimmering against the gray.

There wasn't much opportunity to further inspect the substance, before I was rammed into by one of the tin soldiers. Losing my balance, I stumbled sideways, fumbling for my weapon. I was only just able to bring it up to a defensive position as the soldier swung its ax down at me with all its might.

"Why are you so strong?" I grunted, failing against the surprising strength of the being, until I was pressed against the ground on my back. It was little more than a suit of armor, less ornately molded, but it caused me to recall my fight with the Red Knight. Peter, who was much stronger than I was, had struggled against that hollow armor as well.

I gasped as my sword was only a hair away from pushing lengthwise into my chest, and I was being driven harder against the muddy earth, clumps of dirt and moss grinding into my hair.

"That's not polite!" Tweedle Dum crowed, and bounced over to aid me, swinging his club madly at the soldier. When it impacted, the metal yielded and caved, and I couldn't help but marvel at the surprising strength the twin possessed.

His brother was in place at the other side, swinging his own blow to the opposite side. The two dents met in the middle and cleaved the soldier in two. It dropped its ax as its torso toppled to the ground, and the blade slipped from my sword. Though it didn't have much velocity behind it, it still carved a deep gash as it collided with my arm.

"Ah!" I cried out, and clutched at my wound, rolling to the side of the fray to avoid being trampled by Bill's scuffle with a group of scarecrows. I bit my lip against the pain. Blood was bubbling between my fingers clasped on my bicep, dark crimson beading down my pale skin like rain on a window.

With a sharp intake of breath I released my hold to tear at the ripped sleeve of my shirt. I made quick work of bandaging the injury, pulling the makeshift tourniquet taught with my teeth.

"Watch out!" Bill tried to warn me, but no sooner had my fingers clasped back around my sword, than I felt a tearing tension at my back. Arching away from the pain, I whirled away to see one of the scarecrows waving a knife around wildly.

The strange hissing was emanating louder and rhythmically from it, as it tilted its head at an inhuman angle at me and began cackling, jabbing the knife at me. I summoned fire to my hand, setting it ablaze not a moment too soon. I scrambled to my feet, panting. From our vantage point, it hadn't looked like there were very many henchmen in this area, however, now I could see that more had come filtering out of the Wonderland woodlands, likely aiding the call of their fallen comrade.

We were being overpowered and fast. Though I could manage against the horrifying scarecrows, I stood little chance against the tin soldiers' superior strength. Bill, the March Hare, and the Card-guards were also in a similar position, not having the physique to fend off the Herculean tinmen. But, they continued fighting nonetheless.

Caterpillar was swooping in and dealing blows at random, serving as an armed distraction, and the Tweedles were merrily bludgeoning a couple of tinmen. Everyone was fighting their hardest but, without an end in sight to the army, there was little chance of us advancing further into Wonderland.

"We need some help," I breathed to myself as I brandished my sword in my good arm, and summoned crackling flames in my injured one. "Bill, Cards, Hare!" I barked, and the group immediately leapt away from their adversaries so I could hurl fire at the targets.

"Your majesty, might we take some of your fire?" Bill queried, his eyes wild with an instinctual desire to flee. I knew lizards to be rather skittish in nature, so his bravery in facing this fight was certainly commendable.

I nodded briskly. "Get something to make a torch out of, quick!" I commanded, and the grouping broke away to retrieve stray branches from the edge of the woods. I started a blaze at the top of each one and handed them off. "Burn them down!"

There was something vaguely concerning about sending the mad, babbling Hare off to play with fire, but I didn't have much time to worry about it as I returned to the fighting fray. I could feel blood rolling down my back, from where the scarecrow had handed a successful swipe, though with more and more adrenaline pumping through my veins, I could scarcely feel the pain in either wound anymore.

The Wonderlandians with the torches, turned the tide on the scarecrows, burning them down as instructed, however the tin soldiers still posed the biggest problem. With the scarecrows serving as cannon fodder in numbers hoping to overwhelm those without fire power, it was the tinmen that acted as solid war tanks. I did my best to use the creative fighting techniques that Wendy had taught me, however there was something to be said of it being much different to spar than to actually fight with and against killing intent. Not to mention, Wendy was roughly my size— shorter and more prim, really— and wasn't overpowering physically. Dorothy probably had learned more diverse attacks in practical applications under her tutelage from Tip, as he was a good deal larger and stronger than her. I kicked myself for not having us alternate partners.

It wasn't long before the area was writhing with tin soldiers and we were once more overwhelmed, unable to keep up with the scarecrows any longer either. I leapt away from the tangle of metal, hay, and madness, to catch my breath, trying to evaluate what to do.

"How are there so many? They just keep coming! Are they all on this flank of Wonderland, or are the others having just as hard a time?" I rambled aloud to myself. I had truly underestimated the sheer volume of foes we'd be facing, my focus always jumping to when I could throttle the ringleader. But, how could I do that if I couldn't get into the land to begin with, let alone cross it. I might have to call for Tink or Lionel afterall, but even then, would either reach me in time, or already be helping someone else?

"Your majesty!" A Card-guard started to alert me, but was cut short as his body was torn to shreds by one of the rabid scarecrows in a frenzy.

"No!" I shouted, releasing a blast of lightning at the creature, unrelenting in my fury. It burst into flames and collapsed, but while I had been reactive, I hadn't heeded the guards warning, and was struck by a hard blow to my head, knocking me face first into the mud.

My head pounded with agonizing pressure, throbbing and receding in brutal waves. I felt cold shame burning an icy heat against the inside of my skin as I lay stunned in the mud, ready to send up a magical flare to call one of our other teams for help. I was supposed to be the queen of this direction and I needed to take it back for my subjects. I knew if I just used the compass' power, I could devastate this army— if I survived using it at all without it breaking. I wasn't strong enough without that power!

Use me. Harness the power you love to wield.

I felt a weight press into my back, and I screamed as it pushed into the raw wound across my spine. A tin soldier was stepping on me, staring down with cold glinting malice set in hollow sockets.

You'd be invincible. Use me. Give in to the Wicked. The compass beckoned to me and I felt immeasurable temptation to break my promise to Peter and use my Wicked power.

The weight continued, slowly crushing me as I shrieked in pain. My allies couldn't get to me as I was surrounded by the tin soldiers, and the Tweedles were starting to tire from striking down the onslaught.

You'll die here in the mud if you don't give in. What's the risk? Use me. The voice of the compass stroked the inside of my mind, cold and soothing against the searing pain. *Give in to the pain.*

"No!" I whimpered, tasting the metallic tang blood in my mouth. "No, I can't. This isn't where I fall," I told myself adamantly.

"Die." The sound of the tin soldier speaking sounded like rocks sliding past each other, low, deep and devastating.

The air was being driven from my lungs, and I couldn't breathe. I squinted my eyes closed and tried to gather what little physical strength I had left to push against the soldier, but I couldn't budge from where it had me pinned like prey, slowly driving the life from me.

"Ah!" I shrieked at the sky, throwing my aching head back. I dug my fingers into the freshly churned earth, tilled by battle. "Wonderland! Please, lend me your strength. Protect me so I can fight for you!" I pleaded, and raised my hand to release a tall blast of lightning into the sky to call for help.

A low growling that morphed into a vicious snarl stopped me from using the last scrap of energy I had, and the pressure against me paused. I turned my head, blinking through the mud, blood, and grit ground into my lashes, and saw an enormous white paw of a beast slam into the ground.

It was the paw of a predatory creature, arched against the forest floor with long talon-like claws that glinted, hungry to ravage. I however, had no idea what this beast was and didn't know if it was friend or foe, until it swatted the soldier off my back, shattering the metal like glass with a single blow.

The shrapnel fell around me, peppering me with shallow scratches, and I curled into myself, gasping to inflate my lungs. I was disoriented and shakily raised my body to gawk at what monstrous creature stood before me, towering and proud. It was far larger than a lion, though it looked to be some otherworldly derivative, with a sort of archaic saber-toothed tiger twist. It's muzzle bore rows of large pointed fangs that were dripping with murderous fervor, and every strand of fur on its body with bushed and bristling. Its long tail swished angrily, and it arched down, bowing to me.

"The beast has come out to play at last," Its booming voice purred with an edge of insanity as it blinked at me with round orb-like eyes of wild, ethereal green.

Green eyes… Insane pur… fclinc… white fur though shorter and sleeker— dappled with ginger patches. The thoughts tumbled into each other, and I couldn't believe what I was seeing.

"Cheshire?" I wheezed.

"Naturally," Cheshire tilted his head, and flexed his claws, each one the length of one of my legs. "If you'll excuse me, this form is very hard to come by, doesn't last long, and I am needed in that direction for the moment." He bunched his haunches to spring at the hesitating tin soldiers clustered around the rest of the Wonderlandians. Then he turned and flashed me his signature feline grin, now full of feral fangs. "You've successfully summoned the Mome Raths, so best be ready to advance when they arrive."

"The Mome Raths?" I echoed, entirely lost. I'd never been able to find a Mome Rath in Wonderland, and had more or less written them off as some sort of nonsense myth.

Cheshire chuckled, his booming monstrous voice rattling my bones, and flicked his tail to the Wonderland forest. "Here they come."

I scrambled to my feet, quickly locating and reclaiming my sword. There was a terrible snarling noise roaring through the trees to the west that set my nerves on end. It was accompanied by guttural shrieks of scarecrows, and the piercing sound of shredding metal, behind the thudding of several feet.

"The Mome Raths!" The Wonderlandians began to cheer, the light of hope returning to their faces, as they continued to fight with restored conviction.

"I *knew* you were the rightful ruler of Wonderland!" Bill shouted victoriously, throwing his scaly green fist into the air. "All hail Alice, our *true* Wonderland Queen!"

The others echoed his cry and I stood, dumbfounded and bewildered. There was some crucial information about the Mome Raths that had clearly been withheld from me.

The terrible discordant sounds drew closer, and I began to see movement, the pouding force making the ground shudder, and the trees sway. Then, a cluster of tin men came racing out of the woods, closely followed by a throng of beasts of varying sizes, not unlike Cheshire in his new form.

Some were as tall as the trees, while others seemed to be small furry balls that could fit in my hand. I quickly noted that they didn't stay tiny balls for long, as the little ones grew and morphed into formidable feline monsters like the rest as they bustled forward. They were all shades of colors, natural and synthetic and everything in between. All had beastly fangs and claws, short cropped fur, whipping tails, and glimmering eyes.

They thundered into the thick of the fight, sending the enemy running east, while remaining careful to avoid their fellow Wonderlandians. Whatever foes weren't lucky enough to immediately evade the attack, were torn to shreds in an instant, even the tough metal of the soldiers tearing like paper in the Mome Raths' claws.

I was rooted to the spot, transfixed. I had called to Wonderland for aid and it had certainly responded in kind. But, what was most astounding to me, and brought a wave of tears to my eyes at the sheer brilliance of it, was when I saw Cheshire standing amongst what I now saw as his own kind.

"You were a Mome Rath all along," I whispered, bringing my hand to my mouth in awe. With the last of the immediate enemy being dealt with, Cheshire trotted happily over to me and bowed. "The only one who let me see you."

He swiveled his ears towards the heart of Wonderland. "Climb aboard, my Queen. We are needed in that direction now, I believe." A sense of clarity, I'd never heard from him before, rumbled in his words.

I swallowed down my swirling emotions and nodded, climbing onto my old friend's back. The other Mome Raths also dipped to allow the Wonderlandians to climb on their backs.

Finding myself at the head of this strange new cavalry, I was filled with hope that burned like fire in my chest. I forgot the exhaustion tugging at my bones, the pain tearing at my flesh, and the hammering in my head. Only one thing mattered and shone crystal clear in my mind like a beacon. I gripped Cheshire's scruff and leaned forward.

"To the Red Castle. I'm taking my throne back!"

Twenty-Four

Dorothy

"Are you sure you know where you are going?" Tip hissed at me as we crawled through the Wonderland undergrowth. It was Toto, Wendy, Hook, and the pirates who trailed along behind me and the grumpy Lost Boy. I was leading since, of the group, I had the best geographical reference for the land. Peter had opted to approach from the southwest, to disperse our waves of attack. Being a primary target, he also wished to keep a low profile to start, and only had Tiger Lily accompany him for backup.

"Yes," I assured him, wiggling my nose as a stray frond tickled it. "Just keep your eyes peeled for mushrooms. If we end up in a mushroom forest then we've gone the wrong way."

"That's not reassuring," Tip grumbled behind me.

"I'm sorry, person-who's-never-walked-around-Wonderland-before. Would you like to take the lead?"

"You didn't have any idea where you were going then either!"

"No, but since then, I have seen a map. So, hush."

"Stop bickering, you two!" Wendy chided quietly from down the line. She was more bright and alert than she had been in days, and I could only attribute it to finding a greater purpose in fighting this battle giving her energy.

We all stiffened as the first sound of battle permeated the air, and looked over our shoulders. It sounded like Alice had engaged the Eastern border. Something shrill and terrifying rang out then was cut short.

Wendy jerked her head in the direction of the sound. "We don't want to be caught in that before we are in place, so keep quiet!"

I sighed and crept forward in silence. The woodlands creaked with bobbing branches, and insects of unusual origins sang out loudly. I felt my hairs standing on end, like I was being watched by something, and had the uncomfortable realization that in Wonderland, there was a good chance something was watching. We had used pixie dust— thought I had to be guided by Tip and Hook to say on the right flight path— to take a wide berth over the signpost to enter from the north east, allowing Alice time to reach her marker on foot, while we landed and began to head inland towards Nonsense Falls. So far, we had managed to remain undetected, but I was on edge, ready for some dangerous and whacky thing to erupt out at us.

I could hear the hammering footsteps of tin soldiers heading to the east towards Alice and the other Wonderlandians and silently prayed she wouldn't be overwhelmed by their numbers. She had been sent there to give her the least amount of fighting to do. We had each been instructed to send a distress flare into the sky if any of us were to fall to the enemy, and the closest group would come to their aid. However, it was also an unspoken point that we wanted to avoid shifting our forces as much as possible, so that we could get our footing on the Red Castle grounds as soon as possible. A drawn out fight was not something we wanted.

"We are here. And look," I whispered to my compatriots, and pointed in the misty light towards a group of soldiers positioned as guards at the top of the falls. Beyond that point was a straight shot to the hedge maze and the castle. "There are the guards."

Tiger Lily had been able to scout out a fair chunk of Wonderland on a previous stealth mission, and had noted that there was an inflated number of henchmen guarding the glass portal in the Fungi Forest, which was why we had opted to make our target the smaller group at Nonsense Falls, so we could make a dash for castle on foot and conserve some energy, rather than having to fight through the largest group to make any headway.

"Ready?" I hissed down the line, and everyone else nodded

solemnly. I inhaled deeply. "Alright, time to bring the firehands out."

I leapt from the cover of the undergrowth first, summoning flames to my fingers, and charged towards the falls. The soldiers whipped their heads around to stare at me, and one of the scarecrows opened its mouth and released a screech, a sound that tore the night in two.

"Fire beats straw," I reminded myself, as the deeply unsettling creatures began crawling down a set of stone stairs. Then, I shaped my fire into a blade and hurled it at the closest scarecrow. The aim held true and struck the creature down by setting its head ablaze.

Then, the tinmen started lumbering in from all directions around me, and I realized they had been hiding out of view and blending in with the gray stones of the falls. One swung an ax at me and I just barely hopped out of the way.

"I'll take this one from here, Lass." Hook appeared from the shadows and faced the nearest tin soldier with his hook and broadsword raised.

"Card-guards are coming from the castle," Wendy called out, also now out in the open. "They must have heard the warning call."

"Dorothy, focus on the scarecrows with your fire, Wendy can handle the cards, and Hook, the pirates, and I will take on the tin brutes," Tip commanded, appearing from a cloak of mist near the stone steps where he pointedly shoved a tin soldier into the pool of nonsense water. It sank like a stone.

"Right!" The rest of us acknowledged Tip's orders and set to our tasks. Wendy dodged and leapt nimbly round her surrounding foes to reach a tree and made quick work of climbing it, dropping down at the top of the falls behind the advancing soldiers. She smiled and kicked out hard against the top tinman, sending him tumbling down into his fellow soldiers. Then, she pulled her sword from its sheath in one hand and unclipped her scythe in the other hand and dashed out of sight to engage with the cards.

Hook was fighting adeptly against his grouping of tin soldiers, and I saw Tip grab the handle of a swinging ax, twisting it out of the tinman's grip to use against him. The rest of the pirates faced off against the sturdy tinmen, which left the scarecrows for me to have it.

Leaving the fire on my hand ablaze, I charged the scarecrows head on, careful to do my best to avoid the flailing limbs armed with notched blades. Only a handful of blows grazed me with shallow cuts. I reached out and touched them wherever I could make contact, acting like a match to a hay bale. I squinted my eyes against their gurgling screams, and gave myself permission to process their deaths in my nightmares later. But for now, I twirled around the clearing, like I was a single dancing flame of destruction— and in truth, that's exactly what I was.

It didn't take me too long before I had struck down every single scarecrow, and Tip and the pirates had done a good job whittling down the remaining henchmen. It was looking like our fight here at the falls was going to be over shortly.

I paused to strain my ears to the east and swallowed, still able to pick up on the sounds of battle emanating from that direction. It told me that Alice's team was still fighting which meant that they were also having trouble striking down their foes with the same ease we had been fortunate enough to have. I wondered if perhaps the forces stationed at the Fungi Forest had gone to face her, and the thought caused a chill to race down my spine.

I jumped as I felt a hand on my shoulder, but relaxed when I saw it was Tip. Despite the apparent ease he had fought with, I could see sweat glistening on his forehead, and his ebony tunic was clinging in places to his torso.

"Spacing out in the middle of a fight?" He squinted at me, his words puffing as he caught his breath. Blood coated his hand and the left side of his face.

"Are you okay?" I asked, ignoring his question. "Do you need bandages?" Turning off the fire in my palms, I poised, ready to flash up any necessary items that I could, hoping I wouldn't get frazzled and produce some food item instead.

But Tip shook his head. "No, it's just minor flesh wounds. How about you?" He gestured to the many tears across my top and blood speckled skin.

"Same," I replied evenly. "Nothing but scratches, thankfully."

"Good. Come on, we can check the others for injuries, and then let's press on."

I nodded, and Hook pushed the last of the Tin soldiers into the water. A sweeping gaze around the immediate area was chaotic at best. Piles of smoldering ashes were scattered here and there from where I had taken down my foes, and there were disembodied pieces of tinmen littered everywhere else. Amongst our fallen foes, I counted two fallen pirates with ax wounds that made bile rise my throat, and my stomach lurch.

"Don't look too close," Tip advised, spinning me around to look the other way. "They are already gone."

"Does… does anyone else need triage?" I called out shakily, blinking back tears.

"No, but I will be taking care of my fallen crewmates. You two carry on, we've done our part to clear the way, and the Lass should have done the rest up ahead." Hook's voice thundered with the commanding presence of a captain, and feeling like I was receiving official orders, I nodded respectfully to the pirate.

"My condolences," I mumbled with a small dip of my head, closing my eyes a moment to acknowledge their sacrifice.

A strange hissing started rattling through the air, and we stared around in bewilderment. My eyes flew open and I jumped backwards as I felt something rush by my feet. Looking around, there was evidence of invisible creatures prowling through the clearing, but they didn't appear to be concerned with our group.

Instead, I saw flickers of varying colors racing into the forest towards the eastern border. Squinting I watched as the strange furry creatures became visibly tangible, some small and round, while others were growing at alarming rates to tower in the trees as magnificent and terrifying feline beasts.

Their snarling ground against my ears, and their large paws thundered against the earth, shaking it in their wake. I gawked after then and sent a silent prayer that they were more Wonderlandians going to aid Alice, and not fight against her.

The latter option made me hesitate, watching intently for any sign of a flare from that direction to signal help. My breath was caught in my chest as I waited, but no signal ever came. Instead all I heard was a terrible shrieking sound that made me flinch.

"Come on, Dorothy. We need to keep moving forward."

"But what if Alice—"

"Trust her to be alright, and come help take her stupid castle back for it. That's what we are here for," Tip interrupted, his voice tight, no room for arguments.

Guilt crawled in my belly, but I beckoned Toto from his shelter on the sidelines and did as I was told. Tip and I briefly voiced our departure to the remaining pirates and Hook merely grunted to acknowledge it.

We climbed up the rocks and looked on as a half trampled briar patch. Just beyond it, we could see the rounded glimmering red tops of the castle. The sun had risen, and our visibility would be undeniable now, but it also aided our own ability to see what we were doing.

There were cards folded and pinned, but not killed, through the thorny thicket, showing Wendy had succeeded at her attack. However, there was no physical sign of Wendy.

"She must have gone ahead to meet Peter at the castle," Tip offered an explanation, seeing my searching gaze.

"I don't see any signs that Peter made it to the castle," I replied, my voice quiet as I looked onward at the otherwise peaceful looking palace. There was no smoke, no flashing, or quaking— Nothing to indicate a fight taking place. "I think we are the first ones here."

"Then let's make it count," Tip grunted. He holstered the ax he had stolen to a strap across his back— Alice had given us all various leather pieces to hold our weapons— and drew his sword.

"Are you sure you're up to facing her?" I asked softly, flinching as I saw Tip visibly bristle.

"I guess I have to be," He sighed, rolling his broad shoulders back.

"Well, for what it's worth. I got your back," I lifted my chin and stared at him, unwavering, resolute in my belief that we would both make it through this next fight.

Tip smiled, and squeezed my shoulder. "I know. And I'll be damned if I don't have yours."

"I know you will," I echoed, feeling a reassuring warmth spread through my body at his gesture. I knew, stepping forward into the briar patch, that there was no one in this world I trusted more to have on my side, and the feeling of unbridled trust in someone else felt dangerous, but also like it held a tangible strength in it too. "We'll be a team. We go in as a team, and we come out as one too."

"Yes, we will." Tip's eyes were hesitant but bright as he looked at me, and Peter's previous words about Tip's heart threatened to penetrate my mind, along with the sudden realization of how attractive he looked in all black with the heat of battle blazing in his eyes…but I willed it away. There was no room for turning such fruitless nonsense over in my head at a time like this. To fight Mombi, we needed our full wits about us, not delusions of grandeur or non-existent hidden affections.

I closed my mouth tightly, afraid sentimentality was going to keep oozing out obnoxiously. I wasn't one of those high school girls that pined after wounded boys. I was still logical and pragmatic. Tip was my friend—my good friend. He was reliable and we got along well. I kept drilling that through my head as we walked, though beneath it, I couldn't help but wonder why I was having to hammer it home in the first place. I felt words lingering in my throat, things I wished to say in case we died, but I couldn't actually grasp what those words were.

Stop it! I scolded myself, clearing the last of the thorns. *You should be thinking about all your fighting lessons and preparation. You aren't going to die, so there's nothing to say.* My hands trembled as I redirected my thoughts, but I reached instinctively for my little knife with the anchored hilt. It had become a sort of centering item to ground me in reality when it escaped me, and in moments of fear, I found myself clutching it for reassurance.

Toto's fur bristled along his spine and he began growling. He pointed his body towards the entrance of the hedge maze, where we could see a lithe silhouette slinking through the opening towards us.

"Bravo," Mombi's cold voice greeted us as she clapped slowly. "You're the first ones to make it this far. How fitting for it to be us three. Shall we celebrate?" She summoned a teapot and poured it slowly into a matching teacup. "Perhaps with a nice cup of tea?"

My eyes instinctively latched onto the steaming liquid and I licked my lips. I could smell the tea from where I stood, and everything in my body wanted to lunge for the cup to guzzle it down. I don't know what was so addictive about the inani-tea, but I knew I had never craved something so badly in all my life. My thirst felt insatiable.

"Cut it out, *Witch,*" Tip growled, brandishing his sword. "We've made our move."

"Oh, come now. You used to love playing games together, don't you remember?"

"No." Tip ground his teeth together. "You were the only one who enjoyed that."

Mombi flashed up a table beside me, covered in teapots and cups, and I recognized it as the Hatter's dining table. She crooked her fingers at Tip and smiled, her lips curling with cruelty. "I'm right here. Come on. Go ahead and try to strike me down. My lovely Wicked pet," She goaded.

I shook my head and pulled my gaze from the alluring distraction of tea. Instead, I bit my tongue to center myself and retrieved my own small sword, steeling myself to fight. Tip launched forward with a vicious snarl.

"I'm no Wicked, and I'm not your *pet!*"

"I guess we will see how well I've trained you." Mombi looked at Tip, and her cruel expression melted away into innocence and alarm. Her icy white hair morphed to a deep brunette that was almost black.

Tip stopped in his tracks, a few paces in front of her, taken aback by the shift in demeanor. Phantoms danced in his eyes, and he seemed paralyzed on the spot.

"Tip?" I questioned, but he didn't seem to hear me. I bristled as Mombi rushed up to him and threw her arms around his waist, resting her cheek against his chest. He was letting her *embrace* him? I had expected some of his described reactions to the woman to be exaggerations, not complete fact.

"Oh, Tippetarius! I thought you'd never come back for me. I've been so afraid of what they've made me do. Are you here to save me?" She asked, her voice silky and sweet, rather than the normal harsh, or deranged, commanding tone she took.

"I… I…" He spluttered, his own typical cool demeanor clearly rattled. I saw sweat bead on his forehead as he dropped his sword and his hand slowly lowered to pat her back, like he knew her— No, like he was *familiar* with her and their physical contact. He'd comforted her before, just like me. He'd probably acted as a calming presence for the false Mombi too, and it set my teeth on edge.

"What are you *doing*?" I demanded incredulously as I witnessed the exchange. I knew he'd told me of their past romance, but hearing it and witnessing it were two different things, and I found my fingers curling into fists. Though rigid on Tip's end, they were behaving so intimately… my thoughts trailed away and my jaw dropped as it escalated further.

Mombi blinked up at Tip and cupped his face tenderly. "I missed you so much. I'm so sorry for how they made me hurt you. You know I love you, though, don't you? Now's our chance to finally escape together! We can be *together.* Just like we always talked about."

"What? Tip, snap out of it. She doesn't mean a word of what she's saying, and you *know* that! You've been down this road before. You told me so," I begged, afraid if I advanced to help, she would strike him like the viper she was.

"You've missed me?" Tip looked befuddled as he echoed her words, still unable to hear me. He was completely spellbound. "You want to be together?"

The depth of his unconditional love for the fake Mombi must have been astounding to make him fall into a trance so easily. But, of course it had been. Tip was incredibly loyal and honest. Love he felt probably could be nothing but deep and sincere, and it stung faintly in my chest to know that had been wasted on a monster like Mombi.

"I could scarcely stand it," She whispered, her tone switching with seductive intent. She pulled his head down to hers and kissed him, one hand sliding to his hair, the other rubbing his chest.

I felt a jolt course through my body as I looked on in utter disbelief. Everything in my head was screaming that this was wrong, so terribly wrong. Furthermore, everything in me was crying out that I didn't want to see Tip sharing this intimate moment with someone.

Tip's rigidity seemed to lessen as his body melted to the advance, and to my further dismay, his eyes closed and his arms tightened around her. There was undeniable chemistry between them. But, how? He hated her! How could he kiss her like that? My gut hallowed, and I felt like I had been kicked in the abdomen by a horse. I couldn't understand why, but watching it was causing me actual pain, and I almost felt betrayed. But that wasn't right, was it?

Mombi bit his bottom lip softly and tugged lightly as she separated from the kiss. Tip's breathing was ragged, and he blinked slowly from the intensity. I felt sick to my stomach, my heart was hammering in my ears from my heightened pulse, and a righteous anger was catching fire in my chest. It was appalling to see how easily and quickly she had reduced him— the constant, sarcastic, and resolute Tip I knew— to a puddle. Just how twisted was this game she played with him and his heart?

My hands went ablaze and, unable to take it any longer, I threw a fireball that went whizzing between their googly eyed faces. "Hey! Get away from him!" I shouted.

Peter had told me to master my random acts of magic and insanity, I needed something I felt convicted to fight for. I had promised to have his back, and I knew fighting *for him* was the all the conviction I needed to carry out this battle. There was something I could do here, that *only* I could do for once that could hold her off. I just needed to buy myself a little time for it to work.

Mombi leaned out of the way and then cuddled against Tip's chest, the picture of meekness. "Tippetarius, My Love. Who is this girl and why does she want to hurt me?" Her voice even trembled as she spoke. The cunning little snake. "Can you get rid of her? She's scaring me."

Tip looked at me finally and blanched as his foggy gaze connected to my burning one. His eyes flicked down at Mombi in horror, and he slowly lifted his arms away from her body where he had been unconsciously cradling her.

"I don't…" He spluttered, lost for words, like he was dipping in and out of a trance. "I'm sorry. I don't even remember how…"

"Don't worry, Tip. I can introduce myself!" I snarled and reached for one of the Hatter's abandoned cups of tea on the table. The Hare had mentioned how the more often you have the tea, the faster it would take effect and dissipate. So, I bore my eyes into Mombi's, taking a single small sip from the cup, before throwing it to the ground, and adjusting to fighting stance. "I'm the witch who's about to out-crazy you. But we've already met, as you damn well know. Now, get your claws *off him*."

"Look at the new girl being so possessive," Mombi snorted, patting Tip's chest slowly. "Didn't he explain it to you after our little game? He's already *mine.* You can't have him."

"Are you challenging me?" I folded my arms.

"Dorothy…" Tip cautioned quietly, darting a look to the ground, obviously trying to surmise how to retrieve his sword. His eyes were wild and frantic as he looked at the stray drop of tea that was rolling down from the corner of my mouth.

"No, I think I'd like to hear her say it!" I hissed, staring down the ice witch coldly, before I smirked. "I threaten you, don't I? Why else would a bitch feel the need to mark her territory?"

"I'm not threatened by you. I just am not the best at sharing my toys with others." Mombi's eyes sparked in opposition.

"No, you just like being the toy that gets shared, right? That's how it is with The Wizard? Oh, sorry. He doesn't *share* you. He just likes to play with all his other toys. Especially shiny new ones… Like Alice?"

"Watch your tongue," Mombi bared her teeth at me. I grinned, knowing I'd struck a nerve. Her fragile ego.

"She's pretty isn't she? Alice, I mean. It's no wonder he kissed her. Young, beautiful, and so *powerful*."

"He did that to cast his spell," She seethed.

"And I'll bet he enjoyed it too. Nothing quite as exciting as what transpired between the two of you, I'm sure. Yet, anyway. Unless he's successful in turning her to his side. Which you're helping him do." I raised my eyebrows, pointing a finger at Mombi. "I think, in my world, we'd call that training your replacement!"

A gasping laugh of mixed disbelief and amusement escaped Tip's mouth. I knew I was being horrible. I didn't know where this wealth of animosity was welling up from— perhaps an overflowing store of things I had wished to say back home, and never had the nerve— but I also couldn't help but *enjoy* riling this monster of a human up. Nor could I bring myself to stop. She'd toyed with Tip, and all of us plenty. It was time to repay the favor.

I took a step closer, then another, lifting my chin to bite my words at her. "But, let's be real. We know that The Wizard still isn't over his dead wife." I waved a hand nonchalantly, taking the insult to injury a notch further. "So, truth be told, no one can replace Ozma on her pedestal. No one will ever be as beautiful, important, and powerful. Not Glinda. Not Avrilia, or Ida, or Emmaline. And not *you.* Which clearly bothers you so much that you're threatened that *I'm* going to take your toy from you and treat it better. Because no matter what games you play, and webs you weave," I pointed to Tip. "He's too Good for you, he's not your pet, plaything, or toy, and he sure as hell will *never* be yours. "

"Hmm," Mombi smirked, rolling her tongue over her teeth before returning to her normal appearance. She snaked a hand up to grab hold of Tip's hair forcefully, yanking his head back by the roots. "Would you listen to the mouth of this one? Are you going to let her talk to me that way, Tippetarius? Or do I need to teach her a lesson myself?" She tilted his head to look at her pouting expression.

"She's not afraid of you! You've just pissed her off." Tip glared back, and I was relieved to see him returning to his usual sturdy self. "And we are going to take you down. She and I. *Together*." He leaned on the last word, like it should mean something to the ice witch for him to phrase it that way.

"Fine. If she's not going to be the one to turn…" Mombi sighed. "Then you will. Just like you were always meant to."

"That's not going to work—" Tip started to retort, determination gleaming on his face, but he faltered and gasped, as Mombi ripped one of her many necklaces from her neck and plunged it into his chest. Then she turned it and stepped away, revealing a key embedded in his heart. Black spindles began coiling up his neck and he dropped to his knees.

I sobered in an instant, terrified. What had she done to him? I rushed forward to help him, but Mombi wasn't messing around with me any longer. She reappeared in front of me, punching me, sending me flying backwards. She stood before me with a knife in her hand.

Come on! Time to kick in, insani-tea! I closed my eyes and called upon the dipping sensation of the tea. My eyes popped open as I mentally grasped at the place between sane and deranged— a clear vision of myself forming.

"No more hedgehogs and snakes in this fight," I let the seemingly nonsensical statement trill off my tongue as Mombi leered at me, poised to attack. An insane giggle erupted from me. "Watch me ignite."

I threw my head back and held out my arms, allowing flames to cover my body in a burst. The fire twirled and grew at my back until it towered over me, taking the form of a bird. The black of clothing serveing as a coal bed to hoast the sparkling embers emanating from me. I shifted my arms forward, pulling my fire wings to the front of me. Instead of flames, however, the feathers that detached and spiraled towards the witch were freshly forged daggers, made in the likeness of Tip's sword. I wasn't weak. I wasn't inept. I was confident and free. I was capable of devastating *power.* All thanks to Mombi's attempted torture forcing me to face my Shadow Beast. She'd pushed me towards harnessing that power and now I was going to take her down with it.

Mombi hissed in surprise and teleported herself out of line of fire. I tapped my head and laughed. Then, I hiccuped and zipped through space and time to stand beside her with my anchor knife aimed at her throat.

"Oh, look. I can do that trick too!" I whispered in her ear, reveling at the brief flash of alarm in her eyes, that hardened to pure hatred in an instant. We started popping up and disappearing all over the immediate area, then began grappling and crashing through the hedge maze. The bushes hissed and shrank from my fire still randomly sparking from my body. My bouncy clouds took form and we ricocheted all the way to the courtyard.

Tip managed to stumble into the maze after us, following the trail of devastation we were leaving behind us. He looked like he was wrestling with a great deal of pain but he squared his shoulders and stood poised to fight if our scuffle brought us close again, sword in one hand, and the stolen ax in the other.

A crash in the distance caught my attention and I turned to see Peter whizzing through the air slinging magic at none other than The Wizard, at the same moment as Alice came barreling out of the woods, riding atop a large beast.

Mombi took my momentary distraction as an opportunity to throw her elbow into my face. I dropped my knife and rubbed at my jaw before grabbing hold of her hair and using it to swing her to the ground. We rolled back and forth, fighting for control of the scuffle. I kicked, clawed, and punched— anything to land a blow on the evil woman. I was shouting incoherent words of rage at her, until she finally got some leverage to pin me down.

"I seem to recall you not sharing an appreciation for my spiders, isn't that right?" She scoffed, bruised and disheveled, and pointed a ringed finger in my face.

I glared at it, before lunging forward and biting it, hard. I could feel her skin pop and tear against the chomp. Mombi yelped and yanked it free, her blood coating my teeth. "You aren't going to Little Miss Muffet me this time!" I spat at her, crimson speckles coating her neck from the spray. A bowl of curds appeared next to Tip, who looked at it in confusion.

More bowls began popping up around the area, and I used the pause of confusion to shove the witch off of me. Reaching for a bowl, I flung the lumpy contents into her face.

"Teach you to throw tea in *my* face!" I bellowed, taking a moment to wipe some blood from my lip.

She washed it away with a wave of her hand, and glared at me with such animosity, I was almost certain I would melt beneath it.

"Ah ha!" Tip cheered, racing up to join me. "Her craziness isn't something you can calculate," He threw at Mombi. "And you can't begin to evaluate her Goodness."

"She's Wicked," Mombi hissed back at the Lost Boy. But, there was a slight air of trepidation in her tone, like she didn't understand why the tea hadn't made me erupt with murderous calamity that she could use against us.

"That's right. Your little impromptu tea party with me in Neverland gave me a serious power boost," I gloated, my visions bobbing and contracting rapidly before stabilizing again. I pulled my hand back to strike her down, only to find my arms being restrained by sticky webbing.

"Oh no," I mumbled, knowing her spider cronies had arrived as backup. Sure enough, a quick scan of the courtyard showed it to be crawling with the balboas purple spider army from Oz.

Tip swung his sword to untether me and I fell backward, staring up at him in appreciation. He gave me a brisk nod, and I could see the dark tendrils getting thicker at his neckline.

"I've got your back." He spoke quietly, almost to himself but his words were full of adamance. "I choose you, Dorothy. You're the light I'm going to fight for and move forward towards. I'm done with her darkness. I'm going to be strong enough this time, I promise."

"I…" I stammered, touched and almost giddy from the sentiment. I hadn't never known I was capable of being a lighthouse in a storm to anyone. I was just me, nothing special. Tip wasn't one for fancy wording though, and usually only said what he meant. I believed him, but words to reply failed me.

"Alice is on her way. Let the crazy out to play, because we are both here to look out for you." He jerked his head towards Mombi, who had stumbled away to collect herself from our impromptu fistfight. "Melt her down with the madness. You lead, I'll follow." He grinned as he spoke our trust metaphor that was all the confidence I needed.

Trusting Tip implicitly, I allowed myself to submerge further into the waves of insani-tea lapping at my mind. No fear, just the conviction I needed to maintain control. Something worth fighting for.

"With pleasure!"

Twenty-Five

Wendy

The suit of Card-guards in front of me weren't really my enemies. However, most of them were detrimentally duty bound to serve whoever lived in the Red Castle, so I'd still have to deal with them.

Behind me, I could hear the clashes of battle echoing around the stones of Nonsense Falls, and there were faint wisps of smoke curling through the air, as Dorothy burned down the scarecrows.

"You just need to incapacitate them," I told myself firmly. "You are a Darling and Darlings do not kill."

"We must acquire the girl as a prisoner!" A Three of Spades called to his suit as they began to clamor through the dense patch of thorns between us. Beyond them, I could see the Red Castle peaking through the dim lighting of budding dawn.

"She's alone. We can grab her and go reinforce the soldiers." The Two nodded, pointing his sword in my direction.

"I don't much care for those things," Another spade complained. "They don't have a solid or flat way about them."

"If we don't, The Queen will have our heads!" The Three chided warily, and I felt sympathy in my heart for these poor guards. I didn't truly believe they *wanted* to partake in any fighting, but they believed in doing their jobs as assigned for fear of the alternative.

"Any chance you could simply lay down your weapons and us not have to fight?" I called out hopefully. I knew I could easily beat them, but my goal was merely to clear the way to allow us passage to the castle— Not to show off, or hurt anyone. Getting to the castle meant overthrowing Mombi, and overthrowing Mombi meant we were that much closer to freeing our remaining old friends lost here somewhere in Wonderland.

Despite my ebbing and flowing battle with inadequacy and loss since leaving Oz, along with the ugly jealousy of seeing Peter with Alice, this was bigger than all that. And, just maybe, if I did my part, the universe would see fit to reward me with my brothers. They were the last light I had left to cling to, so I'd do anything to find them. Then, when everyone else went their own way, we would be there to help Peter pick up the pieces. It was my new dream and everything else was a means to an end to protect it.

"We wouldn't dare defy our orders. It would be treason," The Two scoffed, not more than six paces from me. It was clear they thought this would be an easy fight— and it would be, just not for them.

"Very well," I coiled the chain of my scythe in my hand, then cast it in a sweeping motion against the nearest guards. "I have my orders too."

The two cards I'd hit bent in two at their middles, and I whisked one of the many daggers I had stashed on my body into my hand as I recoiled my scythe. Pushing forward, I leapt towards the discombobulated cards and pinned their folded forms to the ground.

"Hey! She knows how to fight. Was that in the briefing?" The Ace complained to the remaining cards.

"We didn't have a briefing, we just ran here," The Seven sighed.

"Sorry," I shrugged with an apologetic smile, though I felt the flames of pride igniting in my chest at my handiwork. I was still the Lost Girl I so longed to be. "I tried to have you surrender."

Springing into action, this time wielding my sword in one hand, and my chain in the other, I managed to make quick work of blocking and disarming the Cards-guards. Then, I folded each one and pinned them down. I kept the knives away from any part I feared might be vital to their staying alive, then paused to inspect my trousers.

"Oh dear. Those dreadful thorns got through the fabric. I'd like to not destroy every outfit I get in this place!" I sighed, stopping to pluck the embedded thorns from my legs. "Black was never my first choice anyway, I suppose."

I stood and stared at the castle ahead. Continuing on alone didn't seem like a wise choice, but I also wasn't so sure I'd be of much use in the fighting back at the Nonsense Falls, since it seemed one needed either magic or brute strength to have much effect. I could try to find Peter, but he had seemed pretty resolute in his decision to keep his party small—something that unfortunately bespoke him doing something reckless to deviate from our intended plan.

Going back to the Falls seemed the best option, but as I turned to return to the group I stiffened in surprise, my hand fluttering to my mouth to cover an astonished gasp.

"Hello, please follow me. I'm running terribly behind." A dazzling white rabbit, adorned in dapper clothing, dipped his head and flicked open his watch. Was this the infamous White Rabbit Alice had never been able to catch?

"Follow you? Me?" I spluttered, pointing to myself. "Don't you want Alice?"

The White Rabbit twitched his whiskers and shook his head. "No. I was sent to take you, specifically."

"Take me where?" My brows furrowed in confusion, and I rubbed my arms nervously.

"To Oz, of course," The rabbit replied in a no nonsense manner.

"I beg your pardon?"

"We really haven't the time to keep going over this."

"I can't go to Oz!" I balked. "My friends are counting on me here. We are in the middle of a battle, Mr. Rabbit. I'm terribly sorry."

The rabbit snorted, and started to wind his clock. "I'm taking you to Oz with my acceleration watch. We have to go *now*, or there won't be time for the extraction."

"What extraction?" I cried in bewilderment as the rabbit offered me his paw.

"One of your Lost Ones of course," The rabbit puffed. "Honestly, wasn't collecting all of them already figured out by the lot of you. We have a limited window while the attention is diverted over here, and if we can successfully get the man out of Oz, then it will weaken The Wizard. He will be able to sense it though, which is why we must hurry."

"You mean Henry?" I gasped. He was supposed to be one of the hardest to get, that we knew of. If I had a chance to rescue him, I should take it right? But what if I only got myself captured again? "What about The Wizard?"

"He will be otherwise engaged here in Wonderland."

"Oh, no. It's Peter, isn't it?" I bit my lip anxiously. "He's seeking him out."

The Rabbit nodded. "And it's not going to be a long fight, likely. However, given that the boy is being led by his anger and desire for revenge, we don't want him indulging it long anyway. Now, *come on.* It doesn't take long for time to catch back up, I don't wish to disturb the connection to the other world too terribly for your friends' sakes, and I can't be away too long myself. Plus, if we don't time it just right, the boy could parish."

I felt like a knife had impaled my stomach, infusing dread into my very core. "He could die?"

"Yes. Or lose himself to his inner darkness. We are playing with fire here, but I was given direct orders that must be carried out to the letter. If you want to protect him, and his light, you'll leave with me this instant."

I inhaled deeply. I could do this! Fighting against magical foes wasn't something I could stand victorious at, but if the cat was away, then I was a mouse that could play. I didn't know who had given the mysterious rabbit his orders, but they had chosen me specifically to perform this task, and it filled my soul with purpose.

There was a small, petty part of me that reveled in the idea that I was the only one who'd gotten to directly interact with the rabbit, and I knew it would drive Alice crazy. I'd return with Henry, and *I'd* be the one to save Peter somehow by doing it. I had to do this for his sake, the sake of finding my brothers, and Henry's wellbeing. Nothing mattered more.

"Right. Let's go then." I accepted the White Rabbit's paw and he mumbled for me to brace myself.

My stomach lurched as the world around me began to warp into fragmented lines of movement. Trees turned to passing wisps of green, the ground a blur of speckled brown, and even the air echoed in a linear transition of white and blue.

Small flickers of frozen moments flashed before my eyes, showing me the others fighting at Nonsense Falls, Dorothy ablaze in mid combat with a scarecrow. I scarcely blinked and caught a flash of towering mushrooms before they too blurred into lines of a rainbow. My breath caught in my throat as I saw the still image of Alice being knocked to the ground.

"Alice! She needs help," I cried out, jealousy aside, alarmed by the overwhelming amount of foe she was fighting, but the Rabbit merely grunted.

"If her heart is truly fighting for Wonderland, then help will come to her soon." The answer was ominous, but I knew that Alice's heart was definitely set on fighting for Wonderland's salvation, so I had to trust what the rabbit told me.

The next flash passed the infamous sign post, then what I had to assume was the ruined former munchkin village, a field of flowers, and finally the Emerald City. The whole trip didn't even take us a full minute of real time, and I swayed from the abrupt shift from rapid motion to stagnance once more.

"Oh dear." One hand clutched at my stomach with the other covering my mouth. "I think I might be sick."

"It will pass," The White Rabbit promised and promptly marched up to the door of what looked like a mostly abandoned building, rapping his paw on it three times. "He should be just inside here."

"I hope we don't frighten him. Henry always was a very sensitive boy," I fretted, looking around nervously. I could see the very top of the Emerald Castle glimmering in the fresh morning light, but I knew it was some distance away. We were somewhere deep in the city.

"For Goodness sake. We don't have time for this," The White

Rabbit grumbled, looking down at his watch, his nose crinkling into a mammalian scowl.

"Are you positively certain this is where we will find him?"

"Yes, quite." His tone was terse. I was asking important questions, but in the rushed air of the moment, I knew they were pointless.

"Dorothy said he had a fancy watch that altered time too. Suppose he left using that?"

"No. My watch can sense his nearby. Think of them like magnetic poles of the timeline. When you move those opposite ends together, they repel with a tangible force. I can't be around it too long or strange things will happen to time itself in the other world."

A slow creaking sounded, and I held my breath as I watched the door swing ever so slighting inward to open. A hooded man appeared hesitantly in the crack.

"Is it really you, Wendy?" The man's voice trembled with emotion, and I felt my throat tighten unexpectedly as I saw his eyes glinting with misty tears from beneath the dip of his hood. "You've gotten older."

"So have you." My words caught in my mouth, and I flung myself forward, shoving open the door to throw my arms around my old friend. There was no doubting it. Despite the change in age, those eyes of his could never conceal his identity. They were too gentle and kind. This was most definitely our Henry.

"We've come to take you home," I sniffled at last as I pulled away at the sound of an impatient huff from the White Rabbit. *Blast it all, Wendy, you can't mess up this mission with your daddling.* I scolded myself, but I felt full to the brim with happiness, I couldn't stop the words from tumbling out of my mouth.

"Take me home?" Henry echoed, dumbfounded.

"Well, we will get there soon. We have to go back to Wonderland first, actually. See, Peter is there with a few new Lost Ones— Oh, well you met Dorothy already. She's with Peter now. And Tip! Tip is back too. And now you. You're here and I can scarcely believe it." I had to swallow against the lump in my throat.

"I'm sorry, but I don't entirely understand. You're going to take me back to my world?"

"Oh, well actually, I just meant Neverland. But, if you want to return to our world, so long as we win this fight against The Wizard, then I'm sure we can figure you into the trip back."

"I can go back to Neverland?"

"Well, of course you can. But, um," I paused, noting that the Rabbit was now tapping his foot and grumbling about how long we were taking, and something about the world's doom being on our hands.

"Listen Henry Dear, I promise you I will explain everything to you, but we have to get moving fast, our timing is crucial to keeping Peter alive. I just need you to trust me. The Wizard had arranged for the Lost Ones at the time to be taken from Neverland and hidden away. You're one of the five missing Lost Ones left in this world, and we have to find all of you to have whatever it is we need to beat him once and for all. So, it's imperative you come with us now."

"I'm one of five you need to find?" Henry repeated my words as a question, causing the rabbit to sigh heavily.

"Look, I don't have the time for you to question every statement and make her repeat it. You must go with her, and you must do it quickly. If you don't, then Peter *might survive* his fight against The Wizard…" He trailed off and darted a look at his watch. "Which should be starting right about now. I didn't budget any more time for this exchange."

"If you really believe it's imperative in saving Peter's life, of course I'll go with you," Henry nodded obligingly.

"Finally," The White Rabbit grunted.

"Thank you, Henry. There's a lot you'll need to be filled in on, but I really appreciate you trusting me."

"There's no reason in this world or any other why I wouldn't trust the wonderful Wendy Darling. Henry nodded and looked at the rabbit. "Alright then, should we use your watch or mine?"

"Yours. I already told you I can't be around his deceleration watch longer than a few moments without causing ripple effects. Don't ask questions you don't listen to the answer for," The rabbit scolded, and I ducked my head. "I am running terribly late, and need to get back lest things go terribly awry. But, don't use it again for a while after or, for all we know, the other world will jump decades." He'd barely finished speaking before he vanished back into the blurring lines of time and space, and I had to seriously wonder what time schedule he was bound to with a timepiece like his at his disposal. It sounded terribly complex, and clearly he didn't not have the time to answer me.

"If I may," Henry offered me his hand after setting his own watch, and I accepted.

"How does it work?"

"It's a deceleration watch, so it slows time for everyone not connected to the watch. As long as we stay in contact, we are merely moving particles in a frozen picture. Since I am not magical in nature, I can only use it for so long. That being said, once I release the peg, we need to race as quickly as possible from this place and make it as far as we can before time resumes. Most importantly, for both of us, we need to get out of Oz before the clock stops or The Wizard *will* stop us."

I reached for where his free hand was holding down the peg and released it, starting the timer. True enough, the world's movements halted around us, but I didn't linger to take in the scenery. Instead I tugged my old friend along behind me.

"Henry? I need to ask you a question," I puffed as we pelted through the stalled Emerald City.

"What is it?"

"Why did you never use the clock to flee Oz and return to Neverland?"

Henry smiled wistfully. "By the time I got a hold of the clock, I was all grown up. I didn't think there was any place for me in a childhood kingdom anymore."

"Surely you know Peter would have welcomed you back!"

"I suppose I should have. But, I doubted my relevance in the grander story for him. I felt I was only ever meant to be without any real impact. In anyone's life, I'm just a blip in their story. A passing character in the background. Not like you, or Tip, or your brothers. To be honest, I didn't really understand why they bothered kidnapping someone as insignificant as me in the first place. I thought, maybe if I could learn all I could here, perhaps some day it would come in handy, but truthfully, I figured I would just die here in Oz someday, and no one would know the difference either way."

"Henry! That's dreadful. I can't begin to fathom what would make you doubt your value or impact on others. Why, you should have seen Peter and Tip's excitement when they realized you were alive. Lionel too! You're more than a blip. You're entirely significant."

"You have Lionel too? He one of the Lost Ones here, I take it?" Henry gasped.

"Yes. Lionel, Pat, Sam, James, and you. We have you and Lionel at this point."

"If you can get Lionel and James back together, those two would be unstoppable. They were always so daring and adventurous, like nothing ever scared them. I couldn't ever hope to have an ounce of their courage and strength. Sam and Pat were always pranksters, and goofballs, but boy were they clever. I'm not sure what I will be able to contribute to stopping The Wizard. Not like the others will. " Henry's tone was heavy and laced with insecurity.

It made my heart ache with empathy. I could already tell that Henry would have a very difficult time facing his Shadow Beast, however it chose to manifest. I knew it would no doubt challenge his sweet and gentle soul with the feeling of quiet despair and insignificance he was already displaying. Perhaps our demons were similar in nature— a feeling of displacement and inadequacy— but one thing I had never lost sight of in my time of captivity was *hope*.

I had never lost my hope in Peter finding me or in returning to Neverland someday. It certainly hadn't turned out as I had hoped, and now I wrestled against frequent waves of loneliness and loss, yet those years of isolation hadn't made me question my value to the world as a whole. That was something I was fighting now that I found myself in a new world for all intents and purposes. However, I *needed* to dream and hope, or I would truly be lost. That was why I had needed to focus on finding John and Micahel so I could achieve my new hope for us. I wouldn't let this one slip through my fingers this time. But, poor Henry had been plagued with such insecurities and doubt, he'd given up not just on Neverland and Peter, but on his own existence.

"Don't you ever let me catch you calling yourself insignificant again," I said fiercely over my shoulder as we raced out of the Emerald City. "You are part of the bright future awaiting us. You are so dearly important to me. Never doubt that you matter, Henry."

"Yes, Mother-Wendy," Henry promised. Something in his tone told me it was going to be an uphill struggle for the poor timid man, but I believed him all the same.

"Alright, now let me fill you in on what we are charging into. There is a lot to cover."

Twenty-Six

Peter

Watching everyone else depart in their small groups made my stomach twist in knots. Only Tiger Lily remained by my side, and neither of us said a word as Tip, Wendy, Dorothy, and Lionel disappeared into the woods with the Imagineds to take their positions. We had nothing to do but wait till it was our turn.

"You have no intention of following the plan, do you?" Tiger Lily finally broke the silence as we took our turn to exit the underwater haven.

I could have laughed it off. I could have swept it under the rug and kept up the charade, but my insides felt like they were being ripped apart from trepidation and rage warring one another with me. So, I didn't have it in me to joke my way around a half truth, and instead stopped to face my old friend. She was created of my mind after all. She had to have some idea of what I felt— Hook likely did too.

She blinked at me, collected and without any trace of amusement in her face. Who knew what terrors had driven Lily to take shelter with the pirate crew to begin with, but to trust Hook for her safety, she surely must have been desperate. Thankfully, though, it seemed that everything had worked out well for her, and as nefarious as I had set out for Hook to be as the villain of this direction, he turned out to be a relatively decent guy when the chips were down. He had outgrown his role and made his own way.

In all honesty, my mind had likely conjured Tiger Lily to fulfill what I had seen to be a normal role of companionship I had witnessed in the Emerald City, but didn't truly understand. I had simply known that there were husbands and wives, and mothers and fathers. Pairings. So, I had imagined a girl around my age to be my paired set.

But, that was before meeting Wendy, who had taught me what that initial spark was supposed to feel like. I learned what it was like to think someone was pretty, and to appreciate her friendship in a different kind of way than the Lost Ones. She had been the one to kiss me long before I ever knew of Alice. She had been too embarrassed to call it a kiss by name and had told me it was a thimble.

Losing her had been my biggest catalyst into anguish. I held her fondly in my heart for a long time, holding on to that spark, thinking that was the most intense feeling I could possibly feel towards another person. But, it was only ever a spark and never a flame. Then I met Alice, and within moments of our first encounter she had already managed to start a spark of her own— and unlike Wendy's, Alice's never stopped growing from a spark to what was now a raging inferno. It taken me far too long to understand it for what it was, and for the longest time I had felt that sharing special moments or affection with Alice was somehow disparaging the memory of Wendy, and having only ever dealt with embers, a full fire made me fear the burns I'd surely receive from getting too close. And yet, I had still been a moth to her lovely flame— even while never truly dreaming that she was also in love with me too. I had gotten burned, but not by the danger of her, but rather the frostbite of her potentially being gone forever.

I stared unwaveringly as the brazen young woman before me. It wasn't just Alice who I stood to lose. It was everyone I had ever held dear. Everything and everyone I had created— those who my mother had created before me in the other directions. I had thought long and hard about my mother's power and her creations. Her countless Imagineds still thrived even after her passing. Whether I lived or died, all their lives were going to keep moving forward.

"I won't lie to you now, Lily," I sighed with a sad smile. "I never was going to abide by the plan. Not after what happened to the pixies. That was an official declaration of war, and I won't let it go unpunished. The plan was for everyone else's sake, and out of everyone I figured you'd likely give me the least guff for ignoring it. However, if you want to join one of the other teams I understand, and you may go."

Tiger Lily inhaled deeply, her deep golden brown eyes reflecting the eerie pattern of fractured light from the dying moonlight bouncing off the ocean beside us. They narrowed, a visualization of her discernment as she weighed her options. Then she loosed a sigh and folded her arms.

"Alright, where is your recklessness taking us this time?" She smirked. "Are we Wizard-hunting?"

I couldn't help but grin back at her. "I'm certain he is going to be watching for sport, hoping to see us all fail. I'm not entirely sure what his end game is, but I think there has been a reason why he hasn't killed any of the Lost Ones, or Alice and Dorothy. Or, even me, for that matter. He still needs something."

"Based on what Alice shared with me about what a book in his library said about *you*, I have to guess that it was all a projection of what he does." Tiger Lily's clipped words hit a bell in my mind.

"You mean draining them of their imagination for power?"

"Just like he did to your mother."

My spine stiffened as a new surge of renewed rage boiled my blood.

Don't worry. I will help you take your revenge. The inner demon's growl slithered through my brain. *I'm counting on it.* I replied back, to which the demon laughed, clearly pleased with my dip into darkness. Despite the happiness I had felt watching Alice undo the destruction and add to Neverland, the Pixie Village massacre had shifted something in me, and I didn't want to be the Good guy today. Not for this important of a fight. I wanted to make the world tremble under the weight of my thirst for vengeance, then rejoice when it saw The Wizard brought to his knees. Had Alice's miracle recovery not happened when it did, I likely would have gone to pick a fight right then and there.

"While Mombi was here, she didn't try to actively kill anyone, other than maybe Dorothy, but even that seemed more like she was just toying with her limits. She was really here to spy and sow seeds of doubt. She did the same thing to Wendy and Alice. But, there was something I heard that she said to Tip that really stuck with me."

"I tend to tune out a lot of her monologues. To be honest, she already was a pain, but after Alice told me about the compass being hers, and Tip explaining it more thoroughly to me, I can't think straight around the woman. She makes me lose my cool." And that was a massive understatement. At this point, I wanted to see her head on a spike so badly I could almost feel it— which caused me to shudder and pull myself back from such violent thoughts. I had to be careful to walk a fine balance in the morally gray if I wanted to be successful.

"As understandable as I'm sure that is, you should always listen when the villain starts getting chatty. It's when they are at their most confident and their most vulnerable. It's like they need to brag about how clever they have been just in case no one ever realizes it before one side or the other falls."

"So, that's when they divulge their best information?"

"Exactly. She said something about *swaying* Tip *just like old times*, and that he just needed to tip far enough. I get she was going for a pun there, but still if you think about what was actually saying, it sounds like her whole goal with Tip was always to turn him Wicked. Same thing with Alice and her compass… and now Dorothy with the tea."

"Tip would never do that though! Second to Wendy, he's the last person I could ever see turning Wicked." I dragged my hands down my face in frustration. "And Dorothy and Alice are *already* Wicked."

"In title, sure." Tiger Lily tapped her foot against the pebbly sand. "But, I think you and I both know those girls are Good at heart, and are far from evil. No, I think there is something more happening there. All of them have been targeted, and while I think hurting you is a driving motivation, there's something else. They need them on their side for some reason. And to get that, each one of them must break. Meanwhile, with the shadows aiding in that endeavor, it benefits them to leave us to stew here, torn down by our own minds while they reap the rewards."

"Alice and Dorothy but have magical items bound to them too. I wonder if that's just a coincidence."

"That part, I'm not too sure about. But why else would The Wizard, who could clearly wipe the floor with you all at the time, choose to play a drawn out game, and let you all return to Neverland where three of you had hidden demons waiting to consume you, and offer Alice and Dorothy tempting offers of salvation for their cooperation? Why didn't The Wizard or Mombi just kill Dorothy and take her shoes?"

"When you lay it all, you're right. Something isn't adding up. When did you get to be so clever?"

"I've always been clever, Stupid," She growled, punching me in the arm. "And apparently I'm the only one with my head on straight and not being turned by someone else!"

"What do you mean by that?" I sniffed. "My head is perfectly square on my shoulders."

"You all have crooked necks. You looking at Alice, Alice looking at you, Wendy also looking at you, Tip and Dorothy look at each other, and who even knows who Lionel is looking at, but I'm sure he's looking at *someone*. It's ridiculous the way you've all just coupled up— well except Wendy. She's a bit out of luck."

"Your point, Lily?" I folded my arms and quirked an eyebrow.

"My point is that, while you've all be half here and half where your other half is, *I've* been thinking. All that gooey stuff might give you motivation or whatever, but it rarely lets you think clearly. So, what I think is that we better get a move on and get our answers."

"Blast! How long have we been?"

"Not too long, so they should still be on their way to their positions."

"Oh, good. Alright, if you're still sure you want to come with me, then let's head out."

Tiger Lily ground her teeth. "You could die fighting him. What happens then?"

I lifted my chin. "If I die, then I'll do as my mother did before me and continue to sustain the world. You all will keep on existing, I'll make sure of it."

I turned to leave, but Tiger Lily caught my arm and, to my surprise, embraced me tightly. "I don't want you to die, Pan. We are fighting for ourselves, but all of us are fighting for *you*. Even though you left and so much happened in your absence, we never stopped fighting for you. Even when I wanted to kill you myself for how foolish you had been, and I blamed you for all of my pain— for my own existence to even suffer the pain in my lowest moments…"

"Lily…" I breathed, returning her hug.

"You can't die. You might not be particularly fond of hearing this, but there's a future waiting for you, and you have to survive to find out what it will be. But, I know one thing for certain is that it will be bright."

"Thankfully, the plan isn't to die then!" I chuckled and shrugged off the tense atmosphere. "You think Alice would let me rest in peace if I went and died?"

"She's going to murder you for being so reckless in the first place. I like her spirit."

I waved my hand dismissively and lifted into the air to head to the edge of the bubble. "I'll definitely lose some points. But, not if she doesn't have to find out!"

"Some things never change," Tiger Lily chided, but she smiled all the same. "Give me some dust, and I'll follow you. Just lead the way."

"Then, I guess we are off to see The Wizard. And Lily, your job, no matter what happens, is to stay hidden and collect all the information your clever mind can hold. It might benefit our side, even if things go awry."

~*~

"Just as I thought. He's here at the castle with Mombi. Disgusting."

"And they are just watching from a balcony… oh look! Here comes Tip and Dorothy. Why is it only them?" Tiger Lily grit her teeth. "Where is the rest of their group? I hope Hook and company are alright."

I wanted to look to the eastern horizon for any sign that Alice was alright in her fight, but my eyes couldn't look away from The Wizard. Mombi was dressed *immodestly* as Alice would have likely called it, since there was more visible skin than I had yet to ever see on a female. She was cuddled close to The Wizard, her arms wrapped around him as they stood at the edge of the same balcony I had sent Dorothy flying away at.

At the appearance of Tip and Dorothy, I saw Mombis face twist and she mumbled something to The Wizard before disentangling herself. He grabbed her wrist forcefully and whispered something to her before releasing his hold in a rough manner. A quick snap of her fingers and Mombi was reclothed, relocating herself to the end of the hedge maze to meet my friends. Narrowing my eyes, I could see that they were beginning with a verbal confrontation, and I only hoped that if Tip couldn't fight her, Dorothy would be enough to protect him. Something told me she wouldn't appreciate Mombi's advances one bit.

"So, you've come to face me at last, Boy?" The Wizard called out, not bothering to turn around. "Struggling to finish that game of hide and seek?"

"Well, I don't think you explained the rules too well," I replied evenly, abandoning my hiding place in the shadows of the tower to fly into the growing light. "Seems that Mother of mine may have given you her power, but none of her prowess, so you felt the need to tweak the odds."

At the mention of my mother The Wizard whipped around. "Don't you speak of her. You have no right."

"That doesn't seem like a very fair thing to be saying with all *that* going on," I growled, gesturing in Mombi's general direction.

"I wouldn't expect a boy like you to understand. Then again, who knows what *Wicked* things you got up to while unsupervised all this time. I was your age once. You've had your share of young ladies around as of late, am I supposed to believe all this time alone and getting older and they aren't all concubines by now? Especially the little blonde one you're so fond of."

I crinkled my nose. "I know you're a villain, but calling them porcupines just because they are girls is a bit below the belt." As usual, people could get as fancy as they wanted with their wording, but it never landed a hit if I didn't understand the insult.

The Wizard stared at me, a brief flash of honest confusion in his eyes before he snorted and shook his head. My hands curled into fists at his patronizing demeanor. He had *no idea* how much I had grown in the last week alone. I was strong. I was powerful. I was ready to end this little game of his.

"I already told you that you wouldn't be able to beat me without completing the first round of the game. I was prepared to stay out of this fight and let nature take its course. If Mombi isn't strong enough to hold her line, well then, I'll move on to someone who is. That's what I told her before she left too. I have no interest in *weak* witches," The Wizard drawled, pushing up his sleeves slowly. He then gestured to where Dorothy had engaged with the Wicked witch. "Yet, you seem to be the one intent on thwarting the rules. Here, I thought you were raised better."

"I've always played by my own rules," I grinned wildly, a fever taking hold of me the longer I looked at the monster in front of me. He was so callous of his own ally, and apparent girlfriend, and was *smiling.* A terror that had caused so much torment didn't deserve to smile.

Destroy him. Let me out.

"So, what's your plan here, Boy?" The Wizard held his arms out wide. "Running away always seemed to be your best tactic, so forgive me for not knowing how to anticipate you actually advancing."

"I'm done running. And *my plan* is to remove you from this world," I asserted boldly, my tone dipping in tandem with the inner demon raging within me. I wouldn't die. He had no idea I was going to unleash my magic on him.

"Is that so? Well, you must have quite the ace up your sleeve. Let's take this outside, if you will. I'd rather not damage the castle. Reera was truly insane, but she did have a good eye for craftsmanship."

"You're right. Alice won't like it being damaged when she takes it back."

The Wizard frowned pointedly. "If she lives long enough, I suppose there's a chance you could be right. Though her options are getting pretty limited. She can continue on and her inevitable actions will break the compass, killing her. Or, she can come to her senses, allow Mombi to fix it for her, and join the cause willingly for her ticket home. Then there's always the chance she will simply turn fully after the compass is repaired, kill Mombi when her purpose has been served, and replace her at my side. I'll be honest, Alice with the power of *four* witches would be quite the trophy."

"She is not a trophey!" I couldn't take it any longer, and using the air at my feet as an invisible wall, I launched forward. The Wizard chuckled and disappeared, beckoning me to follow him over the forest adjacent to the hedge maze.

A quick glance down, and I saw Dorothy and Tip's fight with Mombi had taken them to the courtyard below and out of range for collateral damage. With a snarl of fury I zipped through the air like a bullet towards him. Years of pent up anger and pain was ready to burst from me. *This is it. I can finally unleash it all!*

I felt black spindles coil around my forearms beneath my shirt, and I knew the Shadow Beast was taking hold to aid me in my rage. *I'm not the Good guy today.* I told myself firmly. *I'm getting results. Heroes never finish the job, and show mercy to monsters. So, I'm no hero, and I will show no mercy this monster.*

I advanced with my sword drawn, still playing the part of magicless boy. The Wizard was staring me down with a scathing and patronizing gaze, a smirk on his lips. There was movement below, and I saw a glimpse of Alice riding a great Cheshire beast— I'd have to ask about that immediately after this was over, if I survived— through the gaps in the foliage, racing to join the fight at the castle. She was safe, and Mombi was now outnumbered. I could focus all my attention on The

Wizard without it being pulled in other directions now. I was more than ready to take out my years of repressed fury on him.

More shadows coated my biceps, moving towards my shoulders as the demon took more of my body, enveloping more and more of me in an icy heat. I just needed enough malice to dance in the gray but not snuff out the light. It was by far the most dangerous game I'd ever played, and I could only hope that a victory at the end of this would be enough to drive the demon away. For now, we were aligned in the desire to destroy the man in front of me— physically, mentally, and emotionally, till there was nothing left.

He wanted my power. He had tortured me just to try to reveal it. Well, I'd show it to him now. I'd wipe the smirk right off his face. My eyes shuttered briefly between shades of black and red. I shook it off. I didn't care. Not if I could end it all here.

I drew my lips back in a feral snarl of pure animosity before I raised my other hand and summoned my first wave of magic. The magic that had come to me most easily and had frightened me all that time ago when facing him before.

Storm clouds pooled above us, static charge flickering in the billows like minnows in a stream. Tethering the electric pull to my finger, I hurled a bolt of lightning with all my might.

The moment seemed to slow as adrenaline pulsed through me. I watched as the lightning parted from my hand and coiled through the air towards its target. I smiled as I saw the flashing illuminate the irate shock in The Wizard's dark eyes as he stared down the first attack.

Then, his jaw clenched and with a simple hand motion he directed the energy around him. My brows shot up and time snapped back into pace. Grunting with irritation, I slung more lightning, one beam right after the other. He dodged or redirected each one.

"Looks like you finally connected with that stolen power, Boy," He growled, a deathly gleam of a true devil shone from his face.

"It wasn't stolen. It was *given.* She chose to give it to me. She knew she couldn't trust you with it," I shouted back, my shoulders raised like hackles. I could feel Ozma's magic rushing through my veins, the same as her blood did. It was part of my existence, and was filled with love, hope, light and warmth. It was her protection and her comforting presence— and wielding it was the closest I would ever come to being near her.

Untethered rage twisted The Wizard's expression as I mentioned my mother again. Breaking his calm and collected demeanor, he flashed up to me and grabbed me by the throat.

"You don't *speak of her.*" He was nearly foaming at the mouth as he spoke.

As his fingers crushed against my throat, ignoring my instinctual desire to to pull the hand away, I pulled a dagger free and swiped at his abdomen. The tearing of the fabric split the air like a clap of thunder and at the flash in his eyes before he teleported away, I knew I'd managed to wound him.

Sure enough as he reappeared several paces away, blood was spreading across the white of his shirt, and his fingers dripped scarlet as he pulled them away from the injury.

I'd landed a blow! I could do this. He wasn't invincible, and I could beat him. Shadows fell across his face and he started laughing like a mad man as he looked at the blood on his hand. It was terribly unnerving, and chipped ever so slightly at my resolve.

Wanting to take advantage of his distraction, I grabbed at the air and pulled it like a rug. The ripple of atmosphere caused him to stagger to the side.

His mad laughter subdued to a soft chuckle as he once more dodged another of my attacks— this time a fireball. He squared his shoulders and inclined his head to me.

"You've been practicing, I see. At least I know you've accessed several of your attributes so they should be easier to return to me now."

"They weren't ever yours. *You* stole them from Ozma. *You* killed her!" I spat, more black and red pooling into my eyes.

Yes, let your pain wash over you. Make him pay. The voice of the demon sounded behind my ear, and I knew he was physically present for the first time since I'd clashed with Tiger Lily. He was waiting to steal me.

"Lies!" The Wizard spat, frenzied once more at the mention of Ozma. "I should have bashed your vile little head the moment I first held you. The moment you came into this world! But foolish me thought just maybe there might be another way and I kept you alive. I should have killed you and taken it back! No, I should have killed you just for killing her."

"She wouldn't have died if you could have controlled your lust for power. You're worse than Wicked. You're pure evil. Someone like my mother had no business being chained to a monster like you," I roared back, and braced myself for his reaction.

A sudden physical strike whipped my head to the side as The Wizard reappeared in front of me and threw his fist into my face. Physical attacks, however, was the area I had the most experience in, while combative magic was still new. I returned a blow of my own, thrusting my own fist up to clip the base of his jaw. The sound of impact was immensely satisfying, and sent a victorious shiver of excitement down my spine.

It was clear to me that hand to hand combat might be an instinctual response to his anger, but it wasn't his forte. He was a little bigger than me since, physically, he likely had close to around ten years on me, but it wouldn't do him much good if he didn't know how to use it properly.

The hit I'd dealt him knocked him backwards and he grabbed at his chin, clicking his jaw back and forth. My cheek was stinging and I could taste blood on my lip from where he'd struck me. I spat and wiped my mouth with the back of my hand, ruling my shoulders back to prepare for another round. Each time he lost his composure, I was able to hit him. That was the dance we were doing, and I could withstand it to wear him down to where I could drive him back or use my magic more effectively. I *knew* I should be strong enough.

"Alright, I'm done playing with you. Are you ready to see *real* power?" The Wizard's voice was quiet and low. "I'm more powerful than you could possibly *imagine*, Boy."

He looked up at me, smiling as several blades formed into the air and pointed at me. Unleashing the barrage at once, the swords and daggers hurtled towards me.

"Oh, bloody hell. I forgot about forging items," I groaned to myself, brought back down from the dark cloud of elation for a moment, as I narrowly zipped to and fro to avoid the whizzing weapons. "Ugh!" I grunted as I was struck by an invisible force that sent me reeling.

"I'm not ready for you to die just yet," The Wizard barked out, whipping at me with strands of wind. "No, you need to see it all crumble first. I've become powerful enough without taking that power back. It will be the last thing I take from you, right after I take *your life*"

I flinched as one of the whips sliced into my arm, but stared back defiantly. "Doubtful!"

"First, I think we will take that lad back. He will be Mombi's plaything should she survive— I won't be stingy with her intimacies, how could I when I will have so many new options myself?" The Wizard chuckled merrily. "Then, the little red head will be next. I bet her cries of pain as we turn her will be simply melodious. I bet her Wickedness will run the deepest of any before her."

"You won't touch either of them!" I bellowed, bringing my arms up to block my face as I was pelted with bullets of pure air.

"Then," The Wizard continued manically. "I'll take the new girl with the silver slippers. She might take a while to break, but I know she will eventually make a very spirited witch under my command. From what I've been told she's got a soft spot for the boy, so no doubt she will follow him— Unless Mombi kills her. Guess with those two it will be a game of last witch standing. Winner gets the boy for a prize. And don't worry, I'll make sure and save a special place on the shelf for your precious Alice."

"Gah!" I darted out of the way of the pellets, my skin stinging from the peppering of wounds. "None of them will ever follow you."

"That's what you think. But, it's amazing how ambitions and alliances can alter when the heart can be darkened enough. *Everyone* will follow me at the end of this little game of ours. Maybe, I'll have Alice be the one to strike the final blow to Neverland. Her fiery personality unleashed would be unbridled calamity. Now just imagine her and Dorothy aligned to wipe it away. Every last spec, destroyed. They share my appetite for destruction after all. Maybe the red-haired one will too, once she's turned Wicked as well. I wonder what her power will be." The Wizard tapped his head thoughtfully. "I'm getting excited just imagining it."

"They would never. Not in a million years," I bit, the dark torrent of bitter anger begging to take over.

"No, but I think Alice would be a lovely alternative for Mombi's *affections*. Did you know that there is magic in this world that could sway her attachments? Ah yes, perhaps I should just allow her to love me, and you could watch. We can accelerate her aging a few years too. She can dress down to what Mombi was wearing when you were caught peeping, you Impish Boy. Can you imagine her in such apparel? Well, I certainly can. It's not nearly enough. Perhaps we could take it further—"

"Shut up!" I charged forward with my sword drawn once more. "*You will not touch her*. Not ever again!" I wanted to drive my blade through the center of him. I wanted to tear him limb from limb for even suggesting affections with Alice and turning my friends Wicked, for threatening Neverland— all of it. Murderous appetite was blazing through me, and I never understood Alice's impulses more than in that moment. The demon almost had me in its clutches, only inches away from being the winner of both battles— the internal one I fought, and the one with The Wizard.

"Ah, I see we found our touchy subject. It's the girl! How cliche. That kiss we shared was delicious, you know. I can see what you find desirable about her, really I can. Her lips taste like rosebuds. It left me with a taste of wanting more."

I was once more pummeled with blind force, the air being driven from my lungs. The sword fell from my grip and I swore inwardly. The Wizard's cold eyes appeared before me as I tried to catch my breath and he struck me directly, only this time, I wasn't in a position to brace for the impact, or retaliate.

"Don't you see? I *hate* you, you vile little imp. I will do everything in my power to bring every single one of your nightmares to fruition before I kill you. And there's nothing you can do to stop me. You're *powerless* in my presence. A gnat trying to challenge a dragon. I will destroy everything you've ever held dear. I will take what I need from your friends, and I will collect even more to add to my wealth of power. Then I will *destroy you*—body, mind, and soul."

Each word was emphasized by another blow against my body. The tide had changed in this fight, and I had clearly been far too confident in my own abilities. I heard the demon snarling at me to fight back, and to feed off the rage of defeat.

"If I don't forgo all of that tedious planning and don't kill you here and now." The Wizard grabbed hold of my bloodied face, and stared me down. "If she could see you now, she would be appalled. She adored my strength. She was strong too. If she knew what a pitiful wretch we had spawned, she'd roll in her grave. So, no more of this talk about her power being given to you, or her choosing you. Your entire life is nothing but a pathetic waste. No one truly loves you, despite the notions you've diluted yourself with. Everyone will leave you. Ozma would be *ashamed* of you, she could never love something so abominable. I will erase you."

"You're wrong," I snarled, gnashing my teeth together, but I already knew I'd failed this fight. My body had become sluggish, and even my pumping adrenaline was fading, leaving nothing but physical pain behind. I *was* pathetic, and I *wasn't* able to stand against him.

"No, you're *done*." The Wizard brought down a final blow against my body, sending it plummeting from the sky towards the edge of the hedge maze. And I fully expected it to kill me, but somehow it had felt slightly weaker than his previous strikes.

I stared blurrily up at my father, to see a look of unease crossing over his face. He had expected the hit to be harder too. I started to close my eyes, unable to fly to save myself, preparing to snap my spine against the ground at any moment.

Please, give my power back to this world and not to him. Protect my friends— no, protect my family. My light can go out, but don't let Alice's. I sent a silent plea into the universe, but the fatal impact never came. Instead I saw gold flit in front of me, and felt my descent slow from a gravity drop to a sinking floating.

"Tink," I breathed the fairies name in relief before I landed in something soft and comforting. The smell of roses engulfed me, and I saw the glimmering white petals and green vines curl around me, concealing my body within their embrace and I felt something kindle into recognition at their embrace. "*Mother.*"

A grating screech of frustration erupted from the inner demon as he was ripped from my body and dragged back into the shadows. My inner light leapt in relief from the smothering darkness it had been freed from. *Ida.*

I'm here. Ida, Tink, and a third voice I could only assume was Ozma's, words intertwined as they tickled my ear. *You'll be protected.*

I fought to cling to consciousness, my eyes lulling closed, but I didn't miss the look of confusion and horror pass over The Wizard as he watched the white roses move to protect me.

"She chose *me*," I whispered. Though I knew he couldn't hear my feeble words, I could tell he'd read my lips as I watched distress, anguish, and pure unadulterated rage roll over him. He started to move towards me, absolutely crazed, but his head whipped towards the east, eyes ablaze, and he had a sharp intake of breath. Then he vanished entirely, and I closed my eyes as my mother's roses finished engulfing me.

Twenty-Seven

Alice

My ears were ringing as I raced through the forest on Cheshire's back. It was sharp and reedy, which caused me to look around for the source of the teleportation happening nearby.

"It's Dorothy and Peter's conflicts," Cheshire commented, his voice simultaneously thunderous and silky.

"They aren't fighting together?" Concerned pooled in my chest, and I felt goosebumps ripple across my body. "Peter doesn't teleport either."

"No, but they are in the same general direction."

"Who are they fighting?"

"Dorothy is fighting the witch. Peter is above us facing the Wizard."

"The Wizard?" I demanded, immediately attempting to peer through the dense foliage towards the sky. Sure enough, though I couldn't spot Peter, I could see his thunder clouds. "Why would he face him by himself? That's why he wanted to go alone. Gah! If he survives, I'll kill him. Reckless, stupid boy!"

"We will leave him to it."

"But, I have to help him!"

"We are needed straight ahead, not straight above. So, that's where I am taking you. If you recall, I mentioned that this form does not last very long."

"Yes, and I noticed you've stopped speaking in contradictions and riddles. Care to explain?" I asked, as we burst out of the woods in great bounds.

"Reera's curse of the Mome Rath. We may not speak directly about anything, or be seen directly in most cases either. We heed the call of who we believe is the rightful ruler of Wonderland, however we can not directly sway this ruler or notify them of this rule in advance, lest it make the call less genuine— This applies to all the dwellers of Wonderland. We Mome Raths are typically elusive creatures, and prefer to stay invisible and small, however, if pushed, threatened or called upon by the ruler, we will have those binds broken and appear as we do now."

"But, you let me see you all the time, and the others too."

"Naturally. It is much more interesting to exist in the open, even if I am bound by riddles and madness. Still, we see and know all that happens in this direction. We seep in and out of the land itself. This transformation is limited, and I will soon return to my normal self in body and mind, so look sharp. We are approaching the enemies. Prepare yourself to fight, but know this, Alice of Wonderland, we will defend you until our time runs out."

I patted the back of Cheshire's head as I looked ahead at the swarm of giant terrifying purple spiders crawling over the last of the hedge maze and the courtyard. I took one last look over my shoulder to see Peter physically strike The Wizard, and sighed deeply. I'd have to trust him. I returned my eyes to the scene in front of me and steeled my resolve.

"Thank you, Cheshire. I will defend Wonderland with my life."

"Don't die. I have a book to reccomend to you, and it is a very imperative read," He purred, a deep beastly rumble that almost sounded more akin to growl. He slowly and dipped his head to allow me off of his back. "Time to play."

He, with the other Wonderlandians and and remaining Mome Raths, spread out to start attacking the spiders. I looked around the chaos until I spotted Tip, and Dorothy was a little in front of him standing opposite Mombi. Tip had black tendrils curling around his neck, though they looked like they were stemming from his veins, rather than any shadow creature. Meanwhile, Dorothy and Mombi both looked ruffled, and there were bowls of lumpy liquid everywhere, telling me Dorothy had gone mad again.

There was no sign of the pirates, Tiger Lily, or Wendy. Praying there was a good reason for the slim numbers at the main point of conflict, I rushed up to Tip, weapon drawn, ready to help take down our biggest tormentor.

"You look like hell," He commented with a side glance at me. Up close I could see his face twisting in concentration and pain, with sweat gathering on his brow.

"So do you. Did she poison you?" I gestured to his neck. "Oh, wait. Did you know there is a key sticking out of your chest?" I gasped and pointed at the protruding object.

"I did, actually." Tip rolled his eyes. "She impaled me with it, but I'm fine. We just need to focus on backing up Dorothy now. She had some tea to bolster her irrational fighting, so brace yourself. She's going into the depths of it."

"Right," I nodded and smiled. "I'm more than happy to lend a hand. Or to take one!"

"What? That sounds like compass talk!" Tip balked, but I was already in motion.

I leapt forward, slipping through space to flash up behind Mombi with my sword, and swung it at her. She turned her head to glare at me, before flashing herself out of the way. My sword sliced through the air and I whirled around to relocate her to the left of the courtyard.

Dorothy laughed, clutching her stomach in a fit before sobering and whispering, "Tea drips red in the morning light, but don't tell the icicles."

"I'll be sure not to," I replied to my insane friend. I spotted her bouncy clouds ambiently around already and jerked my chin at them. "Tip, come on. We need to lessen the space for her to teleport."

Tip followed my gaze and nodded, advancing towards the nearest cloud to get into the air, sword ready. Dorothy swayed on her feet and clutched at her head, eyes glazed and bright.

"I've got this sinking feeling. Do you feel it?" She called, and began melting into the ground.

"I thought you said she was going to be useful?" I snapped at Tip as I advanced towards Mombi again.

Tip leapt to another bouncy cloud and glowered at me. "Well, I believe that was her intent, but it's not an exact science!"

Mombi vanished from me and appeared next to Tip, surprising him by slapping him across the face with her ringed fingers. I saw a splatter of blood hit the cobblestone as the metal of the jewelry dug into his flesh. She grabbed the key and turned it a little further, satisfaction curling her pouty lips as he cried out in pain.

"Hey!" Dorothy cried out in anger, her face puckering with a dark look. She teleported over to Mombi and grabbed onto her wrist just as she flashed away, taking Dorothy with her. When they reappeared, Dororthy was digging her nails into the witch's face like an animal. "Stop breaking things!"

"Get off me you vermin," Mombi screeched, plucking Dorothy from her as she tried to drive her thumb into the ice witch's eye. I spotted a knife in her hand but when she swung it at Dorothy, Dorothy caught the blade with one hand and materialized her own knife in the other.

"Chop chop!" She sang out, completely unphased by the bare blade in her palm, and the blood now running down her arm. Then she shattered it with a giddy chirp. She clutched the fragments in her bloodied palm and then tossed them into the air, marveling as they exploded like small crimson fireworks.

I used the opportunity to swoop in next to them, and brought my knife down against Mombi's hand before she could move out of the way. There was a satisfying crunch, as my dagger severed her pinky and ring fingers from her hand. Her shriek of pain was positively melodious to my ears, and I picked up the finger as she fled backwards again.

"Well, it wasn't the whole hand but it'll do," I purred, swinging the fingers in front of my face, then I popped over to hand them to Tip.

"Here are two. Eight to go."

"You cut off her fingers?" He gasped, fumbling in disgust with the amputated digits. "Why?"

"I don't like those rings of hers. Jewelry is dangerous in her possession, so go ahead and take those ones off," I replied with a shrug. I saw red seeping into my vision and I was walking a dangerous line, but I wanted to hear her scream again. "So how do you want to die?"

"Lucky, shot. Her insanity won't last forever," Mombi raved as she tore part of her clothing to wrap her injured hand.

"Glinda, I stabbed and cut out her heart. The Red Queen, I cut her throat. And Avrilia I tore limb from limb." I walked menacingly towards her, ticking the witches off on my blood stained fingers. "So what'll it be for you? Or shall we do something new? I'd personally love to see you turn purple as I strangle you with my bare hands. It is your color after all, and suits you so much better than red. But, is it enough?"

"Dial it back, *Witch.* You're letting the Wicked swing too far," Tip warned me. I bit my lip, and tried my best to swallow my animosity down. "We can make her pay without having to bury you at the end of this."

I heard thumping from within the castle and looked over my shoulder as a fresh wave of Tin soldiers and scare crows came pouring out. Whipping back around, I saw that the Mome Raths were beginning to vanish, leaving only a normal-looking Cheshire smiling in the courtyard strewn with dead spiders. Then he too vanished. Their time was up.

"The book will have what you need to restore the protection of Wonderland. It is hidden in the castle." Cheshire's dreamy voice echoed in my head. It was likely the last sane statement I would be hearing from him, and I was grateful he had been able to pass along the information before decending back into his cursed madness and riddles.

"Fine. Time for the second wave of our own since you seem to have an infinite supply of these bloody things," I growled and raised my hands, calling to my own reserve forces. "Destroy!"

My single command was met with palpitating silence before a screeching sounded in the distance. The screams sent shivers down my spine as I recalled the terrifying hybrid creature that had ripped Avrilia to shreds.

Mombi looked sharply in the direction of the obsidian castle, her cold eyes narrowing at the cloud of beating wings heading our way.

"What?" I tilted my head coyly. "You forgot I had control of the flying monkeys? You remember Avrilia's favorite little pets, don't you?"

"What are these flying monkeys?" Tip grunted from where he had engaged with the first wave of soldiers. "Fire please?" He called out for either mine or Dorothy's aid with the scarecrows, while he used the blade of the ax he held as a shield, and attacked with his sword.

But, Dorothy was staring at the monkeys flying towards us, her eyes as wide as saucers. She brought her fingers to her eyes, curling them in towards her palm and running her thumb over each one.

"Rip, rip. Tear," She breathed to herself, and I had a sinking feeling as I realized that I had once set the monkeys after her too and she had torn them apart in her frenzied state.

"What's wrong with her?" Tip's words were strained. It was clear he wasn't in a proper condition to fight the soldiers and needed the monkeys' help, but it wouldn't do us any good if Dorothy attacked them and her fear took over.

"Um," I began hesitantly. "She might have been terrorized by them once or twice before."

"Witch..."

"Not now! We need to snap her out of it. What's the trick?"

Mombi, seeing her opportunity to attack, flashed over to Dorothy and tackled her to the ground with a knife poised to strike.

"Damn it," I swore and teleported over to help her only to have Mombi relocate back over to Tip, once more twisting the key in his chest further while he was braced against a tin soldier. I puffed a sigh of frustration at the round of musical chairs we were playing. "Dorothy I need you to snap out of the tea trance," I instructed before flashing over to Tip, knocking back several scarecrows with my flames.

Mombi was back to her teleportation rounds, flashing around the area to avoid my immediately following her, or the monkeys including her in their war path. My residual cracks were burning beneath my clothing, and my energy was waning quickly. I groaned and inspected Tip chest instead of giving chase.

"Can't you take this thing out?"

"Can't you take off your compass?" He replied dryly.

"Fair point. Maybe I can take it off or break it like my compass was broken?" I offered.

"It could kill you for all we know. Just leave it," Tip rasped, his eyes beginning to glaze.

"You're in pain…"

"I'll be fine," He insisted.

"But—" I was cut off by a sharp scream from Dorothy.

"Dorothy!" Tip croaked weakly, falling to his knees and clutching his chest. I bit my lip and grabbed at the key, praying silently that it wouldn't kill me as I bent the end down to break it.

After a heartbeat of waiting to see if either Tip or I would die, I whirled back towards Dorothy as another shriek rang through the air, and Tip doubled over in anguish. Dorothy's pain seemed to be linked somehow to Tip, but not in the physical sense or else catching the knife in her hand would have affected him too. No, Dorothy's suffering in front of him was causing the pain. Mombi had her pinned and was dragging the knife across her knees, marring her.

"Let's carve you up." Mombi leaned against Dorothy and stroked her head. "Tip, you can save her if you give in to the Wicked impulses stirring in you and strike me down. Or, " she turned and glowered at her hostage. "Maybe he will just kill you instead, if he spirals in his hate far enough. That'll break him twice over when he see's you dead at his hands."

Twenty-Eight

Dorothy

Pain seared through my legs and I thrashed beneath Mombi's hold. The insani-tea was fading, and clearly I hadn't used it effectively enough. I needed to strike her with something— anything!

"Get away!" Tip scrambled weakly to his feet across the courtyard, but Mombi just laughed as she looked at him and Alice then back at me.

My brain was throbbing from the tea, and the terrible pain I was in. I blinked, everyone's words around me dipping in and out of audibility. The spiders were nothing more than carcasses littering the area now. A cursory glance to the sky and I could no longer see Peter and The Wizard warring. Monkeys were ripping apart tinmen and *eating* the scarecrows before they could repair themselves. The sight of them maybe me instinctively shrink away, and I felt terrorized anxiety tumble through my entire body.

Toto erupted from the side lines as Alice and Tip advanced towards me for assistance. Tip's face was distorting between fear, anguish, and rage as he raced towards me with his weapon lifted. Alice was saying something to him about holding back to see what Mombi had meant by her previous statement, but she too looked ready to rip the ice witch apart like one of her Monkeys. In fact, couldn't she just command one to do the job for her? No, the seemed too busy with the soldiers.Thanks to the tea, I was woefully out of the loop.

Alice swung her sword at Mombi and I flinched as she had to stop short just above my torso when Mombi vanished appeared behind

Tip where she whispered something inaudible in his ear that made him instantly stiffen. Fighting someone with teleportation abilities was extremely obnoxious and aggravating.

Toto was barking fiercely at them, his tail tucked. Seeing my beloved dog in distress sent another wave of anger through me that stifled the burgeoning fear of the terrifying monkeys. I had the power in me, tea or not.

I sat up sharply, casuing Alice to stagger sideways with a curse. "Don't worry, Toto. Snakes don't like *fire*." My phoenix cloak returned and dove forward at Mombi. I didn't like her nearing Tip again, and so long as she had the ring, I could still use my magic on her.

The monkeys grew agitated by the phoenix, and having destroyed the wave of soldiers, they scattered back to the sky. Alice balled her fists in annoyanve as even more soldiers marched out of the castle.

Before she could summon her minions back though, Mombi appeared behind her and knocked her to the ground. Sliding her fingers into Alice's hair, she banged her forehead against the cobblestone and Alice instantly went limp.

I flapped my wings forward again, only this time, I imagined two towering cyclones of flames forming to sweep up the soldiers in their currents. I could feel the air rushing through my body and out through my fingers, coiling with the fire. I had to use both powers, whether I had control of the wind or not, we were out of options.

The fire tornadoes complied to my will, incinerating the scarecrows and picking up the tinmen, before continuing wildly through the hedge maze. Chaos unleashed. Smoke choked the air, as the hedge caught fire, flames racing in all directions. I raised my hands to sky, calling to the wind, and I brought a gust down onto the maze like a blanket that snuffed out the flames with a hiss.

Tip looked to be battling something internally, as he grabbed at his head and hunched over. Toto continued to growl and bark at where Mombi kicked Alice's limp body to the side. She groaned, the only indication she was merely dazed and not unconscious or dead.

"Fine, you irritating creature." Mombi turned her attention to my dog, and she raised a bloodied hand— And I realized that two of her fingers, along with the rings, were missing. With so much blood coating the area, I couldn't discern which rings she'd lost, so I could no longer trust being able to strike her with my magic. "Time to shut you up."

Instinct brought me to stand in front of Mombi's hand, shielding my precious Toto. "You won't touch my dog. Toto, go find the Wonderlandians and stay safe. I'll find you when I am done here," I instructed my dog, and was relieved when he whimpered but complied. Then, I turned my attention back to the ice witch. "I *will* kill you if you so much as try to hurt him."

"Fine. You'll do." She smiled and grabbed my throat.

"Dorothy!" Tip cried out, finally lifting his head to look at me. He didn't look quite right though. There was something burning in his eyes that felt dark and evil, born of torment.

I clawed at Mombi's hand around my throat. Then, feeling desperation coursing through me, I laced my fingers together to make one solid fist and slammed it into her elbow with all my might. A sickening crunch sounded, followed closely by a shrick of pain from Mombi as her arm fell limp to her side. I took the opportunity to snatch another ring from her hand, hoping it would take away one of her loophole abilities.

"You little bitch," She spat at me. "I think I might forgo the Wizard's plans and kill you instead! Once I add your power to mine, and take your shoes, je wpm't need his collection of witches anymore."

She raised her free arm up and pointed her index finger point blank at my chest. To my shock and dismay, she unleashed an invisible force against me and I was thrown against the hard stone ground. Apparently, she still had the glass ring.

"I learned a lesson with that moral compass and Avrilia's meddlesome loopholes with it. This key is different. There's no way to break its pull like the compass," Mombi called out to us smugly. She stood facing Tip, waiting as she stared at where I had landed.

Then she struck me again, sending me bouncing across the

cobblestone courtyard. I felt my body bend and crunch in ways it likely shouldn't and I cried out. Tip gasped in tandem with me and clutched at his chest.

"The rebound..." Alice mumbled shakily as she tried to lift her own body from the ground.

"Looks like you took the wrong rings," Mombi laughed maniacally wiggled her fingers in Alice's direction. "Each one of these cheats a law of magic here. And, this one, here has some of The Wizard's power in it, which can strike and kill a witch." She pointed the same finger at me again and struck me once more with the invisible force. "Though, my dear Tippitarious does have my star ring I showed you the other day. I like to stack my odds with back ups for this very occasion.

Another tumble against the stone, and I wasn't sure how much more battering my body could take. I needed to fight back. Alice was struggling to get to her feet, blood running down her face, and Tip was frozen watching Mombi beat me down. He was just as immobile as when she had baited him at the maze entrance.

"Tip, what's wrong?" I called out hoarsely to him, his mechanical stance feeling increasingly unnerving to me.

Mombi laughed and tapped her chest. "I've unlocked his potential for complete darkness. He feels things *so* strongly under that handsome exterior, his potential is positively boundless for love. But the flip side of that is the bottomless pit of hate he is capable of too. His heart is filling with such deep hatred, the moment he commits and strikes me, with killing intent, he will be a Wicked and under my control. Then he will kill you like a good obedient little pet without a second thought. He might get some power— who knows how the transfer works between a witch and wizard since there haven't been many murderous men around before— and I'll finally get the shoes. They won't go to a wizard. Glinda made sure of that."

"That can't be true. He wouldn't..."

"With the right motivation he will falter and give in. Funny all this talk of defeating me *together* but it's your being here *together* that's going to finally turn him!" She walked confidently towards my broken and aching body and kicked me before flashing her knife back to her hand and bending down to drag it across my shoulder. "Well, you turned out to be my wild card afterall. Remember, I gave you fair warning not to take my toys!"

I screamed at my flesh tore against the blade, but could seemingly do little more than try to scramble away. I reached up feebly and managed to tear one of her necklaces from her neck and melted it down in my hand, and my arm went limp with exhaustion. My body didn't feel like fighting for my life was important anymore apparently.

"He always hated being tortured, and no matter how badly I hurt him, all I had to do was promise I loved him and he'd accept me right back. The fool was so *desperate* to validate his love. How desperate will he be to protect you from the same thing I wonder?" Mombi smiled cruelly and held the dripping knife in front of my face pointedly for a moment. My eyes widened as I realized it wasn't her knife. It was mine. It was the small dagger with the anchored hilt I had made to represent Tip. How had she known?

"You evil monster!" I puffed at her.

She swiped my knife shallowly across my neck, just enough to knick the surface, with a delighted trill of laughter. Then she flung the bloodied dagger at Tip's feet, and kicked her foot against my chest to knock me back again. I yielded against her blow and collapsed fully to the ground, blood dripping from my many wounds, the gray stone turning crimson beneath me. I tried to push myself up but all my energy was gone, I didn't know if I could save myself this time.

"Enough!" Tip's furious bellow clanged through the courtyard—his eyes fixed on Mombi with clear predatory resolve. "I told you that you wouldn't touch her!"

"You did a pretty poor job protecting her, Tippetarius, my love."

"I'm not *yours*, you demon!"

"You didn't like me playing so rough? What are you going to do about it? Seems like most of the time you watched the beating. I guess you are still too *weak* to face me. I always did take more of the domineering role in our relationship, didn't I? You were so submissive, and let me do anything I wanted to you— Though if we are honest, you didn't hate all of our heated moments together. I certainly enjoyed them. Now, I guess you're going to let me do terrible things to her. Less heated, of course, though she does make sure pretty faces when she's in distress." Mombi goaded, moving to stand several paces in front of Tip before crouching down to her knees to wait.

It didn't escape my notice that she hadn't teleported and I hoped with everything in me, that it had been the teleportation magic I had removed with the necklace. I had to cling on to hope, and tried to push away that desperate frustration that neither Peter nor Wendy had been here for this final altercation like we had planned.

Still, ss cocky as she was being, she was in bad shape with a broken arm and missing fingers, not to mention every other injury she'd received in our first scuffle of the day. She was at the end of her rope too and she *needed* Tip to turn in her favor for her to win at this point. Despite Alice and I being in terrible shape as well, we still outnumbered her— especially if Wendy, Peter and the others did show up and join us— and it was seemingly clear that Wizard wasn't planning to come to aid her.

"Tip," I whispered warily as I watched him raise his sword, and the black tendrils had reached into his hands.

"Tell me, Tippetarius. You've done a lot of posturing so far, but little to defend her. What changed?"

"What changed is that I'm finally going to kill you, *Witch.*" He was transfixed, murderous vengeance spreading over his face like venom. He was going to kill her. "I am not *weak* anymore!"

"No!" I gasped, though the idea of Tip suddenly becoming a powerful wizard, like Peter, and taking Mombi's power from her did sound a bit enticing, it couldn't happen like this. We still ran the risk that she'd take control of him and he'd be turned as a weapon against us— not to mention she likely wouldn't even die— despite Alice snapping the key. "She's trying to turn you Wicked."

I was up and moving in an instant, ignoring the sting of shredded flesh on my body and my bludgeoned bones as I pelted forward, fresh adrenaline coupled with desperation taking over. He couldn't give in to Wickedness like this. I wouldn't let him taint himself. Especially not with me as the final straw. *He was Good, dammit! An honest, caring, sarcastic, infuriating, impolite, selfless man.* He would not fall to her. Not now after he'd endured so much from her twisted Wicked games with his Good heart.

His face was contorted by blind hatred— the infinite capacity he had within him to feel— and his sword was poised to strike her clean through. *I just needed to be a little faster!*

Closing the last of the gap between us, I let my body take over, flinging myself over Tip's back, clutching at his arms to pull him back, despite the fact he was much stronger than me. Tears had begun streaming down my face as my desperation to save him overflowed.

"Stop, Tip! You can't. You mustn't. This isn't you," I shouted, my eyes screwed tightly closed, clinging with all my might. My voice rose into something between a scream and a sob as I continued to plead. "You're Good, Tip. You're Good! You can't go Wicked, because you're my rock here in this place. You're Good, you're the best. Just don't do it. Don't kill her!"

The intensity of emotion that surged through me made my head spin, and I once hadn't thought possible for me to care this strongly about the fate of anyone other than Toto, Uncle Henry, and Aunt Em. But, now I *cared.* I cared so deeply it physically hurt. I cared what happened to these people I now called friends. And of them all, I knew I cared about Tip the most. I couldn't lose him to the Wicked anger harbored within, anymore than I could stand to lose him to death. Because, if he became Wicked he would stop being Tip, and that was as good as death. I felt his muscles bunch beneath my arms, ready to lunge anyway. I gave it one last plea.

"Please, Tip," I whispered directly into his ear from where I was clinging like a burr to his back. "I can't lose you like this. I'm alright. You've already saved me, again and again. You have to stay you. Please. I need you to stay with me. I choose you too. You're the light for me too. I'll be yours and you be mine. I'll lead and you'll follow, right? Well, follow me out of the dark prison she has you in. Just please. Please. I need you."

Finally seeming to break through the red haze, Tip's body slacked. Alice, who had also finally managed to get to her feet again, slipped into place with her own weapon to keep Mombi hostage just as Tip's sword— the one he'd asked me to make him with a little piece of me to remember if he made up his mind to stay in this world when I went home— clattered to the ground.

Quicker than Mombi could react Alice ripped off her remaining necklaces, and grabbed her wrist to stay tethered in case the witch tried to teleport away again. She pulled off the remaining rings one by one while Mombi stared defiantly back at her.

Tip slunk slowly to his knees, breathing hard and fast, eyes wide and wild like a cornered animal. I quickly slipped around to face him, once more ignoring my own wounds, and the world around me, to kneel before him. I gently lifted his chin with the tip of my fingers so we were making eye contact. The euphoria and lingering adrenaline at breaking him of his hate-fueled trance at the last moment made my hands tremble. That and my own realization of my true feelings starting to take root. Feelings that so clearly now went beyond friendship. I was out of excuses.

"One, two, three," I inhaled, mimicking the calming technique he'd used on me, relieved as Tip complied too. "Four, five, six. Good. Seven, eight, nine, ten."

Slowly, he began to sober, rationality once more lighting his eyes that bore into mine. They were filled with such emotion. I could see it all swirling around like dye in water. Pain, grief, remorse, shame, relief, gratitude. With his guard down for once, I could see just how much of an open book Tip was at his core, and how Mombi might as well have built his walls brick by brick with her own hands for all the damage she had caused him.

"Thank you, Dorothy," He croaked, reaching out a shaky hand to wipe my tear soaked cheek, lingering there. The gesture was so tender. "Did *I* make you cry?"

I leaned my face into his cupped hand, surprised at the reassurance it brought— the same comfort as when I buried my face in Toto's fur.

"Only a little," I sniffled and worked up a playful scowl. "Don't do it again, you rude boy."

Tip's lips twitched into a tired smile and he looked at me with open affection I didn't expect.

"I—" He started and faltered. Instead, he put his arms around me and hugged me close. "Thank you, for being you, Dorothy Gale. The Wicked witch that just couldn't stomach the Wicked. You turned out to be exactly what I'd hoped for. What I needed."

"You were like another mouse caught in a web to be freed," I laughed, hugging him back tightly. He was solid and sturdy beneath my arms, making my heart flutter alarmingly. "I couldn't not free you."

Before we disentangled from the embrace, I felt him press his lips to the top of my head and sigh. "And thank Goodness for that."

We separated and stared at each other unsure of what to do next. He'd kissed me? But no, not really. The top of my head, not the mouth. Kissing my head was more like I was a child, than someone he fancied more intimately. Like how he'd kissed Mombi. Wait, I *wanted* him to kiss me? When did that happen? It felt affectionate though, and the thought of the closeness made my heart skip. *Damn it! What does a kiss on the head mean?* My thoughts bounced aimlessly in my head until I was certain I was beet red and wanted nothing more than to burrow into the ground where I sat.

Tip cleared his throat, obviously feeling just as perturbed by the now palpable awkwardness and ambient tension as both Alice and Mombi were still right next to us. Battered, broken, and bruised, sure, but still able to see whatever the hell just happened between me and the Lost Boy clear as day.

"We still have to deal with her somehow." He jerked his head at Mombi but didn't actually look at her, instead keeping his eyes fixed firmly on the ground.

"She still deserves what's coming to her," Alice's voice was low and menacing as she stared down the witch that had made her Wicked. She and Tip both had all the reason in the world to want her dead, with Peter as a close third. I wasn't far behind at this point.

"But, how do we deliver justice without becoming Wicked? Maybe Wickedness is not ours to judge or condemn. Maybe—"

But Alice snarled, grabbed Mombi's battered head by the hair and dragged her knife in one swift movement across the ice witch's throat. "For me, for Tip, Avrilia, Glinda, Peter, Dorothy, and for the fairies."

There was a moment of sickening gurgling that turned my stomach, mixed with the splattering sound of blood hitting the cobblestone, before Mombi gave a final hiss. Her cold ice blue eyes faded from malice to blank orbs, and her body went limp. No more games, tricks, or magic. She was dead. I felt bile rise in my throat at seeing a life end right before my eyes.

"You killed her," Tip gasped as he peered up at Alice in awe, the black spindles fading slowly from his skin.

"I am already Wicked," She replied, her body stiffening a moment as the surge of power transferred from Mombi to her. "What's one more witch on my hands?"

"But, Peter—"

"Will understand it was better my hands bloodied, than forever staining yours. Besides, I kept my promise and didn't use too much Wicked magic."" She lifted her chin, and nodded to Tip, who looked at Alice with new found respect and gratitude.

"Thank you, Alice," He said—choosing to address her by name instead of witch, like he always did, for his words of gratitude— and meant it. Another stroke of power taken from Mombi and her coloring of Tip's opinion of young women with questionable magical origins.

"Come on, you two. We need to go figure out where Peter and Wendy have gone off to. Wonderland is ours again, but this war is far from over."

Twenty-Nine

Dorothy

I rested my head on a plush pillow inside the red castle and groaned. "Are you certain you don't know *any* healing magic?"

Alice rolled her eyes from where she was sitting across from me, washing the blood and mud off her face and hands. "For the tenth time, I do not know any healing magic. You have to just get through it."

"The good news is, you have some bone bruising but nothing seems to be broken, surprisingly. You're a resilient fighter," Tip commented quietly from where he was finishing inspecting me for broken limbs.

The sensation of his fingers against my skin burned and I shifted a little to pull my arm free of his grip, letting it plop at my side. I groaned again at the impact. "I've never ached this bad in my life. And I told you about wrestling that goat. Hell, the tornado that brought me here did less damage."

Toto jumped onto the sofa and curled up against me for comfort.

"Oh, stop complaining," Alice grumbled as she inspected one of her many wounds. "I need Peter back so he can try and stitch this one up for me."

"I know how to stitch wounds," Tip offered, shooting an awkward look at my retracted hand before he rose to his feet. I hadn't meant it to seem like I was pulling away, but I was in too much pain to even remotely contemplate what had transpired between us out in the courtyard, nor did I have the energy to awkwardly fumble my way through any conversations about it. It could wait. Then maybe I would have a little more time to try and figure it out myself first.

Alice frowned. "Thanks, but I'd rather Peter do it. He might be able to use some magic to at least numb the area beforehand." She glanced at the gash and shuddered. "Remind me again why we are sitting in here and not looking for the other two?"

"Because *I* took the most direct damage out there and I want to lay down for five minutes. Besides, we need to check you for a concussion before you're trusted anywhere with anything." I pointed to myself, towards the exterior of the castle, then to Alice in turn. "Tip, do you know how to do that with one of your many wise and all knowing tricks?"

Tip jumped when I said his name, looked confused as he had a delay in assimilating my request before nodding. "You make it sound like a parlor trick," He mumbled as he knelt in front. Alice. "But yes, I do. Follow my finger, Alice."

"Eh. Call a spade a spade," I said then chuckled deliriously at my unintentional pun. "That's funny. Because the castle."

"She's the one that needs her head checked," Alice muttered, though she smiled nonetheless at the stupid joke.

"We don't have that kind of time," Tip sighed.

"Rude." I feigned indignation and was pleased to see Tip perk up a little at the reference to our typical banter. I wasn't being weird. He was being weird. I was too tired to overthink everything like usually I did. In fact, I still felt a little drunk from the tea. Perhaps I'd imagined the affection and ambiguous head-kiss.

"Hey, guys?" I started, staring up at the ornate golden ceiling.

"Yeah?" Tip and Alice chorused.

"I'm glad none of us died. I'd miss me if I died but I'd miss you both too. Wait, did that make sense?" I squinted in confusion at my own words.

The other two started laughing.

"We know what you mean," Alice replied, then completing her evaluation, she rose to her feet.

"Congratulations, you are concussed," Tip declared with sarcastic enthusiasm to the witch.

"Wonderful. I'm going to find Peter now with or without you too." She turned to leave and Tip instantly looked panic stricken.

He must be feeling insecure about nearly turning Wicked. I rationalized to myself before my mind wandered further. *And then kissing my head like I was a child after this whole big embarrassing gesture...* "Ugh!"

Tip and Alice whipped around to look at me at the sound of my growl of frustration.

"Damn. That last part was out loud wasn't it?" I cringed.

Alice smirked and waved farewell. Tip stood staring after her in bewilderment before taking a hesitant step to follow.

Good grief, I rolled my eyes, but felt a bubble of affection stir in my stomach at his awkwardness. It was endearing.

"Did you see what happened to Peter and The Wizard?" I called over to him and he turned around slowly, shoving his hands in his pockets.

"Um no. Sorry, my attention was... elsewhere." He fished for words.

"Right, right." I nodded along, suddenly feeling small and nervous myself.

"Listen, Dorothy," Tip started, taking a deep breath. "I think I need to tell you—"

"Hello!" Wendy's cheerful voice sounded from down the hallway, cutting off Tip.

"Tell me what? Don't leave me in suspense!" Curiosity burned in my chest to know what he'd been about today.

"Later," He sighed and called to Wendy to let her know where we were.

"Where were you?" I demanded as soon as she walked through the doorway. "We could have used your help! I'm a mess, Alice is a mess, Tip almost turned Wicked. Peter locked horns with The Wizard. You missed everything!"

Wendy's eyes widened, the smile slipping from her face. "I'm so sorry. I… I, um," She stammered, wringing her hands in agitation.

"What?" I snapped impatiently, feeling justified in my annoyance at her disappearing only to show up completely unscathed at the end of the big fight— and she was one of our senior fighters!

"Dorothy," Tip warned, shaking his head. "At least give her a chance to answer before you go for another bite."

"Hmmm." I narrowed my eyes at him and set my jaw. "I'd just like some answers from the spring daisy over there while I nurse my wounds."

"I went to Oz," Wendy blurred out.

"You what?" Tip and I balked, and I sat up too abruptly with a tiny yelp of pain.

"The White Rabbit took me to—"

"*The* White Rabbit? The one Alice is always talking about?" I interrupted her explanation then waved my hands apologetically for her to continue.

"Yes, he said I needed to go with him right that very moment to get Henry. He said I needed to get him out of Oz to help Peter in his fight with The Wizard," She prattled off her story, then stepped aside to reveal the same kind-faced man who had saved me in the Emerald City.

"Henry!" I gasped, and despite my pain, I rushed over and gave him a hug— everyone in this group was very touchy-feely, so I assumed it was probably alright. "Thank you so much for saving me. And look! You turned out to much more than a blip in my timeline afterall! Sorry, don't mind the blood. I was used for knife-carving practice today and haven't had a bath yet."

Toto wandered over and sniffed at the man's feet before giving his boot a single lick of approval.

Henry returned the embrace with a shy laugh until Tip came over and nudged me gently away. Then he grabbed fiercely onto his old friend.

"It's so good to see you," He breathed, and Henry looked pleasantly surprised at his reception.

"I'm glad to see you too. And I'm so relieved to know you got out of Oz and found your way to Neverland, Dorothy."

"Yeah, it's been a rough go since I left you at that gate," I smiled happily. "But I am still alive. Barely." Tip winced at my joke and kicked myself once again for my insensitivity. "Uh, Tip helped. Defeated a lot of tin soldiers. Strong ones. Killed a spider too..." I trailed off, mortified by my uncontrolable rambling.

Wendy's eyes ticked from me to Tip, and she mercifully changed the subject. "Where is Peter? We passed Alice but she was on a mission and only told us we'd taken Wonderland back."

"Alice killed Mombi," Tip blurted out and Wendy gasped.

"What?"

"Yeah, it had to be done," I glanced sternly at Tip. "Um, Alice is still looking for Peter."

"What?" Wendy asked again, concern etched in her face. "We came back in time right?"

"I don't know. He was fighting The Wizard and then the next time I looked they were both gone," I replied, uncertainty in the Fairy-Boy's fate starting to make me nervous. "But, I had some tea, so best ot ask someone else. For all I know, I imagined everything after that point." I shot a look at Tip, who scuffed his foot.

"You didn't imagine anything. It all happened."

"He's at the White Castle." Tiger Lily waltzed into the room next, pausing to briefly acknowledge Henry with a friendly pat on the shoulder.

"Hey, where were you, Lily?" Tip folded his arms crossly.

Tiger Lily shrugged unapologetically. "Following orders. The Wizard dealt him a pretty nasty blow and he fell into some white roses. Tinker bell slowed his fall though so I'm fairly positive he's alive. Um, then some rabbit showed up and took him. Tink came and told me where to find him."

Only that slightest dimpling in her cheeks over her grinding teeth gave away that she was worried for Peter's safety beneath her cool, brash demeanor.

"Let's grab Alice and head there then." Tip nodded and made to leave the room before pausing to address me. "Er, sorry. Can you make the trip?"

"Yes, yes. Come on. We need to make sure that idiot is alive." I waved the group out the door, and my concern for Peter's fate tangled with the relief of knowing his whereabouts.

"I trust you a lot to look after Pan, but I'm taking this one back to Neverland with me and Hook. We need some extra help to carry our wounded home, and Tinkerbell told me something about his watch interfering with something at the castle." Tiger Lily intercepted Henry, by placing a hand on his shoulder.

"But Peter will be so happy when he sees Henry!" Wendy argued.

"Then you can tell him he better be well enough to make it home too. We will be waiting for him." Tiger Lily's gaze flitted to the ground, her voice soft. Then as quick as the softness showed, it was gone. "Come on, Lost Boy. Lionel can get you filled in on the Shadow business you're going to have to sort out. My priority at this point is getting Lost Ones back in Neverland."

"Oh. Alright, of course!"

"Here, take this jewelry with you. I want to look it over later." Tip reached into his pocket and pulled out Mombi's rings and necklaces and handed them to Henry.

"There's something in the silvery glass one, so take extra care of it." I smiled warmly at the man who dipped his head and exited with Tiger Lily.

Tip, Wendy, and I rushed out of the room and only just barely caught Alice while she was still perusing the hedge maze. Once she heard Peter was involved she teleported us through Wonderland in short jumps until we stood outside the luminescent white palace.

Tinkerbell greeted Alice at the entrance to the castle, explaining something in a rapid series of jingles. Alice's eyes widened and she gasped, looking completely gobsmacked. Tinkerbell jingled something else, then zipped into the woods in the direction of Neverland, and I swore I could see tears of sympathy in her eyes as she flitted past Wendy.

"This castle was sealed by Ozma. And only the Queen or *King* of Wonderland could open it.

"Is Peter the king?" I asked, walking shakily up the stairs, blinking appreciatively as Tip walked beside me to steady me.

"No," Alice breathed. "It's the Hatter. Before he went insane, I guess he must have been their King with Reera."

"So that's why they kept him. They wanted inside this castle. But why?" Tip asked as we cleared the last of the marble steps to stand beside Alice at the door.

"Tinkerbell just said there was something important being protected inside until…" she trailed off and looked at Wendy.

"I hear it again." Wendy perked up, cupping her ear. "I hear the voices. Two voices. So there must be two Lost Ones in there!"

"Protected until Wendy could come here and set it free." Alice finished.

"Me?" Wendy looked stunned and completely flabbergasted. Then her eyes sparkled with hope and clarity.

Her brothers. She hopes it's them inside.

"You're the Queen now right?" She asked Alice, her hands trembling. "Can you please open the door?"

Alice nodded and complied, walking over to place her hand on the towering ethereal doors. Light shown from beneath her splayed fingers and with a loud creak, the entrance yielded, opening wide. Wendy pelted inside as fast as she could manage.

"Something isn't right," I whispered to Tip and Alice, and Alice nodded.

"Tink was entirely too forthcoming and kind in regards to Wendy. I don't know what we are going to find in there, but I do know that Peter is already there and safe."

We each took a breath to steady ourselves, then crossed the threshold into the magnificent castle. The Red Castle foyer had been pretty grand, but it didn't hold a candle to this one. The whole room was bathed in stardust, shimmering and pure, with little mirrors dappling the walls to further reflect the cascading light, and glint off the ever- tumbling particles that swirled through the air just below a crystal ceiling.

Wendy had already located Peter sitting on a sofa, outside another set of doors. The sight of him, battered and subdued, reminded me of a waiting area at the hospital.

Alice and Tip both raced to his side, a flurry of questions tumbling from their lips. Peter answered a few of them around his and Alice's emotional embrace, but once he knew all of us had survived, he pushed the rest of the inquiries off for later.

"I've been waiting for you to open the doors, Love." He rubbed her face gently, then scowled. "I'm going to need an explanation on that giant Cheshire I saw by the way, but first Tinkerbell refused to tell me what I was waiting to see, the little pest. So, as I'm sure you can see, I'm dying to get inside and see what my Mother has protected for me— and for Wendy oddly enough." He flicked a perplexed gaze over the redhead and shrugged.

"I think, maybe you ought to prepare yourself for the possibility that what is beyond those doors might not be… Happy," Alice tried to caution Peter and Wendy gently.

"Nonsense!" Peter waved her off. "I heard my mother's voice for the first time today, Love. Her spirit is still alive in the white roses— the ones you threw paint on unfortunately— and she's somehow saved something for us here. How can that not be happy?"

"Alright…" Alice conceded and repeated the motion to open the second set of doors.

We were met with a gust of cold, glittering wind and stepped inside to some exterior ballroom of sorts, under a perpetual twinkling sky— the entire area covered in white roses. They coiled around large pillars, and formed grand archways over a small path that was paved with some sort of shattered glass.

Alice vented and picked up a shard, looking mystified. "Bubbles?"

"That didn't sound insane at all," I mumbled under my breath.

The path inward was also framed by the white roses that led to three small steps and a platform, likely once used to hold royal thrones. Instead, laying on the ground on the little level, wrapped in a bed of roses, were two bodies.

At last, Wendy. You've come to set us free. Two small voices whispered in the stilling breeze as the air settled around us. Wendy's eyes filled with tears, and she leapt forward.

"John! Michael! I found you."

Peter and Tip's jaws dropped and they followed Wendy, thundering over the broken glass, leaving Alice and I behind to share a skeptical glance as we followed more slowly.

"I don't like the look of this," Alice whispered, her brows knitting together. "The glass is from Glinda's bubbles that preserve memories and moments in time. I don't understand why there would be bubble shards here at all unless…"

"Oh, god. No," I exhaled with dread as I saw Wendy kneel next to what I could now see were young boys as the roses slowly uncoiled from around the bodies. I knew from her stories that Michael had been six, and John ten when they'd vanished. It looked like not a moment had passed since then.

"John, Micahel! I'm here. You can wake up now. Peter and Tip are here too, and we can all finally go back to Neverland together," She babbled euphorically as she reached out to jostle John's shoulders, then pulled back and looked at her fingers in confusion. There was a residue of stardust, falling like pieces of glitter, as she rubbed her fingers together.

"Oh, no…" Tip's clipped sigh, though barely audible, might as well have been a thunderclap around the room, and understanding lit his eyes. Peter looked ready to throw up, and I knew he had realized the same thing. The two boys in front of them weren't alive.

"Why?" Peter whispered, his breathing quickening and his hands balling in fists. "Why save them like this? What kind of cruel joke is this?"

"Um, come on, John," Wendy laughed hoarsely, her eyes looking wild and frantic as she shook her brother's shoulders again. "John! Wake up!" Her voice pitched in panic and she shook him harder to no avail.

"Wendy…" Peter started, but she couldn't hear him, lost in her own denial.

"Michael, please wake up. Look, here. I have your teddy bear with me. Aren't you happy to see him?" She pleaded desperately, and retrieved the small stuffed bear from her belt, shoving it towards the still boy's chest. "Michael!" She screeched, all of her hope dying in that single wail.

"Wendy," Tip tried this time, and I saw his lip trembling as he reached for her. "Wendy, they aren't—"

"No!" She shouted and jerked away from Tip, tears pouring down her face. "No, I refuse to believe this is happening. They are going to wake up any second and we are all going to go live in Neverland with Peter for the rest of our lives. This world isn't taking that away from me too!"

My heart lurched at the aggressively disheveled girl, spiraling in her own devastation, unable to process the fact that her brothers were dead in front of her. I bit my lip. They were so young. The Wizard truly was a monster. And, furthermore I had to wonder why he wanted this castle so badly to get to the boys in the first place.

"They have waited a long time for you to find them here, Wendy." A voice sounded, and we all turned, startled, to see a fully dressed white rabbit slipping out of the roses. "It's time for you to say goodbye and let them go. They are at peace now."

"The White Rabbit!" Alice hissed, her eyes latched onto the mysterious creature, though she had the decent sense to not chase after him this time. It spoke volumes of her personal growth of putting others first since we had met.

"You and I will talk later," The rabbit nodded to Peter, and vanished out the room again, causing Alice to ball her hands in fists, but she still didn't budge, her eyes staying firmly locked on Wendy.

"No. They are not going anywhere. They are going to wake up," She whimpered pitifully, still trying to get Michael to take his bear from her. "Please. Please wake up."

Thank you for finding us, Wendy. A boy's voice spoke directly into our heads. *And thank you for the adventures, Peter and Tip. You were and always will be our big brothers.*

Goodbye, Big Sister. Please take care of Neverland for us! The second voice spoke, and I knew it belonged to the younger of the two. A lump rose in my throat at the sound of his tiny, happy voice saying farewell, like he was merely going off to school or something. But that would never be the case for him. His story ended here, along with his brother's.

Goodbye. We love you. The voices called a final farewell and faded into silence.

John and Michael's bodies shimmered with an ethereal glow.

"Don't! Please don't!" Wendy begged, as her brothers' bodies began to dematerialize into silver stardust amongst the bed of white roses. Their faces were peaceful, soft smiles beneath their forever closed eyes.

The gentle breeze returned to sweep through the room, swirling the glimmering particles into the air and away.

"No!" Wendy cried out, grasping desperately at the air, her eyes wild and pleading. "No!"

She scrambled on her knees and paused, her hands still outreached toward the last essence of her brothers being carried away to rest at last. Peter and Tip dropped to their knees beside her, tears unabashedly running down both their faces. In a single, unified motion, they threw their arms around her from either side and held tight.

Wendy's arms dropped and gripped at her abdomen as she inhaled and loosed a guttural scream of agonized grief.

Her wails reverberated around the walls, an otherworldly screech of unbridled mourning. Her body shook with sobs, but Peter and Tip cradled her, their arms overlapping to hold on to each other at the shoulders along with Wendy—a solid unit of support and pain. Their faces, too, were twisted with grief and tears.

"I can't…" Wendy choked her ragged whispers were barely audible. "I can't bear this. It's too much. My heart can't take it. I can't!" Her voice grew in volume as another screech of emotion erupted from her, causing Peter and Tip to hold on tighter. Their own stifled crying grew stronger too, eyes tightly screwed shut.

My heart broke into a million pieces at the devastating sight of loss. I looked to Alice who's own face was gleaming with tears upon her cheeks, and her hands were clasped at her stomach and heart in empathy. She nodded and we both approached slowly. Alice went to Peter, and I crouched down beside Tip. In another blanket of support, we connected our arms around the grieving trio, allowing all three to collapse into their sorrow, knowing we were there to hold them as they did.

I ran a finger through Tip's hair after a moment and pressed my forehead to his temple gently. All boundaries and awkwardness gone for the moment, as he leaned into my embrace and allowed the sobs to take over fully.

Alice's hands rubbed gently at both Peter's and Wendy's backs in silent solidarity. Peter had also dropped the last of his restraints, turning into the grief he and his friends shared so palpably.

"This pain will ease," I whispered softly. "This will be the worst of it now. But take heart, grief is a valley of great depth. And the depth of sorrow only reflects how much love you shared. But for as deep as it runs in the pit of that valley, and as long as it takes to find your way out again, the strength you garner when you crest the other side is ten fold. The heights you reach with the love in your memories are up to you," I echoed the words Uncle Henry had told me on my first night on the farm as he sat with me and Aunt Em looking up at the stars while we grieved the loss of my parents.

"You'll get to that other side in time. All of you will," Alice added in quietly.

"So, take your time. While you find your way, we are right here when you need us. For now, for this sacrifice of heart, two more Lost Ones found their way home at last," I finished the sentiment, and Alice and I rejoined hands around the trio, as if we could somehow shield them from the pain in our embrace. Tears cascaded from my eyes, and I willed away the agony with all my heart. Alice's hand in mine, I could tell she was doing the same.

We stayed like that for an indiscernible amount of time, forgetting about The Wizard, forgetting about the shadows, forgetting all the magic and castles. We'd won the battle, like Alice had said, but we still had a long way to win the war, and I knew in my bones, these two boys would be avenged by us all.

Our fight had only just begun and we wouldn't fail.

Keep watch for the next book in the series:

When Wicked Runs *North*

When Wicked Series

Book One
When Wicked Runs West

Book Two
When Wicked Runs East

Book Three
When Wicked Runs South

About the author

Marissa Miller is an author/illustrator with two illustrated children's books under her belt. She currently resides in Northern California with her husband, and small herd of cats and dogs. Most days you can find her frolicking outside, drinking her weight in tea, immersing in Disney antics, or doing something to a creative end.

Miller's first published work is the wonderfully imaginative children's book, *Chasing Figments.* Following her picture book, Miller published an illustrated middle grade book, *The Grim and The Fantastic.* Both books embody Miller's motif, which is finding the splendor in one's life, no matter the circumstance, and using imagination to overcome obstacles. She has proudly added her first young adult sereis, *The When Wicked Series,* to her list of publications, with the first three books in the four-part series, *When Wicked Runs West, When Wicked Runs East, and When Wicked Runs South.*

Other works

Chasing Figments
Available on Amazon, Bn.com, and other online book retailers

The Grim and The Fantastic
Available on Amazon, Bn.com, and other online book retailers

Follow the author
on Social Media

Instagram:@marissamillerbooks

Twitter: @BooksMiller

Facebook: Marissa Miller Books

Goodreads: Marissa Miller

Youtube: Marissa Miller Books

www.ingramcontent.com/pod-product-compliance
Ingram Content Group UK Ltd.
Pitfield, Milton Keynes, MK11 3LW, UK
UKHW012248290726
14090UKWH00013B/527

9 798218 054816